The
SUMMER
of
BITTER
and
SWEET

The Summer of BITTER and Sweet

Jen Ferguson

Heartdrum
An Imprint of HarperCollinsPublishers

Heartdrum is an imprint of HarperCollins Publishers.

The Summer of Bitter and Sweet
Copyright © 2022 by Jen Ferguson
Beading © 2022 by Kim Stewart
All rights reserved. Printed in the United States of America.

Library of Congress Control Number: 2021950863
ISBN 978-0-06-308616-6

Typography by Laura Mock
22 23 24 25 26   PC/LSCH   10 9 8 7 6 5 4 3 2 1

First Edition

To all the angry girls; to the Indigenous girls
carrying worlds on their shoulders; girls
who ride or die for each other; the girls
still in the process of becoming—

A FEW THINGS ABOUT THIS BOOK

ONE

This book is about an ice-cream shack, yes, but it's also about the real traumas that teens face. There are discussions about and references to a violent sexual assault; an instance of intimate partner abuse; instances of racism and physical assault toward Indigenous and Black teens; discussions of drug use; underage alcohol use.

TWO

This book centers the traumas faced by Indigenous women, girls, and two-spirit people, and one narrative of the ongoing human rights crisis happening now in the colonial nations of Canada, the United States of America, and Mexico.

More broadly, this book includes discussion of generational trauma from residential schools, and the living, contemporary systems that overtook residential schools: the Sixties Scoop, the Millennial Scoop, and other instances of child welfare systems serving the needs of colonialism through mechanisms like birth alerts.

THREE

With the exception of one unnamed cow, who is humanely euthanized off the page, nothing happens to any of the other cows or the dogs or other animals, this I promise. Mooreen, the udderly delightful Cowntessa de Pasteur, and Homer are okay.

FOUR

Why do I tell you these things mere moments before the story begins?

Because: More than anything, I care about you. Your health, happiness, safety, and well-being matter more than reading this book.

If you're not ready now, that's okay. This book will always be here. If you're never ready, that's okay as well. If you're reading and need to stop, guess what, totally okay. And I'm the author saying this, so believe me. I found healing writing Lou's story, and if you do read it, I hope you find what you need too.

<3 Jen

CHAPTER 1
June 12

RED: Winter isn't colorless—it's full of shine, depth, and shades we often refuse to see. But many of us find winters long and dull. When the season opens at the Michif Creamery, we start with reds. They contrast loudly, wake us up, as spring announces itself with what seem like impossible buds on trees.

We're a sight. Three pickup trucks traveling down the highway, each with one of the Creamery's picnic tables hanging over the tailgate. And me, in the lead, in my old bronze F-150, my best friend, Florence, laughing from her shotgun seat. Summer arrives to the prairies slow—and stays for such a short time. But Florence and me, we're tough enough. We've wound down the windows all the way, because it's tradition.

Last year this time, we were so giddy for summer, for freedom. Florence is trying to bring us back to that place. Her red hair whips around the cab like a storm. It tickles my arm, my cheek. We're singing along to the radio—bad country music because, again, it's tradition. If doing something two years running makes for tradition.

But it's not the trucks and Florence's wild hair causing us to

1

stand out on Highway 16. It's one of the cattle dogs, with his orange-and-white coat, riding atop the picnic table I'm hauling like he's surfing. Homer's a character—an old man with the heart of a young pup. He's the star of cleanup day.

It's not the best day of the season. It's not the worst. But it's certainly a show.

When we approach the turn into the shack's lot, I slow down carefully, watching Homer's dog-smile out the rearview to be sure he's ready for this. It's a balance, and keeping the balance is my job. Homer trusts me. We pull into the clearing, where the shack has sat all winter, and before I can park, an orange-and-white blur jumps off the truck, kissing the land with a little thud. He settles in for the day, in the shade against a stand of trees, where he'll watch us, like he watches the cows. Coyotes, bears, and other predators don't get too close, not with Homer standing guard.

As we wait for my uncle Dom and my mom to arrive, Florence examines her freshly painted nails, all red like blood. She's decked head to toe in black. Her skinny jeans are artfully ripped at the knees and across one thigh. We're giggling over the song lyrics pouring out of my speakers—trucks, girls, and ice-cold beers, like that's all there is to life—when Dom raps on the side of the truck and says, "Let's get started!"

"Loading the picnic tables and the paint and all these supplies wasn't part of the job?" I ask, climbing down.

Throwing his head back so his gorgeous brown hair flutters, Dom grins.

Once we unload the picnic tables, my mom lugs her massive

beading kit from her truck. She's brought the portable stadium seat along—the one she drags to the pool when she watches me swim. She's here to keep us company, not to work. Last week, she quit her hellish job at the 911 dispatch to dedicate herself to art. She spent the first fall we lived here learning the craft. Her fingers bled first, then callused over. Now, she beads while she watches TV, beads while she eats.

If she could, she'd do it in her sleep.

She's leaving me, leaving us for the summer. But she's here today. Teasing and cackling at me, or her brother, with entire lungfuls of air.

No one asks where Wyatt, my boyfriend, is this morning. And I'm glad for that. Glad too, in a strange way, he hasn't shown. As we paint boards with a new layer of whitewash, Florence squeals with delight when drips stain her jeans. In September, she'll wear these on her round-the-world trip, and people will think they're designer. We've already cleared the mousetraps and removed any spiders who've taken up residence by relocating them to the bush.

Next weekend, we open.

When my uncle Maurice joins us, he's bearing lunch. But instead of heading for food, Florence smears a big gob of paint from her palm onto mine. She smiles, radiant.

"Gross," I say.

"Follow me." With a paint-smeared grip she pulls me around back of the shack. We're butted up against the trees. Day by day, they're turning vibrant green. The ground, too, is covered with spring growth, and errant rocks. "Kneel."

I do.

She doesn't release my hand. Hers is warm, the paint between us turning sticky, like glue—like Florence is trying hard not to let me go. Not yet. When Florence insists we lie on our backs to reach under the shack, we do it—hands still clasped—even though it takes some maneuvering. Under here, it's cooler and the good rot of the undergrowth is strong.

"Okay, now that our gymnastics routine is complete—I give us a six out of ten, by the way, and the Russian judge merits it no higher than a three, in case you were wondering."

I grin.

"Press your hand to the wood. Like me."

"Why, exactly?"

"You're asking why? After all that?"

I shrug with one shoulder.

"To mark our place, of course, Louie."

The rough underside of the shack sucks up paint, Florence's print next to mine. A drip stains my cheek like a tear.

"There," she says, quiet and not like Florence at all. "Now we'll be here as long as this shack of yours stands. No matter where we are, we'll be here too."

My skin breaks out in gooseflesh, and my lungs expand and contract like I'm swimming hard.

Florence wipes paint from my face carefully. All she can manage is a nod.

What she doesn't say: Next summer, we won't be here. I'll be at university balancing lectures and fieldwork—hopefully training with the competitive water polo team on weekends. And

Florence, she'll be who knows where. Thailand, on a beach, or the Australian outback working a season on a sheep farm, or Kenya—photographing Mount Kilimanjaro from her campsite.

"Come get lunch, you two!" my mom hollers.

Before we rise from the ground, Florence tries to speak. A strangled sob escapes. She's hardly ever without words.

"I know," I say, and help her up.

We rejoin my family. Dom hands me a wet rag to clean my hands and finally asks after Wyatt. "Where's that boyfriend of yours? He said he'd start work today."

Some paint rubs off, but most of it stays stuck. "Probably still in bed."

My mom's left eyebrow is arched high. "What do you know about his bed?"

I pick at the paint along my cuticles. "You all know what I mean."

"Lazy arse," Florence says, building herself a sandwich. "I didn't sleep well." Her bipolar disorder messes with sleep—big-time. "And I was here, almost on time," she adds, peering over at Dom.

Technically, it's a family business. But the Creamery is Dom's project.

Maybe making excuses for Wyatt is what I'm supposed to do. Like it's my job as his girlfriend. But I can't quite defend him. Can't offer words of support. Even now, talking about him, I'm low-key happy he didn't show.

"This doesn't bode well, my niece." Dom's head drops the tiniest bit, but it drops.

I continue picking at specks of paint until I switch over to ravaging unmarred skin. "He'll be here next weekend."

Dom's brown eyes are tight. And though he doesn't say it, he's thinking that hiring Wyatt was my idea. At the time, it seemed a good one. To spend one last summer with my best friend and my boyfriend.

Out of the corner of her eye, Florence watches as I pick, pick, at my cuticles. She swats at my hand. "Stop it."

My mom glances up from her beading.

At the far end of the picnic table, Maurice's words barely carry against the traffic on the highway. "Fewer employees means less overhead. Can't the girls handle this on their own?"

"Two isn't enough. Three's pushing it." Dom shakes his head. "We'll survive."

That word.

Survival is always in the back of our minds. What if the locals don't rally this year? What if we need another loan? What if Mom quitting a job that made her miserable, that loaded her down with trauma shift after shift, to sell beadwork on the road is a huge mistake? What if Wyatt goofs off all summer and that's the deciding factor to my family's survival?

"Hey, the sun's coming out," Florence says.

I ignore my uncles' chatter to focus on this good lunch, on the sun helping dry the paint we've liberally applied to the shack. For now, it gleams. Later, the shine will dull. By summer's end, it won't look like we did this at all.

Finished with her meal, Florence climbs on top of the table. She wiggles the ponytail from my hair and starts to play.

My mom pulls a long length of thread through her design. "Your braids are too loose, Florence."

"It's pretty this way."

"Tight braids highlight the cheekbones."

They're teasing each other. It's how they've always been, since I brought Florence home to finish a biology project after she joined our class in the middle of the semester our grade-eleven year.

"There's more than one kind of braid," I say, and my mom stops teasing. A tightness claims her eyes. She almost looks hurt. Like even this basic statement weighs her down with the pain of my old lies.

Florence just says, "Oh, shush, you."

I don't know which of us she's shushing. Mom falls silent too. It could be the beads—she's hurrying to fill her stock. It could be what I said, what she thinks I implied.

Florence continues finger-combing little tangles. "You could still abscond with me? Ditch the boyfriend and run?"

I sigh.

My mom clears her throat. We're supposed to hear it. She's contributing to the conversation again.

"It's not like a gap year means she'll never go to uni, never play water polo, Auntie Louisa."

My mom's face lights up. "My daughter could be the next Waneek Horn-Miller! Lou could go all the way to the—"

"Olympics," I say at the same time as my mom. Some days, I believe it's possible. We moved so often I didn't have a picture for *home* in my mind's eye—but I've always had my mom, my fascination with dinosaur bones, and water polo. These days, my family is bigger. My home is a single-story farmhouse with a cool, comforting basement.

We leave my mom to finish the edging on the earrings she started this morning—deep-gold ponies—to work for a few more hours. Near the end of the day, we crack open the shoebox filled with photos and mementos of the Creamery's first two summers and paste them along the back wall.

Florence peers at me, holding a photo of us.

She needs to hear me say it. Again. "I can't go with you on your amazing trip. I'm sorry I can't. But we still have the whole summer."

"We'll make it the best one, then."

I find the tip jar and tape a weathered Albertosaurus sticker that doesn't stick on its own anymore to the glass, positioning it next to the cash register. It's bittersweet, but it's part of this place.

"And we're done!" Florence claps. Her energy is contagious. A little like sunshine.

We're done, but we're not ready to leave yet. Dom settles next to my mom. Florence perches on top of the picnic table, scrolling through her phone. Soon enough, my uncle has drawn us from our corners, and we're snorting over one of his stories. That leads my mom to correct Dom's story, and Dom to correct Mom's, and suddenly the story's evolved into something completely new.

If the white SUV hadn't stopped, we'd have sat around that picnic table, me petting Homer's soft fur, all of us laughing so hard it almost hurt, until the mosquitoes ventured out in search of blood.

But a white SUV with tinted windows turns into the clearing. The interruption sets me off. The almonds we've been snacking on turn bitter on my tongue, grit against my teeth. Homer rises, leaves my side, and takes up watch.

The passenger window glides down—halfway. A blond woman with gaudy red lips leans, nose first, toward us. "When do y'all open?"

Dom doesn't approach the vehicle. "Sunday next. Eleven to eight."

"Fine," she says, and the window climbs, concealing her face.

The white SUV reverses toward us to make the turn. The license plate is one of those vanity plates. They're such a waste of money. Wyatt's been wanting one. This one says: FREED. It merges back onto the highway, heading for town.

Florence stands. "They weren't the friendliest of ice-cream fans. You know them, Dominic?"

"She's older than me. We wouldn't have gone to school together. If she's a local. Louisa?" Dom asks.

My mom compares one earring to its pair, her face lopsided. "I screwed up the pattern. There's too much gold here. Not enough little yellow ones."

"Mom? That woman, do you know her?"

"I'm going to have to tear this apart."

"Mom?" I say again, knowing how she can sink into her art, sink so deeply she leaves us even while she's in the same room. Plus, she's anxious around strangers. Only consented to come out here today because the shack was closed to the public.

"I know she's not a natural blond," my mom says lightly, and then she starts ripping out stitches. "Couldn't see the driver. Could you?"

Dom shakes his head. "Should we pack this up? Get home to our supper?"

I whistle at Homer, who lobs over, his fur covered in burrs. Later tonight, I'll pick them out. Maybe by then, the nervous feeling in my stomach will have settled.

CHAPTER 2
June 14

RED: As a color we associate it with
passion, and with anger too. As a flavor we think it's
childish. A good red ice cream or sorbet is all those things
at once. It's a marvel. If you're lucky, you can be one too.

On Sunday evening after we'd set up the Creamery for another season, I sat on our farmhouse's wraparound screened-in porch, picking dried paint from my skin, my phone on speaker, while Wyatt made his excuses and seamlessly planned tonight's date. Now, I'm rolling with anxious energy, ravaging my cuticles again, as if ugly hands will turn him off. Only a few days stand between us and graduation. It's impossibly hard to concentrate on anything. But the cows in the close pasture munch happily on what the fields have to offer and it's nice for the sun to be in the sky after supper. I try to remember this, sitting still. But I crack, can't settle, can't stop picking at my nails.

Forty-six times. We've kissed forty-six times.

Tonight, in this suddenly-summer sticky heat, if Wyatt has his way, we'll break fifty.

I check my phone again, worrying at the green case. Most of

the color has rubbed off by now, but the outline of the T. rex saying "My name means king of the tyrant lizards in your language" is still mostly there.

Seconds tick slow like they do in the water, when the other team is up in the last minutes of the final quarter. By now, Wyatt really should be driving west along the highway in his red Range Rover—an early, ridiculously expensive graduation gift—to pick me up for our date. Some summer's-here blockbuster. And typical Wyatt, he's late. We're going to miss the previews.

My earrings are big enough to be showpieces. Leather tassels tickle my neck. Forty-six times we've kissed and I haven't felt a thing. No sparks. Not even one pitiful flicker. Not the first time his lips pressed hard against mine. Not since.

The porch door creaks.

"That's what you're wearing?" my mom asks, her hands overfull. She situates her work in progress on a side table, next to a plate of beads she's using to bring a PopSocket to life with a bold pink bison.

I don't say anything. I raise my eyebrows.

"This is a date, eh?"

"The theater will be cold."

My mom laughs her deep belly laugh, like she knows more than I'm saying. Like she can read my mind. We've been two stars orbiting around a common barycenter all my life—so maybe she can. Maybe I'm that obvious.

Wyatt's always late, but he has timing. He rolls off the gravel and onto our looser dirt road with a great big tire spinout.

"I wouldn't go back to eighteen if you paid me in unlimited

beads and moose hide," my mom says.

I know what she means. This—Wyatt—it's too much. But she's saying something else too. Something about her eighteen, not mine. All I ever say when she's in one of these moods is *I love you*. And so I say it.

She reaches out to hold my jean-covered knee. "You're dressed like you're going to a job interview. And it's a job you don't really want." She doesn't comment on my earrings.

"Thanks."

She laughs again.

Wyatt honks the horn. It's a little noise. Nothing like it fits the Range Rover.

My eyes tighten.

"Impatient, isn't he? For a white boy running so late we ought to check his family tree for an ancestor."

With a backward glance, I say, "Lol, Mom. Super funny." But then I'm running down the porch steps to his passenger door, running in jeans in this heat, like my hurrying will actually help us get to town in time.

I yank on the shiny red door handle. It's locked. "Wyatt!"

He laughs inside the cab. To him this is the funniest thing. When he's done, and his wavy, too-long surfer-boy hair is pressed back into its perfectly messed-up order, he clicks the little button to let me in.

I try the door. Before I can manage it, he locks me out again, a wicked grin on his face.

"Wyatt. Seriously."

"Okay, okay." He unlocks the door for real this time.

I climb inside. Cologne weighs down the air in the cab. I taste it. Cleaning supplies and sad, stale sandalwood candles on the bottom shelf at the dollar store. Underneath it all, the burn of new car lingers. My mom watches, her thread and needle paused in the air. I ignore her and focus on my boyfriend.

"Get your ass over here," he says, and I lean toward him and let him kiss me on the mouth—wishing for one spark. One little something.

What I get is skinny fish lips.

Now, that's not nice, just as not nice as my own mother calling my very planned-out jeans and lacy, high-necked top an interview outfit. But both things are honest. And I'm really working on honesty.

So, skinny fish lips stand.

We rip out of the farm, tossing up dirt like it's rural confetti. As we cruise into town, doing ten over the speed limit, we're listening to Wyatt's music. New country. The nightly countdown. We're two songs away from number one and the movie starting. My boyfriend, he has a hand gripped onto my thigh. It's a bit too warm tonight, yeah—the first real hot night of the year—but I'm happy. In denim, he can't worm his hand under my pants.

Still, he'll try.

Wyatt flicks the leather tassels hanging from my ear. His cologne wafts toward me, fuller than before. When I gag a little, bile rises up. I fake a cough to be polite.

This is what sets Wyatt off. Or, helps him to be brave. He turns the music down low, pumping the button on his steering wheel, like suddenly he needs to concentrate extra hard. His thumb rubs rough circles into my jeans.

I'm going to bruise.

"So what do you say about tonight, when the lights are low and no one's watching, giving me a little . . ." He breaks off suggestively.

Now I'm supposed to read his mind. And it's either his thought is so obvious, or I know him pretty well, because I sort of do. I try to say something, anything, and it's like he knows I'm going to tell him that I'm not sure I want to give him another hand job in the movie theater. Well, if I were being super honest, it would be more like, I don't want to have your dick in my hand at all. But I can't find the words.

Wyatt smiles at me, that smile his parents paid bank for—perfect, straight, too-white teeth—and he says, "Come on, Lou. You don't have to like giving BJs for you to, you know, go to town."

Just pretend. Just swallow it down.

Okay, bad pun.

But this is an escalation from *It's just your hand on my dick, Lou*. And maybe moments like this are exactly what bad puns are for. Still, wordplay won't get me out of the hell I've somehow found myself in, dating a guy who can't stop, won't stop.

It's creeping. And the gaps between when I give in and when he asks for something else, they're getting shorter. Which means this won't ever quit. Not until Wyatt wants it to. That rolling in my stomach, the bile, the way I can't argue my way out of this one—my mind's blanked on excuses, on the lies that used to come so easily—that's how I know we have to break up. Not soon. Right the right now.

Before I can do anything but slide the window down to clear some of the cologne from the Range Rover, Wyatt says, "'Cause you'll learn to like it. You really will."

I don't say anything.

One of his hands grips the steering wheel of his new toy, the other my leg. I'm thinking of the venison that sat on my plate tonight. How, to Wyatt, I'm just exactly that: meat.

He opens his mouth again. "I'm done waiting." He slowly raises the music back up. "If you're not going to take our relationship further—and don't make that face, you know exactly what I mean—then, well, bae, tuck and roll."

The pressure's off in here. The window whoops and pops. We need to equalize it.

Even though it's a cliché, I clear my throat of a bad taste and say, "Wyatt, we need to talk."

He's watched enough movies, he should know what's coming, but he only smiles, his hand working farther up my thigh to rub at the crease where my leg meets my hip. It's not sexy. It hurts.

I push him away.

That feels good. So good. My voice is firm, even, when I say, "I'm breaking up with you. Sorry."

"You're what?" he asks over the song. We drift toward the grassy median.

He overcorrects, the Range Rover pulling hard, jarring my neck. The stem of my left earring needles into skin. I reach for something. Under my grip, the dash is clean. I focus on the digital clock's glowing red numbers. The previews have started already. It's my favorite part of the movies. When everything is possible—when nothing's exploded yet—when the butter on the popcorn is warm and the salt still tastes like the best thing.

From the driver's seat, Wyatt glares at me.

"I'm ending things with you," I say, like somehow he didn't quite hear me.

He takes his foot off the gas. This time, he drifts to the right, across the rumble strips. He points at the passenger door and says, "Get out."

"Are you being serious?"

"Get. Out." We're moving too fast. The song's building to some deep heartbreak, and Wyatt, he clicks the volume higher. My ears rattle. "Tuck and roll, Lou," he yells.

I'm sure he'll stop once he's had his fit, but he never quite does. His cologne stings the roof of my mouth. New-car smell, I read once, is a mild poison.

Someone passes us, honks three times fast. Wyatt ignores them and keeps slow-driving on the shoulder.

We can't be going more than a few kilometers an hour now. I have one hand curled around the door handle, but I'm staring back at him. It's a stalemate. One of us has to blink first. We both know it'll be me. Wyatt won't ever simmer down, pull a U-turn, and drive me home. The stinging in my mouth intensifies.

Sometimes, life gets super clear. Tonight, it's like that. Crystal like my favorite lake, the one where I've gone swimming a thousand times, the one where my uncles fish, where my mom sits beading in the shade, pretending the tragedies she once spent all night listening to at the 911 dispatch—the drinking and driving, the overdoses, the suicides—haven't altered her on a fundamental level. For a Métis woman without a high school diploma, the night shift at the dispatch was the best paying job she could get. That's clear to me too. Why she did it, why she suffered through it all. For us, her family.

Here, now, either I'm slipping out of this boy's vehicle and onto the shoulder of the highway, or while something explodes on-screen, I'll be down on my knees choking. In the pool, when I lose control of the ball, I dig my nails into my palms out of frustration. The crisp bite of half-moons centers me. The door swings wide, its hinges screeching. I release my seat belt and grab my leather bag with the good fringe from the floorboards.

Unlike my ancient truck, a moment later, a sensor kicks in. *Beep, beep, beep.*

I don't wait for it to sound off again.

I jump.

CHAPTER 3
June 18

RED: Usually, raspberry. Grainy and lightly sweet.
Seeds in. The key is to balance the sugar with the
sour. So the mixture is somehow both. Riding that
line means you've made a proper Michif Red.

Four days after Wyatt stormed off and I walked home like I used to when I was hiding my family from everyone in town, suddenly we're high school graduates. In my bedroom, in the back corner of the farmhouse basement, I change out of my deep-blue ribbon skirt into skinny jeans and a Black Lives Matter tee. I hang Mom's original-design deer-hide-backed earrings on the wall display Maurice crafted for me out of old chicken wire and reclaimed wood. Next to the earrings the braid of sweetgrass Dom gifted me curls gently, one end wrapped in leather, the other in purple yarn. At the edge of the display hangs the silverwork choker I don't wear anymore but can't seem to give away. I drape my graduation cap over it. I glance at my dry swimsuit, folded on top of my dresser, itching to change into it and drive to the pool. But I've missed free swim for the day.

Tomorrow, I can practice tomorrow.

My bedroom door is closed, so my mom doesn't see me jump—as if the choker is proof she's caught me lying again—when she hollers, "Hey, Lou, you can mope over that boy, or you can be useful! Which are you going to choose?"

She's dragging plastic bins upstairs. It's not really about the heavy lifting. She only wants to spend a little more time with me before she starts her epic road trip. The first summer we'll be apart in our whole lives. Her star needs to circle another sun, and I'm ready too. High school is over. I'm an adult, legally and otherwise. I close my door behind me, pushing the choker out of my mind to heft up a bin. "These are loaded down!"

"Can't weigh more than a tub of ice cream and you haul those fine," my mom says, carrying her bin toward the stairs. I follow. When she cracks a knuckle against the handrail, she curses loudly. We emerge directly into the kitchen, as if when the farmhouse was built the basement stairs were an afterthought. She rushes to the sink, to run cold water over her hand. My mom and I only moved here three and a half years ago, but this place is filled with our presence. My swimsuits drying out on the line. The Lego dinosaur kit Maurice thrifted on the kitchen shelf surrounded by Dom's recipe books. My mom's beads, on hanks, all over the house.

This is the place we've lived the longest. She knows I'm safe here with my uncles, that she can take time to heal. She started beading one weekend after Maurice uncharacteristically left his supplies out before heading to Edmonton. It had been a particularly bad night at the 911 dispatch. She said she couldn't sleep with those violent images in her head, and she needed to replace the pattern. She's been beading ever since.

Outside, a truck pulls up the drive. I don't have to peek over the sink through the kitchen window to know there's a cloud of gravel dust slowly settling. Dom's home. My uncle's footsteps fall hard, so I have a bit of time to adjust my face before he joins us. Dom's an empath. He senses everything—even the things you don't want him to. And since the big lie, he's always watching.

The scent of hand-rolled cigarettes wafts into the kitchen. He's wearing his nice shirt and dress pants, but since the graduation ceremony ended, he's ditched his traditional finger-woven sash somewhere. I say ditched. But Dom, he wouldn't do that. It's probably hanging nicely in his closet, the colors bright against the rest of his neutral-heavy wardrobe.

"Taanishi, yaence," he says, greeting me, before switching over to English. Dom is trying to keep Michif, the language of our people, alive. So he uses bits and pieces every day, especially at the house. "Sample my new flavor yet? It's in the freezer."

Sometimes I speak to Dom only with my eyebrows. Mustard ice cream is never going to fly. It doesn't matter if mustard is a local herb. Or if whomever this secret person Dom's been going picking with loves the rich color of the finished product. This is the new man's influence. But Dom won't tell us a thing about him.

Secrets, it seems, are different than lies.

Life is easier now. Being able to catch a lift with one of my uncles even when they're decked out in beaded bolo ties, not insisting to be dropped off around the corner. In the early days living here, it was such work keeping all my lies from tangling into an impossible knot.

It was cosmic fate, like the end of the dinosaurs, that eventually my lies would implode.

Dom drops a stack of papers on the kitchen table my great-great-moushoum made with his hands out in one of the barns that we've long since torn down. When Dom spots my mom at the sink, still running cold water over her knuckle, he tucks the rest—today's mail—under his arm. Turning, he walks out of the kitchen and down the long hallway to his bedroom, but I notice exactly what he's trying to hide.

Another letter from Victim Services.

"Anything for me?" Mom asks, hovering over the sink.

From down the hall, Dom's voice carries. "Nope."

These arrive a couple times a year. Notices on parole hearings, mostly. Requests to update Victim Impact Statements. Dom handles all of it, even if it's my mom's name—Louisa Norquay—on the envelopes. But this one is off-season. I can't quite figure out what it contains. Still, if it's important, Dom will tell us.

A fly is beating itself against the big window above the sink. I scoot next to my mom and shoo it outside. For days now, not one of us has bothered to do the dishes. Maurice, the one who cares about keeping things relatively tidy, is out of town. I brush crumbs from my quick lunch onto the floor. Once it gets dark, the dogs will be happy to find a treat. That's when I notice it, on top of Dom's stack of stuff, all color coded and printed on the heavy paper he usually reserves for important business documents.

A new schedule.

It's not Wyatt's name that throws me. When he became my ex I figured he'd probably still put an apron on for the summer and scoop. As he walked the stage this morning, I closed my eyes, and when I collected that rolled-up piece of paper everyone pretends is your diploma, I forced myself not to even glance at his row. My everything hurts from leaping from his Range Rover. My ego still smarts after walking home.

Instead, King Nathan's name lodges in my throat. I choke on nothing but air.

King's back.

That's unexpected. After the way he left.

My throat's dry, itchy. I pour a glass of iced tea into my happy dinosaur mug, a thrift-store find I bought long after King disappeared.

11:00 a.m.: Lou, Wyatt, and King.

The silverwork choker won't leave me alone today. If I were braver, I'd get rid of it—and all the memories of lying to King too. How I deflected: when he came to the farm on a service call with his dad, I'd drag him to the hayloft immediately. How I hid anything that even suggested my family might not be prairie settler stock when Dr. Nathan and King joined us for dinner that first time. How I pleaded embarrassment, how I kept my uncles, still so anxious that Mom and I would leave, behaving exactly how I wanted them to when King was around. After all, it's not just Native men who wear their hair long, and Dom sometimes performs that crunchy granola vibe—with his obsession for local, local, local when it comes to the Creamery.

The choker, that's where the lie seeded itself. Dom gave me money to buy something, a no-reason gift, after my first Christmas at the farm. A few days before I started at the high school, my mom dropped me at the mall. This glamorous Dene Tha' woman, down from Bushe River for the weekend, was selling jewelry at a table. And fourteen-year-old me fell in love with the delicate silver and the milky pink stones.

The fifth time I walked by and stared, the woman said, "Try it on."

"I don't have enough."

"Try it on," she insisted.

I liked it because it was Native but not so loud as all the stuff my uncles wanted me to wear. I liked it because it was Native but didn't have to be. It wasn't forcing an identity on me or forcing me to be seen as Indigenous in the place where my mom was hurt so badly. And that made so much sense when we moved back to the town where I was born, the town we'd been running away from for years, that I slipped on the necklace and into the lie at the same time.

We'd never been the kind of people to celebrate our heritage, me and Mom. We downplayed it so we could rent a decent apartment, or we ignored it, hoping the world would ignore us—until we moved in with my uncles.

In the kitchen, my mom juts her chin at me. "What's that face for?"

I stare at the schedule, and King Nathan's name. "You don't know?"

It's too early for dinner, but Dom returns and begins riffling through the fridge. It's fend-for-yourself night. With Maurice in the city visiting his ex-wife and daughter, and Mom preparing to leave the day after tomorrow for her summer selling Louisa's

Fancy Beads across the powwow circuit, no one wants to make an effort to cook.

"Hey, why is King Nathan on the schedule for the shack?"

Dom's finding the last clean bowl, quick-washing a spoon, and digging into leftover stew, almost at the same time. He's like that, moving too fast, always, always in motion. "Oh, you found it, eh?"

"Clearly."

"I hired him."

"Why?"

My uncle shrugs.

Mom claims the spoon from her brother. She fakes a gag. "Too much pepper."

"Just the right amount of pepper."

These two bicker. It's almost always good-natured. You can disagree but still love. That's easy to see here. They grew up together, shared the back bedroom until nouhkom died. We don't talk about it: Dom, he was a kid, but somehow, he understood what my mom needed when she was newly sixteen and hospitalized for weeks, recovering. When she was sixteen and pregnant with me.

Only months after I arrived in this world, we left town like Mom was being chased by one of those big, black dogs Maurice sometimes whispers about—Rougarou. I never believed anything was chasing us. But when Mom told me a little about what happened to her, I understood better why she couldn't stay. Now, I understand why she needs to go. She didn't share 911 calls often. What ended up in the local newspaper was squeezed into facts, and what happened to bodies, to the heart, the rest of us got to forget. Mom carried those stories, holding callers while the worst day of their life was happening.

"Focus, you two. King Nathan, why's he on the schedule?"

"Dr. Nathan did me a big favor. And he asked. What could I say, yaence?"

"You might have asked her," my mom offers.

I let Dom see my eyebrows spike. "What she said."

Mom laughs, but changes gears. "It'll keep a body between you and that ex-boyfriend."

I snort.

"Whaaaaat?" Uncle Dom's a gossip. "You broke up with Wyatt? Or, ouch! Did he break it off with you?"

"I ended things."

"Why?"

These days, I hate lying to my family. After I bought the necklace, I pretended to be fully white. Told people my mom was Catholic Ukrainian if they pressed me, never let anyone but King visit the farm, and that was under controlled conditions. Ignored my uncles, my mom, in public. It was safest that way. But I wore that choker every day so at least when Dom asked me why I wasn't wearing the moccasins he'd gifted me, I could shrug, point to my necklace, and remind him about the Dene Tha' woman.

She sold me the choker for thirty-five dollars instead of fifty and told me to wear it and think of my ancestors. I guess she could tell.

But with Wyatt, what can I truthfully say? I'm frigid and he's all hormones-on-fire, the exact opposite? It's strange living inside my body. Where holding hands doesn't do anything. Where lips against lips—and tongue—feel wet and chapped and gross. I sigh—and this isn't acting—because I truly don't know where to start except to wonder if my beginning might have soured something essential. And, in this house, we don't talk about what happened to my mom at sixteen.

So I lie. "He . . . he's sort of boring."

This time, Dom laughs. "Yeah, high school boys, we can't blame them, can we, if they're a little one-note. They're brewing, in the process of becoming."

"Wyatt's a high school graduate now." I face Dom. "And he's still . . . bland."

Mom walks toward the fridge, but she stops behind me to run her hands through my hair. "It's only been a couple hours, daughter. Growth takes time."

My scalp tingles under her fingers. "But is it actually possible to grow a personality?"

Dom places his empty bowl in the sink with a clatter. "Well, maybe you'll find he gets mighty interesting when you spend all summer in the shack with him. There's not much room back there."

"Unlikely."

Both Mom and Dom leave it.

I don't know how in the world they bought that lie. Wyatt's the last person you'd call boring. He's extra. And he's been over to dinner enough in the past few months that the whole family's gotten to know him. He makes them laugh.

He made me laugh. Most of the time.

Mom quits playing with my hair. She glares at her brother pointedly. "Help me load the truck, would you?"

"We're going to miss you," Dom says, clasping his sister on the back, giving her one of those awkward side-hugs. He doesn't want her to go. But they both select a bin and leave me alone.

I set the kettle to brew. This time, I'll drink something hot and sweet and hope it drowns out the bitter. At school, my friends, especially King, bought my lies: I tan well. My mom travels for work. I can't have anyone over. I don't have a culture. Laugh-laugh. And I kept lying. Even when King told me all these really hard things, how everyone in town, his friends, his teachers, would comment on how much darker he was than his dad—like there's acceptable Black and too Black—how he missed his mom, how he worried about her and her sobriety, working it alone in Toronto. How he was sure his writing would never be good *enough*.

Eventually, I traded the choker for a silver cross on a long chain, and people stopped asking *where I was from, really*. I had friends like King. No one treated me badly—or at least worse than any other girl. Even if my Native classmates looked at me funny, even if they knew my uncles and were among the few who could make a direct connection between my uncles and me, they weren't going to out me. They might have wanted to be white sometimes too. Or maybe they were ashamed of me.

One time, while my mom was beading the vamps for a pair of mocs, she called Wyatt handsome when she thought I wasn't listening. But right after, this stormy look possessed her and I sort of knew what she was trying to tell me. Mom's hair is pin straight. Her eyes are this pretty brown, same as both my uncles, same as my nouhkom are in photos.

But Wyatt's eyes are a muddy blue. Like mine. If I had to bet on it, if I bothered to dig up the newspaper articles, if I wanted to find out for certain, I think, that's exactly what color eyes the man who raped my mother has too.

The kettle begins its high-pitched whistle.

I let it echo, and revel, very quietly, in its tiny scream.

CHAPTER 4
June 19

RED: Sometimes, strawberry. The little wild ones. Not
underripe, not over. Where this recipe can go wrong
is strawberries can run the risk of being expected,
of being compared to something store-bought. To
elevate the flavor profile, add lemon and basil.

I'm lugging this week's batch of Yellow out of the insulated box in my truck bed—a creamy blend Dom says will remind customers of dandelion wine—when I catch sight of King Nathan. His shoulders are still wide, but he's a half foot taller. Six one or six two in his tan boots. His hair has grown. It's not the tight fade he used to prefer. Now, it's more like a little halo. His long-sleeve shirt is untucked, the top few buttons open. In no time, those sleeves are going to be covered in the flavors of the week.

"Hey," he says, his back to the tangle of overgrown trees behind the shack.

I nod. Because what else do you say when you haven't seen someone in three years? In the age of social media. When they left without a goodbye. When they left after you burned it all down with your lies.

It wasn't a little fire. This one raged. It might yet smolder.

He approaches to help, hefting another batch onto his shoulder. His head is cocked to the side, so he doesn't freeze against the tub. Smart move. But King was never without smarts. In this town, when he found trouble, he always had his reasons.

"So you're back."

It's not a question, but King Nathan, yeah, he answers it to make sure I know this situation is only temporary. "For the summer."

"You going to talk about where you've been?"

"No," King says hard, but he smiles. It culls the bite—a smidge.

A crow in one of the trees caws down at us. And I think, yeah, yeah, I know. This is weird. King was my first friend here, when I showed up in the middle of ninth grade, brand-new to a town where most everyone had known each other since birth. He saw me in the hallway, leaning against my locker, wearing a ball cap and hoodie inside. Told me the hat and bunnyhug—the ridiculous local term for a hooded sweatshirt—were dress code violations. Peeling off the layers, I made a mess of my hair and he laughed quietly. He offered his locker mirror so I could fix up my look before homeroom. Inside, his locker was stacked with nonschool books: Ian Williams, Téa Mutonji, Natasha Ramoutar, Dionne Brand. He asked if I had anyone to have lunch with—invited me to join him.

Our end arrived fast and furious, like a sparkler burning out. Right now, right here, I can't dive deeper into that pool. Not while rushing to get ice cream into the freezers before it thaws. Not when I catch the thumping bass from Wyatt's Range Rover. It clashes with the country song blaring from the speakers—but that's Wyatt. He rolls onto the lot way too fast, like he always does, swerving close to the picnic tables, flicking gravel at me and King. The crow takes off, spooked.

"Is that who I think?" King's tone is unreadable. At least to me.

"Yep," I say.

"Is he still a bit of a dick? Funny but a dick?"

I fight the urge to roll my eyes. Or to tell King everything, like we're still friends. The only safe thing to do is nod.

We stand in silence as Wyatt climbs out of his vehicle. He's wearing expensive jeans. He doesn't let silly things like work side-swipe his style. Doesn't let silly words like *no* get in the way of what he wants. My ankle aches, weighed down by the ice cream. The urge to slap him sparks along my palm, radiating down my fingers. But hitting people isn't my style. I don't claw or do violence, even underwater where the ref can't see. Maybe I used to, out of water, for a while after King left. This new version of me, she plays entirely aboveboard. In the pool and on dry land.

The old King was friendly. This one, he's clad in shiny new armor—when over the in-between years I've finally managed to peel most of mine away.

This is a bad idea. Wyatt, King, and me working together. But I can't stop it. The kindling's already catching.

While they clasp hands and do their guy thing, I form a resolution. I won't play along like nothing went down. I won't make it a big deal either. But I don't have to let Wyatt off.

"Lou, you didn't tell me the King himself was back," Wyatt hollers, though I'm close enough yelling isn't required.

To unlock the heavy wooden boards that will lift up, creating our storefront, I climb on top of the freezer. From outside, King latches them easily. "She didn't know."

Wyatt stares at us as we work. "Black man of mystery, that's what you are!"

It's always like this with Wyatt and his friends: they idealize Blackness as *the coolest* and smash what they've taken into their upscale-country-boy swagger. And then they expect King to perform something that's not King but rather this TV stereotype for them. Even if he's not going to let me get close to him again, and I can't blame him for that, I won't let this bad behavior stand.

"What's wrong with you?" I ask Wyatt from my perch on the freezer. He doesn't get it, laughs at me, like I'm the one playing the fool. Like he didn't call me his Native girlfriend, over and over again—emphasis on *Native*, not *girlfriend*. "Why do you have to point out he's Black? Why can't he just be a man of mystery?"

Wyatt, he shrugs.

"It doesn't bother me," King says, staring at me. "*Black* isn't a bad word, Lou."

It's a scold.

Even though he told me how sick he was of the people in this town asking him to perform for them. But because it's me, he won't own up to it. Or maybe since he's been gone, he's changed in some fundamental way.

I have.

It's fair King has too.

Oblivious to the undercurrent, Wyatt untucks his shirt, quietly mirroring King. "I'd pay good money to have hair like yours, for, like, a night. The girls would be nonstop into it."

It's Wyatt who hasn't changed, can't seem to care that he hasn't grown. After that speech, he does the unthinkable: reaches his skinny arm out as if to rub at King's hair, like he's a pet.

"Man," King says, "don't," throwing a hand up in the air. It's not a threat, only a move forcing Wyatt to step back. And before Wyatt can do anything else, King deflects, "There's more in the truck that needs to get in the freezer."

I'm glad because it stops me from having to tell my ex to get to work. While I might be part of the family who owns this business, the four of us working this summer, we're supposed to be equals. That's important to Dom.

King steps close, leans in the serving window, and deadpans, "The caucasity." He smiles at me, big, wide. Even though he moved to the big city, he didn't fix his teeth. Something he swore to me he'd never do, full of pride in his own self, before things between us went bad.

Without thinking, I grin back at him. Maybe I'm seeing King all wrong too. But still I wish he'd called out my ex properly.

We don't have time for much more than stocking the freezers before the first customers roll up. I throw Wyatt an apron and he smiles like he used to, before I agreed to be his girlfriend. When he was simply charming and paying lots of attention to someone no one else really bothered with. Mostly because the rest of my classmates had been burned by my lies too. Little ones, but they'd observed the fallout from the bigger fires. Before Florence moved here, only Tyler, one of the bused-in rez girls, wanted anything to do with me—and even that friendship couldn't last, went up in smoke.

King plugs his iPhone into the aux cable attached to the old radio. Electronic synth-pop explodes, like cotton candy, sweet and empty and wonderful. It reminds me of the first musician we discovered together. Ria Mae. For weeks, she was all we listened to.

Our customers, mostly teens, begin to dance. Wyatt, watching them, tries out a few moves. Awkward and wrong. Last night's lie sits badly. Wyatt isn't boring. He throws everything he has at the people around him, hoping something will land a response. King caves first. I'd forgotten how he laughs, all uninhibited, mouth open so that his front-teeth gap is on full display, his nose flaring, eyes pinched almost closed. He laughs with his whole body. If he's wearing armor, it's not rigid. When he isn't paying attention, I study him, searching for the soft, friendly, funny person I used to know.

My chest relaxes a bit. It's finally, finally summer. Yet inside the shack it's still winter musty, and underneath my laughter, I'm full of quiet rage.

A little after four in the afternoon, the parking lot empties. The highway traffic simmers down low. Even the crows are silent. King sits on the prep counter, his legs long enough to reach the floor. He's fiddling with his iPhone, checking his messages or something. "Where's the Honeypot? I didn't see it when I drove up."

The PopSocket on his basic black case says I *CAN'T BREATHE*, and I know someone around here will call him out for being political, like he's stirring shit. If it's Wyatt, I'll reconsider hitting him.

"Not here yet." I'm leaning over the freezer, making a list of what to restock. The first day's always great for sales.

"I'll take a stroll, then."

"Watch out for those pesky drop bears," Wyatt says, snacking on his free cone. He dug into the sample batch of mustard with a *what could go wrong* attitude.

That joke, he's been playing it for months, after he heard it in a bad movie. Nobody but his buddies finds it funny.

King blows air from between his lips, raises a hand in a mock salute before he disappears. I'm wishing for customers. For so many customers that my ex and I can't manage anything but work.

But, of course, no one saves me.

I refuse to face him. If I don't catch sight of his blue eyes or remember what it's like to spend all day laughing because Wyatt's ridiculous, I will survive this.

"You won't maybe reconsider?" Wyatt asks.

My sore ankle throbs in sync with the song. "Nope."

"We had a good thing, you have to admit. A real good thing. I gave you a social life, and you—"

This is when King returns. He knows he's walked into something because Wyatt shuts up and I fiddle with the cash machine, my cheeks hot.

King hovers in the doorway. "Okay. We gonna talk about this?"

"No," Wyatt and I say at the same time.

"Louder music?"

"Please," I say to Wyatt's "Yes, man."

Even after more customers arrive, we don't get back to that rhythm, that happy-enough space. By talking about it, Wyatt's ruined everything. The whole summer. To escape my ex and this new King I can't quite figure out, I check on the backup generator three times. But every time I do it's set to auto and the fuel indicator points to full. Five minutes before our shift ends, I'm counting cash into a deposit bag.

Out by the picnic tables, Wyatt pretends to clean. He's talking to a table of our old classmates, all low-cut tank tops and shorts that barely cover their butts. He's laughing too loud. He's leaning in close, brushing Alice's sister's bare shoulder, again and again.

"You jealous?" King asks from behind me and I jump. "Wow, wound tight, eh?"

I don't say anything. But I stare him down.

"So I'm guessing at most of the story . . . but you two had a thing?"

"Extra emphasis on the past tense, please."

"You still seem—"

"Mad."

"You said it," he says. But he's smiling.

"Short story, okay? The very censored version. Tuesday, that one picked me up at the farm to go see a movie. We had a fight over something I'm never telling you about—so don't ask—and then he drove off, leaving me on the side of the highway."

King's eyebrows shoot up high. But he doesn't speak. Whatever he's thinking—good, bad, or ugly—he's holding his cards tight. Nothing like how we used to be, when I was the liar and he was wide open, vulnerable.

"It's not the kind of thing you can fix. We're not . . . compatible."

"Fair."

Outside, they're having a good time. They're laughing, all full of bravado.

"I'm sorry if it's making things weird."

King glances at his phone again. "I think things are going to be weird for a while, Lou."

I return to counting bills. Empty the tip jar—trying not to stare at the Albertosaurus sticker—and split the contents three ways. I push a blue bill from the register and a loonie across the counter toward King. "It's not much."

"Your uncles pay us more than minimum wage, and I've got an academic scholarship to the University of Toronto in the fall. So I'm not super worried about tips." He's proud of himself—it comes through in every word.

"Wow. Congrats." I'm happy for him. A little jealous. But I push happy to the top. "English and writing, right?"

"Yeah, that hasn't changed."

We hear Wyatt approaching. "Hey, people I work with. Can I take off? Elise and her bunch have plans. First the liquor store, then a partaaaay."

King defers to me.

I shrug. "Sure, yeah, we're almost done."

"I won't make it a habit, promise," Wyatt says, but before I can even offer him his tips, he's gone. Through the serving window, I catch him lifting Alice's sister off the ground like there's a fire somewhere. She squeals. Out on the highway, on the shoulder, but not in the lot, the same white SUV from last weekend idles. I can make out the plate: FREED. We're open, like we said we would be, but they aren't buying.

King bumps me in the shoulder with one of his elbows. "So, you're still into dinosaurs."

From my very first viewing of *The Land Before Time*, and its sequels, I was obsessed. The box set of DVDs Mom found secondhand and wrapped for my sixth birthday, I still treasure them, still watch them sometimes. King doesn't mention that the sticker on the tip jar was something he slipped into my locker after our grade-nine science teacher recommended me for a really cool opportunity at the Royal Tyrrell Museum. And he wouldn't know how my obsession has only grown the closer I've gotten to university—where I can properly study the massive beings who walked this land long before me. "Some things don't change."

The white SUV takes off, pulling a U-turn, and I'm flooded with a bitter taste. Wyatt's gone. I should feel better. I try to sweeten myself the best way I know how. I dig into a spoonful of the Red and savor it.

"You're still for Calgary?"

The unspoken words . . . *like we planned.* Back then, that's how I knew I'd made a friend; we schemed for months into the future, things like concerts and shopping trips to the cities. We had plans for after graduation, which, back then, was forever away.

"No. The University of Alberta." I fiddle around at the sink, cleaning errant scoopers. "Calgary has a grad program I like though."

King grabs a drying towel because he's not one to stand around empty-handed. "You'll get in."

I can't see his eyes. Can't see if he's playing me. What I thought was armor, maybe's it's only a new layer of city polish, the kind that glosses over sincerity. It's shiny, but hard.

And then he asks, "Are we good?"

"Yes," I say. "You must have had your reasons for leaving without a goodbye."

King laughs at me. "Well, that's nice to hear. But I meant for the shack. For my shift."

With still-wet hands, I pull at my ponytail to tighten it. And then I ramble, "I'm going to restock tonight because it's way cooler than trying to get this done when the sun is at full height. But you can totally—"

"You want some help?"

Does he mean it? But I'd be lying if I said I wanted to spend my first Sunday night as a high school graduate hefting frozen tubs alone.

I'd be lying. I'd be lying to King. Again.

I level my voice. "Yes, please."

"I wasn't really vibing with keeping my dad company while he sits in his boxers and rewatches Caribbean Premier League cricket games he recorded on VHS years back for the second night in a row. He knows how these games end. Where's the drama?"

King follows me to the truck.

"If you come over to the farm, my family's going to make you stay for food, and you won't get to leave until you've played pinochle."

King doesn't even blink. "I'm counting on your ma having a can of veggie chili in the pantry."

I volley a warning back at him. "It's probably expired."

Inside the truck, King doesn't ask, just starts fiddling with the radio as soon as he settles onto the long bench like he used to do. "Don't even. Your ma restocked as soon as she heard I was gracing you all with my presence for the summer."

I laugh quietly and remember how even when it wasn't easy, when I was lying to everyone, it was easy being friends with King—right up until it wasn't.

CHAPTER 5
June 20

ORANGE: Classically, Michif Orange is made with the skunkbush berry, also known as the sourberry. It's sticky, fuzzy, and extremely tart, so this recipe uses more sugar than most. Variants include lemonade sourberry and sourberry orange. Fun fact: while the sourberry bush looks like poison oak, it's totally, completely harmless.

The crows are quiet today as I park the truck in the lot. My hair is heavy and wet, my whole body tired. Since my mom first got it into her head that I should be a star, water polo has been my escape—but the sport claimed me too. The water is home in a way nowhere else has been, at least until we moved in with my uncles. Mom made sure there was a community pool nearby every new house and we had money for lessons. And in every library, I could find books on dinosaurs—even if they were outdated—and on just-because cake days, we'd always check out the dino-shaped pans.

Florence waits, perched on top of a picnic table, her feet dangling over the edge. Her hair has dried into her signature curls. It's this all-natural glamorous look here on the prairies, but back home, in Ireland, she says everyone looks like her.

"I know, I know. I overslept." She holds out an Iced Capp. "I forgot to set my alarm and last night the lads talked me into one too many. And, well, you know, my head is killing. It's not like I could have managed to actually swim. But point being, it will never happen again," she finishes with a huff.

I swirl the straw in the frothy drink. "It's okay."

She pushes herself off the table to follow me and the excuses don't stop. "We only arrived home yesterday afternoon, you know. And I texted. Saw Wyatt with a younger blonde. Ellie? Elory?"

"Elise," I say.

Florence doesn't remember what else she texted. Or if she does, she can't quite say it. She promised, cross her tarnished heart, hope to die young and beautiful, that she'd join me at the pool. But I know her promises don't always hold true.

"What happened, Louie? I only left town for a night. I didn't even go anywhere good. The parents wanted to visit Saskatoon this time! It's no Dublin." She runs out of steam.

It's still novel to Florence, how our town sits on the border of two provinces: making it half of one thing, half of another. I unlock the big front windows. Florence helps. Today, we have the day free of Wyatt—he's thankfully not on the schedule—so it seems okay to talk here. At least, until King arrives. "He was pressuring me. Like, Flo, he couldn't wait. At all."

"That's shite." Her hands are on her hips. "Want me to rough him up for you, pet?"

"He's not in today."

"He called off sick already? His second shift?"

"New schedule." I dig her copy out of my leather bag with the

43

good fringe and pass it over, admiring her orange nails.

"No way," she says when she reads the printout. But she steps closer and hugs me tight, her arms bony but strong.

When King pulls into the lot and backs his dad's forest-green Subaru next to my truck, I nod against her soft cardigan—alpaca or sheep's wool—something she didn't buy locally. "Yep."

King stretches, his plain white tee pulling up a little too high.

"He's a stunner." Florence sighs.

When I don't answer right away, she elbows me. She's seen pictures of fifteen-year-old King. Now, he's grown. Aesthetically, yes, he is beautiful. But physical beauty, for me, shows up in what others would call flaws: his slightly rounded body, his gapped teeth.

"Right, Lou? You must see it. You have eyes." Florence's long-distance girlfriend lives in Ireland, but Flo is very bi.

I'm trying to decide if I tell Florence the truth about this morning, her behavior lately. She shouldn't get away easy as this—with an iced coffee and a hug. She's unreliable. She's easily distracted. She doesn't mean to be: it's all symptoms. At Florence's highest highs she's impulsive, at her lowest lows, basically unreachable. She's my best friend, but there's no balance. And no time for another argument, for more excuses. King's stepping into the shack like he owns it, and Florence introduces herself, handshake and all. "My dad's in radio, my mom's an engineer. Relocated here partway through eleventh grade. Lou is my BFF now, but if you're lucky I'll share."

"King," he says. "I know who you are. I've caught your photos on Lou's Insta."

I don't even have time to enjoy King's admission that he's been scoping me out. That he might not be as chilly as I thought. That we might need time to figure each other out again. A horn sounds twice. This morning, it's not customers arriving first, but the guy delivering the port-a-potty.

Florence passes me an apron and then extends one to King. She touches his hand when she does. "We're going to have loads of fun this summer. Try and stop us."

There's nothing subtle about Florence and normally I adore that. Today, it's wearing on me. Maybe it's that throwing a bright yellow ball into an empty net is work. And this morning it hit me: all this laboring might not be enough to earn me a spot on the competitive team at the University of Alberta. "I'll get it," I say, and slip out, still clutching the apron.

The driver's new—not the guy from last year. After he unloads the portable bathroom, he hands over the delivery notice. He stares at my chest. "What's your shirt mean?"

I'm wearing my "Not Today, Colonizer" tee. "Inside joke," I say, shoving the invoice into my pocket.

"You must think I'm dumb," the driver says. "I'm not." His smirk is mean.

It was always easier talking to people like this man when I was pretending to be white. They didn't notice me. And I didn't provoke them. I shake my head, like no, you've misunderstood me, and glance toward Florence and King. They're close by. But they're not paying attention.

All the driver does is narrow his eyes and bark a rough laugh. "It's called the right of conquest, girl. Done and done and done."

Every time I wear this tee, I'm flooded with adrenaline. The urge to run. To fight. Someone else would stop wearing it. But

I can't. I'd be giving in. Giving up. Turning my back on my family—again.

The driver leaves the caustic burn of exhaust in the air.

Inside the shack, Florence's hand is on King's bicep, and she's describing the tattoo she'll get with her summer pay, sketching it out with her fingertips. They're standing close and whispering like they're conspiring. Or worse, like they're flirting. And for a minute, the old King is back. He was always fully focused on his friends and so easy to talk to because he gave all his energy to his conversations. I used to be granted that.

They're still completely absorbed in each other when a busload of kids from the local summer program runs for the shack, and Tyler, their leader, orders the children to form a nice line.

"Okay, here's a little bit of hell," Florence says. "Trouble, and not the good kind."

King laughs. "Ty and I, we went to kindergarten together."

For a moment, I imagine what Tyler might have been like at six. A little Nehiyaw *terror*. Now, she's all red eyeliner and ink. MMIWG2S surrounded by a sweetgrass braid on her right clavicle is my favorite of the bunch. I held her hand while the needle worked.

Tyler doesn't walk, she stalks, slow and precise. She never makes a move that isn't deliberate. Today, she's throwing a McIntosh apple up in the air. Throwing and catching. She takes a big bite, exposing the white flesh, and chews.

One of the kids whines, "Auntie Tyler, I need to pee."

Florence laughs darkly. It's like she worries I'll leave her for Tyler. It's a one-sided rivalry because Ty doesn't care. All I say is,

"The port-a-potty arrived. Just in time."

"Honeypot," King corrects me.

I ignore him. But secretly I'm thrilled he still cares about words, about finding the precise one.

Florence takes over. "Okay, pets, I recommend the Red, but if you know you're a little boring, just settle for the Blue. Stay away from Green—it's a gross, adult flavor even grown-ups don't enjoy."

The kids listening in laugh. King does too, not very quietly. Tyler's black hair blows in the breeze, but she only rolls her eyes. She doesn't find Florence amusing.

We begin to scoop. Ten minutes into the process, my combination water polo/scooping arm cramps up. It's possible I wasn't as much practicing as exorcising bad energies this morning. Now I'm paying for it.

I switch arms, accidentally elbowing King low in the ribs. He steps as far away from me as he can get while still doing his job.

"Oh dear, take a break." Florence forcibly removes the scoop from my hand and pushes me toward the door.

The line is dwindling now.

A half-eaten apple sits on the closest picnic table, white flesh exposed all along one side. Tyler holds out a baggie with all the kids' change in it. "The Red is good."

"I'll tell Dom." I'm listening for the crows, listening to the kids, because I'm not sure what else to say.

"How's your mom?" Tyler asks, not letting me get away with silence. "I'm addicted to her designs."

"She's fine."

Her gaze drops to the half-eaten apple. "I only wanted to say hi, cuz. We don't see you around much anymore."

It's a dig. She means the Friendship Center. I used to volunteer there. We answered phones, did odd jobs, tutored drop-in students, and we'd hang after our shifts. "I'm swimming a lot now. School, university apps. Life got busy."

It's true enough. Still, it tastes like a lie. Now, I'm staring at the apple too. As if it's a message. When I needed to break away, Tyler let me go easy enough—but maybe she's not over it.

"Relax," she says. "We miss you is all." Before I return to work, Tyler gestures at Florence. "Watch that one, eh. She's getting herself in deep."

I'm shaking my head before I realize it. They don't get along. Could never be friends. I steady myself. But it's not like Tyler to waste words. Or to expend energy on jealousy. Since Mom decided she was really leaving, I haven't been watching Florence as closely. Instead, I've been cataloging the dark circles under my mom's eyes.

Still, Tyler telling me what I should already know, Tyler telling me my business, when we don't talk anymore, it bites—almost as much as her half-eaten apple does when I try to interpret what it means.

And out by the road, past the bus, a white SUV is parked. It's far enough ahead that I can only just make out the license plate. FREED. When the bus drives off, all first-gear loud, the white SUV follows. In the shack, Florence and King are laughing again, the way I used to laugh with King—and I'm wishing Homer were here, next to me, vigilant, his eyes on the people I care about, barking to warn us of the dangers that lurk all around, even deep inside ourselves.

CHAPTER 6
June 21

ORANGE: The least popular flavor in ice cream,
but one of the most popular sorbets. There's
no explaining this fact. It just is. Sit with it.

I t's too early. I've slept too little. I grab yesterday's swim bag from
the floorboard of the truck. When the smell hits me, it's bad.
Like stagnant waters. But trying to squish all of me into a damp
suit will be worse. With Mom gone, no one reminds me to do the
things I forget. Like dry my stuff.

Last night, my uncles talked in restrained whispers until well
after midnight. Sound travels in an old house. The three main-
floor bedrooms are taken. The winter we moved in, after Maurice
got tired of seeing my mattress in the corner of the basement, he
framed me a room, hung drywall. Feet overhead have become easy
enough to ignore. Words filter through, but not whole sentences.
Can't keep . . . Expensive . . . Organic . . . Debts . . .

The community pool's sliding doors open with a swoosh.
At his desk, the receptionist waves. I scan my pass, and he says,
"You're late."

"I know!"

"Just kidding, whoa. Have a good workout."

In the change room, I catch myself in the mirror. I'm wearing a skimpy tank top with a bralette. The things I sleep in. When I realized I'd snoozed through my alarm, I scrambled out of bed and inhaled minty toothpaste. I don't have a clean shirt or an actual bra. As I fold myself into the wet suit, my body is all extra fat. Cut high on my hips, it makes me look wider than I am. Most mornings only me and a few seniors who swim patient, calm laps after their breakfasts are around.

And I'm thankful.

Today, out on the tiled deck, I'm not alone.

If it were Florence, I'd high-five her and get us in the water. I'd buy a lottery ticket, something I never do even though I'm eighteen now and it's legal, if it were my mom. I remember slowly: she can't be here, she's gone.

I don't know what to do with King Nathan.

"Morning," he says, perched on the pool's edge, his feet lost somewhere in the salty teal water.

"Um, hi."

"I'm not stalking you or anything. I like to swim."

I nod, wetting my goggles in a hurry. "You really didn't used to."

"My ma got me into it."

If he's talking about his mom, things can't be that weird between us. So I'm brave. "Actually, I didn't think you could swim."

"Racist," he says with a smile.

"No, seriously. You wouldn't go into the lake farther than the top of your suit when we were hanging with your cousins that time. You literally told me you could not swim. And only went in deeper the night we were . . . drinking," I say, in lieu of skinny-dipping, which we were also doing one early summer weekend back in the day.

"So I couldn't. . . . But now I can. And I like it."

"You're such a jerk."

He slips all the way in, grinning at me from under his swim cap.

We occupy lanes next to each other, and while I count laps, I'm paying attention to King. How he's got pretty good form. How he's taller than me. I push harder to keep firmly ahead. After all, swimming is *my* thing. The old King wouldn't have ever taken up the sport. Something about alligators and other predators waiting in the waters.

When I'm done—ten extra laps than usual—King's at the water fountain, drinking. "So, Florence tells me you're in training and she's a bad trainer."

"Florence is definitely not my trainer."

"You ought to tell her."

"Safer not to," I say, pulling myself out of the water. I try not to think about my hips. Or the fact that the last time King saw me in a swimsuit I weighed at least twenty pounds less.

"Well, I'm happy to stand in the net. In the shallow end," he says emphatically. "If you want to throw your ball at someone."

It's what Florence would be doing, if she weren't in bed—hungover, or depressed—or at her desk, manic, researching all the places she'll visit next year. He's sweet to offer. Yet King's Toronto shine is back in full form. As if he could take it or leave it, body language all aloof, even with his swim shorts inelegantly plastered to his thighs.

I walk toward the equipment room, trying hard not to fix my bottoms. If I do, it'll draw attention to something I really don't want him paying any mind to. "Actually, I'd love that."

He follows behind me. "Cool."

We work out, not speaking more than we need to, until the toddlers arrive. Upstairs, there's a glassed-in viewing area for parents to watch while their children learn how to float, how to stick their faces in the water. I have a hard time imagining King as a beginner, but we all start somewhere. With swimming, it's this.

As we return the net to the equipment room, he says, "I'm starved. Want to grab some breakfast before our shift? Wyatt's opening, right?"

Water runs down my braid in a line, pooling on the gray deck. "I shouldn't."

"I'll pay, if that's it."

"I can't."

"I owe you," he says, employing his charm. "When I left, I think it was my turn."

He's trying and I need to try too. I owe it to him, but I owe it to myself just as much. "Look, King, I want to." Kids funnel out of the equipment room, pushing between us. "And you're right. You totally owe me a meal at the diner, but I left the house on autopilot this morning, without a dry T-shirt. I'm not going to breakfast in my wet swimsuit."

His eyebrows climb. "Honestly?"

That word bites. I aim for level when I say, "Yes. By the time I make it home, change, and drive back into town, it'll be closer to lunch. And you're starved."

He shrugs carefully, as if I have the power to hurt him again.

"I have an extra. In my bag." He points toward the men's locker room. "It doesn't feature a pithy statement about a social justice cause. But it's yours, if you want."

He's big enough so it'll fit.

King's all hyperfocused, watching me. Like I'm rebuking his attempt to triage our friendship, and so I circle my head around, my braid throwing off water, wondering if I should tell him I don't have underwear either. I settle on that being too much truth this early in the day. And maybe between King and me, too much truth ever. "Fine. Okay."

"I'll get it for you." He disappears briefly. When he returns, he hands me another of his plain white V-necks. "Take your time."

Today, I unbraid my hair to wash it. Once it's clean, I knot it on top of my head, dressing quickly. My bralette is black, and this tee is just thin enough that my outfit can only be called a very bold fashion statement. I tie the extra fabric at my waist and shimmy back into my sleep shorts.

They're pink with a silky ribbon tied in a bow.

I peer in the full-length mirror and roll my eyes. I'm glad it's Florence's day off. She would go hard over this look. She'd laugh so long, she'd cry. I wouldn't blame her one bit.

In the lobby, King's waiting, his gym bag hooked over a shoulder, an Afro comb stuck in his hair. Back in the day, he never used to be so carefree about his hair. It was always tight and perfectly done before he left the house. Now, he's comfortable in his own skin. I never noticed that perfect was a kind of shell at fifteen, a way of blending in as much as he could.

"Wow. You really did not bring anything."

"Told you."

He stares at my shorts. At the pink bow. "You want to go home? I can wait—if I down a granola bar or two."

"Let's eat."

"You positive?"

I don't answer, just walk toward the exit. "Yours or mine?"

He nods over at his dad's Subaru. "I can drive."

As we head through town, we don't talk. When we pass an empty lot, right off the main road, both King and I avert our gaze. Now, it's only low-level rubble and shards of weathered glass. For fun, people smash bottles against the concrete. Still, the roadside sign stands tall out in front of the mess: O'Reilly's. Ever since that night, when I pass this place, I taste smoke. It doesn't matter if the air is clear, fresh; for me, it's acrid. With King beside me, I swallow the bad taste and begin picking at my ragged cuticles. But I stop myself. I curl my hands into tight fists. If Florence sees this as a tell, so will King—eventually. He doesn't miss a thing and never used to shy away from hard talks or hard truths.

A block later, I relax. The diner's parking lot is full but we find a spot next to the vape shop at the strip mall. Not that long ago, I sat on their fake leather couch with Tyler for hours. Florence isn't entirely wrong. Ty and me, we sort of ran around stirring up hell. After King left. Losing friends is a habit of mine. A habit as bad as lying. Part of me wonders if Florence is next. If I push her too far, if I notice out loud how hard she's been struggling. I wipe my palms on my shorts, shimmying them down my thighs at the same time.

Inside the diner is all chrome, the decor reclaimed from the 1950s. The coffee and food is cheap and good. At the far end of the counter, Tyler's baby sister, Cami, wears a frilly pink apron and aggressive winged eyeliner. She's fifteen and has this massive smile but doesn't show it much. She's a bit sullen. I try not to take it personally. The two of them lost their mother, violently, and that's not something you get over. She arranges new stock, earrings on a sale rack, while she waits for the "order up" call. They're my mom's.

King and I flip our coffee cups on the red-checkered counter-top. Our server fills them without asking and King loads his with sugar.

I say what I'm thinking out loud: "That hasn't changed."

"Never will," he promises. "Coffee beans are real bitter."

The bell above the front door rings and a pack of white guys I graduated with rolls in. Wyatt's friends. Marcus and Doyle. Some others. They join a table in the back, pulling out their chairs roughly, making their presence known by reminding the world how big they are.

I pick up my mug and sip. Someone's kid screams. A table of seniors laugh. Marcus, Doyle, and their buddies keep one-upping each other and yelling "Bro, no!" or "Yeah, bro, yeah!" The cook flips a pancake, bacon sizzles, a toaster pops, and one of the servers, she's singing along to "Billie Jean." This is my favorite place in town, and I haven't been here, not since King left.

King stares at me, waiting. He must have said something. "I was asking about that program, the one at the Tyrrell. Did you get accepted a second time?"

Our food arrives. Eggs and bacon and carbs and butter for me. Everything minus the meat for King. I dig into my eggs. "I did."

He covers his with hot sauce. That hasn't changed either.

"But the scholarship they offered wasn't enough," I say between bites. I claim the hot sauce from him to douse my eggs too. Another thing I haven't done in a long while.

Two weeks at the Royal Tyrrell Museum, working alongside their lead paleontologist, was my high school dream. But no way could I let half a year's university tuition plus room and board go toward a glorified science camp—even at the Royal Tyrrell. Instead, last fall, I visited the public-facing displays with Florence and her parents. I wandered around in awe, tried not to regret anything.

"Lou, I hate that for you."

I change the conversation, to avoid the sting of missing out on something I wanted but couldn't have, to avoid his compassion when I'm not sure I deserve it. Even after all that went down between us, King can still dig deep into his well and care about what I wanted for myself and never got to have. "Did you like Toronto? I mean, do you like it in Toronto?"

"Yeah," he says all low-key. Calls it the 6ix, but makes sure I know while it sounds exactly like the number, it's spelled different. Between bites he tells me about the city's vibe. Drops a little into the language he uses there, that he doesn't use here: flexing hard on Queen West and eating at poutineries, the ones that stay open until four a.m., with the broskis, about fake IDs and dancing, sweating in the club, about scooping his sister from her Scarborough foster home and treating her to Blue Jays games, way, way up in the nosebleed section. He calls it the SkyDome even though it was corporatized before we were born. King believes strongly in what things should be called.

He doesn't mention his Toronto friends. And I don't ask. Even if part of me worries that his whole speech was another performance—studded with slang that no one here will get without an explainer. But he's letting me in, talking about his sister. "She's what? Fourteen?"

"Thirteen. And sweet and smart and so fucking angry."

"I mean . . . relatable content."

King laughs like I've made a joke, but I'm serious. I remember twelve, my constantly flaring nostrils. And thirteen, the way I'd cut anyone off, not let them speak to stop them from hurting me. At fourteen, I started grinding my teeth. It got better for a little while, and then after King left, worsened again. I'm not angry anymore. Not like that. I can't afford to seethe—like Tyler. After a night of flame, anger can burn out. Anger can simmer under the surface, waiting, too.

The server drops off the check and King swipes it, extracts a few bills from his folded brown leather wallet. We've been in the diner for over two hours. Talking almost like we did when we used to be friends. Maybe this, what we're doing now, is a new shot at friendship. I don't want to ask him, won't ruin it. I smile to myself and jump off the high-back bar stool. Even if the anger is waiting, this, right now, is nice. I'm full, and the kind of tired that comes after a good workout. I practiced for real today. I ate at the diner. And I'm hanging out with King, getting to know him again, without active lies hindering us. But in this town, this brand of happiness can't last. Maybe your anger comes for you. Maybe it's something else.

Between King and me, the fallout, the betrayal, remains alive. It has its own heartbeat. It lives in the hesitations, lives in the things King didn't tell me about his Toronto life: the people he left behind when he came here for the summer, the ones who miss him, the ones he's been missing back. The ones he's always checking his texts for.

On our way out, weaving between tables, I hear a voice I shouldn't. Not here. Not now. In a corner booth, Wyatt emphasizes some point with a *bae*, and then swoops in and locks lips with Elise.

I inhale loud. King notices. He scrambles to pull the schedule up on his phone like this is his fault. "I swear we were both in at noon."

"We are," I say, stalking toward Wyatt's booth. I clear my throat, but that doesn't force them to pull their faces apart. Elise's hands are buried in his greasy hair and it looks like she's into it, but I remember eight days ago when that was me and his tongue was a boiled fish in my mouth. "Hey! Hey, you two!"

Wyatt extracts himself. "Oh, sheeeeet."

"Yeah."

The excuses flow. "I swear I forgot, and then we'd already ordered and—"

"Enjoy your day off," I say.

"Lou, don't be like that," Wyatt counters.

I hold one hand up in the air, and it works. He shuts up. Behind me, at the counter, Doyle and Marcus are cashing out. They laugh loudly at some bro-this comment, flinging a couple of quarters in Cami's direction as a tip.

Hours later, we're closing the shack. With a washcloth in hand, King, who's been friendly and funny like the old days all day, blasts me with a serious look. When he says, "It's really none of my business," my stomach drops.

We've been getting along so well. I try for trust. I have to be strong enough to handle his honesty. It was always the thing I admired most, even while I was lying to him, to everyone, constantly. "Go on."

"Are you planning on letting your uncles in on Wyatt's big miss today?"

I shrug—a little, sharp gesture. While I tell my uncles a lot more than I used to, I don't have to tell them everything. "We handled things."

King exhales, in the way that, even back in the day, meant someone had disappointed him. Had failed to live up to his super-high standards. I grind my molars to stay quiet. I thought we were making progress. I thought wrong. When King unplugs his iPhone from the aux cable, I say something like "See you tomorrow," and he asks, "Are you hiking to the pool to get your truck?"

I close my eyes when his gaze intensifies into something much too much. I've managed to disappoint him again—already. I start at my cuticles but force myself to quit.

In the Subaru, the music means we don't need to talk. There's no traffic on the highway but we're stopped at every red light. And we say nothing. We really are strangers after all. Three years is a very long time.

Still, part of me wants to tell him how last week I walked home almost all the way from town on a bad ankle, to hear what he'd say. King would have all the technical words to describe Wyatt's bad behavior and he'd *care*. But King doesn't know. No one does—except Wyatt, who found a replacement for me so fast. She seems to like his fish lips.

I'm going to have to learn to swim in these new waters.

Once we're safely parked next to my truck, I grab for the door handle and say, "Good night—" at the same time as King says, "Look."

He points at the sky. Little explosions rocket off in the distance. "What do you think they're celebrating?" he asks.

"That they're still alive, still breathing. Or they've been drinking and everything, including playing with explosives, sounds like a good idea right now."

He laughs wide enough for me to get a glimpse of his teeth. "Good night, Lou."

"Night," I say over my shoulder, clutching my gym bag. "I'll wash the shirt later this week."

"Keep it. It looks good on you."

My cheeks throb. Waving awkwardly, I climb up into my truck. The night air is cool and almost smells like rain is coming. I dig into my bag of wet things, searching for my lip balm, wondering if it's just rained here or if the storm is still on its way, when I discover a letter. It's in a plain envelope, *Louisa* written on the outside in blue ink. My mom's name. But she's gone, and this isn't my mom's gym bag. I tear into it.

THE FIRST LETTER

Dear Louisa,

We've not met. There's not been a clear avenue of approach until recently. It's a winding story, and one the courts believe I hold blame for. You've heard your mother's spin, her understanding, no doubt. What I want to tell you—father to daughter—it's not about her. It's about us. There was an incident in the prison, a year and a half after you were birthed, where a man died by my hand. My sentence was extended indefinitely. You have to understand what being caged is like. What eliminating man's God-given freedoms does to strong, proud males.

You and I. We have the right to meet each other. I have the right to mold you into a woman—like any father does. We've had too much time taken from us already. Louisa, as your father, the time has come for me to step into that role. We'll arrange a time and place to meet.

Yours,

Peter England

780-555-0356

CHAPTER 7
June 21

ORANGE: Generally, a hard color to create without poisonous dyes. Since we don't use anything like that, I'll share a trick. You think of turmeric for yellows, I know, but turmeric will bring out the color you're seeking. Just don't use too much. A tablespoon is plenty. Any more and you're making turmeric ice cream—which we might try someday. But not today.

Under the community pool's parking lot lights, my hands shake. A second page slips from behind the letter. It's a copy of my birth certificate. On the line for *father*, Peter England has written his name in confident all caps. My insides thicken and then there's pressure. I haven't eaten since breakfast, but that doesn't matter. I fling the truck door open wide and lean out, gagging. This is worse than that freezer-aisle grocery-store smell, worse than Wyatt's cologne.

I lean too far, slip from the bench and tumble to the ground. Palms and knees dig into the rough pavement. I gag again. Nothing comes up. The pressure intensifies. Acid burns in my throat, my fire seeping out.

The do-not-contact order has been in place since before I was born. But it ends the day he's released. It's something I've always known.

For him to write me . . .

Now I do vomit.

What my mom told me: Peter England, he's as white as they come. Old, old settler stock. She knew him. They didn't travel in the same circles. He attended the Catholic school. And one night, out on the land, at a bush party, he tried to convince her to go off with him. He flirted. They'd both been drinking. She said no. She didn't want him. He left. She hung with her friends. But her friends evaporated, one by one. To fill up their drinks. To chase warm bodies. And when she was alone, he returned. He'd been drinking. He asked again. She said no. When he hit her across the face, she tumbled to the ground. His breath tasted like rye. He hit her again. When she woke with underwear missing, her jaw was broken, she was alone—covered in bites from mosquitoes and black flies, bruised, unable to do much more than crawl to the road.

She crawled a kilometer or more.

A local farmer found her first. He was riding his tractor between fields. He said he'd call an ambulance. And he must have. But he left her there. Bleeding and broken like she was an animal.

He left her there.

He just left her.

I wipe at my mouth with the back of my hand. When my stomach settles into a stone, I brush fine dirt and blood from my knees. I shove the papers into my bag with my wet things and drive home like I've forgotten how, at night, deer cross this road in droves and if you don't watch the shoulder for their glowing eyes, you're risking your life and theirs. I can't care. I can't. I'm reckless.

Beneath the sting of stomach acid, under all that burn, I taste smoke. It's up in my hair, like it was the night I stood next to Tyler in the back alley of O'Reilly's, watching, watching as flames took hold.

I rip onto our dirt road. The wheels spin out for a second before I let off the gas. Maurice will lecture me if he isn't plugged into his headphones. Something about grading the road. Something about what it costs to fix mistakes. I'm lucky that while Maurice is composing, he's not quite in this world, listening to the old songs, laying them in new arrangements, like my mom is when she beads. Unlike Maurice, Dom won't berate me. He remembers what it's like to be young here. But he *will* ask what's wrong. And that's equally horrible. Telling him about the letter in my swim bag will lead us nowhere good. Telling him will lead my family to break apart, to splinter —and my mom will suffer most. Strange laughter bubbles up from my stone stomach. I'm happy, for the first time, truly happy, my mom's gone.

If he's free. If she knew. If she ran into him at the grocery store. If she had to face him, she'd run, again.

It's for the best, her being gone. It's for the best, keeping secrets like this.

I rub at my eyes, using the half-ruined-from-age truck mirror to investigate the damage. Swollen, all puffed up, and what mascara I managed to put on after swimming has run in goth-girl-gone-bad streaks down my face.

If I could sleep in the truck tonight, I would.

But my uncles will come fetch me if they catch me out here too long. Something about responsibility to their sister, to me, their kin. I wipe my eyes the best I can on my gross swim towel, staining it permanently.

In the mudroom, I kick off my flip-flops. One lands in the middle of the pathway. The other smacks against the far wall.

My uncles aren't eating or playing cards. They don't look up when I enter the kitchen. They're arguing.

"You're not letting me express—"

"You're expressing yourself fine, Maurice."

"Then you're—"

They finally hear my footfalls and stop.

Instead of dropping my bag in the mudroom, grabbing some tea, and checking the fridge for leftovers, I'm waving at my uncles with one raised hand and pushing through our crowded kitchen to the far corner in a hurry. The basement stairs are my escape. My uncles let me pass without comment. No *Taanishi, yaence.* No *How was business today?* And as soon as I'm clear, they resume their fight, quieter with a witness in the house.

At the very bottom of the stairwell, I'm breathing carefully so they won't know I'm listening.

"We're swamped and we can't wait to see how Louisa does. She'll lose most of her profits on gasoline and motels anyhow— you know it. She's doing this for herself, not for the family, which should tell you all you need to know. We can't wait to see if your ice cream saves us this year. We must decide soon."

After everything she's done for me, she's allowed to be selfish.

She's allowed to take care of herself. Still, she's my mom. Mine. And I want to be selfish too, want her here to run her fingers through my hair and to sit with me on the porch, sitting, saying nothing, as much as I'm glad she's gone. Her text to me today: **I had the best bison burger just now—so juicy. Tell me my brothers are feeding you well?**

Upstairs, Dom says something I can't make out, all hard consonants. It could be Michif. More likely it's English, and I'm too far away from the conversation to understand words shaped by anger.

Everything falls silent.

I'm waiting for Maurice to push onward, but he refuses.

Soon, it's chairs grating against the floor. Soon, it's dishes being cleaned, a little roughly. Soon, Maurice travels down the hall. His equipment turns on, and a few fiddle notes blare out before he connects his headphones and disappears. Soon, even Dom extinguishes the light and steps onto the covered porch to smoke his hand-rolled cigarettes. Soon, I'm in my bedroom, ripping my earrings out. I'm riffling through my bag to reread the letter.

Blue ink bleeds across the page like a wound.

Dear Louisa,

We've not met. . . . I am your father. . . . Peter England.

My eyes burn. He can't be out. He can't be. He can't. Perched on the edge of my bed, I dig through my bag for my phone. It's like I've disappeared. Sunk down under the weight of what I know, and I'm waiting at the bottom of the pool to be rescued. But no one is coming.

My phone is damp. The screen doesn't respond to my touch.

Using the long blade from my Swiss Army knife as a pry tool, I crack the case open and wipe the moisture away on my sheets. Then I open my text message chain with Wyatt—quiet since the day of the breakup, when we were joking about sneaking into the theater and not buying tickets at all—and I type.

> **Did you . . . ?**
> **Tell me you did it.**

Immediately those three little dots appear.

> **What you talking about bae?**

>> **The letter.**

> **Wait. I don't get it. ???**

Fury slips into my body. It runs along my veins, pumped forward with each heartbeat—and then it jumps the fire control line. He's out. He's really out. They released him. I pull my hair from its messy bun, ripping out a handful of strands at the end, when the tie won't come loose.

Wyatt's name pops up on my screen again: **Lou, what's the punch line? What's the joke?**

I launch my phone across the room. Something cracks.

For a while, curled on my bed, my knees drawn to my chest, I open and close my hands, forming powerful fists, stopping myself with will alone not to see if I have the strength to punch holes in the drywall that surrounds me.

I fall asleep wearing King's T-shirt.

CHAPTER 8
June 22

YELLOW: They tend toward the mellow. Dandelion wine or
golden currant. We blended a white peach recipe once, but
that wasn't local and honestly, didn't seem to fit, at least
for us. That said, yellows can be shocking too. When they
manage this, they force us to reevaluate softer flavors and
that's utterly powerful. All life exists on a spectrum, after all.

After knocking three times, Maurice leans into my room.
"You not well, Lou? I have wild-mint tea I can brew? Or
licorice?"

I sit up, my legs tangled in a pile of blankets, like I've been
flutter kicking in my sleep. "W-what time . . . is it?"

"You've got twenty minutes to dress and drive to the shack,
ch?" He nods in his way, slow and without meaning much more
than he's here and he's listening. "Unless you're unwell and then I
can ring up Florence and request she subs in."

I shoo him out. "I'm good. Really. Thanks for waking me."

As soon as the door is closed, I'm running a brush through my
hair painfully fast, settling on another messy bun, switching over
to underwear, to my favorite thrifted linen skirt, all while wearing
King's T-shirt. Eventually, I have to change. Put on a proper bra.

I grab a tee out of the pile at the end of my bed, clean clothes I haven't put away yet, reach for it because it's yellow and bright. It's from a local Students Against Drinking and Driving chapter's fundraiser: Students Do It Sober!

When I arrive at the shack, barely in time for my shift, Wyatt is scooping alone. He waves at me, all carefree smile and too-long hair.

I reach for my phone. I will sit out here and text until the clock says it's exactly noon. Hairbrush, hair elastics, wallet, and two handfuls of candies from the diner are all scattered along the bottom of my leather bag with the good fringe, alongside three pens. But there's no phone. Then I remember throwing it across my bedroom—hearing the crack. I slept hard, but I don't feel like I did, sitting in the sun, knowing Peter England isn't locked up anymore.

I squeeze past Wyatt and start working without a word. If someone wants a Red or Orange or Yellow, I point and let them order from him. Today, I'm serving the darker colors. Today, I'm in the mood for oregano. So I recommend it to everyone.

"It's spicy and fresh and really unique. Care for a sample?"

"Sure, yeah," a customer says. "Who turns down free sweets?"

Wyatt butts in. "But really, the Red is better this week. Why would you want spicy ice cream?"

"I'll try that too."

Wyatt rushes to fetch a mini bamboo spoon, knocking a scoop off the ledge.

"Oh, wow," the customer says. "You're right. This is . . . Wow. I don't need to try anything else. Two scoops of Red, bro. Great recommendation."

I pick up the scoop, wash it, seething inside. Customers show up, in ones and twos and fours, well into the afternoon. When King arrives, he plugs his music in automatically—today, it's old-school R&B, his hair newly fashioned in little twists—and takes over the cash. It's hard to get used to him with anything other than a tight fade. Before his mom left, she used to do his hair, didn't trust anyone else in town—I've listened to King's stories about having to sit perfectly still for hours, while his mom multitasked, the forever dramatic story lines of *Passions* in the background. After, without his mom around, it was easier to keep things simple. But this isn't simple—and I can't help but wonder if King is reacting to what Wyatt said that first day, if he's showing Wyatt that no, this cannot be copied, and King won't quietly fall back into the spot Wyatt and his buddies carved out for him in kindergarten.

The ice-cream-sample battles rage on even with King present. We don't draw blood, but we're vicious. After I lose another and audibly say, "Fuck off, Wyatt," King, always the peacemaker, the one to deflate a tense situation, lays both hands on my shoulders and gently navigates me over to the worn stool so we can shift places.

I huff, removing my eco-decomposable food-prep gloves.

King leans close, his breath warm against my ear. "Now, I don't want to tell you your business. But I think I have to or you'll end up kissing him again. Or killing him right here in this shack."

My eyes widen. I pivot to face him. "This isn't one of your stories, King."

He smirks. "Enemies-to-lovers is a popular trope for a reason. It happens."

"It's not happening here. But I'll knock him on the head with an ice-cream scoop if it will up the drama," I say a little louder.

Wyatt throws up both hands in surrender. "We were having fun. Weren't we?"

King doesn't give up, attempts again to keep the peace: "It takes a level of chill to serve ice cream on a hot day. Get me?"

"He's—"

"I know," King says, and returns to tidying things while Wyatt excuses himself to smoke his silly vape pen on one of the picnic tables. "But, Lou, you're behaving badly too."

My cheeks burn. He's right. I'm acting like a child. Maybe I'm acting like Peter England's child. No, no—I'm acting like I did when I ran with Tyler. I furtively check my hair for lingering smoke. While it's quiet, I shift bigger bills from their slot to under the cash tray. Without a workout this morning, I'm wound tight. I won't get what I want if I don't work for it, and that makes this feeling worse. Like sleeping is self-sabotage.

After the dinner rush, Elise's boring sedan glides into the parking lot. She lingers at the closest picnic table. Wyatt delivers her samples, absconds from the shack every few minutes. When he finally scoops a massive Red sorbet for his new girlfriend, I snap. "Seriously?"

"Christ, Lou, take it out of my tips."

"You know free ice cream is for staff only."

"I said I'll pay. What else do you want?"

"Most people do that before they consume the product."

King leans against the counter between us. He taps his thigh in time with the music.

"Lay off the jealousy. It's not hot. And it's not an ice cream, it's a flipping sorbet," Wyatt says, and storms off.

"Feel better?" King asks once he's gone.

I want to lie so badly. But King is the one person who won't forgive me if these little lies build up. "Not at all."

"And I'm sorry for that. But he's right about one thing. You can't have it both ways. Either you're dating him or, to borrow a Wyatt-ism, you ain't."

"That's not even the problem," I say, and regret it. I don't want to get into this with King. Especially not here. Wyatt's a few meters away, happily flirting with his girlfriend.

But I can't lie. Won't lie. There's got to be another way out.

Peter England's out, a little voice in my head echoes. *Out, out.* I fall quiet. "Please, King, can we drop this?"

He exhales harder than usual. But then shrugs and lets it go.

Wyatt abandons his tips again, leaving with Elise, who has the nerve to come up to me alone at the door—not the window—before they do. "Hey, I'm sorry. Do you want me to pay?"

"Your boyfriend's got you covered," I say.

"Cool." She smiles. She's just finished tenth grade. She's a baby. Only last year, she had braces. Now her teeth are perfect—like Wyatt's. "For the record, in the future, I'll pay. I don't want there to be anything weird between us. Or Wyatt and you. I know it's not great seeing him with—"

"Please, it's not even." A little part of me wants to warn her, to suggest she run now, before he's ordering her to jump from a moving vehicle. Another part of me can't get involved in Wyatt's business.

"You're sure?"

I lie: "Totally."

Even though I don't want him back, don't want what he wants, I'm all boiling water, all screaming inside the kettle walls watching him be a fool for someone else. I wish, really wish, it were okay to do it like we did when we were kids. Throw a fit, kick and wail, and then pick yourself up again, move on with your day.

Instead, as we close shop, I clean, washcloth in hand, while my mind runs this in a hard loop: *He's out. Out. Out, out.*

In the parking lot, King only says, "See you, then," and leaves.

And I hate myself, standing alone for ten minutes, while mosquitoes swarm, bite into my skin, wishing he'd asked if I wanted to hang, wishing Wyatt would stop flaunting it, wishing Florence would quit texting at five a.m. promising she'll be at the pool by six. All impossible things. Wishing I didn't care about any of them.

But one thing sticks from today. King isn't holding back from telling me the big truths anymore. And if I spend all my energy on my ex, I'm going to burn out, and everything I'm working for this summer will be that much harder.

At home, the lights are on. The kitchen table is strewn with paperwork. Bills and legal documents. My uncles shuffle around somewhere in the basement. They were deep into it last night.

I pull up the first invoice. Vet fees for the cows.

Dr. Cornell Nathan.

Under it, another. For the dogs—shots and yearly checkups.

Dr. Cornell Nathan.

Under that one, a bill for repairs to the production freezers after they failed a month ago. We lost our early stock and had to do major retrofitting. It was expensive. Like we-needed-another-small-business-loan expensive.

Under that one, an invoice for my truck's water pump—something I told Maurice I'd figure out myself because how-to videos exist and my labor would be free—but he refused. Three hundred and sixty dollars owed to Sadie's Automotive Repair.

When my uncles' footsteps reach the bottom of the stairwell, I rearrange the papers in a perfect stack and bury my nose in the fridge.

"There's hamburger soup on the middle shelf," Maurice says when he sees me. "And some fresh bread care of that one to go with it."

Dom elbows me. "I'll get it out."

He's out. Out, out.

"I'm not letting you microwave this. Sit, sit."

I do. In my chair, at a table covered with bills no one is talking about. At least not today, not now that I'm home. It's a weird realization, that my uncles, that my mom, they have a whole life that keeps going while I'm not with them. I wonder what my mom's doing right now. The thought swells like a blackfly bite. Hot, swollen, itchy. Today, she's only texted *love you*s and bison emoji.

He's out. Out, out.

Maurice notices my eyes wandering and hurries to clean up. "I was filing these. They certainly do not belong on the table where we eat."

Lies.

Dom, from the stove top, where he's heating up the whole vat of soup, asks, in that forever meddling tone of his, "So, yaence, how's King Nathan working out?"

"We should be talking about Wyatt Thomas."

Or Peter England. But I can't. This life I've been building, it comes apart as soon as I mention his name to my uncles, to my mom. As soon as they know, everything will change. All that pain my mom has carried from move to move, it will be reborn.

"That bad?" Maurice asks, carefully returning the bills to a worn brown accordion folder.

He can't know what I'm thinking. Can't read minds.

"Oh, that one, he has a new girlfriend and she hangs around a lot and he's getting sloppy."

"Already?" Dom says, carrying my soup.

It doesn't matter if he means Elise or Wyatt's ridiculous work ethic. It just doesn't matter, so I nod.

This time Dom uses his eyebrows to talk.

The aroma of soup, and Dom's tobacco, are delicious. The only thing missing is my mom. Sitting on her chair, beading or laughing, or both. I dig into the meal. Add more pepper and a dash of hot sauce. *He's out. Out, out.*

"Let me know if I need to have a talk with that boy," Maurice says, kissing me on the forehead before excusing himself. He carries the accordion folder away with him.

Dom passes me a thick slice of rustic bread. "Seriously, though, how's King doing?"

"Great," I say, my mouth full of soup.

"Doesn't sound like I should believe you."

"I'm eating!"

"Excuses, excuses," he says.

"Really, he's . . . great."

Dom sits next to me, in my mom's chair. "But?"

Out. Out, out.

"It's just I thought we were learning how to be friends again and today, it felt off. Weird."

The bread, some recipe from a book Dom bought at the Goodwill, is slightly sour and fully crusty. It drinks up the broth without falling apart. It's heaven, for someone who failed to eat anything but two granola bars for breakfast, and whose lunch was a double scoop of Indigo. I rise from my chair to cut another slice.

"You know he called here this morning. Early hours."

"Who?" I ask, because suddenly I'm worried we're talking about Wyatt again. Or worse, Peter England. Because he's out.

Dom says, "King," like it's totally obvious.

I swallow hard. "What for?"

"To make sure you were alive. You stood him up for swim practice?"

"Oh."

"He said you weren't answering your phone. I checked but you were asleep, snoring a little. It was super seukrii."

I raise my eyebrows at the "sweet" comment.

"So I left you there."

Out, out.

"I forgot my cell at home today. It was probably on silent. Maybe that's why I missed my alarm?"

"Sure you aren't coming down with it? Maurice told me he

found you curled up like a hibernating bear at almost noon o'clock. That's not like you."

I reclaim my seat.

"The soup will help," Dom says, patting me on the shoulder. "You know what? I think King wants to be your friend again. And you two need to agree you're going to talk about things like this. Talk even when it feels . . ."—Dom throws up scare quotes— "weird."

"Talking to him is both the easiest thing and really, really hard."

"I know, Lou."

"He's always waiting for me to lie to him."

Dom's face still falls when he remembers those lies. But he recovers fast. "Well, you did tell him a few good ones back in the old days."

I nod slowly, chewing the bread. *Out, out.*

"I'm in the production studio all tomorrow, so I should get some sleep. Plus, Dr. Nathan is looking at the cows again. Mooreen and a few others seem . . . off." Dom places the lid back on the soup, readying it to return to the fridge after it cools. "Oh, and your mom called. She's in Lethbridge for another night, then she's off to Montana. After that, it'll be Wi-Fi calls only—she wanted me to remind you. She sounds . . . happy."

Worry roots in Dom's eyes—probably the cows. Some days, his whole heart belongs to those animals.

"Love you, Dom."

"In Michif."

"Keesha kee taen."

"Same," he says, and walks down the hall. Soon the shower begins to run.

It's right, keeping this secret from my family. I abandon my dirty bowl and race downstairs, taking the steps two at a time, to find my phone. Screen's cracked, but it's not too bad. A jagged line across one corner. Battery's low, but not so low I can't go cordless. Changing into pajamas—King's T-shirt and a pair of shorts—I sit on the covered porch, my legs tucked underneath me.

Twenty missed text messages from an unknown number. A 416 area code. I look it up: Toronto.

> **I'm at the pool.**
>
> **Still here.**
>
> **You all right?**
>
> **Maybe you stayed in bed.**
>
> **That's fine.**
>
> **Calling your house, to check.**
>
> **Making sure you're alive.**

All of them just like this.

I text back.

> **Slept in, left my phone at home,**
> **literally a mess. Thanks for checking**
> **on me. But—real question?—why**
> **didn't you say anything?**

He answers immediately:

> **Seemed like you were having a hard**
> **enough time.**

Something relaxes. Just melts. My stomach is full, my phone is okay enough, and King was waiting at the pool for me. I banish all thoughts of anything but this. I can be selfish. *He's out.* That might be fact. But I won't contact Peter England. I won't answer him. At all. And that's how I'll move on. How I'll keep my mom safe.

My phone vibrates in my hand. I smile.

Without my adding to it.

I sort of got the feeling you were upset with me.

Well, if I was, it wasn't really with you.

Three little dots.

I wait.

And wait.

Eventually this pops up:

Okay, I was cheesed. With the you I thought I was dealing with. The old version. I didn't want to give you the chance to lie to me. So I was preemptively in a mood? Maybe?

It's fair enough.

What are you doing right now?

Nothing.

Come over and we can talk to the cows in the hayloft. They probably won't recognize your voice, though, so you know. Prepare yourself.

80

Three little dots.

I don't think I'll cry.

Okay, I might cry.

Bring tissues.

LOL.

Fifteen minutes.

I wait on the porch for King's headlights to swing into the drive.

He's out. Trying to reach for me, to claim me. My mind flashes to the white SUV, the one lingering about the shack. And I worry Peter England's already too close. It's exactly loud enough, that vanity plate. The kind of thing a man like him would do. Part of me worries I'm paranoid—that if I had a mirror, I'd reflect my mom every time, in the weeks before she decided it was time to move to another city, another house, another school. Those haunted eyes. But King arrives, and like he used to when we were friends before, he bypasses the house, heading straight for the barn. I follow a path I know well. The barn's red paint is peeling. Soon, I'll be far away from here. At university studying real dinosaur bones, not just reading about them on blogs. And that might be far enough. Mom's already talking about joining me in Edmonton. Maybe I can have my own blog. I'll call it *Notes from the Land before Time.*

"Hey," King says, and hugs me. He's warm, in a baggy hoodie and sweats. My head fits against his chest. "Sorry about blowing up your phone."

"Sorry about ditching this morning. I slept until almost noon."

"It's cool," he says, and means it.

We climb the old wooden ladder up into the hayloft—King first, since I'm wearing sleep shorts—and open the window. From here, the stars are bright and we're a little closer to them. Back when Dr. Nathan had to drive King out here, we used to pick out constellations and tell stories. King's were wild, full of plot twists and unexpected turns of phrase. It was always clear he was a storyteller. I wonder if he still writes seriously—hope he does—but I can't ask him—not yet—not until we find steadier ground.

"Still wearing my shirt," he says.

"It's soft."

He smiles, his eyes crinkling.

"Thought you were getting this back, eh?"

"Like I said. It's yours."

And then he starts mooing gently at the cows below us. I lie on my stomach so my head sticks out the barn window, and for the first time in a long time, I moo too.

CHAPTER 9
June 23

YELLOW: It's hard to get ice-cream and sorbet recipes as sharp as nature's own. For a smooth yellow, sometimes you need to cheat. Turmeric can muddle the delicate flavors. Saffron isn't local, but it works too. Here, at the Creamery, we don't mind a yellow that's a little less vibrant if the flavor shines. Flavor is prime. But hey, really, you do you.

I've fallen into a summer rhythm. Scooping at the shack, training in the pool, and spending time with my friends. Tonight, King drives me out to the bonfire so we can hang with the people I graduated with not even a week ago. Neither of us is drinking because it doesn't seem fair to leave the other person out. Somebody needs to drive. And it's no fun to drink alone.

Or at least I'm hanging out with one of my friends. Florence is absent, again, tied to her computer. Planning her trip. So she says.

I'm waiting for Peter England to show up, but he hasn't—yet. As we drive through town, and then out into the bush, I watch for a white SUV, his, not his, depending on how worked up I am in the moment. But it's gone, as if I imagined it. Florence has told me about her ghosts, what she calls her Thevshi, how sometimes, her reality isn't the same as mine. For her, the side effects of certain meds twist things, until their very *thingness* is suspect. I worry I'm slipping into an in-between space. Will I be safe there? Without my mom to ground me, how will I navigate?

It's hot still, close to midnight. I'm sitting in a clearing in the sparse woods on a fallen log someone has made into a fairly comfortable bench. King excuses himself for a moment. Underneath it all is the thing I'm not saying: I can't shake the feeling we shouldn't be here. I'm low-key itchy. And it has nothing to do with Peter England. The last time King was out in the bush like this, he disappeared for years. The last time I was . . . I don't remember what happened, how I got back to town, how I found myself on that ratty couch in that row house, sleep crusted in my eyes. I woke Tyler and we stumbled out before any of the men noticed.

I'm letting Wyatt be Wyatt, and Elise is trying so hard to be friendly it's almost too much. With King, sometimes I'm sure we're over the past. The lies. And Peter England, I'm pushing him out of my thoughts. *Out, out.* Pushing this nagging voice that tells me Dom must know—my uncle must have gotten the release notice—*out, out.* Because if he held it in his hands, at the start of the summer, and lied to my mom's face, I don't know how I will forgive him.

Music thunders from someone's truck's speakers. Luke Bryan and the Zac Brown Band, and later, for sure, there'll be some Garth. Willie Nelson, when he shows up, will have everyone cheering.

High-pitched laughter cuts through the music. Tyler and her friends swing into the clearing and claim seats all around me.

Ty's baggy black hoodie brushes her knees. SKODEN, in red ink, almost like it's been spray-painted on, is stamped from corner to corner. All her tattoos, except for the ones on her neck and knuckles, are tucked away. I half expect her to pull out an apple and throw it in the air, taunting me. Cami's winged eyeliner is just as extreme as the last time I saw her—and perfectly balanced.

I nod up at them.

"Welcome back," Tyler says.

Cami laughs. A couple of the others do too.

Tyler throws them all a look, like *simmer down*. "You haven't been here in an age. It's nice to see your face."

"I've been busy," I say, again.

"Busy," Cami says. "That's such an excuse."

She's wearing a pair of my mom's earrings. Shoulder dusters. The night my mom beaded them, *Dirty Dancing* was on TV and we sang along to the soundtrack. Damn Cami for surfacing this memory tonight, for disturbing the careful waters.

My patience runs low. "Is that what you came over here to say?"

"Chill, cuz." Tyler spreads her arms wide.

That's when King wanders back into the clearing with two guys in tow. "Look who I found."

It's Marcus and Doyle. Frick and Frack. They were both there that night too—King's last night in town—according to the gossip. Marcus was one of the crew who helped King home. Marcus nods at me in that bro-y way, like, 'suuup. Like we didn't have English together the last three and a half years. Like I don't know how on his sixteenth birthday he cried after failing his driver's test.

But Doyle only says, "Bitches, where's your drink?" He's slurring his words, laughing it off.

I've been asked this question a hundred times already tonight. "I'm driving," I say. This should be enough. This shouldn't be a discussion. Shouldn't be an issue.

But Doyle doesn't let it go.

"But you're, like, Indians," Doyle says. "Right?"

King's kissing his teeth. His usual desire to make peace with these fools nowhere in sight. And I want to puzzle over this, this change, but I don't have time.

Tyler and Cami and their friends explode. A mix of "Fuck you, asshole" and "What are you trying to say?"

It's exhausting hanging out with drunk people when you're sober. I don't know why, but I stand up from the bench. "It's really not worth it, Ty."

Marcus says, "Relax, man," to Doyle.

But none of this stops what's about to happen. The trees around us throb with it. Their leaves and needles flutter, excited, ready. They've witnessed this before, and they'll witness it again and again, as long as the grass grows, the waters run.

My mother knows this.

It's generational.

Tyler says, "Let's get gone," but Cami says, "No," and she struts into Doyle's space, right up against his too-tight Volcom tee. "Say that to my face."

"He didn't mean it." Marcus has one hand on his buddy's shoulder, restraining him. "Ladies, he's wasted."

Tyler grips the back of her sister's pink hoodie and holds on until the seams pop. We all witness the little snaps of thread. "He's not worth it when he's sober either, Cam. Let's go."

"I said . . ." Doyle pushes against the much shorter Cami, throwing his chest at her, breaking out of his friend's grip, with enough force that Tyler's jarred back a few steps. "All you bitches are drunks."

It happens fast.

Cami knees Doyle between the legs, and he crumples. But as he falls, he pulls her down with him. Someone outside our circle watches it happen and chants, "Fight, fight, fight." The whole party rushes from the fallow cornfield into the wooded clearing. I'm enveloped by bodies, elbowed in the cheek by someone—Ty, I think—as she tries, and fails, to get her sister off the ground.

I'm pushing to free myself of the mess, head tucked low, shoulders high. In the dark, I stumble over a loose rock. Barely catch myself from falling. I turn, scanning for King's blue baseball cap in the crowd.

While my neck is twisted away, searching, someone grabs a handful of my loose hair. "Dirty fucking Indian, that's all you are," Doyle says, pulling hard, slurring worse now. But not enough that I don't hear each word cuttingly clear.

King's behind me somewhere, calling my name, his voice deep, loud, angry.

"Over here!"

Doyle yanks me forward and down. I fight against it a second. Pure instinct. But if I don't follow Doyle, it feels like he'll rip my hair from my head. I reach to push him away but can't get a grip. Instead, I press one hand against my scalp to stay the hurt, to relieve the building pressure.

Next to me there's a crumpled pink hoodie, Cami's form on the ground. She's knees-to-chest to protect herself. Boots keep kicking at her. One pair. Two. Three. Heavy work boots with the steel toes. The kind my uncles wear when they're with the cows. The kind these boys wear to school. One of my hands presses against my head, holding, holding on, and with the other, I reach for Cami. I keep saying, "Stop. Stop it. You have to stop." But no one listens.

Sound rips in my left ear. Doyle's fingers flick awkwardly at the buttons on his jeans. One-handed, it's not working. He's laughing, running his words so hard together. "Gotta empty . . . tank."

It was a thing, for a while, in this town. If you found one of us sleeping it off, outside that bar downtown, it was your job to drain the main vein, shake out a golden shower. Those words. He's going to piss on me.

"Rip . . . a wicked leak."

The ground thunders as if it's fighting back. Marcus comes flying in, tackling his buddy. But Doyle doesn't release my hair as he's knocked to the ground, still attempting to free his fly.

I topple shoulder first. The impact is rough. My throwing arm crunches against a rock or a tangle of roots. With enough force, finally, my hair rips. Marcus strikes his buddy, once, twice with a heavy fist, until Doyle lets go.

I roll away, roll small.

My hearing has gone weird. All echoes. Like I'm underwater now.

Doyle's still close—too close. "I was only going to leak a piss, man. Now look what you've gone and done. I'm fucking . . . bleeding!"

He's holding a clump of my hair in his closed fist.

My hand comes away from my scalp wet. In the half dark, it doesn't look like blood. Too void of color. But it's sticky. Reeks like wet metal.

Someone reaches for me.

I swat them away, nails out. I catch skin.

"Lou, shit. Let me help you." It's Marcus. "I'm so fucking sorry, Lou. Let me get you to your truck at least."

When I don't budge, he reaches down, yanks on my arm. My shoulder screams. My vision goes black. I retch against the ground.

Somewhere off in the distance, in the fallow field next to the road, a cop car turns its siren on.

The echo, I can't trace it.

Everyone flees. Marcus drags me toward the road. My feet barely touch the ground, and the more Marcus pulls, the sharper I know something's wrong. Pain veers through my shoulder, down my arm. I clench my teeth.

Suddenly, King is next to us, carrying Cami. He's looking for a way out, a way around the copper in the field. Even at nine years old, he was getting lectures from the RCMP while the white kids on the playground got stickers and other swag. This is the last thing King needs in his life.

Tyler says, "Fuck, fuck, my ride's gone."

"Where's your truck?" Marcus searches the field. Cars drive all over the place, cutting fast near us, and ripping out onto the road. Some of them head north, others south. They don't care. It doesn't matter as long as they aren't stopped and searched.

The siren continues to blare but I can't locate the source.

Wiiiiooo, wiiiioooo.

My knees buckle. I sink to the ground and try to throw up again.

King says, "This way," and Marcus continues half dragging me to the Subaru. Eventually, he presses me into the front passenger seat, sweaty, alcohol on his breath.

Tyler climbs in next to her sister.

"I'm so sorry. So damn sorry," Marcus says, staring right into my eyes, his wide and bulging, and then he cuts out too.

I track him a minute. He launches himself into the back of a random truck, sinking down low against the cab, until he fades into the dark. Too many clouds tonight for the moon to show its face.

King's throwing the Subaru into reverse but bisects the field carefully like he knows even off-road he's got to follow the rules. Once we reach the road, he's about to turn left toward town and the hospital when the flashing lights take over behind us. King's eyes tighten and he whispers something under his breath, something I don't catch. The siren bites against my teeth.

Wiiiiiiouuuuuu, wiiiiiiiouuuuuu.

"Pull over now," the cop orders through his loudspeaker. "All hands where I can see them."

King exhales like he's in a yoga class, long, measured. He shifts the engine into park and rolls his window down. These moves are mechanical. Then, he removes his baseball cap, pressing it into my lap. His hand isn't steady. I finger the brim, worrying it with blood.

From the back seat, Tyler utters, "Fuck," and pulls her hoodie up. She's cradling her sister in her lap. Cami, eyes closed, moans intermittently.

The cop is tall and blond. I don't recognize him. Not someone's older brother or cousin or father. Not one of Dom's classmates, who on occasion drive out to the farm for drinks. There's a cop or two in that bunch—even if it riles Maurice to have them on our property. To have anyone who is part of the System in our home upsets Maurice.

This cop leans down to flash his heavy light into the vehicle. We recoil. Collectively. Even Cami moans louder.

"What's going on here?"

"They were attacked, sir," King says, polite but firm. He won't let the cop see the real King. This is a performance too.

"That's not what the last bunch told me. They said the Natives started a brawl. One of them tried to rob one of the others."

"They were attacked, sir," King repeats. "And I'm trying to get them to the hospital."

"Been drinking, boy?"

King shakes his head, controlled, oh so carefully.

I can't help it. I wince at *boy*, the mean spit of the word.

"How about the rest of you?"

"A little," I say, so Tyler doesn't have to admit her underage sister has been too. I lie and I wait for King to rebuke me for it. If not now, later. When he's not controlling himself so carefully, trying to keep himself, and all of us, safe.

Tyler nods. Cami just cries.

"That one okay?" the cop asks, finally.

"They kicked her," I say. "They threw her to the ground and booted her over and over."

"That's a lot of blood on you."

"Head wound."

"Okay," the cop says. "I won't cite y'all. But did you ever come to think maybe the bunch of you shouldn't socialize out here anymore?"

It's not clear if it's a threat.

King thanks the cop, like he's talking to a grocery-store checkout clerk, and rolls up the window. But his hands, they're still not steady. He doesn't say anything until we get back to Highway 16. When he speaks, it's in a series of questions. "Hospital? Or . . . my dad's? Or . . . ?"

He's not himself, swimming in rough waters—in shock. We made it through that encounter whole, but King's still stuck in that moment, being held hostage there.

Tyler says, "I don't know. I don't know."

"The hospital," I say. "For Cami."

At the emergency room entrance, King and I extract Cami from the vehicle, while her sister stumbles inside to find a wheelchair.

She comes back running.

"Do you want us to stay?" I ask, bracing myself against the Subaru's cool green metal. It's holding me up. Entirely.

She juts her chin at me. "You should get checked too, cuz."

The emergency lights flare out in beautiful arcs. "I'm fine."

"You're still bleeding."

I reach into the Subaru and pull King's baseball cap onto my head. It's roomy, doesn't press against the wound. "It's fine."

With Mom working at the emergency dispatch for the past three years, most of her local friends are nurses. They worked the night shift too. If they see me like this, if they treat me, they won't hesitate to text my mom. To forget confidentiality, to rat me out. And then everything comes undone.

"Your choice," Tyler says weakly. "No. Go on home. I'll call Jaxon for a ride. He'll come."

Her stepfather is off in the oil patch for weeks at a time. But when he is home, Jaxon's steady. "Let me know how she is. How she's doing. Will you?"

"Cam's tough," Tyler says. "Thanks to both of you. For . . . you know . . ."

"It was nothing," King says, somehow more himself now that we're out of the Subaru.

"Bullshit." Ty rolls her eyes and half smiles. "Fuck. They're totally going to call CPS."

King says, "They won't," but there's no faith behind his words. He knows Child Protective Services. Knows what they do to families as well as we do. His sister lives in foster care instead of with their mom.

I'm dizzy, and tired, but I know in my gut we can't leave Tyler to face this alone. We can't. Even if I'm not her friend, even if I can't be the friend she needs, I can do this. For one night. "Ty, we'll stay. At least until we know you're both okay."

King nods.

"There's no point in all of us getting in trouble," she says, but it's without rancor.

Leaning into King for support, and maybe supporting him back, we follow Tyler into the too-bright building.

CHAPTER 10
June 24

YELLOW: Delicate things require a delicate touch. We've found, when you're trying to craft these recipes, it's best to leave all your baggage outside—before you step into the kitchen. Trust us, people can taste bad vibes.

Cami has to spend the night. Even though they don't have beds available upstairs, they admit her. They're worried about internal bleeding. Her spleen, maybe. We can't stop the staff from calling Child Protective Services when they go back to the nursing station, but we're collectively thankful they don't call the cops.

We've been lucky tonight already. With the police, it won't happen twice.

Tyler insists on sleeping right next to her sister in an uncomfortable chair. I pull my hoodie high over the baseball cap, so the nurses can't get too close a look at me. My mom would overreact, if she knew. She'd be reminded of all the things she's trying so hard to forget. I bite my cheek through waves of pain. If I stand still, I'm almost okay. The numbness spreads.

But as King and I leave, I'm walking less smoothly, trying to protect my shoulder from how each step feels like a knife in the joint. "Take me home."

"Hell no," King says. "You're pale. I can't believe the nurses didn't force you to get examined."

He doesn't mention how I offered a fake name when they asked. Or the lie I told the cop. But he helps me walk to the Subaru.

Hospitals keep records. Of this kind of thing. And those records, they can be used against me. Against my mom, my family. It's what the government does to people like us. They employ their systems to keep us down, to watch us. Maurice's time in foster care damaged him and our family. Maurice is hurting still.

I exhale roughly. Can't pull the seat belt across my lap. Try, but can't.

King settles the strap against my good shoulder with care, watching me. He's always got the words, but right now, he's struggling as much as I am. He manages, "It's dislocated, right?"

"I think. Maybe? I don't know."

"We're going to wake my dad."

Before he was a vet, Dr. Nathan worked as an army medic. That's where he met King's mom—while he was stationed in Trenton, Ontario. After vet school, they came out West, relocated here. I swallow down the taste of smoke. I can't stomach any of the old guilt right now.

We cross over into an older suburb. The streetlights are dimmer, the roads narrower. King's dad's house is tucked at the end of the street, on a cul-de-sac, and though the lights are off, the door, like it always was back in the day, is unlocked. We walk right into the living room.

King floods the space with a yellow glow and yells, "Dad, wake up. Can you come help? Lou's hurt."

Dr. Nathan's used to emergencies. His hair is graying along the temples. His glasses are thick black frames that make him look like some kind of model, even in the middle of the night, wearing a white tee and a pair of loose sweatpants repping his favorite cricket team—the Trinbago Knight Riders, of course. His hands are gentle.

After a whispered "Lord help us," he doesn't ask questions, just works to assess what's wrong. "Shoulder's dislocated from the joint, young lady."

In the middle of the night, the island accent he swears was worn away by schooling, his stint in the military, his time on the prairies in a town with too few people who know the islands as a real place and not only as a playground for all-inclusive weeks away from winter, is fully present.

This is a different Dr. Nathan than the one I know from the daytime.

He removes his son's baseball cap, bloody now, and lays it on a nearby end table, next to a framed photo of the family, from long ago, when King was small, on vacation in Trinidad and Tobago, a red, black, and white flag fluttering in the distance. Probably, this is what Dr. Nathan did the last night his son slept in this town three years ago, placed a bloody ball cap on his end table. Above the photo, on the wall, there's a crucifix. Black Jesus. The mementos from their trips to Jamaica to visit King's mom's people aren't on display. But in this shot they look happy: before King's mom's accident, where she wrecked her back, before Aliya's birth.

King's smile, it's an exact copy of his mom's, down to the front teeth with the gap.

"The tear will need sutures. A medical doctor would do better, with less scar tissue."

"I'd rather you do it, Dr. Nathan."

He's staring at me with tired eyes. Staring hard like he sees right through me. Maybe he smells the smoke too?

"All right, young lady," Dr. Nathan says. "Move to the kitchen, where we have light. These eyes are getting old. We reduce the shoulder first. Son, over here, like so. Hold on. And, child, you have one job: breathe. All right? One, two, breathe."

There's pressure and then my shoulder pops.

At first it sits exactly right. Perfect. Like it should be. Like when I'm strong and swimming. Then, everything shifts. Pain floods my body. "Ouch, ouch, ouch. It hurts. It really hurts."

"Are you allergic to any medicines?" Dr. Nathan asks.

"Um, penicillin."

Dr. Nathan pauses. "Ever had codeine before?"

He's examining me, long and hard.

I'm going to throw up; it's not pain, but smoke, a bitter, acrid burning. "No, no, no. I'm fine. I'll be fine."

"Son, in the medicine cabinet."

King's sweating a little.

So am I.

But I'm not hot. I'm freezing. My teeth chatter, too big, like I'm faking.

Dr. Nathan says what we're all thinking: "She won't tell anyone I gave her this."

And with that, King walks deeper into the house toward the bathroom.

My eyes are trained on what's left of a plate of now-cold KFC. A bachelor living alone until King showed up, I think. If I wasn't hurting so bad, I might tease Dr. Nathan about his habits. Next to the plate is one of the imported Caribbean beers Dr. Nathan favors: Carib Lager. Over dinners, he's said it more than once: this beer tastes like home, even if he's been living in Canada since his teens, even if he only drank the stuff for the first time on a trip home to bury his paternal grandfather—a man who never left the islands, not once, in his long life.

"Hey, now, child." Dr. Nathan sinks to his knees slowly, like his joints are protesting, even though he's not that old. Only in his midforties. "You'll be all right. It's a bad cut. But it'll be all right."

When King returns, Dr. Nathan offers me one pill at first. Then he changes his mind and hands me another, even as I start to protest. "No back chat," he says, but smiles at me. "Son, water and a wash rag, a clean one."

By the time the tear at my hairline is stitched, I'm all woozy. King helps me back to the living room, an arm wrapped tight across my back.

Cleaning up his supplies, Dr. Nathan finally says, "What happened tonight?"

I'm laid out on their long couch. Yellow lights pulse at the same frequency as my heartbeat. King is at my feet, a hand rubbing back and forth along the bare skin of my calf. I'm trying to remember the history of each of the cricket bats hanging on the wall above me—but I'm fuzzy.

"I'm not waiting all night for you both to talk." Dr. Nathan's hands are on his hips. "This business here is serious."

I'm thinking of my mother. How she crawled a kilometer or more. How a local farmer found her first. How he was riding a tractor between his fields. How lucky I am to have King and Dr. Nathan caring for me. Still, I can't tell the whole story. I'm holding on to the past, and on to this one piece of tonight. "He was going to urinate on me."

"Doyle Younger's a fucking racist," King says to follow me up. "He knocked this fifteen-year-old girl down because he hates Indigenous folks. And then the rest of the party exploded."

Dr. Nathan makes a sound in his throat but doesn't reprimand King for swearing—like he usually would. No one suggests we call the cops. We get quiet, lost in our own nightmares.

My lips are heavy and it takes work to ask King something I've been wanting to ask a long while. "Back then, you know, way back then, why did you leave?"

His hand stills on my leg. "You for real don't know?"

Dr. Nathan rubs at his eyes, lifting his glasses from his face to rest them on his head.

"I wouldn't lie to you," I say, and stumble over the thickness of my mouth. Of my body. "I mean, I know when you left, but not why."

King releases a big, ragged breath. He thinks and he waits. Eventually, he speaks. "You know about my ma, and her . . . issues."

I nod, a tiny movement, but he continues.

"Part of it was to be with her, to help my ma stay on the

methadone. She taught me how to swim because it was one of the things she did for herself when she first moved to Toronto, learned all proper, in a class for adults in the neighborhood. She said swimming laps, in a pool, it helped her focus on what she wanted, and it was good for her back. And part of it was—Kenny Marks—you remember that senior who had it out for me all that year?"

"He's locked up now. He was caught transporting . . . cocaine. Like a car full of it. Behind all the panels, buried inside his seat, in caverns of ripped-out stuffing." I sway, though I'm not moving. "Everywhere."

Dr. Nathan kisses his teeth, echoing his son.

King ignores my statement, wrapped up in his memories. "That night, that ignorant asshole took it too far. I punched him and I kept throwing my fist. You weren't out there, at the party."

What he doesn't say is by the August long weekend before the tenth grade, we weren't on speaking terms.

". . . But someone yanked me off him and someone else took me home before I got myself arrested. I knocked out one of his front teeth."

The pull of the medicine is making it difficult to follow King's words.

"I thought I killed him. I told my dad. And Dad had me loaded on the Greyhound less than eight hours later."

I almost whisper it. "He told people he was in a car accident, Kenny Marks. He joked about a hockey puck knocking out that tooth."

"It was a fifty-five-hour trip, one way." King shifts on the couch, pulling me to the left.

I bite down on my tongue.

"So, you see, I didn't have a lot of time to say goodbyes, Lou."

It's true, but it's also not.

I'm getting tired, so tired, but I have to say this. "That was one good reason. To leave super quiet. But it expired as soon as you found out he didn't press charges."

King stares at his hands. "Lou, I was fucking ashamed."

"Son," Dr. Nathan says. It's not a rebuke, it's comfort. As much as Dr. Nathan would rather we keep our language clean in his house, in his presence, tonight, in this room, where the crucifix hangs, he's not going to insist.

"He called you—"

"Don't say it."

"Wasn't going to," I reply harder than I mean. "He called you that horrible word all the time. What was so different about that particular night? That particular instance?"

"You know?" King throws his hands up in the air. "Nothing at all. Something inside of me just said, *That's enough. I've had enough.* Enough of Kenny Marks but enough of everyone else who might have slighted me smaller but slighted me just the same. It was enough."

The room quiets. Just three people breathing.

"You should both get some sleep," Dr. Nathan says eventually. "It will take a lot of healing to move past this."

I close my eyes. They flare open. "No swimming?"

Dr. Nathan shakes his head. "Young lady, nothing for a while, with that shoulder."

My eyes burn.

King exhales hard.

Dr. Nathan simply takes his son's hand in his own, and without any irony, says, "This fucking town."

The couch shakes gently from King's strangled laugh. "Dad," he says, "I didn't think you had it in you."

The two of them talk quietly and I sink under into sleep, the rough beating of my heart like one of Uncle Maurice's drums.

CHAPTER 11
June 30

YELLOW: Honestly, best consumed in winter when the
Creamery is closed. That's when the subtle flavors of
yellows do something for the soul. We never appreciate
what we have when we're sitting in it, when we can revel
in it. No one will fault you for enjoying a Yellow during
midsummer, but really, save these recipes for the dark days.

My right arm sits in a heavy black sling. Eating breakfast, scrambled eggs and thick-sliced bacon Dom fried in our cast-iron pan, with my left hand, is awkward. But I'm getting better at coordination. The bruises on my face are fading. My cheek is easily covered by foundation now and my hairline, it's so itchy. That's how I know I'm healing.

Maurice clears my plate. "You promised you wouldn't scoop for at least another week, eh?"

Dr. Nathan didn't say how long I should wait to start swimming again. The internet says six weeks to three months is normal. I'll be lucky if I can even try out for the competitive water polo team in September now. If I can't practice for weeks, I might not even make the rec team. One thing I wanted for myself, for my future, and now I can't have it. Because of Doyle Younger.

"Just cash, yeah, I know."

After the party, Maurice was furious, but Dom and I made him promise not to tell Mom. We all want to protect her from more violence. We're not lying to her—we're holding something back. It's not the same thing. It's not. Horrified, and to give me time to rest up, Florence took my morning shift though she was hungover from her own little private party. After work, she brought flowers—bright summer yellows—to the house. "Because I knew you'd need something sunny." And sat with me on the porch, gabbing about all the town gossip, until I kicked her out. King and Wyatt scrambled to cover the rest of the week. It's what we promised we would do. But it's also the three of them looking out for me.

Even Wyatt.

He texted me: **I'll kill him.**

Don't.

Okay. But that asshole's dead to me.

In the kitchen, Dom stands with his hands braced in a knot across his chest. "If that Doyle kid shows up, call me."

Maurice is the one who went to jail for an assault he won't talk about ever except to say, calmly, all monk-like, that violence is a mistake. But Dom has the power in him to break someone too. I can see it for the first time, maybe in this whole time I've lived with him, bubbling up, in the days after the party. He's quick to smash his hand against a hard surface, his knuckles bruised.

I lie. "Promise."

Lately I'm lying more and more. Little things only. Things I think are right to do. But still. The little things, they don't stay small. Like any other living being, they grow up. And yet, I'm coming to believe, with lies, there are different flavors too. Some are bitter, some sweeter.

If Mom knew, she'd return immediately. But that's not the real problem. Once she'd taken Doyle Younger and his parents to task, she'd have had me packing my bags and we'd be moving somewhere new, no questions, no calming her. We've done it before. She knows that child welfare is the modern version of the residential schools. Maurice was taken from his mother in the seventies—and only met his younger siblings years later, after he was grown. Mom and Dom escaped that horror. But it's not over. The government is still removing Native kids from their homes to be raised by white families, still sterilizing Indigenous women and girls, still acting shocked when another mass grave site is discovered at one of the old residential schools. When that neighbor in Lethbridge called the RCMP because she hated how Mom smoked on our porch, and the police showed up and mentioned child welfare, we left that very night. It's what she does, to stay okay enough.

My uncles know it. Three plus years might feel like forever to them and to me, but my mom needs to run. She's running now. From something she can't see. If my mom knew Peter England was out of prison, we'd be gone. That's why, when Dom got the news—the Victim Services letter that arrived after my graduation ceremony, it had to be the release notice, an update—he didn't tell us. Dom can see farther than I can, lied to keep my mom safe.

We're all keeping secrets, each of us living in our circle, overlapping—uncle to niece, mom to daughter—but never fully knowing the whole truth. And all this, it's why I passed as white when we first moved here. It was safety. It was a way to put all that trauma off to the side—at least for a while. A way to hide in plain sight.

At the shack today, Florence keeps asking the others to leave space around me, so no one jars my arm, while she finger-combs my hair. She's gone all mother bear. And King's taking over the cash every chance he gets, leaving me to do nothing, even going so far as to ignore his phone when it buzzes with messages from his Toronto friends. Wyatt, well, he's working, without jokes, without wasting time. Eventually though, King bumps into me, and I make a rough sound, somewhere between *ouch* and *stop*.

I reclaim the cash stool. "Okay, I really appreciate you . . ."

Wyatt beams at me.

"Jesus, yes, all of you," I say. The breakup seems so small now. Tiny and insignificant. Except my yes tastes exactly like no, like bad fiction. Wyatt didn't exactly force me to do anything I didn't want to, that's true. Other than force me to jump out of a moving vehicle. I drew my own line, when I realized it needed to be drawn. But he sure didn't listen, didn't pay attention to me, didn't care to miss his movie to drive me home. I swallow that down and bury it. "Who is supposed to be on shift? Like the original, pre-this-happening"—I point at my sling—"schedule?"

"You, me, and Flo," King says.

"I'll happily jet." Wyatt's loosening his apron ties. "My girl-friend has the day off. We might go see a movie before the Canada Day long-weekend crowd invades town."

Even though Elise seems content, I worry.

"How many movies do you see a week? Six? Twelve?" Florence asks, but Wyatt only smiles in a way I used to think was all charm.

After he rips out of the parking lot with as much disturbance to the gravel as he can manage, we settle in, me on the stool, Florence on the back counter, King leaning against the door.

"I can't believe I wasn't with you that night." Florence stares at me, and then at King, with these intense, meaningful glances, as if we're holding back on her. But honestly, she hasn't been around. She's made her choices. Florence still believes the world revolves around her. Even this caretaking, she's doing it for herself.

It's all we talk about now. What happened to me and why she wasn't there.

"You were video-dating your girlfriend," King reminds her.

"I can't wait until the fall and we're not using phones to see each other's faces!"

"Young love." King's not mocking her. He's a romantic at heart. The proof is in his e-reader. It's loaded with romances written by Black women: Talia Hibbert's Brown Sisters books, Alyssa Cole's Royals series, and a Rebekah Weatherspoon book about a Black doctor with twins and her buff nanny. His family didn't get a happy-ever-after, and neither did mine, but King still believes it's possible.

"Oh, I forgot," Florence says, offhand. "Someone came by with a real-paper letter for you yesterday or the day before."

My leg shakes uncontrollably.

King confirms it. "It was Monday."

"It's in the cash, under the drawer. I thought to deliver it, then, well . . . forgot," she finishes with a tiny throwaway shrug.

He's out. And I thought ignoring him would be enough.

I press Sale once, and then, when this old thing Dom bought

at a flea market in Edmonton sticks, I strike the key twice more. It rings, pops open. *He's out. Out, out. And he won't stop until he gets what he wants.* I lift the heavy drawer, extracting the letter awkwardly with my left hand. The second envelope has the same handwriting, *Louisa* printed across the front in blue ink. This one has never been wet; its paper hasn't dried in crinkly waves. From the outside, it could be identical.

Sweat gathers on my upper lip. I wipe at it. I need to say something. They're waiting. I manage, "Oh, thanks."

"Aren't you going to open it?" Florence asks. "It could be something we need to deliver to the authorities. This is exactly what Doyle would do—try to—"

King's shaking his head.

I'm not sure what she's letting slip her mind. That I'm Native? That King is Black? Or that she's white and pretty and exactly the kind of person who can get away with anything in this town? But all I say is, "It's not from Doyle Younger."

Now they're both looking at me funny. And I have to decide. Lie and keep this to myself. Lie and refuse to split my heart open here. Lie and deal with the consequences later when they come rolling into my life. Wait for them to arrive. Anticipate how they'll ruin my friendships.

But secrets can burn down friendships too.

It's hot in here. So hot. If I turn my head, I'm worried I'll catch the scent of smoke.

I could do the unthinkable and tell them about the first letter, how it's in my bedroom, tucked inside a book I never returned to the school library. I fill my water bottle at the sink. "Who dropped it off?" I know, but I need to hear them say it. I need them to tell me.

"Some bearded guy. Older. Sorta hot. You know, weathered."

"He was white," King adds.

He's out. Out, out.

"What was he driving? Do you remember?"

Florence shrugs. King doesn't know either.

But I do. I'm not overreacting. It was an SUV, and if they'd seen the plates, there would be a loud proclamation. Certainty thrums through me, carrying with every pulse of my heart.

"Okay, we're waiting. But, like, you're scaring us. Right, King?" Florence is impatient. But then again, Florence doesn't care when I lie as long as it's a good story. She believes we all deserve our stories—even if they verge toward fiction.

"I trust Lou," he says.

Damn, King. Why'd you do me like that? Now I have to tell them.

"Um, so," I start and then have to sip from my water. I'm all dried up, primed for flame. My body tries to fight me here— to keep my secrets inside where they're safe, where they can be shrouded in smoke. "It's not a lie, more of an omission. Because it wasn't any of your business."

King's face slips into neutral. Eyebrows sitting level, lips relaxed, not smiling, not frowning. Even his eyes are balanced, watching me. He's waiting for me to prove I haven't changed.

"No one is stressing over things that happened like an actual eon ago," Florence says.

"He cares."

"Oh, King." Florence pats the prep table gently, as if it's King's arm. "Give it up, love. She was a child then."

King rolls his eyes at her, reaffirming his position on the matter, but Florence isn't watching.

"Keep going," he says.

"A week ago, remember, when we went to the diner."

King nods. "This isn't the first letter."

"It's not."

"Fill me in," Florence says. "Seriously, you two. I need to stop letting you off on your own if when I do, secret correspondences appear and dramatic, horrid fights break out."

"She didn't tell me about it, if it helps. It's not like I'm taking your spot as her best friend forever, Flo." His voice is light, but he's not smiling—not the way he would if he were teasing Florence for real.

"It wasn't on purpose." I want King to really hear me. "We were hanging out and I didn't find the letter until way later that night, and when I read it, I couldn't process . . . I just . . . could not."

King doesn't give me anything. I can't tell if he's pissed or only waiting for me to carry on.

"Are you sure it was me taking dramatic arts last year, and not you?" Florence deadpans. "Sure you want to be a scientist of the dinosaurs and not a glam Hollywood star? 'Cause you're really doing the drama, Louie."

It's so hard to say this, so I tell them that.

"Now you're really scaring me." A true quiver lives in Florence's voice.

"You don't have to," King adds, like he's realizing how heavy this is, how I'm sinking—me, the swimmer. "You don't have to tell us."

"It was from my . . . father."

"Jesus H. Christ on toast," Florence says.

King's jaw works but he never manages to say anything. They both know enough about Peter England—the very basics—to know this isn't good news.

We stare at one another. When the camp bus pulls into the lot, honking its horn twice, we jump.

"Can I take a minute?" I ask, holding the letter.

My friends, they look so worried, so scared for me.

"We can handle this," Florence says. "I'll even be pleasant to you-know-who."

I try to smile.

King isn't as easy—because he's not sure I will be okay if I walk away. "Are you positive? Should I call your uncles?"

"No. They cannot know about this. Nobody else can. Please."

I wait for my friends to nod their consent before I slip out to cower behind the shack, pressing my back against the wood, trying to sink into it. I expected to be followed—but I thought I'd have time, and I thought it would be King.

Today, Tyler's all tattoos, wearing a cut-up tee, more strings of cloth than anything else. "Am I interrupting?" she asks, clutching a bag of change.

"Yes."

She laughs but leans into the shack too.

"How's Cami?" I ask, staring at the trees. I grip the letter hard.

"Mending. You?"

"Same."

Kids scream and laugh, getting full up on sugar and good things Dom harvests from the land. Next to me, Tyler waits, rests, stands with me. When we were running together, we were always together. She knows more than anyone about Peter England. "Ty, would you do something for me?"

"Probably."

The envelope is smooth, almost slippery. "Can you not ask anything from me? But stay here. Exactly like this. No questions."

Tyler stares at the trees too, doesn't even move. "Yep."

THE SECOND LETTER

Dear Louisa,

You're beautiful. I needed to tell you that.

Call me. Or text. We must speak about the past and our future. With your mother out of town, this is kismet. Delaying our reunion longer will not help either of us heal from wounds she caused. If she returns, you will be able to show her what you want. She will not be able to stop us.

I could help you, if you'd let me. University isn't cheap. Especially if you're planning to attend graduate school, as I've heard from friends around town.

I've attached a copy of my first letter, as it's come to my attention you may not have received it. Without your phone number, this is the only way we can communicate.

Your father,

Peter England

Behind the letter, there's a printed photo, of me and Florence sitting on a picnic table, leaning close to each other, and another copy of my birth certificate. This time, he's written his name in red—like he couldn't locate his blue pen. My hands shake.

"You want water, cuz? Something else?"

I glance over at Tyler. She's still staring straight ahead, focused, but she's here with me, and like we used to be, she understands something I haven't had to speak.

I fold the photo in half and shove the papers into the pocket of my dress. "That's a question."

"Fair." She laughs. "Still, I'm serious. If you need me."

"I'm good." I nod at Tyler. Needing her is too much. We leave everything with singed edges, buried under ash when we need each other. "My break's over."

"Shout if you need . . . ," she says, "something."

She hands over the money. On the inside of her wrist, new ink: it's a shiny red apple. I want to ask her about it. I don't want to know. Both of these things are present. With Tyler it could be anything, and it could hurt.

Back inside the shack, Florence's lip curls, but she keeps quiet. Seeing me with Tyler is hard for her. Flo thinks she tore me away from a toxic friendship—and she did. Only, she's wrong about Ty. The two of us together, we're combustible. But each of us alone, we're only two girls made heavy by our baggage.

King steps close, peers at my stitches. "My dad says you can take these out."

"I'll ask Dom. When he has time."

My uncle's been gone more and more too. Either in the production barn or visiting his secret beau. Usually, Dom's boyfriends come to the house, eventually. But this one, Dom's hiding him from us.

"I can do it after we close tonight," King says. "Or my dad can."

They're ignoring the letter. They're letting me have this. They're good people, my friends. "Please, would you? They itch madly."

"Can't be much different than with a horse. I've done that. I'll YouTube it." He laughs. "Only not in here. That's not food safe."

Florence manages a laugh too. She's not happy, but she really is letting this go.

Still, nothing is okay. The picture means he's watching me. He knows my plans. People in my life are talking to the man who violated my mother. I'm not okay. Not okay. But I'm pretending to be. I have to pretend until I'm home, and safe, and I can figure out what to do.

I finish out the shift, with the photo and papers in my pocket like stones. We close up quietly. Florence hugs me and whispers, "Call the house later," against my neck, in the parking lot before she drives off.

King points toward the Subaru—so we can escape the bugs.

I recline the front passenger seat all the way back. We turn all the interior lights on. He leans over me.

It's sticky hot. The cool nights I remember from last summer, the summer before, and the summer King left refuse to show up. It could be climate change. It could be spirits with the power to do these things are tormenting me. I think of the pool and of cold water. How I can't even get a break with a hard, long swim.

No relief.

My eyes burn, pulse. Anger and underneath the anger, sadness. I won't be back in the pool—or swimming—at all this summer. Not anymore. I can barely eat, barely do my job. My muscles tense, my shoulder aches. Peter England and people like him are taking my safe places from me, first the pool, now the shack. And King, my friend, swears extracting these stitches from my head is no big thing.

Clutching the armrest, I hope he's right.

Behind me, King sighs. He fiddles with my Swiss Army knife. "There's no reason you should have told me about the first letter. I want you to know that."

He passes me the baby tweezers. The littlest knife is open, the blade too shiny when light catches its sharp surface. It's small. But it's still a knife. Near my face. Near a wound some careless person only recently made. "Maybe we shouldn't do this? Is this a bad idea?"

King leans against the seat. "That man. I thought he was in prison."

"And I hoped he would be there longer." The knife isn't anywhere near me, but I begin sweating.

"Fuck," King says vehemently. He doesn't push. Doesn't try to make this about him.

"I'm glad I told you both. I am." I brush baby hairs away from the stitches. "Thanks for not . . . pushing."

"It's your business. It really is. I worry about you is all." He shifts closer. "Let's do this. When, if, you're ready."

"Okay, ready."

He gives me a look like, *no you're not.*

"But I am. Ready."

"Actually, hold up. The scissors will work better."

Scissors are utterly basic. My mom's beading scissors are sharp, but they are only a tool. Her texts today, they were about spending too much money at the bead store.

King tucks the knife away. He replaces his hand on my forehead. Clip. Clip. Clip.

"Tweezers, please."

My leg is shaking, so I press a hand to my thigh to still it. I try for a joke. "Yes, doctor."

"Listen, if I make it all the way to my PhD, I'm not going to be that kind of a doctor." But he laughs and it helps obscure the sound of the stitches as they slip out of my skull. Long rips. My eyes fall closed again.

When he's done, his hands travel to my temples. He presses there, his thumbs moving in full moons. My skin is hot and cold. I shiver.

"Hey, fam," he says.

"What's that? Like hey, cuz?"

"No." He laughs again. "My friends in the 6ix would be cracking right now, listening to you."

"So, word person, give me the definition."

"It's like, my people, the ones I trust, the ones who are like family but not blood family. Get it?"

I nod. "You think Tyler and me are actual cousins?"

"You're not?" he says, mock-seriously.

I laugh. It's warm in here. I'm warm. My heart beats in my ears. One, two, three heartbeats.

Four, five, six.

He's been quiet too long.

And then he breaks the quiet, his voice low and serious. "I've been meaning to ask you this thing for a time now."

My stomach does a flip. Then drops. There's something I don't like about his tone. How it's a new kind of intimacy. "Okay, that isn't ominous."

He continues rubbing my temples gently, then stops. I hear him sigh again and he leans back against the seat, far away from me.

I twist to stare at him, my hairline throbbing. He matches my stare. This is bad. I can't stop thinking about the fire and what will happen when he learns I caused him that pain too.

"Do you maybe want to go out with me one night?" His shoulders rise and he seems so young and vulnerable in this moment.

My skin tingles—hurts. This could be worse than any of my other secrets. I should tell him I really like his company and that he's been one of my best friends—and might be again—and he's such a good person, but no part of me wants to kiss him. I should tell him it's me, not him. I don't want a replay of what I went through with Wyatt. Not with anyone. But especially not with King.

Only I don't have time to say anything.

Or I use up my time freaking out.

"Forget about it," he says softly.

"Sorry," I say.

And then I'm reaching for the door handle, climbing out of the green Subaru, and I'm half waving behind me, half running to my truck, abandoning my Swiss Army knife. This time, King lets me drive away first, as he sits in his vehicle, the glow of his cell phone illuminating his face in the starless night.

CHAPTER 12
June 30

GREEN: Typically, oregano. It's spicy, for people who like things both hot and cold. Our mint-and-wild-greens blend is especially wonderful as a palate cleanser or with flaky chocolate pastries. You'll have to secure your own before trying that particular pairing, though. We're really actually quite epically bad at pastry.

After everything that's happened today, the thing I can't stop thinking about is how much I miss my mom. Little things. Her smell and the way her touch grounds me, holds me together. Sitting alone on the screened-in porch with a glass of wild-mint tea isn't helping. Normally, my mom would be next to me, swearing in whispers she'd pretend I couldn't hear when her beading needle slipped and drew blood. Then she'd laugh—with her whole body, as if under the spell of some joke, and she'd draw me in too.

I check my phone for the fourth time in two minutes.

Hearts and kisses from Mom, who has gone to bed, on Lakota Nation land in a motel room she's sharing with three Kainai friends. She's having the time of her life, she tells me. And she deserves this. But she's so far away. From me. When I need her. When she needs to be away. From here. From *him*.

He's part of me.

But he doesn't have to be part of my mom's life. Not anymore.

I can't text Florence. She's struggling—I can't burden her. Text by text these days, she's proven I can't rely on her, even if there are totally valid reasons why. For months last year, she was either in bed ignoring her phone as she tried to sleep through the worst of her lows or struggling with rough meds and texting nonsense. There was the ten-day run last summer where she claimed that doing cocaine balanced her out. A few days ago, she lost her phone in a random field.

I haven't reached out to King either. I don't know what to say. How to erase earlier, to rewind to where we were. Being friends. Just friends.

Picking at my phone case, and at my cuticles, doesn't stop me from checking my messages again. Nothing. My fingers itch. I shouldn't do it, but I need to. If my mom were here . . . she'd run her hands through my hair.

I text King.

I'll be waiting out in the barn.

If you want to talk.

I do.

It'll take me 15 or 20.

I'll warn the cows you're on

your way.

I head there immediately, climb the ladder and sit in the hayloft, staring out the window at the road for forty minutes trying to figure out what to say—to King and to Peter England—before I realize King's not coming. He's changed his mind. He's not over what happened earlier. Me not wanting him that way.

The dogs bark up a storm out on the eastern property line. Deer maybe. Something the dogs want to chase, but it's not King.

Peter England. He's out. He's out and he's not going to stop.

The evidence is still in my pocket. That photo. His name on my birth certificate—as if it belongs there.

As if he's earned the right.

Dom's doing the final barn check before bed. He sees me backlit in the window from the glow of my phone. "Can I come up?"

I nod.

He scales the ladder. "I remember playing up here with your mom."

"Until—"

"That." He pauses.

Neither of us will say it. *He's out. He's out, Dom.*

But Dom doesn't notice what he should—how I'm all torn up. He only says wistfully, "Or maybe it was a few years before. She was such a teenager."

"What was it like growing up here?"

"Cold."

In spite of myself, I laugh.

"And nice until nouhkom died, until our dad did too. It got better when Maurice's adoptive family told him where he came from, when he came back to us. And when you were born."

"I was born out of . . . a mess."

"Oh, Lou. You were hope," he says, and pulls me into a side hug. His hand-rolled-tobacco smell tickles my nose. It's warm and natural—nothing like commercial cigarettes. When did I start thinking of this smell as home?

Homer wanders into the barn and, like he has hands and feet, climbs the ladder to lie against my hip. With my good arm, I pick burrs out of his orange-and-white fur. "Why haven't we paid any of those bills? Dr. Nathan and the repair guy and my truck."

Peter England offered to help pay for school. He has the money. His custom plates prove it. He offered for a reason. Someone who knows me told him I'm in need. This, what counts as news in a small town. Already, he's back in, he's part of the fabric of this community—as if what he did is over, done, finished.

Dom stretches his hands behind his head. "You're not floating around this place. You pay attention." His face crunches. "I told Maurice you should be looped in."

"We're broke?"

"We owe a lot of people a lot of money. Well, people and the bank."

"Same deal."

"No, it's an important difference. We have creditors. They'll let us hold out all summer, and if we manage to rake in a small profit, if we don't have another mechanical failure, if we don't need to replace the roof on the farmhouse, if none of our creditors call in their ticket early, we can manage through to next summer like we have since we started the Creamery."

"The roof is going?"

"It's old. One of the first metal roofs installed in this area. My mother was ahead of the curve. But nothing lasts forever. The barns could use updating too."

"This is bad."

He thinks about how to answer. "It's next door to bad. It's what it's like running a small business. Or two."

It's not the question I want to ask, but it's the only one I can. "Does Mom know?"

"She does now. She's fired up that we didn't tell her until after she left on this road trip of hers."

"She would have stayed," I say, knowing it's the truth. "She would have kept working at the emergency dispatch. Even though it was killing her." My voice breaks. "But, for us, she would have done it." And she would have been here for me. And she would have been here for Peter England to harass, to target.

"That's exactly why we waited. She needs this summer in a way I'm not sure you can rightly see. She needs to be somewhere else right now. For her own reasons. For her own healing."

Why right now? The buildup of listening to other peoples' trauma finally hit a boiling point? It's not like something specific happened to her to make *this* summer the one she needed to be gone. Mom might not have planned it, but Dom knows *exactly* why his sister needs to be away. He encouraged her to go—has been encouraging her since Christmas. The worst possible thing that could happen to my mom is coming face-to-face with Peter England randomly, at the grocery store or at the gas station. Part of me wanted to believe in government incompetence, in the failure of Victim Services, so I could believe in my uncle. But the system works exactly as it's meant to.

In looking out for his sister, my uncle has failed me.

Dom exhales, shifting his legs so they hang out of the big window. "We used to jump from here into the hay below, when we were kids. Now it seems . . . too far."

I can't look at him.

A firefly picks up outside. We watch it buzz and glow, buzz and glow, as it travels across the lawn, living in the world. The cows are shifting on their legs, mooing in a way I've learned means they're calm—happy even. Against me, the dog breathes deep and heavy.

Dom knows. He really knows. And he didn't warn me.

I steel myself, bury my anger. "Could we go back to commercial? Is it the organic thing that's hurting us?"

"Plain milk that we ship off to be bottled under some generic label, and we sell the rest to folks who make cheese. Sure. We could." His voice is sad. "But I don't want to. It's waste—millions of gallons get poured off."

"We wouldn't have to lose the Creamery."

Dom pulls out his cigarettes but knows better than to light one in here. "We would, Lou." When he catches me watching, he tucks the small box—a beaten-up packet from a store brand—back into his shirt pocket.

Dom's sentimental. I bet it's his boyfriend's. Someone he can't convince to switch over to the practice of hand-rolling.

"It doesn't work if we're conventional. Conventional milk under government subsidies needs to be used for particular purposes."

He knows. Dom knows. And he didn't tell me, his niece, his kin.

The most recent Victim Services letter wasn't just another parole update—it was something worse.

"We could fire Wyatt?"

Dom breaks into a laugh. For a second, I think he's going to fall. I grab for him. He catches hold of the window frame and, still laughing, backs away from the ledge. "Thanks for offering."

"Glad you didn't jump there. We can't afford that."

"Now you're getting it. We're balanced up high and the wind is blowing. But if we keep from tumbling to the ground, we'll be fine."

He helps me pick burrs out of Homer's coat for a while. The dog grumbles in that contented way. We work silently. I can't ask my uncle why—why he didn't tell me. Even if Dom couldn't tell my mom, why couldn't he warn me? I'm still here. I need protecting too. I tear a burr apart, pricking my fingers.

"I should go off to bed. I have a loan meeting in the morning." Dom pushes himself up from the hay bale. "But—"

"Don't tell Maurice!"

I wonder if *he* knows too—about Peter England—or if Dom is managing all of this on his own.

Dom chuckles, nodding. "Let me tell nishtaish." He's halfway to the ladder before he turns around. "What are you doing out here anyway? It's cooler on the porch and there are fewer bugs."

"I was waiting for King." I rise too. "But it's clear he's not coming."

"Meeting a teenage boy in a hayloft?"

I throw my eyebrows up.

"Like noonk like yaence. I had so many boys up here," he says, laughing again, all the louder.

I want to join him, but something inside me is newly broken.

In the farmhouse basement, in my bedroom, I slip into King's T-shirt. I'm frustrated he ghosted but weirdly angry at myself too. That muddle cancels out my ire until it's nothing but a faint sadness.

I didn't even try. With Wyatt, I tried going on four months.

The house is silent. I leave my underwear on the floor in a puddle and lie on my back, my head propped up on a pillow. I grab my phone and find a playlist with my left hand awkwardly. Something that reminds me of King. Of us at fifteen. Of a summer that felt like it would never quit burning. Of the time we went skinny-dipping, and the water was so cold we told bad jokes to stay warm, and the whole time King worried something with teeth stalked under the surface where we couldn't see. I didn't mention sturgeon, a living "dinosaur" of the fish world, because they live in rivers and don't have teeth, but when I whispered about the dreaded northern pike and its multiple rows of sharpened fangs, King grabbed hold of my arm and pulled me out of the lake while I laughed.

I slip my earbuds in.

Ria Mae's "Stars" floods over me. I inhale, exhale.

I press the fingers of my left hand over the soft fabric of the T-shirt hesitantly. I try to imagine it's not my hand, but his. Pretty, short nails and long fingers. Pressing firmer until my body responds.

My hand sinks lower.

I can do this. My breath catches and my skin warms—fast.

My phone buzzes, dimming the music a second, no more.

I let it go.

Between my legs, this part of me works. But every time I try to imagine doing this with someone—with King—I tense up.

My phone buzzes again.

Bad timing, I think. Ignore it, I think.

I exhale hard.

Every time I start to feel good or think of the person who wants to date me, I get too much in my own head, think too much about what I'm doing, and my body stops trying to unfold. Instead, I lock up.

My eyes fill with tears of frustration. Something else too. The knowledge that what happened to my mom, maybe it's changed me fundamentally.

I wipe my hand on the sheets.

The idea of sex is fine. Sex on TV is fine. Sometimes, you know, at night, in the dark, this is nice enough. But seriously, with Wyatt, nothing. Nothing at all. Just pieces of my body and pieces of his, and gross sounds and too much spit.

My rupture, I think it started early—way early—like first-two-cells early. It bloomed as the cells did. Two became four and four became eight, and when I was born, there's no part of me that wasn't laced with it. The violence of my getting is woven into me. I carry it—all the passed-down traumas, as my own. Science supports me here. Epigenetics are real. I'm proof.

I stop. Give up whatever this was. This awkward trying.

I should brush my teeth, pee, but I can't stomach running into my uncles right now. My mom, I want my mom. My phone buzzes for a third time.

I rip the earbuds out, glance at my notifications. Three missed messages. King. Of course.

Long story—flat tire.

Longer story: My dad's hurt. It
doesn't look too bad. We're at the
hospital.
Okay, even longer story now that I
know something. We tried to change
the tire in the dark and the jack
failed. His hand was crushed, for like
a fucking second, before I lifted the
Subaru off. The doctor here is telling
me we have to go to Edmonton—
tonight. Dad needs surgery if he
wants to keep full functionality.

Oh my god.

Do you need anything?

Tell your uncles I'm so fucking sorry,
I won't be at work tomorrow.

Don't even think about it.

Thank you, Lou. Really. Thank you.

Text if you need anything.

Tonight. Tomorrow morning.

Whenever. I'm here.

I plug my phone in next to my bed. Whatever I was going to
try to say to him will keep. But what I realize, what haunts me for
hours, it's not waiting for a text that never comes. It's the nagging,
horrible ghost thought of those vet bills and what we're going to
do if Dr. Nathan can't wait to get paid. I wish so hard that he's
going to be all right, that we'll all be okay enough, that I don't
notice when I stop wishing and slip into a sweaty, dreamless sleep.

CHAPTER 13
July 1

GREEN: Okay, it's not local, but once we whipped up
a batch of avocado ice cream. It's strange and perfect
and terribly expensive. If you want to give it a try,
experiment. The only pro tip we'll offer: underripe
fruits work if you have a good arm—or blender. We
lied, one more pro tip: be careful with your blender.
That afternoon, we also went to the hospital after
an unfortunate accident. It wasn't pretty, friends.

Since Florence volunteered to open the shack on her own, say-ing she needed to stay busy, and of course, as a favor to me, I have time to run into town. I want to buy Dr. Nathan a get-well card. When they return from Edmonton, it'll be waiting in their mailbox. They'll know I care.

I wonder if there's a *Sorry, I can't date you, I'm a mess, I swear* card in the drugstore too. Two years ago, I searched for an *I'm sorry, but we can't be friends anymore because of that thing we both did that neither of us can talk about—I don't know about you, but I still smell the smoke* card and noticed greeting cards aren't all that specific. Or my problems are abnormally weird. Non-mass-market problems.

It's a holiday, but the mall has always been like this: half the storefronts featuring For Lease signs. Right now, though, it's decked out in celebration stuff: red and white streamers and loads of Canadian flags.

The popcorn place went out of business the winter we moved here, but no one would know from the chemical butter smell lingering in the carpets. I like to park near this entrance, even though it's a longer walk to the drugstore. There's something grounding about seeing the mall like this. Half-empty and somehow still around.

It's relatable.

I'm here. I'm mostly trying. But I'm never quite failing in a way that means I should stop. Florence is pretending I'm breakable—that she could crush me. And so she treats me as if I'm glass. King . . . he's gone radio silent, but that could be for lots of reasons. No power cord, no outlets in the hospital waiting room.

I walk past the store for tweens that's all bright purples and sassy statements in sequins on tank tops. The gate is pulled shut, but inside, everything glows. We could never afford this stuff. But as a kid I begged for this brand in the Goodwill when Mom took me shopping. My style hasn't changed much. Today's T-shirt is "Love Is Love Is Love" in glitter. I found it for two dollars secondhand. That's where I find all my tees. Where once-activists donate their uniforms when they give up the fight. Or, where they dump their gear when the fight isn't cool anymore.

The first big lie. It was born at this mall. When I found the silverwork choker. When it was half gifted to me. And the first lie led to the others and to losing control with Tyler.

I'm so in my head, I walk past them, their faces smashed together, before I realize who I'm seeing. Wyatt and his girlfriend.

But Elise notices and pulls herself out of Wyatt's grasp. "Lou! Hey, Lou!"

I stop, pasting on a big smile.

"Oh my gosh. I'm so happy to see you," Elise says. "We want to invite you to a barbecue. Don't we, Wy?"

She glances over at her boyfriend with stars in her eyes. Maybe Wyatt's behaving. Maybe he's careful and gentle and kind to her.

"I keep forgetting." Wyatt has his hands in his pockets now that they aren't on Elise's ass. His lips are red and chapped. "We're having a little party tonight."

"The July one thing," I say, nodding.

"Yeah."

"I'm working." I shrug. "Sorry."

"But it's Canada Day," Elise says.

"You want to tell her, or should I?" I ask Wyatt, putting a little pressure on him.

"Um," he says. "See, Lou doesn't celebrate."

Elise's eyes are wide.

"Listen, bae," Wyatt says. "Her whole family doesn't."

"Oh gosh. I mean, I'm sorry . . ."

At that, I laugh. "Elise, I'm Métis. It's not a holiday most Indigenous people are really excited about. Colonialism and genocide, the mass graves of children at residential schools and all that."

"Colonialism, genocide," she says, and peers at Wyatt. "Um, well, we wanted you to come. Oh gosh," she says again. "We should let you get on with your shopping now."

132

Behind her back, Wyatt mouths, "Sorry."

But she's not done. "Happy un–Canada Day then!"

"Thank you, Elise." I turn to my ex, trying to tell him something, like *I know what you did to me, and you'd better not be doing it to her too.* But all I say is, "I really like her."

And Elise makes a cute sound like she's not entirely human, she's animated, and Wyatt says, "Me too."

Maybe they're perfect for each other. Maybe that's nice. For some people. Not people like me. Or maybe, just not me.

Inside the drugstore, no one from security follows me. They have before. Especially when I'm wearing my mom's big beaded earrings or when I've been with King or Tyler. While dating Wyatt, I never got followed in here. Or during those days when I was playing at being a hundred percent white.

I check over my shoulder, worrying I should be watching for a man with a beard and blue eyes. That I should have surveyed the parking lot for his SUV.

I pick out a card, a simple Get Well Soon with an illustration of a little girl holding a bunch of wildflowers. At the checkout, I try to buy a scratch ticket too—Dr. Nathan used to love the Scrabble ones—and I get carded.

The male cashier glances half-heartedly at my driver's license and then back at me, two, then three times. He does the mental math. "You're eighteen, eh?"

"Yeah."

The fluorescent lights are bright, unflattering. He's Maurice's age or older. The corners of his mouth are red.

"You're a pretty thing. Exotic looking." He scratches at his stubble. "Legal, too. You have a boyfriend?"

I stare at his name tag. "Is that any of your business, Tim?"

"Feisty. I like 'em feisty."

My hands tighten on the fringe of my leather bag. I square my shoulders like Tyler taught me. "I want my stuff now. Please."

I spot a camera behind the cash desk, peering out at us. They might tape over the footage nightly. They might not care. But I could complain. This is a chain.

"You're part Indian, aren't you? I can tell. It's your sexy hair— long, easy to grab onto. Those cheekbones too. I'd really like your number, baby."

"Not going to happen. Just give me my stuff."

He thinks about it for a second. "If not your number then, what about a blow job?"

My skin burns.

I'm back in Wyatt's vehicle. Back in that body. Right there. Being told it doesn't matter what I want, it matters what he does. The road is under me, bumpy when Wyatt rips off to the side— right over the rumble strips.

"You slow? I don't care about none of that. It's those thick lips I need."

Tuck and roll, Lou. Tuck and roll.

I ditch the card on the counter and escape.

"Hey, hey," he yells. "Bitch, your ID!"

I don't turn around. Can't.

Because I know there's something worse than my hands shaking, than the dizziness I'm suffering. I need to run before I pass out and I'm left alone with that creep.

CHAPTER 14
July 1

GREEN: With desserts, generally, a little unlikable. Frozen
peas produced mixed results in the test kitchen. Some
loved the pop, the bite. Others thought we were way
off and should quit the ice cream biz entirely after that
experiment. We prefer green mix-ins, to keep the color fresh
and complementary, but no one says in your kitchen you
can't try cherries or even, yes, chunks of dark chocolate.

When I arrive at the shack for my noon shift, I can breathe again. Driving helped. Sitting inside my truck cab, I side-eye my phone. No new notifications. King hasn't texted me. Not once. Not at all since last night. I roll up the window real slow.

With no customers this early on a holiday, Florence is outside enjoying her melancholy. Even with my window closed, her sad music leaks in. Singer-songwriters, all women cursed with bewitching voices. I steel myself. I know what she'll want to talk about today: the letters, my father, and her 'round-the-world hostel-to-hostel trip. Since yesterday, she's painted her nails a glossy black. Her at-home femme-icure, with two shorter nails and the rest long and glam, changes colors depending on her mood. Black is either a great sign or a toxic one.

When she notices me, she waves a bit like the Queen of England might. "It's just us today, I figure. King's stuck in the city with his poor da. I mean, I wouldn't complain about being stuck in the city. But wow, the accident. That's not good. Just terribly not good."

"I heard what happened."

My phone remains quiet, but hers seems to be his choice method of communication. The silent treatment sucks. He's blaming me. That's clear now. If I hadn't invited him over . . . then Dr. Nathan wouldn't . . . He'd be fine and King would be here. I'm blaming myself too.

"The lazy one hasn't texted me back," Florence says. "Though I tried to convince him to come in today. Time and a half and all that jazz. I really tried. I did. But Wyatt doesn't care about money, does he? His parents are very well-off, eh?"

"He's busy." I roll my eyes. "At the mall. With his tongue down Elise's throat. And later, they're having a holiday barbecue. I just bet there's going to be fireworks!"

"Oh my. Tongues. Jesus H. Christ, prince of scrambled eggs and bacon, I miss my girlfriend. So damn much. She's incredibly far away and it's tearing me to pieces, Louie."

The music makes complete sense now.

Normally, we'd stand out here and laugh until someone decides they need a scoop. At least, that's what we did last summer. We applied SPF and talked about our escapes: hers to Europe to look at paintings that need to be repatriated; Japan for the food and the Ghibli Museum; a tour of capitals of the African continent—Cairo, Addis Ababa, Nairobi, Dar es Salaam, Cape Town; Australia because beaches; New Zealand because LOTR sightseeing and the accents . . . and mine to a paleontology degree I could afford with a side of water polo. I wasn't thinking of the U of Alberta then. Just reading my favorite blogs, *Why I Hate Theropods* and *Paleochick*, practicing my offensive swim, drive, and countermoves, and daydreaming about where I'd go if Calgary wasn't my only option. We were sitting around talking during one of the first days of the season, exactly like this, in the picture my father sent.

You're beautiful.

Florence is still going on—flitting from topic to topic like a bee gathering pollen, telling me about her girlfriend's new haircut and then about how to secure your belongings properly in a hostel to avoid theft. When she's in one of these moods, grabbing her attention is impossible.

"I'll join you in a minute. Let me get some water," I say, and step into the shack. The freezer hums louder than usual. I shush it. "Do your job. Your one job. Please."

A truck passes on the road, loaded down with something heavy. The shack shakes gently and the freezer hums louder in response. I hang my bag on one of the hooks, its leather fringe softly fluttering against the door. I stare at the freezer as if this might convince it to play nice. It's a beast. An industrial-sized monster on wheels. Dom got it secondhand, at a great price—promising he'd replace the thing when we could afford to. I kick at it, gentle, friendly like.

It lowers to its regular register. I remind myself to tell Dom to check on it. Before something bad happens. Something we can't recover from.

Outside, in the sunshine, Florence's eyes are closed. As if she's run out of steam. "I've missed this. Just you and me here."

I nod. "Me too." But I'm watching the road, watching for a white SUV.

"Last summer, it all felt less . . . complicated."

I sit on top of the picnic table, next to Florence, but not too close. "Exactly that." Now, everything is changing. I used to be good at this, at finding myself somewhere new, at leaving people behind. But it's like any other skill, like water polo: if you don't do something regularly the muscles atrophy. I haven't packed my life up in years.

She doesn't wait. Once I'm seated, she says, "Maybe we should burn those letters. Both of them. Right now. Right here."

It's utterly impulsive. Totally Florence. I laugh. "Start a fire? In the middle of the prairie? During the driest summer we've had in years?"

She nods primly. "Let's."

I met Florence only a few weeks after O'Reilly's burned. Smoke lived in my nose almost all the time back then. Tyler's need for me was overwhelming, hot and all-consuming—and then there was Florence. She didn't know she was saving me, but she did. I clear my throat because I can't say all of that. I only say, in a tone much breezier than I feel, "My uncles would kill us if we burned down the shack."

Florence laughs a little, under her breath. "That's a certainty."

We fall silent. The crows are in the trees, jumping around, watching us, and watching the road too. And Flo seems so much more balanced—present, here for me, in this moment. "Florence, you know what?"

"What?"

"I think you're right. I shouldn't be out in the world without you."

She claims my hand. "Does that mean you'll come traveling once we've finished our final summer as small-town ice-cream queens? You'd love Romania! Vlad the Impaler's castle is a must-see. Don't you agree?"

Before, I didn't think I would tell her. At least not right away. I hoped King would be here. And it's always a good idea not to talk about sex with someone you literally ran away from when he asked you on a date while inhabiting the same tiny space.

Who you then tried to think about while you touched yourself. Tried and failed. Miserably. Just last night. I'm overheating, dizzying, and to hold myself together, I drop Florence's hand and pull my knees up to my chest. "The cashier in the mall drugstore tried to get me to give him a blow job today."

Her long red hair is in a high ponytail, but she doesn't look her regular angelic self. She's sickened. The lines of her face change. "First the bush party, now the mall."

Another truck rumbles on the road—carrying long lines of heavy pipe. The pipeline's been approved and the people who wanted to stop it have been silenced. They aren't on my social feeds anymore. The oil workers haven't gone anywhere though. They never do. They live in town, mostly in run-down motels, during their two weeks off, and they drive out to the shack a few times a year in their big rigs and try to flirt one of us into the truck, back to the motel, for a good time. But we're old enough now; we know to watch for them.

When I first moved here, I didn't.

Not until King warned me about that row of motels. Where his mom went, a long time ago, after her prescriptions ran out of refills. Where her daughter was conceived, King's little sister. After King left town, running, running from this place, Tyler and I, we parked my truck in those motel lots, knocked on those doors, seeking that kind of trouble on offer.

When the highway quiets enough again, Florence asks: "Did you suggest instead a kick in the bollocks?"

I shake my head. "I left. Without my purchases. I had to be . . . not there."

My ID. Abandoning it was bad. Driving without it is worse. But I'm not sure the clerk would have returned it even if I asked. Not without me giving up some fuzzy and unclear thing first.

There was a camera.

He couldn't have really hurt me. Not without evidence.

But that's what finally got the owner of O'Reilly's convicted for murdering Tyler's mom. His own security footage at the bar, how he didn't care it was filming, how he didn't care enough to destroy the footage after the fact.

My shoulder aches. I extract my arm from the sling, ready to reclaim my life. The pool, the friends I'll make next year on the water polo team, after I've lost Flo to her trip.

Florence recovers from a yawn, lifts her sunglasses to wipe at her eyes. "We need to do what we need to do in the moment to survive it." Her phone buzzes. She checks it midthought. "King again. He'll be in on Wednesday. His dad has surgery booked."

She begins texting back, typing for a long time.

When she began dating her girlfriend, last summer, we agonized about how to word everything. With King it doesn't even matter. She's smiling an odd little smile, catching her bottom lip between her teeth like she does when she concentrates.

He might have asked her out. He might have been coming to the farm to tell me. He leaves without saying goodbye. He probably moves on quick too. Maybe Florence is tired of the long-distance thing. Maybe that's why she's drinking so much. She wants to go into law eventually. She told her girlfriend both times after she kissed someone else, drunk, at a party—even though her girlfriend would have never known. I thought Florence had a grasp on ethics in a way I don't.

Maybe I'm wrong.

"Great," I say, but it doesn't sound like I mean it.

Of course, they could just be friends.

That's possible too.

At least I hope it is.

Another truck rolls by on the highway. It doesn't matter it's a holiday. Oil is money, and money is everything.

Even though I can't date him, even though I love Florence, it's selfish and unfair, but I don't want King seeing anyone else. Not this summer. After Labor Day, King will go back to Toronto and to his *fam*, the people who know him so deep they don't need definitions for his words because they share his language. But until then, I want to monopolize his time.

His and Florence's too. Because when the shack closes for the summer, it's all changing.

It's the middle of the day, as bright as it can be, and at the house across the highway, they're setting off fireworks. I can't tell why. It's not like we can see the colors painted against a bed of sky. Maybe they just crave explosions.

CHAPTER 15
July 6

BLUE: Usually, wild blueberries. Though, of course, you
know blueberries aren't actually blue. They're a deep
purple. In nature, not much is true blue. Potatoes and
corns have blue varieties; and yes, both are wonderful
and creamy and occasionally find themselves on the
rotation. It's rarity that makes true blues special.

My body wakes at quarter to six most days. I've taken to
reading my geeky blogs at the kitchen table and drinking
too much iced tea, my dinosaur mug smiling at me like it knows
something I don't. This morning, the sinking feeling is worse.
Maurice is gone again—back to Edmonton with his daughter and
ex-wife. Dom's out to tend to the cows, and to work on production. It's too hot during the day, and the production barn is coolest
in the very early morning.

It's quiet in this house.

Too quiet.

My mom's off-key singing to pop songs is missing. Her
spoon clicking against the mug, stirring the universe in her tea,
is missing.

Six fifteen. I should be in the pool already, running through front-crawl laps. Hair in a braid, goggles on, working on accuracy and then, when I perfect form, on speed. I shouldn't be anxious, my shoulder out of the sling for the first time since the accident. Waiting for someone to bump into me. Anticipating the pain to come.

I snatch Dom's laptop from his room and try to sink into Reddit's Paleontology feed. A picture of a twelve-million-year-old praying mantis encased in amber is pretty. There's a bunch of really cringeworthy T. rex tiny-arm memes. I crack a smile. And a discussion on how many people an American mastodon could feed that's interesting in a *hey this question doesn't matter, not for real hungry bodies* kind of way.

Today's tee is bubble-gum pink and says "There Is No Planet B."

I thought it would cheer me up—but I can't stop my brain from traveling to the bad place. How many letters will Peter England send before he forces his hand? I've typed his number into my phone a hundred times. Once I open the text chat, I can't manage a word.

Not one.

Not even the only one I want to send him.

No no no no no no no no no no no no no no no no no no no no no—

My phone buzzes. I peer at it as if it has teeth.

It's a text from King. He returned to town late last night.

Where are you?

         At the farm.

The pool is waiting all blue and full
of salty water.

My shoulder = no swimming.

Aqua-fit? Like the little old ladies
with bad hips?

Hell no.

Three little dots.

If you won't Aqua-fit with me . . .
meet me in the far parking lot, at the
trailhead. Bring good shoes.

I want to tell him I'm not in the mood. To talk. But that wouldn't be entirely self-serving. If I stay, I'll only keep rereading the letters Peter England sent me. Not that I haven't memorized his words already. *You're beautiful. This is kismet.* Eventually, I'll break. My fingers will slip on the keys. I'll start googling him. I'll learn too much. I won't be able to go back to thinking of him as someone whose life has nothing to do with how mine is unfolding. He'll become a part of me, and me a part of him.

His eyes are blue. I know it.

If my mom were here . . .

But she's not.

There's stuff you can't text another person. Instead, I open our thread and type: I miss you, Mom. When are you coming home?

It's early. She won't be awake yet.

Before I stash my uncle's laptop back in his room, I log out of my account and open his. He knows I know the password. I delete his desktop photo—a picture of Mooreen—and replace it with the worst of today's T. rex tiny-arm memes.

Finally, I reply to King. **See you soon.**

Downstairs, I dig a sports bra out of the bottom of a drawer. It's old and barely fits. A size too small from the start. But it's all I have. And compression matters if we're going to do what I think King's proposing. If I can manage to run without pain. I ditch my pink shirt for a much looser one commemorating some long-ago antisuicide 5K.

King will whoop me at soccer, if that's his plan. I'm not good at sportball on dry land but he played as a kid. His childhood team photos hang on the wall at the Tim Horton's near the mall. That was when his mom was still in the picture, before his sister was born, when he was the only Black kid on the team, when his hair was always styled exactly so.

He must miss her too. Even if he's not talking about the hurt, we have that in common.

I check myself out in the mirror. I feel ridiculous. Swimming is my talent. Where I'm at my best, even though my hips are big and my boobs are bigger and my shoulders don't fit into delicate dresses. In the water, I'm strong.

The bra cuts into my rib cage. I fiddle with it for a second, smoothing out the seam. On my bed, under a pile of blankets, I find my bag with the good fringe and jet.

The drive into town takes no time at all. I'm in a Jade Bird mood— like I could be that kind of woman. Harnessing my rage, all my pain, and turning it into art. That's what my mom is doing this summer, while I'm scooping ice cream for the locals.

The parking lot near the trailhead is empty, except for the

Subaru. King leans against it, all long legs in basketball shorts and a hoodie. "Morning."

We haven't spoken in days, and I say, "I'm bad at soccer."

"I'm a bad swimmer," he says.

"That's not true. At all." The birds are loud, chirping from the trees—somewhere, just off from where I can see. We're too far apart. We're off. We're not friends at all, but I need to know. And unlike asking after his mom, about Toronto and his life there, this is safer ground. "How's your dad?"

King shrugs. His eyes are a bit glassy, and his head hangs low, his usual refusal to fold himself small to make others feel better around a tall Black man missing. Today it's like his neck can't support the weight. His skin is ashy, drawn. He's not sleeping well.

Neither am I these days. The codeine pills Dr. Nathan slipped me are long gone. It was a kindness. No doctor around here would have given me, a Métis girl, opiates. Even if I needed them for a while. King's mom wrecked her back and even when the pain remained too much, her doctor refused to renew her prescription. The way King tells it, his mom's old boss, Mr. O'Reilly, was more than happy to help her with what she needed, no doctors, no pharmacists.

Now, when the ache gets too heavy, I down a few Advil.

But basic painkillers don't help you sleep.

"It was bad." King's head hangs further. "They've reconstructed what they can. But . . . he's not going to be working much, for a while. And he might not be able to do what he used to even if things heal right. It'll take time, before we know, one way or another . . . We have to wait it out."

147

This is bad news for my family. But it's much worse news for King's. "I'm so sorry."

He perks up a little. "But actually, that's what gave me the idea for your shoulder." He pulls a roll of bright orange tape from his hoodie and throws it in the air, only to catch the orange blur a second later.

"I don't know how to use that stuff," I say. But what I mean is kinesiology tape is expensive.

Too damn rich.

I'm already behind in savings, after I had to take time off to heal. I can't afford anything else if I want to pay for U of A on my own. Without taxing my uncles, my mom, the farm. Without upsetting the delicate balance keeping us from falling. And I need to finish paying off my balance at the bursar's office before they'll lock in my schedule.

"I watched a bunch of videos in the hospital. Drained my data, so I'm screwed for the rest of July, but hey." He's tossing the tape from hand to hand now, like he can't stay still.

King's hands. They're so pretty. Those perfect half-moon nails. He doesn't know I tried, I really tried, to feel something for him. I can't keep staring at his hands or I might tell him that. I peer around the parking lot like I'm tracking the birds. Every streetlamp is still decked out with Canadian flags, hanging limp in the windless morning.

"The videos I watched. I think I can tape up your shoulder." He waits. "So strip."

I don't have a poker face—not anymore. When you have to peel it all away to become a person again, you learn hiding behind

148

a mask hurts everyone. My skin prickles. My lips are dry.

I can't.

I just can't.

"Lou, look, I asked you out and you basically ran. I get it. I took some time away, to focus on my dad." He holds the tape in the air. "This is only to help your shoulder." His voice lightens. "But thanks for absolutely crushing my ego. Again. My Toronto friends say I should drop you. But I enjoy your company too damn much."

He's smiling at me—not like he's laughing and not like he pities me. He's just smiling, carefully, warmly. This is King. One of my best friends. At least he was—before. We're trying again now.

Truthfully, I don't know where we stand. Except, he's asking me to trust him. I strip my T-shirt off, draping it over the Subaru's passenger-side mirror. "What do your Toronto friends know? Your ego can take up a little too much space in any given room. So you know, I'm doing the world a favor."

He laughs, then steps behind me, steps close. Puts his hands on my bad shoulder, gently. "Hold on," he says, then, "Can I?"

I nod.

He slips the bra strap down my shoulder. He probes with light pressure for underlying muscle. The first piece of tape hugs shoulder to bicep.

King talks to himself: "Deltoid, twenty-five percent tension."

He keeps handing me little pieces of backing. I gather them in my good hand, forming a scratchy ball. Next he presses my bad arm across my body until my palm cups the swell of my alternate shoulder.

"Stay like that for a hot minute." He tapes along the backside of my deltoid, pressing the orange fabric against skin, rubbing harder at the ends. "Okay, release your hold."

"Is that it?"

"No. Next you need to take your injured side and . . ." He swings around front and slowly lifts my arm higher than I've dared since the accident.

It's uncomfortable, awkward, a little too sore. My face says it all—pained eyebrows—and then King's grabbing my good hand. He takes the paper backings from me and shoves them in his hoodie.

"Here. Use your other arm to . . . yeah, perfect."

He shifts behind me again. Even when he isn't touching me, I sense him there—like there's spider silk strung between us.

"Don't freak out. But I need to get behind this fabric. Like, this is not a big deal," he says. "It really isn't."

My skin warms under his touch. King must be feeling it too. This, touch like this, is exactly what I'm missing with Mom gone. Touch with no threat of wanting more.

Maybe not exactly like this.

We're against that line.

"I can take it off, I guess?"

His throat is tight on the words: "Don't. Please."

"Okay."

He shifts the other strap, trying to push the elastic up along my rib cage far enough. But it's so tight, it's not moving.

"Stop," I say after he's tried fiddling with my bra while keeping it on a third time. I'm sweating properly now all along my hairline and my new scar. I work the straps back up my arms carefully, and then work the bra over my head, babying my shoulder, trying to keep my body straight so I don't flash him—or a random jogger. "Please do this quickly. I'm literally topless in a public park now."

I resume the position he'd come around front to set up without being asked to. For my own safety.

He rolls my bad shoulder inward to create a big stretch along my back. The tape travels across me. He presses it down smoothly. "Fifty percent." Another piece of tape snakes along my back, sneaking lower. He's inches above my shorts. Still not quite touching my low back, the swell of my hips.

I think I'd like it, if he did.

It's a ghost thought.

But it whispers at me. At the worst possible time. I shiver.

"Relax your arm. Last piece." He swings around, keeps his eyes high up, places tape right on the swell of my shoulder, pulls my arm out to the side, and his breathing brushes against my neck when he secures the tape at the front. My neck cools when he secures it in the back. He rubs at the last piece for a long while, assessing his work. "Some wrinkles, but I think this looks good enough for our first time."

When his hand drops, I test out the shoulder. It's supported. Aches but feels . . . secure. "Wow. This is almost good."

"I know, right?" He's a little breathless.

So am I. Before I turn around, I squeeze back into the bra.

"You're supposed to wait like an hour before physical activity, and two before swimming, but—"

"I can swim in this stuff?"

He smiles big, his teeth all on display. "Yes! I mean, it's just supporting your muscles, which support your joint, but the tape is meant for athletes. So they can get back to training sooner."

"Wow," I say again, stuck on repeat. But really, it's how I feel.

He walks over to the driver's side door and strips his hoodie off until he exposes a loose workout tank—the fuchsia striking, pretty against his skin.

It's hot. Even this early in the morning, it's too hot. I quietly ask the land for rain.

Not now. But soon. I don't have tobacco or anything to offer like Dom taught me after my big lie imploded, so I just say, quickly, very quietly, "Please." When I get home I'll say thank you properly.

King is still over on the other side of the Subaru. "I know you're gonna hate this," he says, fixing up his hair. "But I bought you a case of KT Tape when I was at the sports medicine clinic in Edmonton."

"You shouldn't have." It's true. But I also won't say anything else. I step around to hug him. "You're a good friend."

He's warm. I'm warm.

It's so unbearably warm.

Another ghost thought: If he'd kiss me right now, I'd let him. I would at least try.

"Not that good," he says, and pulls away. "If you're sick of this parking lot, we can walk and talk. Or if you'd rather be close to your truck, in case you want to ditch, we can stay. You won't like what I have to say."

It could be anything.

We've put off talking about what happened the last time we were hanging out for as long as we can.

"If you have to talk, I'll listen." I walk toward one of the paths that cut all through the park. I'm calmer than I thought I'd be. At fifteen we roamed here, a bunch of us from school, acting silly. When things were deep frozen, we skated on the lake, King so much more confident than me. In the warmer months we'd sit on a bench or in the grass and talk about our lives. That deep talk. Well, he shared bits of himself, his history, his hopes, and I lied. Not about everything. But about too many of the foundational things. At sixteen, I walked here with Tyler after the Friendship Center closed, smoking stolen cigarettes. Once, she cried on one of these benches, and I rubbed her back like my mom used to do when I was young. It felt wrong, her mother missing—not yet found—and the two of us sitting and breathing and being when both of us knew how the story would end. Last year, I didn't come here at all.

He's walking next to me, close but not touching. "So, I straight-up lied to you about why I came back for the summer. My dad wasn't expecting me. At all. I should have trusted you with that."

"King, you don't owe me anything."

He ignores me, continues: "I did something real foolish. Sort of kidnapped my sister, Aliya, during March break. Her foster family refused her the trip, and Aliya didn't tell me that until the situation went critical. We drove to Montreal in my friend Malik's car and we had this really great time, catching a John Orpheus show, getting a fresh copy of *Saga Boy* signed. We goofed off at the

Science Centre, scoped out the McGill campus, ate poutine for every meal to see if it was better than the stuff back home. Even though Aliya's foster family agreed not to involve the cops, just to note the incident with her social worker, when we got home, my ma, she was so angry that I might have ruined her chances of getting custody again, she kicked me out of the apartment. Threw all my stuff, all my books, from the balcony into the courtyard and told me she was done with me."

I'm leaning close. I'm listening so hard.

"I slept on Malik's couch to finish out the year at school. I could have stayed there forever. He didn't care. As long as I kept filling little baggies on the kitchen table." King clears his throat. "This wasn't legal weed. I wasn't selling it. Wasn't smoking much of it. But I could see what was happening. I could see how if I stayed on that ratty leather couch, if I kept on as I was keeping on, I'd compound my betrayal to my ma, and I'd be betraying myself too. More than anyone else, my ma believed I'd have my name on the spine of books. Not just one book. But lots of novels and a collection of short stories too." He trails off. He slows, kicking at the loose gravel.

I continue walking.

But King stops.

Later this park will be full of families enjoying their summer holidays. Fireworks have raged it seems for five nights straight. They make dogs cower. Today, people will come out with picnic blankets, and beer they shouldn't be drinking in public, and they'll celebrate Tyler's mom's death, forgetting whose land this really is. And tomorrow they'll do it again. And again. Until the weather turns cold.

This park makes me sad.

"What exactly do you need me to say?" I ask.

"Nothing. I don't know. Something."

I want to sit down on the gravel here and just breathe. I want to be out in the bush, picking berries with my mom. I want forgiveness. I want a lot of things I can't have. I turn back toward King. The sun is bright. I squint. "I understand."

Surprise and maybe relief flood King's eyes.

He unravels. "It takes a lot to let things like that go. To be able to do it. It hurt so damn much when you lied—over and over again—and did everything to keep us, keep me, thinking you were this basic white girl."

I sink into what King must have felt back in the day. Really sink. How lies are more than words. How they take root, crack foundations, until eventually when enough ground slides, the whole friendship crumbles under pressure.

"It hurt, Lou. Because if you wanted to be all white, how could that self-hate not make you think that I was less . . . human."

He falls silent and I'm not sure saying *I understand* again will serve anyone. We resume walking slowly around the lake.

Eventually, he grabs my hand. "Last week, I wasn't over it. You lying. Back in the day. Because you're obviously a different person now. And no one can move forward if they keep getting called out for doing the same shit all of us do all day long. That's not fair. I'm so sorry for not seeing this earlier."

My whole body reacts. Like my blood comes alive, moves faster in its push toward my lungs, my heart. It's not his words.

I don't want to say anything.

I don't want him to think the wrong thing right now.

"Friends can hold hands, Lou," he says.

"I didn't ever believe you were . . . less. If I hated anyone, it was myself. Not you. Me. And coming back here, where my mom was . . . violated, where I was born—it seemed safer to actively blend with the rest of them."

He's not judging, just speaking a truth, when he says, "Some of us can't do that, Lou."

And in the silence between us, I offer myself forgiveness. For thinking only to keep myself safe, instead of how to do my share to keep my community safe, healthy—my share in supporting community members who can't hide behind whiteness.

King's not done. His voice is low but it's the only thing I hear: "In this town I'm too Black—hell, on the prairies I'm too Black—but in my ma's hood, at Westview in my classes, in my friends' eyes, I'm not always Black enough. They only say things in jest, but you know that those jokes are onto something. When I moved to Toronto I had to learn to live in a place that's not all white space, I had to learn how to live with other Black and brown people. Don't you think, Lou, that I would have been the person to get what you were going through, to understand why conforming to whiteness felt like safety?"

His hand tightens on mine. It's insistence, it's his body asking that I hear him, really hear him.

"But it's not that, Lou. It corrupts. It creates too Black and Black enough. It's what made you think you needed to hide yourself. But you know all this now, and here I am speechifying."

"It was a good speech," I say, because that's the truth. King's good with his words. Still, I can't help myself. "But don't you think that when Dom discovered what went down, that he wasn't serving me his version of this same talk, three plus times weekly, at the dinner table?"

King's laughter is rough, but he doesn't drop my hand, and we don't stop walking—held in another kind of safety here, the kind the land offers—surrounded by trees in the stillness of an early summer morning.

After we've made a circle, we wind up at the far end of the parking lot. There's a white SUV, parked, near the entrance to the pool. It's too far off to be sure. I drop King's hand—stuck in indecision. To approach. To run away.

"I'm exhausted, but I can't imagine sleeping. Feel like going for a run?"

I turn away from the SUV. "When I say I'm bad at soccer, what I mean is I'm not a runner."

"You have excellent lung capacity."

It seems obvious, but I gesture at my body. Like, um, all this.

Hips and curves.

King can't stop himself from looking.

I let him. It feels good, him staring at me like this. But it can't last. Can't go anywhere else.

He points toward the trailhead. "Okay, okay, forget the word *run* entirely. We'll jog. Slow."

"Running is jogging. You're the word person; you should know they're the same thing."

"But they aren't. Not at all."

I let out a big puff of air as we start out, ready for that rain now. Footfalls jar my shoulder, but not bad enough to make this unbearable. Not bad enough to stop this. Not bad enough for my excuses to be the whole truth.

"So, the pool tomorrow?" he asks.

"There's no way I can get up . . . early enough . . . to have someone tape me . . . and be at the pool by six in the morning."

"Didn't I mention it? The tape lasts five days."

"What?" I say because it's all I can manage.

And he still looks tired, but yeah, happy too, nodding back at me.

I push Peter England out, push the white SUV out, out. And it's thanks to King. Whose friendship feels right and good, whose words reminded me I have changed. He'll leave this town when he's ready to go home, to Toronto, to his Toronto friends. But that's not for eight weeks. Give or take a few days.

I'm burned out on celebration. But I surprise myself and find one little thing to celebrate this week. King Nathan.

CHAPTER 16
July 28

BLUE: Borage flowers and honey make delicious
sorbet. In cream, the honey stands out louder, and
so it's really a floral blue honey rather than the true
flavor of the borage. Most palates won't mind. But
people who love the taste of borage should opt for
sorbet. This is a life lesson: sometimes what you think
you want isn't always what you'll realize you like.

The weeks go by like this, in a whirlwind, with no new white SUV sightings. Mornings at the pool, practicing modified water polo drills. Every five days or so, King meets me near the trailhead and I strip down, silently, while he replaces the orange tape. Those mornings, we jog. Sometimes we go to the diner afterward, King wearing his flat-brimmed We the North snapback, me with my hair loose; other times we go to work. And on my day off, or his, we're making plans to meet up later. The movies, the barn, game night with my uncles, Jamaican jerk chicken and tofu, rice and peas, or roti dinners at his dad's—goat for the meat eaters, potato for King. Like old times—but different.

While King applies the tape to my shoulder, I try to remain like stone. Unfeeling.

But it doesn't always work.

It's not that I'm topless. That's nothing.

It's his hands on my skin, pressing against my body, like he cares. With my mom gone, touch is something I'm missing so much. It's only that. Her texts are always there—she doesn't miss a day—but they aren't touch.

It's late-July hot now. Wildfires north of us send smoke into town like a heavy blanket. Something is brewing too. Underneath it all. The cows feel it. They're anxious and their calls to each other are strained. Even normally chill Mooreen, the udderly delightful Cowntessa de Pasteur, is upset. And Florence, she's hardly sleeping—running herself ragged. Texts all hours of the night. Sometimes they're unreadable. Words without context. She's trying, but those messages, they only make me lonely for my best friend.

I want what's coming to be a storm. A big one. The kind that takes all the pressure and lets it scream and snap into rain. We're good for those on the prairies. I want a storm but what I get is a quiet invasion. When the third letter appears, it's taped to our front door. Not the porch screen, but the wooden door, painted red.

This is my home. My mismatched chairs. My dent in the porch floor from when I dropped an ice skate, the blade narrowly missing Dom's moccasin-clad foot. We laughed about it, staring at the newly sharpened skate so close to Dom's toes.

This home is ours.

Where anyone could have found the letter. Maurice or Dom or even my mom. If she were around. A small voice deep inside

wonders if she'd recognize his handwriting. She's canceled her
first three trips home. Told us it would cost more money to return
than she's making—even on Greyhound. And that sounds fair.
Totally fair. Except, it isn't. She should be here. When she first
started talking about her road trip, she promised she'd be here
for me. We sat on our porch, wearing parkas but enjoying winter's cold. Dom brought us tea. She joked I could come along, if
I was bored of this town. But she knew we couldn't afford that,
that I couldn't afford a summer away from the pool. And we both
laughed, our breath making clouds. Still, she texts every day when
she finds a Wi-Fi signal. Sweet messages. **You'd have loved the
jingle dance yesterday. Lou, dinosaur earrings are a thing
now—I've seen at least two pairs.** 😌 **The sunset last night
was like a painting, only I was missing you.** Her sweetness,
her joy, they make it hard to reply with serious things when I'm
staring down at a series of six emoji. How do you say, *My rapist
father has come to our front door?*

I want my mom. It's primal—this want.

But more than almost anything, I crave the rain.

Smoke in the air burns my throat, and I cough into my elbow.
Before my uncles come to investigate, I rip the letter off the
door. Clean the left-behind tape with my nails until no evidence
remains. Scratch the paint a little and know if my family notices,
I'll lie.

My uncles are in the kitchen, arguing again, so even though
it's beyond hot in the barn right now, that's where I need to be.
I drink water directly from the sink. It runs down my chin, my
shirt. My uncles don't stop talking, don't even seem to notice me.

The house reeks too—all the windows are open to harness the breeze, to cool us a little. I push out of the screen door and while walking to the barn, tear the envelope open. My hands are damp. My eyes focus on the words so hard, my vision blurs. But I see what I need to. The third letter isn't patient anymore.

It's a threat.

THE THIRD LETTER

Dear Daughter,

Eighteen years of patience is something you cannot fully understand. I am not a patient man any longer—not after my time in the cage, where I was treated as less than an animal. But all that time, I have been your father. I have legal recourse and will use it as necessary. I can prove you belong to me. I can't sue for custody. You're of age; it's your choice to meet me.

I'll incentivize you.

I'll pay your tuition. For four years. We can discuss further schooling later. All you must do is meet with me. Afterwards, we'll see my lawyer to have your birth certificate amended.

Another thing I need you to know. It's cruel to write this, instead of telling you while I hold your hand, but you've left me without choices. Your mother has abandoned you. She left. She did not come home when that boy beat you bloody. She did not avenge you. Did she ever tell you about the abortion she attempted? Those pills? She wanted to shed you from her body. She tried to legally murder you when you were beyond defenseless. I saved you.

Let me tell you how much I don't want to do this. I don't want to. Believe me, Louisa. But I can take the farm. The cows. The useless guard dogs you have on the property. I can take the businesses—all of them. But I'll take the land your ice-cream cabin sits on first of all.

The choice is yours—be my fierce warrior-girl.

Your father,

Peter England

I press my hands together to still the tremor, and when I do, I tear the paper.

The barn door is open. I slip inside. I scale the ladder.

It's one of the first things Dom taught me—what it means to be claimed, for us, the Métis. We claim our relations and they claim us back. In this way, we create a circle of kinship. My first lie, I've never thought of it exactly like this, but back then, when I pretended to be white, I wasn't just claiming the safety of whiteness, I was claiming Peter England too. Now, he's come to finish things—to complete the circle. I'm crying without sound, water leaving my body, running into the hay, the letter gripped tight in my hand like I can't let it go.

When I wake, a storm is throwing the barn window closed and yanking it open again, rattling the old hinges like the force could, if it wanted to, tear this whole building down. Lightning cracks. I jump into a sitting position, pulling at hay stuck in my hair, scratching my face. Lightning cracks again. I lean out to catch the worn pull cord, scramble to heave the wooden windows closed. Secure them with the pin.

Homer's here next to me. He's been on the farm his whole life. A real cattle dog. He knows how to get out of trouble.

It's not raining yet, but the wind is fierce.

If Homer's in here, it's trouble out there.

The cows have returned home on their own and they're worked up too. Loud and panicked calls echo through the barn. Even Mooreen is upset.

It's wrong, this weather.

I shiver but I'm not cold. Dizzy, disoriented—like I'm forgetting something terrible has already happened.

Dom steps into the barn, frantic. "Lou? Lou!"

My throat is dry. "I—I'm here."

He climbs the ladder, his hair askew. "What the hell are you doing?"

"I fell asleep."

"There's a tornado on the ground." He yells to cut through the noise. "North of us, tracking this way."

I push my body, sore from sleeping slung between the curve of two bales, toward the ladder. We don't run, but we hurry to the house and directly into the basement, Homer at our heels—watching for danger. The other two dogs are already curled up on a blanket, like this is any other day.

Maurice rises from the kitchen chair he must have carried downstairs and hugs me, hard and tight and long. "We couldn't locate you."

My fingers curl into his back. "I fell asleep," I say again.

When he lets me go, I search my pockets covertly.

Empty.

The letter. It's in the hayloft.

While we wait for nature, I pick errant bits of hay off my clothes, dropping them on the floor even though the mess must be driving Maurice batty. Once the storm passes, if the barn's still standing, if the cows survive, I'll retrieve the letter. I'll clean the hay from the basement floor. And I'll do something other than bide time. I can't sit around waiting for what's next, and it's not the stress of the impending tornado pushing me to action.

I'm done with the man who calls himself my father like he's earned that name. Even if I made a mistake, and by doing so, claimed him in a way—we've never spoken. Peter England can't threaten to take the land we care for, our very home. If it wouldn't drive us apart, I'd tell my uncles. Violence begets violence. After the bush party, I've worried what my uncles would do to protect me. How much violence they'd enact. In their weaker moments, my uncles must think about what they'd do to Peter England if they could. I can't give them the opportunity. I won't.

I'm sitting on the floor, low, next to Homer. He's soft like a puppy, though he's old. My uncles and me, the three of us, we're quiet a long while. Five minutes or eight. We're never quiet this long in this family. But the wind is loud. We listen to it speak.

The rain is thunderous on our metal roof. When it changes over to hail, we lean closer. I'm waiting for water to pour through, travel down the stairs in epic, movie-like proportions. Waiting for the next bill we won't be able to pay.

"This is God-given," Maurice says at some point. "Why can't you see it, Dominic?"

Dom's somewhere else. He breaks. His whole face crumbles inward, like he might cry. "If you want to leave so badly, leave us. Don't blame this on some god."

Maurice is soft-spoken. He's careful with his words, doesn't use his Catholic God's name in vain. That's how I know he means what he says next. He talks slow, word by word. "If this all comes down around us, we won't have the opportunity to sell. To recover our losses. We'll be stuck here, with nothing."

"Nothing but the land," Dom says, as if that should be enough.

"Did Dr. Nathan call in on what we owe?" My fingers are buried in Homer's fur. "That was thousands of dollars."

"Not yet," Maurice says, and then, "Let me guess, this one told you?"

We ignore him.

"He won't," Dom says. "Not for two thousand and forty-six dollars. Not because his hand is in a cast."

My eyes burn. "Will one of you fill me in already? I keep hearing whispers. The two of you are fighting so quietly."

Dom says, "Your uncle wants to sell the farm."

Maurice says, "Dominic wants to risk everything we have on the Creamery."

The hail stops. The rain keeps on. This thing is much larger than I could have imagined. It's not just bills. It's the entire farm. It's our everything. "And my mom, what does she want?"

"She refuses to decide. Told us to sort it out between the two of us. She'll stay, she'll go. She won't break this tie." Dom leans his head in his hands.

"No, what she's afraid to break is your heart, Dominic. Can't you see? This town hates her, hates us. Your own niece was beaten simply because she's Native."

"It's no better in Edmonton!" Dom yells. "Police brutality. Our people freezing to death on the streets."

"You're listening too much to that Henry Reina if you think the same thing doesn't happen here. We're not in a better place because our family's lived a long time on this land. History doesn't make this a better place."

It's quiet for a moment.

"We're not . . . seeing each other anymore," Dom says without his usual speed. "For the best."

Maurice nods once, curtly. Like this is a thing they've been fighting about too. But the news doesn't rein Maurice in. "Your own niece went to see a vet to get her injuries fixed, because she didn't feel safe at the hospital! When she was born, CPS flagged her. They watched our Louisa so closely—here and in Lethbridge and in Winnipeg and Vancouver. They watched her with so much focus simply because she was a Native mother. If Lou ever has a child in a hospital in Canada, they'll be called to assess her parenting skills simply because she's Métis. They're taking babies away from parents at birth! Here, in Edmonton—everywhere!"

"Don't you think I know that?"

My fingers tighten on the dog's fur until he whines. They don't need Peter England to tear this place apart—they're doing it themselves. "Stop it. Both of you!"

My uncles recoil.

I lower my voice. I need to hold us together, not help drive us apart. "Do I get a say in this?"

Dom nods, believing I'll be on his side.

Maurice thinks it over. When he talks, it's full of intention. "You're eighteen. If your cousin Molly were older, I'd let her say what she thinks too. This is her inheritance as much as yours. What's left of it."

I'm acting on instinct. "Give me until the end of the summer."

Dom nods.

Maurice is slower but he relents.

"I need until Labor Day to decide. Five weeks."

Outside, the rain is slowing. It's not over yet. This is either the calm after the storm, or its eye. We'll wait it out. Whatever happens.

The dogs pant.

We fall quiet again.

When Dom's phone erupts into a series of notifications, the reports say we're safe. On social media, images of the destruction start popping up. Friends of ours. People we know. Just up the road.

"We're lucky." Maurice collects the kitchen chair he'd been sitting on. "We won't always be lucky."

Dom's tired. "We just agreed we'll wait."

"For what?" Maurice asks. But he doesn't stay around for an answer. All three of the dogs follow him up the stairs and out of the house.

When I make it back to the barn, to read the letter again, to memorize it, maybe to do exactly what Florence suggested and burn it—the letter is gone.

CHAPTER 17
July 29

INDIGO: Saskatoon berries should be on every commercial ice-cream company's rotation. Pies and tarts—there's even a good Saskatoon butter tart variation out there—and jams and muffins and cocktails, this berry works everywhere. To start a Michif Indigo, first you'll make a classic jam. Blended into our base, you have a nutty, creamy frozen treat. You can limit the extent of the blend by adding the jam so it forms ribbons of flavor. As always, trust yourself. Try things. See what works.

Tyler calls in the morning. Direct to the house. She's never done this before. Not even when we were hanging together almost every day.

"Oh, hi." She pauses. "Lou?"

I recognize her voice immediately. "It's me."

We haven't spoken since she stood watch at the shack.

Tyler clears her throat. "I'm calling to see if you, and your uncles even, want to help the Friendship Center with our cleanup project? A couple of farms were hit, and only one of them is Native-owned, but we want to assist. It won't be anything major, unless you can handle a John Deere."

I tidy the kitchen as we talk. "Sure. When?"

"The meet is tomorrow at eight a.m. in the parking lot. Boots and leather gloves mandatory for safety. If you have extra—gloves or boots—bring them, would you?"

"I'll dig around in the barns."

The line succumbs to static. Then clicks in. We've been on speakerphone.

"Listen. We need to talk. Later. When you have time. But not now. One of the aunties here is staring me down. Like, work harder, Tyler. Work faster, Tyler. I've got to go. I'll see you."

She ends the call.

My good hand grabs at one of my earrings. I finger the beads—wondering what Tyler needs from me. What she wants.

What I'll give her.

For an hour, I track down mismatched gloves and boots we've outgrown. I pack them in the bed of my truck, wildfire burn stinging my nose. In the basement, in the drawer of an old desk, I find a marker, and in the depths of my closet, a piece of bristol board I used for a presentation on why there should be gender-bent *Hamlet* productions in provincial schools. On the back side I write, CLOSED FOR THE DAY. CLEANING UP OUR COMMUNITY. I hand-draw a rough map, circle the tornado damage zone, and sketch a pair of boots and gloves. I add the Friendship Center's phone number along one of the long edges, in case someone wants more information. It's not perfect, but it'll do. The poster winds up in the cab of my truck.

At the shack, Wyatt's serving while King tracks down stray napkins the wind hasn't carried off yet.

I catch King's eye. "Can you do my tape after work? Tomorrow

I'm going to volunteer with the Friendship Center. Help clean up the farms that were hit."

"Instead of resting," he says without judgment. He bends down to grab part of a cone, covered in ants, and throws it into the bush. "I'd come along but I'm on shift."

If I'm going to really take control not just of Peter England but of my life, I need to begin somewhere. "Actually, about that . . . I'm closing the shack tomorrow. So you can get paid and do something other than scoop with those arms." I don't realize how flirty my words sound until they escape my mouth.

King settles the spray bottle and a rag in one hand. And totally ignores my weird comment. "I was out there with my dad this morning looking after some injured livestock."

He's moving slow. His eyes are bloodshot.

I can tell before I ask, but I do anyway, to hear King say it. "Was it bad?"

He nods for a long time. "We had to put down one of the cows. She was too far gone. Debris and—" He cuts himself off. Sinks into one of the picnic table benches.

I sit close but not too close. "The owner didn't just shoot it?"

"My dad wouldn't let him. Said if the owner wanted him to come out that way ever again, the owner would pay to relieve the cow of its misery humanely. No cattle-bolt shit. No hunting-rifle amateur shooting, hoping it does the job—eventually."

Dr. Nathan is a good man. He won't call in the debt we owe until he has to do it. That's comfort.

King seems like he wants to say something else but doesn't. He straightens. His hand ends up next to my thigh on the bench. It stretches out, clenches in. I think about grabbing it. Taking his hand and holding on—but a big truck passes by with a screech and King sighs, pushes himself up, and returns to cleaning picnic tables as if it's the most pressing thing on his schedule.

"So I'm being clear," I say, walking with him from table to table. "No pool tomorrow, okay?"

"Clear. Yeah." He's in his own head. "But we'll tape your shoulder tonight. Good plan."

Inside the shack, Elise perches on the prep counter. Her legs are bare and she's kicked off her shoes. Pink toenails. Freshly done, by the looks of the polish. There's a place in the mall. Twenty dollars for nails was always too steep for me—and with a friend like Florence, there's no need. Only we haven't had a nail-painting session yet this summer.

"Hi," Elise says, full of cheer. "Wy said this was cool as long as it was quiet. Is this fine?"

"Whatever. Today, I don't care."

Wyatt finishes ringing up the only customer in the lot. A dad with two young girls. It's an ice-cream-for-lunch kind of day, I agree, realizing suddenly I'm starving, and like normal these days, I didn't pack anything.

The tornado has me all out of sorts.

It wasn't Tyler's call.

It's not Peter England.

It's nature.

"We're closed tomorrow, just FYI." Wyatt probably needs a harder sell than King. "You can have your birthday off like we planned next week, and I'll cover for you the day after so you can treat that hangover right. If you'll help with post-tornado cleanup tomorrow in the a.m."

Elise jumps in. "I'm free too. Actually."

I can't help but see the sparkle in her eyes when she looks at Wyatt. She's got it bad for him.

"The movie theater fired me for sneaking this one popcorn." She leans toward him.

Wyatt cleans his hands at the little sink. But he comes over and kisses her, all wet. She squeals but returns the kiss with an open mouth.

I could never be like that.

I will never be like that. It doesn't matter how much I want to. I can't.

"We'll join in, right, bae?"

Elise nods emphatically against him, her legs open, her hands holding the little indent I know sits under his shirt, right above his hips.

In my head, he's still wearing a shirt, but his board shorts are Velcro open and pulled down his legs just far enough, and his dick is in my hand. My other hand is tucked into that groove and I'm doing what Wyatt wants. I'm getting him off. My hand isn't steady. I'm not comfortable. He doesn't notice. He's eyes-closed, saying, *Yeah, Lou. You're so good at this. God, Lou. Yes, Lou. Yes.* And then quickly, *Oh fuckkkk.*

Elise is so comfortable, happy to be touching him. To being touched by him. For me, the memories of what we did are as sharp and as cutting as when they were new.

Still holding his girlfriend's body tight against his, Wyatt turns toward me. "I don't have big b-day plans. And you don't have to swap me a day. This is what we do."

He says it like we hold each other up in this town. He says it like Cami wasn't beaten so badly she ruptured her spleen. Like I'm not still taping my shoulder so I can train, so I have a chance at recreational water polo—all dreams of joining the competitive team ruined now—like I'm not still driving around without my ID because I'm too afraid to ask for it back. He says it like he didn't push me to get him off over and over again, to hook up, even though I told him no a lot in the daytime. Even though in the deep part of me I didn't want to. It took time for me to understand that meant I shouldn't cave to his demands. That, maybe, my consent wasn't offered. That maybe he coerced me.

My T-shirt says "Be the Better Person," and damn if I didn't randomly pick the one I'd need today.

Help is help.

Some would say this is how you build a community. Some would say, maybe you forget the past. Maybe you forget their ignorance.

I can't believe that. If we forget, they stay ignorant. Calling us Indians. Or worse, all those slurs they love to throw around. All the violence, the stuff that's seen, the stuff that's still to be uncovered. Wyatt should know the community he's a part of. "Is this what we do for everyone? Really?" I ask pointedly.

He pulls away from Elise, squares his shoulders, sticks his chest out. "It's what I do for everyone."

I'm not afraid of Wyatt. "You weren't friends with Doyle Younger? Before he grabbed my hair so hard he tore my scalp?

Before he threw me to the ground and fucked up my shoulder? The guy whose friends kicked Tyler's little sister—a fifteen-year-old child—while she lay in a ball crying? You didn't used to shoot the shit with him? After school. Every weekend. Your whole entire life."

King stands in the doorway now, the spray bottle forgotten somewhere, watching the way he does. Even though he's beyond tired, he's here. Ready to step in. If he's needed.

Elise's hand covers her open mouth. Her fingernails are pink too. A sweet, pretty pink. I'm watching her shock. Watching her fall out of love with Wyatt Thomas.

"We were with him and a bunch of his friends last night. You told me that was a rumor. That he had nothing to do with what happened." She pushes herself off the table, landing on her feet with a thud. She gathers her shoes in her hands. "Did you really know he did that to Lou?"

Wyatt nods, quick and curt.

"I'm leaving," Elise says. "This is done, by the way. Over. Don't follow me."

King lets her pass and then resumes his position in the doorway. His shoulders are big, bridging the gap. Wyatt paces the shack, from me to King, a few times before he tries to give chase.

King stands firm. "No, man. You heard her."

Wyatt's chest puffs out again. This time, all his country-boy charm evaporates. "Move."

"Or what?" King, always best with his words, asks. And it's not to tempt Wyatt, to rile him up, but to get him *to think*.

Wyatt's voice climbs. "Move. Now. It's the last time I ask. Next time I'll just do."

King's body doesn't change. His face doesn't change. He doesn't become someone else here. "She asked you not to chase after her."

Wyatt turns as if to climb over the freezer and launch himself out the serving window. Before he can, Elise's little sedan exits the parking lot.

"Why couldn't you just take what I offered and shut up, Lou? You can't ever shut up."

He steps toward me. The backs of my legs press into the stool. I'm leaning away from his body. Wyatt doesn't care that my neck is bent rough. "Doyle almost killed a girl."

Over Wyatt's shoulder, King's tense. He's waiting for me to ask him to step in. He's trusting me to handle myself. But he's here for me too.

"She was drunk, Lou." Wyatt doesn't scream it—he spits it. "Drunk and getting pissed over nothing. Empty words."

"A white man murdered her mother."

"It wasn't fucking Doyle."

"He called us drunks. Because we're Native."

"She *was* drunk, Lou. So was her sister. And last year, you would have been fucked-up too. Indians drink. There's a pack of them right now on the sidewalk outside that trash hotel downtown and you know it."

"Leave," I say. "You're done here."

King steps out of the doorway to let a furious Wyatt pass.

But he isn't ready. He turns fast, approaches until his breath hits my cheek. His head snakes left, then right. "I knew there was something wrong with you. The first time we kissed. You were frigid. You're frigid still. And that doesn't go away except when you're drunk. That night, that's when you were half-okay." He grabs his keys from the counter, abandoning the shack. Outside, louder now, so even the family enjoying ice cream at the far picnic table can hear him, he says, "We can't cure cold bitch, Lou. Turns out it's terminal."

A half minute later, he tears out onto the highway.

I collapse onto the floor. The cooler hums loudly, vibrating against my back, and I'm not asking nicely now. This time, I smash my right elbow hard into the metal door. Once, twice, three times, until the humming falls a hint lower. My shoulder protests.

King offers me space.

Later, I'm sitting with my shirt and bra in my lap, in the back seat of the Subaru, facing the window. It's dark, after midnight. My poster board is duct-taped to the shack.

"He was angry, you know," King says. "No one should treat you like that. And he's wrong."

It's the first time King's mentioned that whole show. Earlier, he changed his playlist to something intense, voices yelling rather than singing. We listened to them scream for an hour before I forced him to fingerprint me into his phone. I couldn't stomach rage for another second.

"We don't open up for everyone." His hands press the tape on my back, kneading in at the edges. "White boy's so wrong about you. You're not cold."

My voice wavers. "Are you sure?"

I could cry here. I could believe him too.

His hand travels to my neck. He shifts my loose hair over to the side carefully. He's not doing anything he hasn't done before, taping my shoulder. "Lou, I still want to take you out one night. Because you're totally amazing."

I can't look at him. "But what's wrong with what we have now?"

His laugh is pure frustration. "Well, for one . . . at the moment, I really want to kiss your neck." He groans, laughs. "But friends don't do that."

"You shouldn't, then. We're good as friends."

"But you're a lot like a fire and I can't tear my eyes away."

His hands are calm pressing the tape into my skin. They wouldn't be so calm if he knew that the police came for Dr. Nathan after O'Reilly's was nothing but rubble and broken glass because of what Tyler and I had done.

I choke out, "Fires burn."

"They do."

"They destroy."

"You know wildfires create," he says.

"Cold things burn too."

"If you need to keep telling yourself that." He finishes with the tape and climbs out the other door, leaving me to get dressed alone.

Before we drive off, in separate vehicles, in opposite directions, I glance back at the shack. It's been bothering me since I read the third letter. "Do you know who owns this land? Legally, I mean."

"Your family doesn't? I had assumed."

"I really don't think we do."

The Creamery opened three summers ago. I helped Dom drive the shack out here on the back of a rented flatbed truck. He said it was the perfect location, for now. Like it was temporary. Like he didn't really want the shack to sit here forever.

King's two feet away now. When I move closer, he steps back.

He rubs at his eyes. "Why does it matter?"

"*He* sent another letter. He's threatening to take the farm, the shack, everything from us, if I don't add his name to my birth certificate. And I'm sure, if I do, I won't ever be able to keep him out of my life. We'll be tangled up permanently."

King's hands are in his jeans pockets now as if he's holding himself in check. "If you need someone to tell you that you get to make this choice and he doesn't, I'll be that person."

"Maarsi, King Nathan. You're a good one."

He smiles sadly at me, no teeth, no real joy in the action. Like he doesn't want to be *good*.

"I need to find out who owns this land." I'm talking more to myself than to him, but he answers me.

"The day after tomorrow?" he offers. "After we get some sleep. After we help those families out."

I wish I could date him. I wish I could be all wildfire—the kind that makes the land healthy again. To kiss him, bury my hands in clumps of his T-shirt, and feel something. But he deserves better than me. He deserves it all.

And I know when I become fire, I destroy.

CHAPTER 18
July 30

INDIGO: Bacon finds its way into everything, even ice cream. Saskatoons and bacon marry to bring salty, nutty, and sweet together. Saskatoons and elk. Any wild game, really. Our house favorite is Saskatoon berry and dried moose meat. It's chewy in a way that will appeal to those of you who, when you were kids, liked that blue horror-story stuff studded with pieces of frozen gum. Try it. The kids, they call this a glow-up.

Maurice and Dom leave the house together, abandoning their dirty coffee mugs. It's a bad family habit. We all do it, waiting for Maurice to tidy up later. Without Mom here, it's easier to see the patterns. Before, it was like she was weaving it all into her designs. When she sat with us at this table, I didn't notice things as sharply.

Our sink is two feet from the table.

We own so many mugs, it would take us weeks to run out if we used a new one every day. They overflow out of the cupboard and onto the counter next to the fridge. Like my T-shirts, they're from everywhere.

But, in this house, we only use the same four mugs.

This morning, full of nervous energy, I sink my hands into

hot, soapy water while I wait for my uncles to drive into town, for people to gather outside the Friendship Center. I need a buffer.

They're either going to love me for this or it'll go the other way. There aren't other options.

I haven't even told Mom about the tornado, about closing the shop to help clean up. Her Insta stories are all laughter—she's so happy. And last week, at the diner, Cami was talking about my mom's sales, like Cami's texting my mom more than I am. When we FaceTime, my mom beads the whole time—half somewhere else, with some other auntie sharing the room, and the TV up loud. She hasn't been home to find out what's going on in my life. That fact itches like a half-healed wound and I know if I scratch, I'll bleed.

Florence lives closest to me in one of the newer suburbs. It spreads out into what used to be farmland. This morning, she's decked out in cargo pants and a tight, midriff-baring top. Her hair is up really high, dramatic and beautiful. Her sunglasses are perched on her nose, concealing her eyes from me. She's been drinking alone in her bedroom. Again. She promised she'd call when she feels this way—and she hasn't been calling. But I haven't been either. She's not in the top spot in my messages window anymore. Both my mom and King text more often.

"You okay?" I ask.

"Don't you start too," she says, climbing into the truck. "I'm a little low. But who isn't?"

"Okay, but—"

"I'm taking my meds, pet. I can handle myself. I don't need you, or King, or my parents biting into my neck at all hours. I need my friends to be fun."

"King's worried about you too?"

"Jesus H. Christ, bringer of fluffy pancakes. Lou, you're jelly, aren't you?"

I back out of her driveway. "You two text, don't you? A lot."

"He's teaching me Toronto slang. I'm teaching him Dublin slang. And we both watch *Drag Race*," she says, like it should be obvious why they're friends. "Besides, really, that boy only has eyes for you. And he's a major step up from the last one, eh, now?"

She's so fully Florence this morning—bright and witty and sharp like sunshine—I let myself quit worrying. At least for today. "We're just friends."

"Whatever you say." Florence throws her neon-pink boots up on my dash, one at a time, to tighten her laces.

When we park in front of King's house, Dr. Nathan comes out to the truck first. "Good morning, young ladies," he says. "How's that shoulder healing up?"

"Better." I lean toward the passenger-side window with a smile. "How's your hand?"

"I'm an old man now." He lifts his casted forearm as if displaying the evidence.

"You're not old, Dr. Nathan," Florence says.

He laughs. "King'll be with you shortly. He's on the phone with his sister."

Florence hops out of the truck, leaving the door open, so when King emerges, he's forced to take the seat right next to me. She winks.

"Jerk," I whisper.

"I'll be that way later," Dr. Nathan says, holding the truck door open, smiling at Florence. "After my follow-up at the fracture clinic."

When King emerges, he claims the middle seat, nudging me with one shoulder. We exchange hellos. As we pull away from the house, Florence waves while we spin around the cul-de-sac. She laughs when Dr. Nathan returns the gesture as enthusiastically.

At the Friendship Center, when we don't spot my uncles in the parking lot, it's a relief, and I relax enough that I start to enjoy this. Riding around in the truck with King and Florence. We haven't done this all summer either, hung out the three of us while not at work.

Tyler catches sight of my truck. Her hair is loose, and she's wearing a shoulder-baring tank top and her classic black skinny jeans, holding a clipboard. "Can we use your beast for dump runs?"

"Sure."

"Great. I'll catch a ride out to the site with you, if that's all right." She peers into the cab. "Truck bed's fine."

We drive north, heading out of town a few kilometers before we start seeing downed trees and overturned farm equipment. At one point, we cruise into the ditch to get around debris emergency services haven't moved yet. King's talking to Ty through the little window. The wind is whipping her hair all over the place. I pull a hair tie from my wrist, press it into King's hand, and wordlessly, he passes it over.

"This one," King says, as we approach a farm road.

The white house is torn in half. Furniture and belongings are scattered all over. In the field, well beyond the house, a red pickup truck is flipped over on its nose—as if it's a child's toy and not a sixty-thousand-dollar machine, probably still being paid off.

Tyler hops out when we stop. "Insurance was here yesterday. It's time to sort what can be salvaged from what needs to go. Lou and King, would you load and run out to the dump? Um, and you . . ." She only half side-eyes Florence. "I'll introduce you to the family and you can work on piling trash here by the drive."

Florence smiles bright from behind her sunglasses. "Whatever you say. You're holding the super-official clipboard."

Between the two of them, this is progress.

A small crowd is already at work. The family too. Brown skin, dark hair in skinny braids—the kids small, wearing diapers and nothing else. It's hot enough. But really, everything they have is spread out along the prairie, tangled in a small run of bent and broken trees, and no one could blame them if their babies aren't wearing pants.

That's a lie. Someone could. Probably, today, someone will.

I don't spot my uncles in the mix. Maybe they're at another farm. That would be lucky. There's already a pile of soaked mattresses and broken chairs. We dive in. When the truck is loaded, I slam the tailgate shut and we're off. King's arm glides along in the wind.

It's too loud to talk with the rush of the road and the wheels running in circles over the pavement, *thump, thump, thump, thump.*

I keep telling myself it's too loud to talk when Dr. Nathan all but gave me the opening to ask about Aliya, and then it's not much further after that, to ask about their mom.

At the dump, I reverse into the pile of things already

decomposing—plastics that won't ever, next to cheap wood-laminate Swedish furniture that will one day, eventually, return to earth. We stand in the bed of the truck and together lift and throw water-laden furniture without speaking.

The collar of King's shirt darkens under a circle of sweat. At some point he pulls it up and over his head, hangs his shirt through the back window of the truck. I try not to stare. His body is rounder than Wyatt's. Friendlier. It's not the first time I've seen King without a shirt. We swim together all the time. But it's the first time I've seen him like this. Not *only* aesthetically beautiful.

As soon as he catches me, I glance away—and focus on a stained mattress, half-submerged in the mess.

"You're acting weird," he says.

"I'm hot," I say. "I mean sweaty."

He leans into the truck through the little window and tosses me the water bottle he brought along this morning. I take a sip, offer it back to him.

I want to ask about his sister. About his mom. But something tells me right now, right here, isn't the time.

"It really smells," he says, wiping his face with his discarded T-shirt.

"Yeah." It's the first time I've noticed it. Really noticed it. My senses are overwhelmed. We quickly finish unloading and return to the farm and fresh air.

Dom catches sight of me first. As I throw the truck into park, he walks over. "Florence told me you were here. Somewhere. She was being cagey."

I nod.

"You closed my shop."

"I did."

"You know we can't afford that. And to pay them." He's shaking his head like he can't stop. He's disappointed.

My shoulder aches in a quiet way. "I'll cover their salaries."

King, still shirtless, standing somewhere behind me, says, "You don't have to pay me."

Dom exhales hard. "Florence said the same."

"I said I would and I will. It's only fair." Across the yard, Maurice is working with the family, sorting through boxes of things from the flooded basement. Old photographs, mostly. "I'll work three shifts without pay to balance it out."

Dom walks off, his shoulders tight. "Yeah, you will."

"Lou, you didn't clear it by your uncles?"

I'm still watching Dom surge off, watching his shoulders knot up. "Nope. I did not."

"Brave," King says, and starts loading the truck again.

I want him to go on, but he doesn't.

Near the wreckage of the house, Tyler peers at me over her clipboard. She signals me like in the old days, two fingers pressed to her heart, and when I nod, she comes running. "King, would you help with the furniture on the second floor? There's some carpet up there that's so wet, I can't lift it." She flexes and her biceps pop. Tyler's fit. "I'll ride with Lou this round, if you don't mind."

King lets her make her excuses and doesn't call her out on them. He heads toward the house, shirtless and lost in his own mood. Maybe he's just tired. Maybe I should have asked after his family even if the time wasn't exactly right. His sister called. I don't think she calls often. But, honestly, I don't know if she does.

Tyler waits until we turn out of the gravel driveway. "Something strange happened earlier this week and it pertains to you. I was at the welcome desk, minding my own, and a white guy, around forty, bearded, wearing his sunglasses inside like he was in a music video, you know the kind, he starts asking questions about you. The personal variety."

I'm driving slow. To keep the stuff in the truck bed from bouncing around too much. We turn onto the highway and I have to pick up speed. I keep the emergency flashers on because we are certainly a hazard.

"He wanted to know about that summer."

"What did you tell him?"

"Not a thing. Are you in trouble?" she asks. "He was a creep. Plus. He has no right to know anything about you that you don't want him to know. I played it like we were never friends, cuz."

I've owed her this for a long time. Somehow, the road, here in the same truck we sat in after we set O'Reilly's on fire, after we took something back from the man who murdered Tyler's mom, this is the right place. "Ty, I tried on the tough-Native-chick thing with you for almost a year. It didn't fit."

Her laugh is cloudy. "You still don't get it? There's not one way to be Native, eh? It's not either this or . . . becoming an apple—red on the outside, white all through the middle. It's who you are. It's being yourself and honoring your family, your people, the land— all living things." She slows, watching my face, and softens. "And it's about wearing big beaded earrings, eh?"

My throat is tight. "Well, I have the earrings at least."

Today, they're running bison, edged with a rainbow sequence.

"Who knows what will fit tomorrow or next week? It didn't fit for you then, but this . . ." She throws out her tattooed arms. "This fits me now. For the me I am now. Right this minute. Right here."

"Thanks for telling me. About the man, the one asking questions," I say, ready to tell her who *he is*, exactly who, just as a siren goes off behind us. I can't see out the rearview, but in the driver's side mirror, I spot the lights.

"Fuckers," Tyler says. "It's like they're out here looking for brown people."

"Neither of us are that brown, Ty."

"Don't go back on your bullshit, Lou. We only just talked about this." She taps the apple tattoo on the inside of her wrist.

I nod because what else can I say? I clear my throat. "He's probably pissed about how we've loaded the truck."

Tyler exhales, sinks lower into her seat. If she had a hoodie on, she'd be pulling it up.

"Morning, Officer," I say when he approaches Tyler's window. It's safer, away from traffic, but I hate that he's closer to Ty. "We were going the speed limit. What's wrong?"

"License," the cop says, glaring inside the vehicle.

It's the same cop from the night Cami was hurt. My stomach sinks. I still haven't gone back to the mall to retrieve my ID. "I'm going to get my friend here to reach into the dash for my pink card. Is that okay?"

His mirrored sunglasses only reflect back my own fear. "Fine."

"My ID," I say as Tyler pulls the insurance card and my

registration from the glove box and hands it over, and I maintain eye contact with the cop. "I left it at the drugstore in the mall, by accident, this morning. The clerk forgot to return it. And I was going out to help with tornado cleanup. You can see from the other documents I'm insured. It's my truck. If you want, I can show you my school ID?"

He peers into the bed of the truck. "You helping the Joneses, the Englands?"

My heart hammers. England. It could be him. It could be a cousin. I picture a flipped-over white SUV and fight against a small smile that wants to enjoy imagined revenge.

Tyler speaks when I don't. "And the Frankfurts and the Bengays and the Delacroix families. They were all hit."

The cop stares at the two of us. "I like seeing you people doing something to build this town up instead of complaining about it."

Beside me, Tyler stiffens. My hand sinks onto the bench next to her as if I might have to hold her back.

"You can go," the cop says, backing away from the truck. "Retrieve that ID. Today. The next time, I'll impound your vehicle so long you'll never be able to afford to get it back."

"Understood," I say.

The cop hits the side of the truck twice, like, get on now, and climbs into his cruiser.

"That was only low-key racist." Tyler starts breathing normally again. She knows me well enough to know I used to be a pretty good liar. "Where's your ID really at?"

"The drugstore. Since before the holiday weekend. I went to buy a scratch ticket and the clerk made me show it. And then when he noticed I was legal, he tried to get me to suck him off. Like I would agree, do it, and then leave the store. Like that's how it is."

"Fucker." She bites at a knuckle. "One of the assistant managers in there once, goes by the name of Hal, wears one of those effed-up Canadian thin-blue-line pins on his lapel . . . Cami didn't have enough for the crap she was trying to buy. He said he'd trade. Sex for nail polish and shampoo. Like in the good old days."

"Jesus."

"She was eleven."

When I told Florence about the pharmacy clerk, she was shocked. Tyler understands. I hate that. But at the same time, it makes me feel seen. I didn't go into stores by myself, not at eleven, not until we moved back here. My mom taught me how to look out for myself, but she was always looking too. I wasn't ever alone. It was a little messed up to be always with my mom when I wasn't in school—but it was also protection against the world. No wonder the first time she let me run about on my own, I managed to screw it up so badly—with lies and fire.

At the dump, we make quick work of the stuff in the truck bed. It's getting hot, so hot. King's T-shirt is on the bench next to me, and I curl my hand into it for a second before I realize it's a bit gross, me holding on to his sweaty tee.

I need a shower.

A cold shower.

I need to get my head screwed on straight.

I need to lose myself in a punishing training session.

On the drive home, Tyler sings along to the radio. Every

191

country song, it doesn't matter, new or old, she knows the words. "Want to stop in there? I'll get your license back for you. Around here, they know I'm a mean bitch."

I smile but shake my head at her offer.

"They don't know you used to be one—once," she continues. "That once, it fit. For a time."

O'Reilly's. The fire. The smoke. I laugh. It's her tone. It's the fact that she's right. It did fit. Maybe too well—that terrified me—and maybe it doesn't anymore. "Our secret has to go to the grave, Ty."

Her voice gets small, but it still rings with truth. "Might it be a long while before I can tell all these fuckers about how you threw the first flaming bottle through that green stained-glass window. How you ran with me. How you drove this truck away from the burn, nice and slow. How we sat in the park and I cried for hours."

I grab her hand. She grabs back.

"I still . . ." I try to say it. Tell her about the smoke. "I still . . . I . . ."

She nods. "Me too."

We're closing in on the work site. I can't pull in there this close to tears.

I clear my throat. "Ty, the England farm, is it next door? Or—"

"It's farther up. The one after."

I focus on the road. On driving. On keeping the truck within the lines.

"Lou, I get you want me to play like I'm not following here. And so I'm playing—but I'm also worried for you."

I slow down before we reach the England property.

192

There's a white SUV parked in the drive, nestled up against a well-maintained hedge, and behind the hedge, there's a big stone-and-log farmhouse. The license plate reads FREED. The damage, it appears, is minimal. A few fences bent, torn. His SUV gleams.

I keep driving, slowly, and then press on all the way to the next farm before I turn around, before I say anything. "I'm worried too."

"That asshole, that's your sperm donor, eh? My mom used to talk about what happened to yours, about a . . . Pete . . . England."

He's so close. Closer than I hoped. I nod.

"Was it him, at the Friendship Center, asking me questions?" Tyler asks.

I keep nodding. It's all I can manage this close to his property.

"Okay," Ty says. "But you'll tell me if you need someone like me on your side?"

That's comforting like campfire.

CHAPTER 19
July 30

INDIGO: This might be obvious, but sometimes
you gotta state the obvious. Indigo stains. Badly.
Avoid wearing white T-shirts while consuming.

When we make it back to our work site, my hands are
steady. There's a lunch on. Maurice is at the barbecue
and a CBC reporter is taking photos. I didn't see Peter England,
didn't confirm it's his farm, his SUV. Not for certain. But I don't
need proof beyond what my body says is true.

Tyler offers me an awkward side hug. For her, this is a lot of
physical contact. "Cami's going to be so pissed when I tell her
about the drugstore. I can tell her, right?"

"Of course."

She's glancing at the house—or over the house, toward the
England farm. "And I'm serious. You know where I lay down at
night. Come get me anytime."

One thing I miss about Tyler. She's ride or die for the ones she
loves.

I press two fingers to my heart. I'm off balance. I'm falling
back into old habits—and they feel exactly right.

Tyler offers me a slight chin-up before heading off.

"Hey, hey," Maurice says when he sees me. He waves, getting the photographer's attention. "Taking the day to help out here was my niece's idea."

"Great," the reporter says, extending his hand. He's white, in his midfifties, maybe. Wears a polo shirt and tan shorts. "I'm with the CBC in Edmonton. We'd love to get a picture of all of you who work out at the Michif Creamery, if you don't mind."

"That's fine," I say. "I'll gather them."

With a thing to focus on, I push away the stress of returning to Tyler, and of my father's coming home. For now.

Across the yard, King and Florence are eating BBQ and picnic salads, laughing together, leaning against someone's car. She catches my eye and mouths, "What's wrong?"

I notice Elise standing in a tee and cargo shorts next to the old oil heater tank, off by herself. She spots me. But her characteristic smile has vanished. Suddenly I like her a lot more. And it has nothing to do with Wyatt's tongue not being down her throat. She's not only rainbows and sunshine. She's human, it turns out.

I fake a crooked smile for Florence's benefit. It's a mixed message, but it's enough for now. "Both of you, meet me over by my truck in five?"

They agree.

I cross the lawn in Elise's direction.

"Sorry about the drama yesterday," she says, screwing up her button nose.

She showed up. She said she'd show and she did. That's responsibility and it's kindness, what she's doing out here.

"When I broke up with him, it was pretty dramarific too." I don't know I'm going to tell her until suddenly, I'm telling her about it. "He made me jump out of his moving vehicle. Onto the shoulder of the highway."

Elise is halfway through shoving a potato chip in her mouth. She starts to choke. When she recovers, her voice gets low. "No way?"

I nod. "I wish I'd told you."

"I wish I'd known."

She offers me a chip from the bag. They're original and not my favorite, but the salt is needed today. "Did he ever . . . do anything like that to you?"

It's too late to change things. But I need to know.

"He's good at getting what he wants. But no, not really. And I had you and King around when it ended." She shrugs. "It's just . . . I'm not the kind of girl guys like. I'm too . . . smart or I don't pretend to be empty well enough, and . . ."

"Oh, Elise, hard same."

She smiles now. "Did you know I won the science fair the year after you did?"

"I didn't pay much attention. To be honest."

"It's fine. My project wasn't as cool as yours—I was programming drones to recognize where to seed-drop native plants after wildfires—and—"

"I love that idea!" I say, cutting her off. It's exactly the kind of thing that vibes with what we're doing at the Creamery.

"Really?"

I nod, animated.

"Well, so my photo was up in the awards case next to yours.

In the hall. The one across from the boys' change room. And I'm wondering if maybe Wyatt just picked us out there, like he was shopping?"

I laugh. It's light and real. "Totally, entirely possible."

She laughs too. "I'll warn next year's winner. In case."

Elise knows what's right. It's what I should have done at the start. Talked to her, privately, and told her what happened to me. An idea shows up, fully formed in my head. It's what I want to do. Entirely. It's what Tyler would do. And so I do it. "Do you by any chance want a job? We have an opening . . . it turns out."

"Really?" she asks.

I smile.

"Yes, oh my gosh, yes! My parents were so angry at me for getting fired. My older sister's never been fired from anything—she's never failed at anything—and then, here I am, getting let go from my summer job."

"Your first task is a team photo." I point toward the reporter. "I'm positive you can handle this."

She grins. "But my sister would excel at it!"

I nudge Elise gently as we walk. I never had a sibling whose shadow I had to live in—only my own. And what my mother's passed down. What Peter England has. A violence that's seeded deep inside of me, that's corrupting my attempts at normal—at kissing and at what comes after kissing. I push that away. Together, me and my friends, we stand in front of the wrecked house, arms thrown over each other's shoulders, me on the outside, King's hand gently resting on my bad shoulder. He can't help himself from feeling for the tape, pressing it into my skin.

It's nice, so nice—and in the photo, I'm smiling wide.

The photographer promises to stop by the shack tomorrow on his way out of town to sample the goods. "I'm a big ice-cream fan. So are my teens. They're going to be so jealous."

"We do pints," Elise says, upselling already, before she's even worn the apron.

When I'm sitting alone, finishing my lunch, Maurice wanders over and sinks down next to me. He's quiet for a while, like he's gathering his thoughts, ordering notes on sheet music precisely so. "I'm proud of you, Lou. This was the right thing to do."

"Dom doesn't think so."

"He's scared. This is the last summer we'll ever live like this. He can feel it and it's terrifying him."

The white SUV—FREED—and Peter England's big house, built out of logs and stone.

My shoulder holding me back in the pool.

Florence and Tyler and King. University in September.

"I feel it too," I say.

My uncle isn't done. He says, "Everything is changing. That's the way of this world. You know, I lived with six different families growing up. Change. It's our world, the one constant. We're fools to think otherwise. To think we can stave it off."

What we're trying to hold on to here, it's like beads—and one thing Mom taught me, beads, they're alive with a mind of their own. Thinking you can control them, that's the first mistake. There's nothing else to say. My uncle and I sit together, both of us lost in our own heads, thankful this isn't our farm. Thankful our change is coming for us slower than a tornado.

CHAPTER 20
July 31

INDIGO: Colors in nature aren't as sharp once they've been blended with cream. In ice they stand out better. If color fade is something you're worried about, amp things up with natural dyes. Or take a different approach and create your indigo in the final stages of the process. Don't blend, fold. But here's our best trick: before serving, add one more layer—fresh borage or other candied flowers from your garden—to ensure an unforgettable experience.

'm supposed to meet King at the public library this morning, both of us taking a day off to do research on Peter England's involvement with the shack. My shoulder aches like I've been hand-grinding roots for Dom on the old mortar and pestle we keep in the kitchen, and last night I swallowed some leftover pain pills I found in our medicine cabinet. The label said my mom's name. But it's mine too, I justified, swiping two and throwing them back without water.

I'm groggy. Not myself.

Summer's coming to an end so much faster than I thought possible, and in a few weeks, King and Florence will be boarding airplanes. I'll be moving into the dorms, taking classes in massive lecture halls, trying to make new friends, and the shack will close for another year.

This time, maybe, it will close forever.

In the kitchen, mugs overflow from our cabinets and pepper the kitchen table, and I think of the families who lost everything in the tornado. It's instinct, this drive to help. First, I riffle through the basement to find a box. Then, I pack up most of the mugs. I leave ours and four more. For guests and accidents.

I load them into the truck bed. I'll stop at the secondhand store drop-off bin before the library.

Probably, my uncles won't notice.

I'm driving into town deep in my weird funk, trying to work through that every time I see a white SUV, I flinch; that since I hurt my shoulder, I'm not excited about university—when Florence blows up my phone. First a series of texts I don't check because I'm driving. Then she begins calling.

This is something we never do. It's an emergency. I pull the truck onto the side of the highway, the rumble strips jarring me almost awake. My emergency flashers tick, echoing like a warning I can't quite make out. I call her back.

Florence doesn't greet me, she explodes: "Lou, it's a mess in here. The freezer died! Everything's fecking melted. And I wore white trainers today, Louie. White trainers in a shop that looks as if a unicorn imploded."

I hit the steering wheel with my fist. My horn blares.

Pain bites in and my stomach rolls. My shoulder isn't pleased with me. After yesterday. I'll have to ease up on training. For a few days.

"Are you driving? Please tell me you're not driving and on your mobile? That's dangerous!"

"I'm on the side of the highway. Close by actually. I'll . . . come and help. Do not call my uncles. Please."

"I would never," she says, and then adds, "It's a real mess in here. Everything is sticky and the flies. Jesus H. Christo, lord of breakfast foods, the flies are as big as birds. What is wrong with this country?"

Vehicles pass me on their way into town, shaking my truck ever so slightly. Before merging back onto the highway, I remember to text King.

> Change of plans.
> Disaster at the shack.
> Everything's melted.
> Flo needs help.

Be right there.

> You don't need to. We can
> handle this.

Three little dots, then:

Don't turn away a hand, Lou.

> Okay.

And then, before I think about it, I add:

> Thank you. <3

Only a little part of me wishes I could delete the message and retract the heart. It's a habit with Florence dropping my love into our messages—and suddenly, it's become one with King. When I pull into the parking area next to the shack, my best friend is dragging colorful bins of melted ice cream and sorbets outside. She's covered in it. In her hair, staining her tank top, and yes, her shoes are ruined. She spots me, dropping the mostly full container she's carrying in exhaustion. It tips over, bleeds red onto the gravel. The melted product is studded with globs of ice.

"It's everywhere," Florence says, miserable.

I pull my hands through my hair. I straightened it this morning. I put on mascara this morning. I'm wearing this black jumpsuit that pops all my curves, with a tiny cutout, a flash of skin above my sternum.

She wipes her hands on her leggings and presses a hair tie into my hands. "You'd better tuck all that gorgeousness away, pet."

"Right."

We stare at the red mess, slowly running down the slope toward the highway.

"This is the hell you never imagine when your summer job is scooping ice cream and sunbathing on the side of the road."

"This almost never happens," I say.

"I didn't read anything about handling melting product in my contract."

"What contract?"

"I didn't sign a contract?" she muses. "Why I am here again? Covered in warmed—slush!"

"You could go home and sit on the couch, talk to your parents. About your life choices."

Florence brightens a little. "This isn't the worst, I suppose."

I laugh. Her parents are wonderful, but they're full of questions.

For thirty minutes, we clean what we can. Yesterday's closed sign ends up in a pile next to the wasted product. My truck bed is loaded with emptied plastic tubs. They'll get sanitized and reused. Later tonight, alone in the production barn, that's what I'll be doing. Either weighed down by guilt, or because it's my punishment for not reporting the freezer to my uncles when I knew it was misbehaving.

I meant to.

I did.

But intention doesn't actually mean a thing. Not really. Dom won't care what I meant to do. There are things I'm sure he meant to tell me. Like the Victim Services letter arriving. Like the news that when Peter England was released from prison, he came back here, to the town where I live. To hell with intentions, I think, wondering why I didn't act when I knew the freezer was failing, why Dom didn't act when he got the news. Maybe we're both cowards. Maybe we did act; maybe doing nothing at all is a very loud action. Ineffective, it seems, with electrical appliances. And with men like Peter England.

By now, the gravel is stained all the colors of the rainbow. Ants swarm. They're marking this glorious holiday down in their history books. The flies would prefer to land on our warm bodies, their little legs tickling us. Off in the trees, a crow watches us with interest.

When King arrives with doughnuts and cold, caffeinated drinks from Tim's, he doesn't ask questions, just surveys the area. He meets my eye and smiles this half smile. I wish I knew what he's thinking. But I shouldn't. He offered his help and showed up with fuel— King putting his words, his intentions, into clear action.

The three of us are working on cleaning the melted, sticky mess sludged along the bottom of the freezer when a truck pulls into the parking lot.

Florence passes me a dirty rag to rinse. "Feck, it's your uncle."

"Which one?"

"The pretty one."

I drop the rag on the prep counter and walk into the sunshine to meet him. He's holding the newspaper, folded over, tucked under his arm. His free hand creeps into his hairline and grabs at a handful when he processes the mess covering the lot.

"The freezer went out. Sometime after we left Friday night."

"For fuck's sake, Lou. This could break us. The bank's calling me every other day looking for last month's payment plus interest." He pushes the newspaper at me, forgotten now, and closes in on the shack. "If . . . if you'd been here like you were supposed to be, we'd have saved the stock at least."

He turns, storms away from me.

From the serving window, King and Florence watch. They heard my uncle. They know, as much as I do, that this is my fault. Only they don't know how I heard the freezer giving off signs.

I glance at the paper. The *Edmonton Sun*. Today's edition. We're on the cover—all four of us. Smiling. King leans toward me a little. Elise is as happy as I've seen her. And Florence's eyes are bright.

"Lou, check the generator," Dom hollers.

"We look good," I say, staring at the paper.

Dom leans out of the shack. "I need to know if it's the freezer or the generator that failed. If it's the freezer, we're done. We can close up right now."

I don't exactly cross my fingers, but I brush the earrings I wore today. They're another pair of Mom's—shooting stars.

Out back, the generator's wired into the shack. Everything appears normal.

Dom yells, "Fire it up."

"I can't," I holler in return. My shoulder won't let me do this— not today.

King slips around back of the shack. He offers to try. Pulls once, twice, three times.

Nothing.

Dom's joined us. He's hovering now, watching. "When's the last time you checked to make sure the gas tank was full?"

I think. I really do, and I can't remember.

"You let it run dry!" Dom yells at me like I basically sabotaged our family. He restarts the breaker that's hardwired into the main power and, thankfully, the freezer begins to hum happily.

I'd apologize, but Dom's not ready. He won't hear me. He won't trust me.

When Elise shows up for her shift, my uncle takes off, and basically orders us to have this place ready to open tomorrow morning. He'll be in production all day trying to replace stock—if he has enough ingredients to produce anything.

He leaves dejected.

If we've lost as much as Dom thinks we have, we really might have to close early. That's what you do when you go out of business. One day, you simply give up. If this happens, I won't have enough money to cover tuition. I'll have to take a job on campus, and that will cut into water polo practice. Already, I've missed almost a week, and I owe three days. I shouldn't have hired Elise. I shouldn't have offered to help the Friendship Center. I should have told Dom the freezer was making weird noises, even if it meant we'd have to pay someone to assess the damage.

It's barely noon and I'm exhausted.

When ice cream melts, it spreads everywhere.

I take a break to scroll my mom's Instagram. Normally when I do this, it stops me from wanting to call her, to break her happiness with my problems. Today, all she's posted is a pair of earrings. They're large. A pair of dinosaur skulls. They're badass and dorky at the same time. My heart clenches: she's thinking about me—she has to be.

I find her in my contacts. The connection isn't great, but my mom's face appears on my phone screen. "Are you at the shack?" she asks.

"Yeah, I am."

"Everything okay?"

I want to tell her. But if I start, I won't be able to stop myself. From telling her everything. I manage: "I miss you. That's all. I wanted to tell you how much I miss you."

There's a pause. The video connection is rough. Fuzzy.

"I—I have to go, Mom."

"Lou, wait—"

The video is trying to reconnect.

"Lou—"

"I have to go."

"Okay, okay. Call later. I'm missing you too."

I shove my phone deep in the pocket of my jumpsuit as if that will quiet the rush of feelings inundating me and force myself to get back to the mess.

The first unfamiliar car shows up a little after noon. It's a family. A couple and three kids, wearing camping clothing. "We heard about you on the radio, and thought we'd support a great community business," the woman says.

"As you can see . . ." Florence waves with dramatic flourish. "We've had a little power failure."

"Oh darn," the man says.

"You have nothing left?" the woman asks.

All three kids stare, politely waiting for their promised treat to appear. The littlest one picks her nose.

"Nope," Florence says.

"But," I cut in—thinking fast. "The production studio is only five kilometers up the road. If you're okay driving out there, I'll sell you a few pints and give the kids a tour of the dairy too."

"What do you think?" the husband asks his wife.

"That sounds delightful," she says. "Right, kids?"

The three of them nod. Even little finger-up-the-nose.

"Great, follow me," I say, and run into the shack to fetch my apron.

Florence is giving me a look. "Well, that's an idea, pet."

"Do you mind if I take Elise along?"

"Go for it. We'll keep at this and send people out there."

Florence, when focused, can clean like she's on some kind of stimulant. She claims she likes cleaning too—that it's relaxing, a way of ordering the world to her satisfaction.

King grabs a pad of paper we use for really complicated orders. "I'll start drawing maps. Are we charging for tours?"

"No. But make sure people know we're not serving scoops. Only pints. Until we run dry. And to bring cash."

I know Florence and King will get things done, and get them done well.

At the farm, Dom hears us drive up, emerging from the production barn, his hair in a net. Elise carries the cash drawer out of the truck and parks herself in the shade against the barn. She's talking to the kids, who have escaped their car and are goofing off with the dogs.

"I don't think our insurance covers this," Dom says. But he opens the production studio wide, pinning the doors in place. He shows Elise where the ready-to-sell pints are kept.

I straighten, pretend at a control I don't really feel. "Right, Wheeler family, follow me. We're going to find a cow named Mooreen and pet her. She's as friendly as the dogs, Mooreen is," I say, emphasizing the pun. "She's the udderly delightful Cowntessa de Pasteur and very much enjoys company. Mind you—the other cows are cows. We don't pet the other cows, okay?"

The kids laugh at me. When we return from the field walk, Dom takes over the tour. Everyone is given a hair net. Dom pulls samples from his concentrated flavor stocks—freeze-dried raspberries, sprigs of wild mint, a fingertip of moose fat—and offers the Wheeler family a taste.

At first, it's only a car or two. Then it's three, four.

As promised, the CBC reporter shows up. He takes pictures.

He talks with Dom and before heading home, buys one of every flavor we have in stock. Dom gifts him one of the big blue coolers we use when we go fishing. I empty the house freezer of ice.

Later, King joins us with foam coolers and bags of ice he bought in town so we can sell in bulk to others. "Florence will stay at the shack until midnight. Unless you want to close up earlier."

"Text her. Ten is fine tonight."

And then, even later, when I'm pouring us all iced teas from the kitchen, I notice there are more cars parked in our lot than ever before. I stop and can't help myself, I count them. Forty-six vehicles that don't belong to my family or my friends. It's kind of incredible.

Once the townies heard, they drove out to get a look inside the barn. But most of the people are from out of town. They're on holidays. They're from Vegreville and Marshall and Cold Lake. They're from farther out, Edmonton and Saskatoon, and one family is from Prince Edward Island, this the best stop on their cross-country road trip so far, their precocious preteen says, digging into the family's carton with one of our mismatched kitchen spoons.

"We're out of Red, Green, Violet, and . . ." Elise checks her notepad. "And Orange. Your uncle—the one with the hair—is thrilled."

Shortly after ten, Florence arrives. She's a brilliant wreck. Stained from head to toe. "You could perform a surgery in that shack, I tell you."

I hug her tightly and she hugs me back.

We finish tours and sales, and we send our guests home with a wave.

Maurice invites my friends up to the house. He's taken a big batch of Mom's all-vegetable lasagna out of the freezer, cooked up bannock, and steamed summer squash from the garden. "Eat, eat, and relax."

Dom's music radiates toward us as he works to replenish what he can. He'll be in the production studio all night.

"Well, that was a fecking trip," Florence says.

We're sitting on the porch, plates on our knees, cups on the floor by our feet. We laugh. We fill our stomachs. I pass my big bottle of hot sauce around. King runs inside to fetch the salt.

Even later, Maurice returns to the porch with a fifth of rye and two liters of Canada Dry. He holds both bottles while he talks. "You've earned this. But unless you promise to sleep over on the couches, I'm not leaving the alcohol right here and going to my bed."

"We promise!" Florence squeals. "Right?"

Everyone nods.

"Call your parents before you get too far gone, now. I don't want anyone worried about where their teenage child is tonight."

Elise leans close. "Does he know I'm not old enough?"

"He's okay, if you're okay. And if you're not, that's okay too."

She smiles. "Can I still stay over? I don't want to go home yet."

"For sure."

Dom refills Red and Green for the morning, but nothing else, and heads to bed, offering us his thanks. The night is hot, and we're sticky with splashes of color marring our clothes, our hair.

It's like Florence was waiting for my uncles to disappear before excavating the deep stuff. "Have you ever . . ." Florence asks, "kissed someone of your own gender?"

It's always Flo who starts this kind of thing. But we always fall into it.

I'm lying on the porch, my head propped up by a cushion. "It's supposed to be *never* have I ever."

"And gender is a social construct," King offers.

Half the rye is gone. I'm radiating heat like a furnace. Elise leans against my hip, pressing a glass of iced tea to her cheek.

"Right, then." Florence tries again. "Never have I ever kissed someone of my own social construct."

After a half second, King drinks.

Florence cackles, and drinks too. "My friend, hello," she says.

And we all laugh. King's watching me for a reaction.

I throw him a lazy smile, my cheeks throbbing with warmth from the rye.

"The point of the game is to get other people to drink, Florence. Not to have to drink yourself." King rolls his shoulders but doesn't say anything more.

She shrugs like she doesn't care about the game. "I was curious. And I was right about you, *Drag Race*," she says, like it's a conspiracy.

"Your turn." He points at me.

"Never have I ever gone to a very serious museum while not wearing underwear."

"Guilty!" Florence says, and then drinks.

"Really?" Elise asks.

King rests his head in his hands. "Which museum? Because if it was the Museum for Human Rights, I'm more worried about

211

you than if it was a bougie art museum like MoMA."

I'm mock disappointed. "It was only the Royal Tyrrell! The best museum in the history of . . . museums!"

He gestures wildly in the air. "Flo, why were you—?"

Florence twirls a long piece of hair around her finger. "I was going through a phase."

I say, "That was six months ago!"

"I've never not worn underwear," Elise adds thoughtfully.

We drink, ask questions, keep laughing and telling stories, until Florence's low-key boredom drives her to get too cocky—because Flo has tried everything at least once and doesn't keep secrets, and she's half in her cups—and she decides to purposefully bring the mood down. But she knew it would, this question. "Have you ever lied?"

"It's *never* have I ever . . . ," Elise reminds her.

"Not what I asked, pet."

We all, one by one, drink. The whole world would be drinking right now. We'd drown ourselves if we had to drink for each little lie.

"What about?" Florence asks, a little too perky.

They all stare at me. Even Elise. Who might not know. But who am I kidding? Everyone around these parts knows. That's what happens when your lies grow too large in a small town. And since I've never told anyone about that night with Tyler, that doesn't count, exactly, as a lie.

"You all already know what kind of a bad person I am," I say, like it's no big deal. Like I'm not sitting next to King Nathan. "We don't need to rehash it here. Please."

Elise grasps her empty glass tight, saving me. "I lied about why I got fired. I don't know why I did, but I guess it was easier. Wyatt and I were caught . . . Well, I was in my ugly blue uniform, on shift, and I was on my knees and . . . you get it. Right? Do you get it?"

So Wyatt got his way, in the end. It just wasn't with me. I wonder how many times she said no. How many times he insisted.

Florence hoots with laughter. "Oh, how embarrassing for you."

We wait. For Florence and King to admit to something. They both drank. They're staring at each other.

Florence breaks first. She peers directly at me, as if she's only talking to me. "Well, you may have noticed, but I'm not doing as well as I could be." She empties her glass. Her voice gets small. "I may have made some statements that are technically false, statements about . . . my medications and ingesting them."

She reaches out a hand toward me.

I curl my fingers around hers. "Oh, Flo, why?"

"I was getting everything done. My schoolwork, not missing video-dates with my girlfriend, making it to work on time, showering, blow-drying my hair, answering every single text, just living my best life. And so I stopped. I was positive I didn't need the pills any longer." She shrugs. "But lately, it feels like I've lost control . . . of myself."

No one speaks. The air is heavy. Charged with something like static. Even the crickets in the field stop their night songs.

We collectively turn toward King.

He takes another sip of his rye and ginger ale. "So we're going that deep, eh?" He pauses.

He's going to tell us a story, I know it. He's readying himself—not for something as simple as a muse, but to share with us this thing that he values above all else, his words ordered into story.

"For a while, I thought they were dreams," King says. "Told myself they were only dreams—not memories. Me, in the back seat of my ma's old Toyota Corolla, not in a car seat, but one of those booster seats. You know that age? Small but not so small as all that.

"She'd scoop me from school, and then she'd cruise not toward our house but toward the motels. Days like this, she left me in the car. For maybe ten or fifteen minutes. I don't know. Time is weird in memories. Some days it felt like forever. Others, like nothing. I know now that she was in pain—real pain—but back then, I didn't think too much about the forever crease between her eyes.

"After, she'd take me to McDonald's, the drive-through, and she'd look behind and catch my eye, not in the rearview mirror, but her eyes to mine, and say, 'We're not telling your father about this, are we?' and I'd agree, thinking we were talking about the chicken nuggets with extra sauce and not the stopover.

"Then she'd drop me with my dad at home, kiss me on the head, and fly off to the bar for her shift. I wouldn't see her again until morning—if I was lucky—but she was always there, waiting after school. Her son wouldn't take the bus, no, no."

King pulls his ball cap lower, then rips it off. He tosses it down the length of the porch and kisses his teeth, full of frustration. "Everyone believes in their gut that my dad burned down O'Reilly's, that he avenged my ma—even after my ma left him. They're so sure, just because she's an addict, because she worked there, because she wrecked her back lifting a keg there. And her boss, Mr. O'Reilly himself, was rumored to be keeping her in Percs, oxy, whatever she needed, whatever she wanted to tame the pain all those years. That's what my dad believes. To this day he's sure the same way he's sure there's a God in heaven and that cricket is the only civilized sport."

In spite of himself, King smiles. He's pinned his dad down so well, and while he might be talking about painful things, the love King has for his dad swells over.

"I've agreed with my dad so many times I've started believing that story too. That O'Reilly was pushing, that O'Reilly planned her accident. That those after-school drives weren't about scoring, not really. That she was doing O'Reilly's work, knocking on motel doors, inviting the men to come for drinks, offering two-for-one coupons with a smile, me out in the car waiting. But there's a line somewhere inside. Where you tell yourself a thing. When you start believing that thing."

He stops. Just stops. For a minute or more. Time slows.

"Oof. That's not what I planned on saying. Um, I was gonna tell you I lie about why I'm a vegetarian . . . Or, how I don't tell the full truth when I . . ."

We sit in silence. Waiting for King to keep talking. Waiting for him to see he's his own person. That he's okay. That we will be okay, all of us, in the end. Instead, with an elbow Florence spills her glass and our intimacy, the moment where one of us could have said anything, it breaks.

CHAPTER 21

August 1

VIOLET: Fresh chokecherries are poisonous. They contain amygdalin. That probably means nothing to you unless you're a chemist or a food scientist, but true-crime TV enthusiasts understand this: as amygdalin breaks down, it becomes cyanide. Funny enough, this little anecdote is the best way to convince people who think they're tough to eat violet ice creams and sherbets. Use this newfound power at your discretion.

The first thing I notice is how far I'm pushed over in my bed. Basically against the wall. Not where I like to sleep, starfished in the middle.

The next thing, a heavy weight. An arm. King's arm. His half-moon nails curl against my belly.

Don't move, don't breathe, don't think. Don't anything. That's my first reaction. Eventually I have to breathe.

And I have to pee.

I shift King's arm so carefully and sit up to find Florence squished next to him. Elise is on the floor, curled into a ball, with my favorite moose stuffed animal tucked under her chin.

My whole lower abdomen is hard. I'm desperate.

The mattress is springy and too soft. Standing is awkward, but that's the only way I'm getting out. With shaky footing I manage to extract myself. Without elbowing anyone. Without waking anyone. I step over Elise.

"We have couches," I say aloud to no one at all and head upstairs.

After I use the bathroom, I notice it's not the middle of the night. It's past ten in the morning. Two abandoned mugs sit on the table. Next to them, a note and a pen. *Ask Elise if she'll help run tours. Ask Tyler if she wants hours on the weekends when camp is out. Gone picking.* —D

I scribble *Will do*—but wonder why Dom didn't text. We're not a write-a-note family. Maybe he's still upset?

With a big stretch and a yawn, King joins me in the kitchen. "Do we have to work today?"

"You, this afternoon. Me, soon."

"It's too much," he says, and collapses into a chair.

And I get it. Being awake *is* too much right now. But I know what will help. "Coffee?"

"Please."

I work on filling the water reservoir. I gesture at the Advil tablets one of my uncles left on the counter, but King isn't watching. Leaning against the counter while the coffee brews in spurts, I'm not thinking about his arm, or the rest of his body warm against mine. I'm not.

Yet my mind stalls here, betraying me.

Warm bodies and touch.

But not generic warm bodies. Nope. One in particular.

King breaks the silence—like he can't help himself. "I couldn't ask you this last night. Not with the others around. So, um, I know exactly why I can't look at what's left of O'Reilly's. But . . . what about you? What turns your stomach rancid?"

I'm foggy. "What do you mean?"

"I've been watching, Lou. Whenever we hit that block, your eyes are anywhere but at the wreckage and you tear at your hands like you think I won't catch you at it, your favorite little self-harm."

The kitchen fills with invisible smoke. It's in my nose, but King can't smell it.

"I know what happened to Tyler's ma," he says, as if that's enough.

I glance at the coffee pot, at the electrical cord, searching for a spark—for signs of burning. But I know it's nothing anyone else can tune into. The smoke chokes me. I cough into my elbow. "Y-you can say it."

"Can I really?"

I wipe at my eyes, worried all of a sudden they're full of sleep.

He backs off. Throws his hands up in surrender.

I've scared him off.

"Go on, King. Say what you have to say."

I carry two mugs and the bottle of Advil to the table. He's not going to free me and I can't speak about the fire, about what I did and how in supporting Tyler when she needed me, I sent the RCMP directly to King's dad's door.

"I thought we were past this," he says finally. "This carrying around bullshit from three years back." He laughs a bit, one of those laughs where you know it's not really funny, winces, and then rubs at his temples. "It's too damn early for this," he says, as if he's done. But he isn't. King meets my eyes, straight on. "Lately, I feel I'm out to make everything awkward between us. From your face, I'm doing exactly that."

I try for neutral. I try not to think ten steps ahead of where we are right now. Hungover and almost talking about it. Almost talking about the fire.

He exhales like he's about to break my heart into jagged pieces. "I know you don't want to hear this. But . . . damn, Lou, I still want to date you. Sleeping next to you was torture. No, no, like the best kind of torture."

Say something, I think. Say, me too. But all I manage is, "Oh."

For the first time, I want to admit to the fire. To take responsibility for the way my actions turned on King's dad. To remember that actions have consequences beyond what we *intend*. But in this kitchen, this morning, we're moving slowly, like goldfish in a tiny tank. I suck back too-hot coffee for strength. Before I can summon my bravery, Elise appears in the stairwell with a loud yawn. Now there's no room for me to say what I'm thinking. No room to ask for clarification. Does he know it was me with my hands on the lighter? Or does he only suspect I'm guilty?

Drinking my coffee, slow now that I've scorched the roof of my mouth, maybe, I admit to myself, I was awake long before my bladder decided it was critical. I liked King's arm over my body.

Elise and he talk quietly, starting and stopping when they run out of energy. Florence will sleep the day away, and since she's not on the schedule, it's fine if she does.

"Already it's too cold at night." Elise holds her coffee with both hands. "Summer's almost over. And you're all leaving me."

We don't answer. If I don't think about September, it won't come for me. If King's been thinking about his return to Toronto, he hasn't said. I haven't asked either. With school, I might be letting my intentions carry me too far. Because Elise is right. We're running out of time. And I've left too many things unfinished. My head aches, but I push myself up to grab Dom's laptop from his too-tidy desk.

When I'm seated at the table again, King reads my mind, nudges his chair closer. "Yeah, we didn't get to that, did we? Try the city website."

"Property assessment?"

"No, that's tax stuff."

"What's going on?" Elise finally asks. She's not as patient as she seems, not as meek.

I really like her.

"We're trying to suss out who owns the property the shack is on."

"You mean, you all don't?"

King looks at me, like, *this is yours to share.*

I enjoy Elise. But I have to trust her too.

I offer up the basics. I've never met Peter England—he's a sperm donor to me, only that—but he's threatening my family, and he said he'd take the land the shack's on first, displacing us. The highway traffic that keeps us alive, visible. It's a lifeline. "He's claiming me. And . . . it's more than paternity, Elise. It's a claim on who I am, on who I will be, on my family, on my people. It's not only a name on a piece of paper."

"Makes sense." That's all she says, then Elise pulls her chair closer too. She points at the search results, tries to drag the screen, as if this isn't a cheap HP. "What lot is your family business on?"

King asks, "How do you know this stuff?"

"My mom's in oil. Surveyor work. This is a staple during dinner conversations at my home. Thrilling, I know." She returns to staring at the screen. "Do you have a guess as to who owns the land?"

"Try my family."

Now Elise takes over the computer entirely. Types my last name. Only one result comes up. Our farm. She shakes her head.

"Try *England*."

"Lots of results. But I don't think it includes the piece of land the shack is on. These are all big lots, well north of the highway, mostly."

I stare at descriptions of parcel sizes and geographic positions, the throbbing in my temples intensifying. "Would you save that? I'll figure out where they are on a map later."

The dogs bark outside, chasing something out of the yard. I check the window, worried about what could be disturbing them. Nothing, it's nothing. King grabs his cell phone from where it's been sitting facedown on the kitchen table, offering to overlay the confusing legal descriptions onto a map for me. A minute later, he passes his phone to Elise. She performs another search. I check the yard one last time, then the stove clock. I'll be cutting it close, not that we have much to sell. But that won't appease Dom.

I'm on my way out the door, tasting mint and coffee, when Elise stops me in the mudroom. "The land is owned by a numbered company. That's all we can see online."

"So we can't find out who's behind it." I stop searching for my other flip-flop. This is it. This is as far as it goes. My bad feeling is going to stick around.

King joins us, notices I'm holding only one shoe and begins to sort through the disaster that is the mudroom. Even Maurice refuses to tidy in here.

"If you have twenty-five dollars," Elise says, "I can send in a request for information. They'll mail out results in ten business days or less. My mom orders these all the time. It might be nothing. It might be exactly what you need. It's a gamble."

King catches my indecision, holding my lost flip-flop out to me. "I have a credit card. Cover it when you can."

I take the shoe. I should say no. I shouldn't let him do this. But I want it too badly. "Can you ship it to your house too? I don't want my uncles to know."

I hate that I'm thinking it. But no one else should know I'm looking into the shack—into how far Peter England's tied up in my life—until I'm ready to share.

Secrets aren't lies.

We all have our secrets.

King doesn't even question it. Doesn't accuse me of hiding something, of building the foundations of untruth. "Sure thing, Lou."

The whole time I drive, I'm not thinking about the shack. That answer will cost me twenty-five tuition dollars and show up in two weeks. What I can't stop thinking about is how nice it was to be close to King. Bits and pieces of last night trickle back. After

Florence ruined our game, it was hard to return to that place, where we were laughing and carrying on. Something was yipping in the yard, but the dogs were inside, curled up in their beds.

Florence trailed off the porch to smoke, first one cigarette, and then a second, lost in her silent moment, while Elise washed her glass at the sink.

Alone on the porch, I didn't think. My hand ended up on King's knee. Just because. He grabbed it and held on. And somehow, when we drunkenly wandered down to my bedroom, King ended up pressed against me. Though all we did was sleep, I am closer to him now. It could be we're finally talking about our old friendship, and what my lies did to us. Or it could be something else entirely. Like little magics, like good medicine. I don't know. I really don't.

I tongue the roof of my mouth and even that small pain doesn't hurt as much as it feels exactly like living. I haven't slept enough. And I might throw up. This hangover is bad. And yet, I don't think any of those reasons are the reasons why I want to succumb to tears, to let them reign.

CHAPTER 22
August 12

VIOLET: Sugared lilac is unexpected out of our no-frills shop. Lilacs aren't native to this land. But the most common plant settlers wanted by their houses was the lilac because it reminded them of the Old Country. They've taken root here. Blossoms in late May and early June; varies, depending on your location.

The shack is up and running again. The day after the CBC airs our story, another reporter produces a bit piece. Two days later, Leif Winters, this Food Network Canada star, arrives unannounced with his crew. He's ruggedly handsome. Hint of a mustache—but no beard. Dark hair and darker eyes. Like a movie star. Or just someone from Toronto.

The crew tries spoonful after spoonful. Even Dom's wild rose, moose fat, and mustard ice creams.

They're filming everything for a special. They interview King and Elise and Florence and me. They travel to the production barn, and Dom and Leif Winters really get on. I mean, there's shoulder touching and they both cannot stop laughing, smiling. Dom takes Leif out into the bush. They leave the cameras behind.

The special airs a week after they leave. And by Wednesday

we're swamped. It's mid-August and Dom can't keep his freezers stocked. Now, we close when we run out of product. Now, the locals know to show up early. It's exactly what we needed to recover from the backup generator running out of gas. I'm lucky the motor didn't burn out, or worse. I could have started another fire.

It's three p.m.; my handmade "Done for the Day, Try Us Tomorrow" sign is tacked on the boards. Now that we've added the opportunity to swipe credit cards, the tip jar isn't doing well. No one else seems worried. At home, my collection of loonies and toonies isn't growing fast enough. I'm trying not to care. But I'm behind now—on where I thought I'd be with savings by this point in the summer. I'll have to ask my family to cosign a student loan.

What I know I'll never do is ask Peter England. He believes it's a little thing, allowing him to put his name on my birth certificate. A thing maybe worth my education.

Except it's not.

"Time zones," Florence mutters. She runs out to catch her girlfriend for a trip-planning session before her girlfriend heads to bed.

Elise is at the farm helping Dom with tours.

It's been eleven days.

Eleven days of this. Knowing what I want. Deciding if I deserve it. If it's fair to ask King to try.

He sits next to me, close but not close enough, talking about the University of Toronto, its downtown campus, the libraries, and the English program and how he's low-key nervous about living in the city again after the way it all went down. All these worries about what next year means for him. But still, he doesn't mention his mom.

My heart hammers like it does before I get the nerve to raise my hand in class. Hammers like it does in the water when I've got the ball and I'm coming up on the net. Only I haven't felt that power since before the accident. In the water now, I can no longer hyperfocus.

"We should go on three dates," I blurt out.

He looks at me like I've lost my mind. Entirely.

I can't stop if I tried. "I keep thinking about how we're running out of time. And if there's something here, if we don't try now, we won't ever know because you're leaving and I'm staying, and Toronto and Edmonton are very far apart. Like, once you leave, we might never see each other again. But only three though. Three dates we can manage. Three won't fuck us up entirely. And then after we'll know, one way or another. It won't be this thing keeping us awake at night for the rest of our lives. What if . . . What if . . ."

He's watching me carefully. Too closely, like I'm a painting—all impressionist and hard to fully, properly take in while this close.

"Okay, now you need to talk. What do you think?" I ask.

"We'll like date for three days and swing back to this afterward?"

My hand rests on the picnic table. So close he could grab it if he wanted. But he doesn't. "No, I mean like three real dates."

"I see you every single day, Lou. We hang all the time."

"But we're hanging out," I say, emphasizing the last two words. "We aren't dating."

"So you want us to keep"—he pauses dramatically—"hanging out like we are and also go on three official dates? That the program? Or what?"

"Is that weird?"

King laughs, his pretty teeth on display. "I mean, yes, very. But . . . I don't think I care."

The weight consuming my chest evaporates.

He's looking out across the highway at a house, the kind that comes off the back of a flatbed truck and gets planted on the land. A family lives there. Their kid is in Elise's grade. He's shy. Sometimes he stands across the road and watches us, but he never walks over to get a cone. He only stands and stares.

He's over there right now. Sitting on his steps.

King waves.

The kid hesitantly raises an arm.

I've never thought to wave at him before. I've been out here three summers now, and I've never just waved. It's so easy.

"I mean, not to freak you out," King says. "But I've been thinking about where I'd take you for months now. I have a plan."

My cheeks hurt from smiling. "You do?"

"Tonight. Is tonight too soon?"

"No."

"I'll pick you up like eight, okay?"

I nod. Slowly, I lift my bad arm and wave at the kid across the street too. Maybe next year, this can be his summer job. Maybe it starts like this.

When King and I finally push up from the picnic table to head home, for the first time in our lives, he kisses me on the cheek when he says goodbye. It's nothing. Nothing at all. But once he's gone, I sigh, and wish we were French, so he'd have done it twice.

At home, I can't settle. Even though it was fairly straight already, I iron my hair again. I'm brushing my teeth and reapplying my beeswax lip stuff after dinner—a meal I barely ate. My phone, sitting on the edge of the sink, startles me. It's exactly eight p.m.

I'm outside.

        Too afraid to come in?

100%.
I love your uncles.
But I'm nervous they're gonna see
me as a threat.
Now.

        You're lucky my mom isn't
            here.
       She's the real threat.

I type it all fast-moving thumbs. But realize my mom has always liked King. She said what I did was wrong. But it was worse because I did it to a friend.

She hasn't come home. Not once.

Today's text: **Dom's adoring this media attention. Are you?**

I know she loves me, even after all the lies. Even though by lying about who I am I erased her. I should text her back. Tell her everything that's going on. But now's not the right moment. King's waiting. I type as I shove my feet into pretty ankle boots in the mudroom.

I holler at my uncles that I'm going out and step into the night, unsteady, because I haven't worn these boots since early spring. Heavier than my flip-flops, with a two-inch heel, they take some getting used to.

"Hey," he says when I sink into the passenger seat of the Subaru.

I hey him back and we fall into an easy quiet as we drive. The music is low, all moody. Our old music. When King turns north, and we pass the movie theater, and reach the edge of town and keep driving, I can't help but ask, "Where are you taking us?"

Both hands on the steering wheel, he's holding on tight. "You really want to know?"

Fields fly by. Wheat and sometimes canola. The canola, vibrant yellow-yellow, thinks it's still full-on summer. And so maybe I can too. "I trust you," I say.

"Good." He pulls an envelope stamped with the city's logo from the console. "It arrived today."

I take it. Hold it.

"I don't want to look. Not tonight. I don't want to worry about all that with you. Is that okay?"

"Your choice, Lou. Totally your choice."

We talk about school. About Edmonton, and the gen ed classes filling my fall schedule when I want to be deep into the paleontology program—where in lecture halls we'll discuss recent discoveries and I can geek out with people who understand how viewing *The Land before Time* changed my life—and too, we talk about the parkland on the North Saskatchewan River we've both visited, but never together, and the hometown twenty-year-old who, years ago, after a night out on Whyte Ave., Edmonton's party street, was stabbed to death. It happened a long time ago, but we talk about it like it happened yesterday. We could talk about the fire—the whole town still does—but King and me, maybe we can't yet.

We talk about his sister. How Aliya's eager for King to get back to town, planning local adventures he can scoop her off to. Still, King's not talking about his mom. I want to tell him how much I miss mine, but it doesn't seem the right thing to say on a date.

We're still driving.

When we cross over an in-ground cattle guard, directly into a pasture, King says, "We're here."

I don't roll my eyes. But I laugh a little. "You took the person who lives on a dairy farm to see more cows?"

The vehicle clunks over uneven ground. There's nothing to hold on to but the armrest. Or King.

I'm not nearly brave enough to do that.

"Not cows," he says.

It's still light. When I see them, they appear immediately—giant and brown and alive. "Bison, my favorite. Oh, they're amazing."

King executes a perfect three-point turn. "The ranch owner told my dad this is fine. They're really comfortable with vehicles, but we shouldn't get closer. And if we do, that's on us."

"Of course. They're living things. They deserve their space." They deserve more than space. They deserve the whole wide-open prairie.

King grabs a blanket from the back seat and tosses it at me

with a wide grin. It's scratchy wool, an old HBC stripe blanket. Everyone on the prairies has one of these. Dom's has been sewn into a jacket. The wool tucked against my cheek, I understand all of a sudden.

Oh.

This was a mistake. A massive one.

King climbs out of the Subaru to open the trunk. When he folds the rear seats down, I toss the blanket back at him. I can't hold it. Can't carry it to him. Can't do anything to suggest that I'm able to do what he wants. My throat is tight and my skin is hot, almost itchy, like little wool fibers have shed themselves on me. Grass brushes against my bare calves. Slowly I walk to where King is perched on the rear bumper. It must be all over my face.

"You afraid?" he asks.

"Terrified."

"Look, I'm not trying to get you naked, Lou. Not right now. And not at all if you're only giving me three dates." He points out into the field and mock whispers, "And certainly not in front of the bison."

I'm standing two meters away. My arms snake tight across my chest.

"Is this too weird?"

I nod a long time before I can speak. "A bit."

He gestures to the space next to him. The trunk is a long flat expanse now. He's tall, couldn't lie flat without overhang. I could. But still I sit on the very, very edge. The Subaru sinks lower.

I'm thinking of all the times Wyatt got me in the bed of his truck. How much work it was to keep him off me. How much guilt, slick and feverish, wormed into my heart. Before and after.

King's eyes focus on the bison. So do mine. They graze, totally ignoring us. They couldn't care less we're here.

"Listen, I want to sit with you and watch these massive creatures eat grass, and we can talk about all the stuff we normally do." He puts a hand on my knee. Tentative and careful, and then, suddenly, he pulls away. "That's a lie. I want all that and I really want to kiss you too."

Deep breath. Fall into it. You can't know unless you try.

I almost chicken out.

I almost can't.

But then, I realize, I can. Because I trust King. If I tell him I've changed my mind, he'll stop.

"Then you really should."

His hands have been on my body since we started with the tape, weeks ago now. But this is different. His fingers against my neck are softer. He shifts my hair, long and straight and always in the way, off my bad shoulder. When he brushes the sports tape, it's like he's touching me for the first time.

He bends toward me and I tilt my head up. My neck burns like fire. Too hot, and then, when his lips graze my skin, I have to reevaluate what burning is.

His lips leave my neck. His fingers rub at the skin he's kissed. It's almost too much—like the roof of my mouth. Tender.

This is a new kiss. Entirely new.

Our lips meet, teeth knocking a second, and he laughs, and then I do too. But we don't worry about the awkward moments. We acknowledge them and pass on by. I don't know exactly how to untangle this knot. The feelings. King, my friend King, as this. Or even this: when my neck starts to ache from the weird angle, I pull away, long enough to stand, long enough to press my knees on either side of his thighs and lean into him. His chest. His arms around me make me feel like I'm small. In the best way.

This, we fall here, for I don't know how long. *I don't know. I don't know. I don't know.* It's all I can think, when I can think.

I'm breathless.

His hands grip the hollow of my back, fingers splayed out. That spot he refused to touch when he was taping my shoulder.

When we take a breath, take the space to feel the cooling air, I just say, "Wow."

He answers, "Yeah." But then he grows nervous. He picks me up, hands on my hips, and shifts me so I'm sitting in the trunk again. So we aren't touching. "Sorry."

His jeans are tented and I don't blush, but I say, "Oh. Right."

And he says, "Can we just not talk about it? That's probably the safest thing."

And somewhere out in the field, we hear a series of low-pitched grunts, and seconds later, a higher response.

Babies.

Both of us crack up, King looking over at me, me looking over at King, both of us staring out into the field, laughing, laughing so hard until we cry.

CHAPTER 23

August 13

VIOLET: At the far spectrum of the rainbow, we expect the most saturation. But violets exist along a gradient the same as all others. Don't compare too much. Don't put too much pressure on yourself to fit the mold. If you're violet, you're a violet. Just enjoy what you have. It all tastes really great, anyhow.

At the pool, something shifts. To start, I forget my pass at home, in my bag with the good fringe, but the clerk lets me enter anyway. King agrees to skip laps, so we goof off in the shallow end. The ball settles okay in my recovering arm. I'm approaching the net as if I'll take a shot—and King walks out, right up to me.

"Too easy," I say, swimming around him.

But he grabs me by my middle, hauls me against him.

The ball floats away from us.

Last night was the best date I've ever been on and I can't stop thinking about it. The competition isn't high or anything. Wyatt drove me around in one of his parents' vehicles and tried to get me to fool around with him during superhero movies.

I steal a kiss from King, and then break away, reclaiming the ball before he can.

It's the best date I'll probably ever go on. Unless one day someone arranges permission for us to check out all the fossils that don't make it into the public exhibits at the Royal Tyrrell. This is what I'm thinking during the whole drive home from the bison paddock, giddy sitting next to King in the Subaru, brave enough to lean toward him and not away. Last night, as I tried to fall asleep, I was thinking about our date. This morning, toothbrush shoved in my mouth, toothpaste foaming, I smiled like a fool into the bathroom mirror.

Here, in this saltwater pool, I'm thinking of the ways bodies touch, me trying to shoot, King trying to block. I'm breathless. Standing in the shallow end. I drop the ball.

"You giving up?" King laughs at me, his eyes crinkling.

Everything stops.

I find the pool clock. Work the mental math. Even if I don't shower, pull my clothing on over my bathing suit, and drive fast, I won't make it home to fetch my bag and the letter and get to the shack in time to open. I could open late. No one will know. Florence isn't in until noon.

Until I can read that letter. Until I know who owns the land. Until I prove my bad feeling wrong, I'm frozen.

But I've screwed up enough already this summer. I owe it to Dom, to my family, to put us first.

"My shoulder," I say to King. It's true but not the only truth. We shower and kiss in the parking lot like we can do this anywhere, anytime, before I drive to the shack, where I work, half-distracted, until we sell out a little after five p.m.

Tomorrow, King is helping his dad on an early vet visit halfway to Saskatoon, as he has more and more while Dr. Nathan's hand heals. I'm in charge of our second date. My mind is a blank. Later, when my brain isn't hyperfocused on the letter, I'll figure out how to impress King.

At the farm, Maurice's truck is parked in front of the house. He's returned from another Edmonton trip. Since the Creamery started doing really well, he's been home less. I'm sure Molly likes having her dad around. And if being away makes Maurice happy, then he should do it. Mom's happier than I've ever seen her—away from us. Yet, sometimes, I wish my uncle would bring Molly here. To our home.

Dom is spending so much time out in the production barn— and fielding personal calls from Leif Winters—that we've been eating the dregs of the pantry. The freezer's long emptied of the meals Mom and I made one fall weekend after harvesting the last of the garden.

I step into the kitchen. Dom's slicing lettuce in long, thin strips. It's just like the stuff that comes from the store. It crunches perfectly. We haven't had Indian tacos since Mom left. But Dom's decided to cook. He's been to the store too.

My good bag with the leather fringe hangs on my chair.

Mom's is empty. She's in Texas now. Or Arizona. It could be New Mexico. It's hard to keep her adventures straight.

"Have you thought any more about what we should do?" Maurice fills fresh bannock with canned chili.

Dom swoops in to the rescue. "Leave her be. We gave her the whole summer. It's not over yet."

I extract the letter from my bag.

My uncles continue to bicker.

I rip open the flap.

They're fighting over whether the exposure from the special is enough to carry us through to next year. They're chewing and arguing.

I read.

It's business formal. My eyes skim down to Registered Owner: Numbered Company 543907 (Peter England & L. Norquay).

Dom says, "We have to take things day by day," and Maurice says, "That's not how you run a business," and I sound so calm they don't hear me at first. I repeat myself. I have to raise my voice. It's becoming a habit.

They're both staring now.

"Who owns the land the shack sits on? Do you know? Because I do." I hold the paper up in the air.

Dom visibly folds into himself.

Maurice clears his throat, once, twice, three times before he can speak. "You'll have to discuss the land with your mother."

None of us is eating now.

I press the letter onto the table beside my fork. "Tell me."

"We can't, Lou," Dom says. "This is your mother's story. Call her."

"Tell me."

Maurice shakes his head.

"Tell me, damn it."

"Call your mom," Dom says, rising from the table, and my

uncle, he walks away from his dinner plate and from me.

"Tell me," I say, staring at Maurice. I won't cry. I won't. "You have to."

"Sorry—"

"No. Just tell me. It's easy."

"I can't," he says. "Dominic's right. This has always been for your mother to disclose, and I wish she'd done it sooner." Maurice excuses himself too, as if to offer me privacy.

Down the hall, Dom slams his door so hard something shatters.

I fold the city stationery in half and then in quarters. Like a robot, I open my phone, to the text chat filled with hearts and kisses and *I love you*s, and message my mom.

> I know who owns the land
> under the shack.

Immediately, three little dots appear.

They disappear.

They appear again.

> I love you, Lou. Remember I love
> you.
> We need to talk face to face. Let me
> find someplace quiet.
> I love you.
> I love you, my Lou.

When the video-call alert goes off, I reject it and the next six calls.

I sit at the table a long time, picking at my cuticles until I bleed. The grease on the stove turns hard in the pan. Outside, the dogs whine. I walk through the mudroom to the door, throw it open. Pour the taco toppings and both my uncles' plates—the mess is attracting flies now—into the dogs' dishes. All three of them wait, watching me.

I walk to the basement stairs. And they're still watching me. Waiting.

"Eat," I say, but since I yell it, they don't know what to do.

I take the stairs slow. Climb into my bed and make myself small. Listen to footsteps above me. Dom pacing. Maurice tapping his foot on the floor, staccato.

My phone buzzes:

Pick up, daughter.

Whatever you're feeling, know I love you.

I love you, Lou.

I love you.

It won't stop.

The footsteps, the tapping, my phone's buzzing.

I turn my phone off. Something I never do. I don't plug it in so it'll be charged and ready in the morning. I don't throw it across the room. I abandon it on top of the blankets. My body moves without thought. My body is strong, even now that I'm injured, and it carries me. In my closet I find my camping gear. My tent and sleeping bag. Things I've collected from secondhand stores over the years. I grab my hockey duffel too. Mom bought it for me when we lived in Winnipeg, before we moved to Vancouver. I fill it.

Clothing, deodorant, a few books, the braid of sweetgrass I was gifted at graduation, and with my bag slung over my shoulder, and my tent tucked under my other arm, I leave the house. Homer abandons his dinner to follow me. We hike across the property toward the western boundary fence. He sits there the whole time I'm setting up the tent, in a field we used to keep the horses in back when we had two pretty brown mares. Before we sold them to save on bills. Before this field became tertiary feeding for the cows.

I leave the rain fly off the tent. Because it's clear tonight. Because of the stars. Because the rain fly boasts a huge tear I didn't notice until after I'd brought the tent home.

I never sat down to fix it. Never mended the broken thing.

My mom's still texting, I know this is truth. But with my phone off, does that mean her messages will come through like nothing's wrong? Or will she get a return message: this person doesn't exist anymore?

The ground is hard, lumpy, the way fields tend to be.

Sleep won't come.

Neither will tears.

Morning light arrives first. Foggy and dull until the sky burns orange.

I wish I'd remembered my pillow. Instead, head cradled on my hockey bag, my bad shoulder up in the air, I curl inward like a baby, and eventually, when I don't think it's possible, I sleep.

CHAPTER 24
August 14

FACT: Ice cream is good. But it can't fix everything.

Eighteen shouldn't be this rough. I crack my neck before crouching to zip the tent closed. My eyes are gritty, heavy, hidden behind my favorite cat-eye sunglasses.

Homer, who sat beside me all night, panting hard, follows me toward the house—but once he sees I'm headed for my truck, he takes off to find shade.

One thing a mostly sleepless night is good for: I have a plan for the date. Setting the plan in motion, that's my only priority today. By the sun, it's after noon. It's gross but I chew three pieces of glove-box-stale gum instead of brushing my teeth.

I can't go back inside that house.

When I lied, when I disowned them with my lies, they were so hurt. Maurice couldn't look straight at me for a week. And Dom, he didn't understand, at all, why I didn't want to own my Native heritage, why I couldn't love being Métis the way he loved it. Maybe after King, my mom was the person who my lie wounded worst. She told me lying about who you are, about your heart and the things that matter to the core of you, that's a big thing.

The Friendship Center was my family's idea of the next step, atonement. I volunteered every spare second. They pushed me into Tyler's sphere—and then Tyler and I, we had to follow the path we were set on. We followed it all the way. While I was volunteering, while I was running with Ty, my grades slipped, and I swam once in six months.

These people, my family, the ones I live with, the ones I love and trust, they've been lying to me too. In a way. For a very long time. Maybe my whole life. I can't believe it's only about the land, that concealing this one thing doesn't point to a whole story—many stories—that my family has kept from me. Because life is a web of relations, and one thing is always connected to others, related in sharp ways.

With windows down on the highway, I'm flying past trucker after trucker in the left lane—obsessing. My family punished me for lying, and all the while, they were hiding so much. So far, the only person who seems to be telling even a sliver of the truth is the man who raped my mother at sixteen.

But he's probably a big liar too.

I'm surrounded by them.

When I near the shack, even though it's foolish and dangerous, I close my eyes. The roads on the prairies are straight lines and I'm pretty sure I'll be fine. Twenty heartbeats and a quarter kilometer away, I open them again. But I still sicken, maybe worse than if I'd looked at the shack.

The truth is I didn't start lying at fifteen. I only got semi-good at it when we moved back to this town. Before, I lied every time I brought a bag of penny candies to the counter and told the corner-store clerk I had a dollar's worth when I had a dollar fifty. When teachers asked me why I moved so much. To men on the street asking my age. Always I'd offer something much younger, like that would protect me.

All the liars in my life, they've made me who I am. Then they punished me for doing the thing they've trained me at.

When I hit the first red stoplight in town, I slow down fast— but not fast enough. Behind me, sirens and flashing lights blare. My eyes fall closed again. Even when closed, they burn. Someone behind me honks a long note. I'm in the left-hand lane. The light's turned green.

I whip into the Husky Truck Stop parking lot instead of doing this on the shoulder of the highway. The cruiser follows. I spit the too-big wad of gum into a wrapper and push the mess into the pocket of my jean skirt.

The police officer approaches, smiling, and says, all friendly like, "Hello. You were going a little fast there."

He doesn't order me to remove my sunglasses. He rests his arms against the edge of my window. It's almost intimate. I get a good look at him. He's young enough. Maybe late twenties or early thirties. He's tanned, spends a lot of time outside, or he visits the salon in the strip mall next to the vape shop on the regular.

"Yeah, I was. Driving fast."

"You're not sorry," he says, grinning. "Most of the time, people at least claim they're sorry when radar catches them speeding."

For a liar, I should be better at this. I should have stories to tell, full of pathos and good, strong feeling. But today, I'm running on fumes. "I don't have an excuse."

"For not being sorry. Or for the excessive speed?"

I think it's called being velocitized. No, it's called not caring. All I say is, "Nothing you want to hear."

"Try me?"

"Don't you want my license? To run my plates to see if this truck is registered or, like, wanted for heinous crimes?"

His laugh comes from deep and low in his belly. "Not really. Not today. I only want you to slow it down."

The thing about being a liar is that you don't ever believe anyone else is telling the truth either. "Do you know my uncles or something? Is that why you're acting nice? Or do you want me to call this into the radio's *Officer of the Week* segment so you can win fifty dollars to eat overcooked steak? Is that it?"

"Okay, fine." He straightens to his full height. He's not that tall. "If that's how you want it. Miss, can I see your license, please?"

I exhale. "No."

"Wow." He's deadpan.

"I don't have it."

He pulls his sunglasses down his nose and that's when I notice his eyes are green—like oregano. "Is it in your other purse? I've heard it all."

"No."

"Where is it?"

"Do you actually care?"

"I've been asking. You might as well tell me."

For a hard minute, I stare at him. He returns my gaze, level and unrelenting. A gun sits on his hip. A Taser too. He's white or white-coded. He's RCMP. He's not playing it by their books.

He should be gone already and I should have a ticket I'll never be able to pay off. He should be gone already and my truck should be impounded. He should be gone already and I should be sitting on the curb, cowering under his low-key threats, his racist words.

Instead, the smell of the Husky Truck Stop grill is in the air. My stomach wants grease, suddenly and with a ferocity I'd forgotten bodies could manage. I didn't finish my meal last night. None of us did.

I'm being reckless—really reckless—but I can't muster the energy to stop myself. I run my tongue across my teeth. Before I make the decision fully, before I've decided to trust the cop will listen, this true story unwinds itself. Like it needs to be told. "About a month and a half back, it was the holiday weekend. I was in the pharmacy, the one in the mall. And the asshole clerk, he carded me."

"Abiding by the law makes him an asshole?"

"Ensuring I was legal before he tried to convince me to give him a blow job does."

"Yep." The cop looks down at his shoes. "So he took your ID from you?"

My stomach grumbles. "No, I left it there. I haven't returned."

"You probably ought to."

"I don't want to go back to that place," I say, and my voice wavers and I'm going to cry, and I hate myself for breaking like this. If only this cop had been a jerk. If only he'd played his part, then I could have pushed through and played mine. Now I don't know who to be.

The cop exhales loudly. "I'll tag along, if you want. I have time."

I wipe my nose on my sleeve and surprise myself by nodding.

"Okay, but drive the speed limit, would you?"

I nod again.

At the mall, I park about as far away from the pharmacy entrance as I can. I slip out of my truck slowly, so when I do, the cop's already leaning against his cruiser a few spots away.

"How do you want to proceed?" he asks.

"Why are you being so nice?" I haven't put it together yet, his name badge and that name Maurice dropped during the tornado. Reina. But when the sunlight hits his badge just so, I do. "Fuck, you were dating my uncle."

"For a bit," Henry Reina says.

"He dumped you."

"He did."

"My uncle was dating the police," I say, to say it out loud. To hear it properly.

"I'll admit it was an issue between us."

"He was ashamed of you. Of what you do."

Henry looks a bit sad and a bit like that's okay, an old wound, a scar he's come to terms with. His eyebrows crease together, but they level out quick.

"He's dating a Food Network star now."

"Is he?"

"Yup."

Right in front of us, someone drives a big boat of a car around in a circle a few times. The teenage driver sticks his head out the window, and says, "Shit, it's the cops!" and peels out of the parking lot about as fast as that boat can go.

Henry glances over at them, unamused, but not like this is the first time it's happened—someone seeing him in uniform and running. "Well, I'll try to be happy for your uncle."

Two of the pharmacy's marquis lights have burned out. It just says PHARMA. Everyone in town knows where to find this place, so the sign doesn't do much work. Still, it looks cheap. It looks exactly like the kind of place where the employees are predators.

"You can stay out here," I say evenly. "I have to handle this."

Henry Reina smiles at me as if I'm doing exactly what he wants me to. But that's okay. Telling him Dom's dating a Food Network star wasn't very nice and telling him Dom was ashamed of him was cruel, and I owe Reina one minor thing for not issuing me a ticket.

If he wants me to be brave and walk in there myself, I'll do it.

What Reina doesn't know: once, when I was younger, I helped a friend burn down a bar. Once, I was braver than I am now. Or, once I didn't care what happened to me. Today, I'm a little bit that girl again. It burns and I like it, the way my tired eyes and the foggy feeling in my head clear enough to hyperfocus on the strength I know I have. Tyler knows too.

The two of us, we used to be powerful.

Today, I'm so tired, so done, if Ty were here to hand me a bottle of liquor, a shredded tee for wick, and a lighter, I'd do it all over again, even with a cop watching.

The automatic door slides open. A bell chimes. I push my sunglasses up into my hair. The fluorescent lights burn but I can't hide behind them here. The clerk leans against the counter reading a magazine. I spot a woman and a kid in the junk food aisle picking out snacks, but otherwise the store is empty, save the pharmacists in the back.

It's not the same clerk.

It doesn't matter.

He follows me with his eyes, peering over the magazine's edge, but doesn't shift positions. He doesn't say hello either. I head down the first aisle because it's instinct to disappear into the store. Staring at a wall of paper products, I'm examining sale stickers because that's habit too. I mentally kick myself and turn around.

I am powerful.

I start talking before I reach the counter. "One of your staff . . . it was about six weeks ago . . . he took my ID and then asked if I was Native, and then asked me to perform a sex act on him." I'm talking loudly. I don't want to go into this meek. I'm overcompensating. "I got scared. And I left. But I'm having a hell of a time without that ID and I want it back."

Wordlessly, the clerk pushes himself up off his forearms, tucks the magazine under an arm, and inserts a key hanging around his wrist into the register. The till pops open with a trill exactly like the cash register in the shack.

His name badge says "Hal, Asst. Mngr." On his lapel sits a pin, the Canadian flag in black and white, the only color on the pin a blue line that matches Hal's polo shirt.

While I study him, he pulls out a stack of IDs secured with a rubber band from underneath the cash drawer. He flicks through them one by one. "Lisa? Naw. Jillian-Marie? Naw, you're not a

Jilly. Louisa? Yeah, this one looks Indian enough. Half-blood at least." He holds it out to me.

There's another ten or so left in the stack.

"You been working here long, Hal?"

"I got a bad back out of the oil patch. Ten years now, eight as management. Pay's shit compared to oil."

He's holding the plastic card out toward me. My awkward sixteen-year-old self glares back at me. Sweat gathers along my hairline where the still-pink scar will live forever.

"You the same Hal who once tried to barter with a child for sex? 'Cause I've heard stories."

He doesn't deny it, just leans back onto his forearms, the magazine still tucked under his arm, my ID in the air between us, and says, "Now, do you want this back or not, Louisa?"

I grab it.

He smiles. "That's what I thought."

He thinks he's won.

"So you know," I say, even though the woman and her kid are staring openly now. "If I ever hear you do anything like that again to a child, I'm going to burn this place to the ground with you inside of it."

When he laughs, I get an eyeful of silver fillings. "Yeah, right, sweetheart."

"I'm not lying," I say, and mean it, and I walk out into the sunshine because he doesn't have to believe me. I pull my sunglasses down again. If I had my phone, I could tell Florence—and Tyler—what I did, what I said. They'd both be pleased, for different reasons. When I get back to my truck, and the waiting Henry

Reina, I exhale noisily through pursed lips.

"That bad, eh?" Henry asks.

"You should know I threatened him and I mean what I said."

"You are exactly like your uncle."

I roll my eyes. "I don't know why I'm telling you this because you're a cop and cops don't listen to us, but that man in there, the assistant manager, Hal, and at least one of his clerks—Tim, the guy who harassed me—they're hurting people. Children."

He throws his hands on his hips. One cups his holster. "Want to come down to the station and file a report?"

I hate that my throat closes up, tightens, that I want to run—but know I can't. I model his body language for him all large. I'm mad, talking to this man like he's one of my uncles. "Now why'd you go and do that for?"

"Sorry." He drops his hands. "I should know better."

"Yeah, you should. About a lot of things." I walk back toward my truck, open the door, and climb in.

"Slow down on the roads, would you, Lou? If anything happened to you, it would kill Dominic."

"Yeah, right," I say, but the bite has gone out of my words.

Henry smiles, but I drive off pretending I didn't see him do it. It's cold. I'm not feeling kind. As I pull out into traffic, heading for my original destination, a white SUV in the westbound lanes honks its horn. The driver throws up a hand in a casual wave—at me, at someone else, I don't know. I suck in air. With my eye trained on the rearview mirror, watching to see if the white SUV pulls a U-turn, follows me, I drive the two blocks to the diner on high alert.

I park around back, so that my truck can't be spotted from the road. But I don't exit the cab. I'm stewing, worried suddenly that this date idea isn't enough to impress King, and that somehow, this whole thing is cursed and what's the point of two more dates if it's going to end, if I'm going to freeze up when King wants more than kissing. We stared at bison together and we made out, and it was fun.

For almost twenty hours, I felt like a regular person.

Next to me on the truck bench lies King's discarded tee from tornado cleanup day. I've had a hundred chances to return it. His baseball cap too. That's in my tent, stained with my blood. His other T-shirt, I still sleep in it.

My fingers curl into the cotton beside me and even when I sink my nails in, I can't hurt myself. I pick the tee up, pulling it to my nose. It's faint, but it smells like him. Warm and icy at once. I don't realize I'm smiling until I register the pressure, my cheeks against my sunglasses' metal frame.

I can't cower every time I spot a white SUV.

If King and I get to live in this temporary happiness for a few more weeks, then maybe it can outweigh all the other things—all the liars in my life.

But we only have two dates left, and then we need to be . . . just friends again.

By the back door of the diner, sitting on a milk crate, Cami wears her signature frilly pink apron. When she notices me approaching, she juts her chin at me. "How's things?"

"They suck."

"You too, eh?" She boots another milk crate toward me.

I sink onto the plastic. "I meant to check in on you after—"

"Don't think on it."

This, another place where my intentions never blossomed into real action. "I should have."

Cami's fifteen. But already, she's so jaded. "Fucking social services show up to my house every month again these days."

"I'm sorry, Cam—"

"Don't tell me you're sorry. You should have taken me home. You know better. You should at least."

It's almost the same speech I gave Reina. "Probably you're right."

"I'm always fucking right," Cami says.

It's a dismissal. I push myself off the milk crate. It's time to head inside. When I ask for this favor, the worst thing that can happen is they'll say no. And once I'm done, whatever they say, I can drive back to the farm, and I can sleep.

CHAPTER 25
August 15

FACT: Ice cream is cold and sometimes we crave warmth. Ice cream will forgive you. Ice cream will be waiting when you're ready. If you have any left. So while you're in the kitchen, make a double batch. Hide some. That way, you know ice cream will be reliable.

'm outside King's house, parked on the street, waiting. I'm too lazy to go inside, to make nice and talk with Dr. Nathan. I haven't showered, but yesterday, while my uncles were running errands, I snuck into the house to grab my pillow, fill an empty two-liter bottle with water, and track down my phone.

Dom texted: **Call your mother. She's worried and so are we. And if you're going to stay out there, if you need the space, take one of the heavy blankets. It's getting colder, Lou.**

Mom texted too. I deleted the whole thread.

I've never done that before.

She tried to video-call me twenty times.

There are four missed phone calls too, one after another. Finally, something's important enough to pay the eight dollars a day it costs my mom to use her phone off Wi-Fi in the US.

She should be here. To fight him with me. Even though she can't know, she *should* know. Some sixth sense, some inexplainable force tying us to each other—no matter how far away we are in body. But she's posting selfies to Instagram, smiling, happy and free. She should be here to tell me my stories. Instead, she hid them from me. I thought I was protecting her. I'm *still* protecting her. But in keeping my stories from me she protected herself most of all. I can't believe my mom would own land with Peter England—that she could ever trust him. And yet, it's in front of my eyes, her name and his, tied to the parcel of land the shack sits on.

She wouldn't.

But what if she did?

Acid scorches the back of my throat. I swallow it down.

Lately, my hair lives in a messy bun. My eyes are shadowed, so in the tent, with my cell-phone camera as a mirror, I used an eye pencil to darken them further. As if I meant to look like I'm not sleeping. It's a bit glam and it's a bit wrong. It's not me. Not any version of me I've been before.

When King slides into the truck, he throws me a gentle double take. "Wow, you look really . . . fierce? And, of course, beautiful."

My smile isn't forced, but it's half-formed. "I'm not sleeping well."

"I'm sorry," he says, and leans across the truck bench to kiss my cheek.

His lips on my body.

I don't mean to do it, but something takes over. Once he returns to his side of the bench, my hand rises and my knuckles rub at the spot where he touched me.

"Ouch, Lou. You didn't have to do me like that," he says, pained.

"I'm sorry. I'm . . . not myself today," I say, which is only part lie.

It's me. It's not me. It's both.

"Tell me about it?"

He's sincere and exactly what I don't need. "Later," I say, hoping later never comes. King hasn't fastened his seat belt yet, but I throw the truck in drive and swing around the cul-de-sac.

When we pull up to the diner, King is smiling. "Really?"

But it's not his real smile, not the one where he's peeled back the mask he wears in this town. "Wait for it," I say, and I stop myself from adding "bac," from talking exactly like Wyatt Thomas did all those months we dated.

Canola is in the air. The processing plant always smells like Thanksgiving dinner. That's meant for fall, for when it gets properly cold again, and nothing about this is comfort. All it does is remind me summer is almost over. Those bright-yellow fields won't stay that way long. Even now, some farmer is harvesting his crop.

The shack closes Labor Day weekend.

University starts the Tuesday after. I've hardly thought about it, hardly cared. Even though it's such a big thing. If Florence were going right away, she'd be obsessed, like the way she is with her around-the-world trip. Even King, who has a scholarship and friends in Toronto already, is anxious for next year, talks about university constantly.

We walk up to the diner, King trailing a few steps behind me. The place is busy, but one of the booths in the back, the one that curves and can fit a party of six, it's empty and waiting. I slide in one side. King picks the other. We're sitting four feet apart. But he stays where he is, and I do too.

I hand him the menus from where they're nestled between the salt and pepper shakers.

"I know what I want," he says.

"You don't even care to look?"

"Breakfast for dinner. Why else do you come to a diner at dinnertime? It's the grand slam for breakfast, veggie burger with tots and hot sauce for lunch, and other assorted breakfast foods for dinner at a diner."

I exhale. "Okay."

"What?" he says. "You're not into breakfast for dinner all of a sudden?"

"I am, I am." Some small part of me wants to roll my eyes.

"But what?"

I can't tell if he's playing at being clueless or if it's something worse. If he thinks he's caught me lying. "Look at the menu. Please."

So he does. It conceals his face from me. But his laugh shows up soon enough. "You didn't! Lou!" It's a little paper insert taped onto the plastic. "How?" he asks with Christmas-morning awe in his voice.

I melt a little. "I said it was important. It's one night only though. So . . ."

"So I'm having King's Favorite Mac and Cheese." He reaches

a hand across the table, palm up, open and waiting. "That was incredibly sweet of you. Thanks."

I take it, though it's an awkward stretch. He's been doing all these things for me, iced coffees, the constant moral support, and now I'm wondering who has been doing nice things for King this summer. Who has been taking care of him? Underneath, he's got to be hurting too. I taste acid again—guilt and too little sleep conspiring against me. "You haven't tried it yet. Don't thank me too soon."

He throws me a look. "I can't believe they ever took this off the menu."

"It's macaroni and cheese. King, it's like the easiest thing to make at home."

"It's the fact, Lou. Most places ruin this dish. They add bacon—"

"Some. People. Like. Bacon."

"Or bread crumbs. Or vegetables. Broccoli. Peas!"

"Bacon is the peak of the conventional salted meats."

He continues ignoring me. "You know, I once saw a mac with a crust of crushed Flamin' Hot Cheetos. Like why would you do that to something that's already perfect?"

I laugh. But my arm aches. I pull my hand free and settle on my side of the pleather booth. "I'm glad you have strong feelings for your meal."

His grin is wide. "It's not the only thing I have strong feelings for."

I scrunch up my nose.

"Bad, eh?"

"A bit . . . cheesy?" I say, and he cracks up.

Sometimes, everything is so easy between us.

When our food arrives, we eat and we try to talk, but even if we can laugh over puns—something's not flowing. We're out of sync. A fraction of a step off. He's here. I'm there. King asks about my mom and I shake my head, like nope. I ask if he's fully committed to his first-year classes yet or if he's still perfecting his schedule and he changes the subject to Florence's trip.

It shouldn't matter. But it does.

It has nothing to do with me ignoring King's admission of how much he likes me. Because that's not news. Because he's told me how amazing I am before. It's not that, right? I ask myself, picking at my cuticles under the table. After I pay the bill and leave a nice tip, I check my phone. It's only 7:10 p.m. I didn't plan anything else. I thought we'd do what we always do: sit and eat, and sit and talk, and suddenly notice we've been lost together for hours.

In the parking lot, we linger next to the truck. Awkwardly.

I flash to running out of the door of the vape shop with Tyler, one long-ago Saturday night. She's not smiling, but she's okay. Her mom's not missing yet. And for now, the two of us, we fit.

We haven't gone entirely dark yet.

We're only painting ourselves in grays, in colors like ash.

"Hop in," I say to say something.

King does and I cruise. We used to do this all the time, Ty and me, for a whole year. And somehow, that led to me being the kind of girl who could burn down a bar. Out of town now and deeper into Saskatchewan, we travel along the highway, through two small towns, and then, when I see it, I know this is where we've been heading all along.

An old grain tower.

Not used anymore.

"Class of '19" spray-painted at the top, and everyone who drives by has to wonder how they managed it. Grade 12 physics paying off? Or some kind of magic? The tower stands so tall it's the only thing in the wide sky worth noticing, other than the stars.

It's too early for stars.

Other graffiti sits on reachable planes. Those marks aren't interesting.

Once, Tyler and I climbed this thing. Later, later, when things were close to incineration. While we were sinking into it. We'd scored beers from the rig pigs at the Starlite Motel, escaping their room as soon as it got too obvious the men thought they'd be getting sex for beer. We shouldn't have been driving that night.

We didn't care.

We hadn't set anything on fire yet other than dated school textbooks, in her yard, and the occasional menthol cigarette.

"Lou," King says as I jump from the truck, landing in the dirt. It's loose and burnt brown. "Not what I expected."

"I've done it before," I say, like that's what he wants to hear.

I strut toward the ladder, tuck my cell phone into my bra, and throw my hands up a few rungs, getting ready to climb. And on the wind, it comes for me. The burning.

"Lou," he says again. "People die doing this."

"Yeah, they do," I say, and push myself forward. If I get high enough, I'll rise above the smoke line.

King ventures over to the bottom of the ladder and I think he's about to follow me—to chase after me. Find the clear air. But his feet never leave solid ground.

"This isn't safe. Please don't do this." He raises his voice, trying to reach me. "Are you hearing me?"

Now he's backing away from the tower to watch.

Rusty metal bites my hands like broken glass, but my feet are strong—they push me up and up and up. Even my shoulder sits . . . almost right. Finally.

He doesn't have to join in.

He doesn't have to like me like this.

We're far from town, but underneath it all, somehow, alongside the smoke, the canola processing plant haunts me—Thanksgiving-dinner smell crowds in, blending with the smoke. Autumn. Crushed leaves. Proscribed burns in the fields. Farmers wielding drip torches. University—and King back where he belongs, in Toronto. No, in the 6ix. Florence gone too. Soon, her text messages will stop coming, like how it's been with every other friend I've left behind.

"I don't know what you're trying to prove right now," King says from the ground, and he's truly angry. This isn't King, the one who holds himself back to maintain the peace, or King who labors to be cool, deflecting Wyatt's microaggressions, or King who buries his anger deep, deep down until it's safe to feel it somewhere private. Even King's patience runs dry when there's enough heat in the air.

That stops me. I glance downward and with all the conviction I have, I say, "Nothing," and that's when one of the metal ladder rungs I'm clinging to gives way. It would be fine, but my bad shoulder is the arm still holding on, and the sudden, immediate pressure of my own body weight is too much.

I fall through the smoke.

The ground is all hard-packed dirt.

"Jesus." King rushes over. "Are you all right?"

"Fine. Ouch." He squats next to me, but when he reaches out, I shove him away. "I said I was fine."

King is done. With me. With tonight. He explodes. "What misguided flex is this? What's wrong with you? You're acting the fool, ridiculous, like my sister, Aliya, when she wants something she can't have. And Aliya happens to be a child."

I push myself into a cross-legged sit—and already know where I'll bruise up, where it will hurt tomorrow. "Are you actually mad enough to lecture at me right now?"

He bites out each word: "Yes. I. Am."

"Fuck." I huff smoky air from my lungs. "This whole day has sucked."

He kicks the dirt, marring his white trainers before he sinks down next to me—the anger still inhabiting his body. He's holding himself back. He cracks his knuckles. "Lou. Tell me about it. Instead of being this person I can't even recognize."

He's not used to seeing me powerful. Not used to this kind of burn.

"I don't know where to start," I say, shifting a bit closer to him. "Ouch. That really, really hurt."

He doesn't speak. I inch closer again until I'm leaning into him. He lifts his arm to let me get closer still.

"I'm sleeping outside in a tent."

"I'm guessing not for the kicks."

King's warm and mostly hard, except where he's soft. It's his soft parts I like. It's the soft parts that remind me he knows how to be careful with me. Even when I'm not careful with myself. And even when I'm not careful with him.

"They're keeping something from me. My family." I don't say *lying* because I can't have him turning against me. Not when I need him. Not when he's already fed up with me. "Something real bad. My . . . Peter England . . . owns the land under the shack. And it's either my mom's name next to his on the title or mine. He owns the property our business is on. Or maybe my mom and him co-own it. Or I do. And my uncles will only say, talk to your mom—like this is something so big, only she can tell it to me. Like if they did, I'd hate them forever. As if my mom is the only person I'll forgive. And *she* isn't here, won't come home. She texts me *I love you*s like that's enough. Because we don't have the money for her to return, because in the end, it's about money."

We sit quietly. It's still fully daylight. Can't even hide my shame after speaking all this under the cover of night.

"And I haven't showered in days. And yesterday, when I was ignoring all of you because I left my phone in the house, and I was too angry to go get it, well, I met one of Dom's exes, who's a cop, and he pulled me over but didn't ticket me. And this thing happened a while ago, and I didn't tell you about it, but I'm telling you now. Please don't hate me." I continue pressing my face into King's shoulder. "Canada Day weekend, while you were in

Edmonton, I tried to buy your dad a scratch card, and the clerk in the mall, he . . . he wanted me to . . . give him a blow job . . . Just randomly because I don't even know why—because I'm a girl, because I'm . . . because he could?—I stormed out, but he still had my ID. Yesterday, I went to the pharmacy to take it back."

"I'm . . . really sorry, Lou."

He hurts for me. It lives in the careful way he says my name. For King, *sorry* isn't an empty word. He's so patient. And he doesn't ask me for anything. Doesn't ask me to carry his worries. The only thing King asked was that I didn't climb this grain tower. We always talk about me, my problems, and we talk about the world, but we only ever talk about parts of him. The safe things. Nothing critical. "I haven't asked you about your mom, how you're feeling, or about Aliya. Not since you told us what happened. I've been making this all about me."

King's body tightens. "Yeah, you have."

I don't waver, but nothing feels steady—even now that I'm on solid ground. "How is Aliya?"

"She's mostly good."

There's story here. If I keep asking, King will tell me when he's ready.

"Your mom?"

His voice breaks a little, then balances out. "Still won't talk to me."

"I don't know what to say." But I lean into him like he's holding me up, and when he leans back against me, properly, I know that I can hold him up too.

"Me either," he offers.

We sit and say nothing for a while.

I should apologize. But first I owe him my story—the part I've been holding back. "It's so boring here all the time," I say eventually. "But underneath the boring, there's this whole other world."

"That's truth."

"What we were almost talking about—in the kitchen—the morning after . . . after the rye . . . ," I say, instead of saying, after you slept, your body against mine. "You were talking about O'Reilly's."

He nods but doesn't interrupt.

"What you have to understand is Tyler and me, we were like stars caught in each other's declining orbit—burning, burning hard. We were fools. We were brave. We were fucking extraordinary. And when Tyler's mom went missing, and when she stayed missing, when her body was found, and when the police in this town bothered to look, to look properly, well, you know what happened."

"My mom's old boss, that bastard, he went to prison, and my dad was delirious. So fucking happy that finally, even if O'Reilly had been convicted for another crime, he was off the streets, he was being punished. Until . . ."

"The fire."

"Yeah, the fire."

"It wasn't your dad—even if everyone thought it was."

King's whole body radiates tension. "Are you going to say it?"

"Do you need me to?"

"Yes."

264

I hesitate. I don't know where to start. Like most stories, the beginning is difficult to pin down. "After the courtroom verdict, Tyler didn't feel any better. It didn't matter he'd do time. That they were calling it murder, and not something like what they normally do, when it's one of us, none of that manslaughter crap. But nothing mattered. And I was her person. I was there with her. I had to follow it through with her."

"I understand that kind of bond."

Now that I've found an opening, I sink into the story. "We bought the liquor with money we found in my mom's wallet. Tyler tore up a T-shirt donated to the Friendship Center that somebody thought was good enough to hand off. It was stained, riddled with tiny holes. And the two of us, we always had a lighter on hand. I was smoking that year."

King has fallen quiet.

"We didn't hesitate. There were no second thoughts. We waited until four in the morning—when night-shift workers would be most exhausted. We lit our bottles and we threw them through one of those ugly stained-glass windows. We stood and watched, longer than we should have."

I think about telling the rest. But I don't owe him that. It belongs to Tyler and it belongs to me.

King's heart beats fast against my forehead. If we were supposed to have fun on this date, I don't think any of what we've done hits the mark. "I've messed this up. This date thing."

"I don't know," King says. His arm tightens around my back. "I'm actually feeling a lot better now. Are you?"

I think about it. "Some, yes."

"Lou, you have to know, they would have come after my dad anyhow. He was a Black man, an immigrant whose accent isn't quite gone after thirty-plus years in this country, who'd been witnessed harassing the owner of O'Reilly's, who had dirt to talk on him to anyone who'd listen. And he'd been at it for years, my dad. He blamed my mom's boss for her addiction, for her infidelity. Even the most incompetent cops in the world would've been knocking on my dad's door after O'Reilly's burned." He clears his throat. "When it happened, at first, I hated that I thought it might have been you. I was scoping you out online, yeah, and it was the pictures you posted a couple nights before, you and Tyler, the background all blurry. Her eyes were empty, and yours were all fire, all focused, all ready to do what had to be done."

"You were scoping me out?"

"Every other day. Couldn't double-tap but couldn't stop." He exhales long and it's like he's breathing it all out—all the hurt. "Back then, I thought if you did it, you knew they'd come for my dad, that you were banking on someone else taking the blame. Why not a Black man. I also think I wanted it to be you, so I could keep hating you."

I rush my words: "No, no, almost as soon as it was over, I felt sick—and when I saw the papers, with your dad listed as a suspect, I wanted to admit what I'd done. But I couldn't do that to Ty. Do you understand? At all?"

"I think I do."

He quiets a long while, and I let him.

"I get that my ma's still fuming mad at me," he says, eventually. "It hurts, but I understand. That's the thing, understanding, for

266

me, that's easy. It's the part I have control over."

I pick up one of King's hands, trace his life line, his heart line, his head line, thinking back to the summer fair my mom dragged me to, to the palm reader's tent, to the feeling I had that summer, that some things were fated. "Maybe you have to keep on trying to apologize, keep on waiting for your mom to be ready to hear it."

"Truth." King nudges me. "So, what non-death-defying things do you want to do now? As you may have noticed, that stunt terrified me. I'm a music-and-books guy. I don't need adrenaline rushes. I'm sorry if that's boring."

"It's not. Or if it is, I like your kind of boring." Out on the highway, cars and trucks rush past, but this has become the calmest place I've been in days. "Can we stay awhile longer and be boring together?"

The smoke is gone. Just gone.

"I mean, we aren't trespassing, and we didn't just break this antique grain elevator. But sure."

I push up to face him. To lean in. "Thank you for saying *we*."

"Welcome." He laughs quietly. "One day, and this is your fair warning, I might write a story about this."

"I want to read whatever you see in this disaster. Though you'll keep any mention of a certain fire very, very quiet, right?"

"Hand to G-O-D." He nods, then whispers, "One day, Lou, I want you to read all my stories."

I don't want to leave. To climb into my truck. To return to town. "Can we stay here awhile longer and, like, make out?"

"Ohhhhh," he says. "Yeah."

I don't want to push us that much closer to the day he's going to want something other than kissing from me. But I'm hungry for this. With King. I sink fully into the present. I kiss his bottom lip tentatively. I taste him. And everything inside me says, more, more, more.

CHAPTER 26
August 16

FACT: It's possible to have too much ice cream. It's possible to burn out on your favorite flavor. It sucks when it happens. And trust us, it's going to happen.

We're scooping. It's me and Florence with our hands in the freezer, while King works the cash, perching awkwardly on the stool, his legs too long for the furniture.

Florence is in one of those moods. They're big and they're exuberant and it takes me longer than it should to realize, yes, she's manic. She's been cycling for weeks.

"I hate to say it, but I'm going to say it. I cannot wait for summer to be done." Florence wipes a speck of something off her face with the back of her hand, ignoring the customer currently asking her for a second spoon.

I reach over, handing it to him.

Florence doesn't even notice. "I'm sick of being sticky all the time! The gentleman—or might it have been a woman?—who invented air con should be a god. Why don't we have air con in here? Lou, air con! We need it. We need it now. Tell the pretty one or the other—your bloody uncles—they must figure it out."

King rings up a rainbow bowl I've just finished scooping for a family of tourists and hands them their change before he says, "It's not as sticky over here. I'll swap you."

Florence brushes him off. She has this lilt in her voice. Too much of too much of everything. "I was up most of the night reading about all the places I'm going to visit, all the weird art I'll see, the foods I'll eat. I'll gain a stone sampling all the gelato Italy has to offer. Did you know they have actual ice-cream sandwiches? Like gelato on brioche? Why didn't my mother move us to Italy? They must have mechanical engineers in Italy. Do they have crude oil in Italy?" She's multitasking. Breaking off to catch a customer's order and then she continues. "And Thailand, they stir-fry their ice cream. They add cereal and wee bits of other things. They—"

King cuts her off. "You aren't sick of ice cream yet?"

"Are you?" I ask.

"Is there something wrong with him?" Florence's sotto voce is all drama. Of course, it's loud enough for King to hear. It's part of the bit.

He laughs. "To be fair, yes."

We have a real line today. That's what most days look like since the Food Network special. And it's not only tourists. The locals have renewed their enthusiasm. Half of our former teachers truck their kids out after dinner. They're thrilled when they recognize King. He was always a favorite: called well-spoken, like he wasn't born in this town, called gentle, like they expected a kid of color wouldn't be. In truth, King's fascinated by words, loves to shape them, to put them to work, to take them apart to see how they tick, and he's kind, because he cares about the world, about the people who walk in it, even if they're flawed.

Florence babbles on about her trip. And we, her audience, listen. Last year when this happened, it was Florence's mother who eventually got her back on the meds. I couldn't convince Florence—and the more I tried, the more my best friend stopped talking to me about the important things.

She's still going nonstop. But King has joined in. And now, it's less weird. Less like she's off balance. I stash my phone on the prep counter and don't think too much, just step closer to King and put a hand on his left hip. He smiles, climbs off the stool, and joins Florence scooping without missing a beat in their *Drag Race* conversation.

But Florence sees something. Stops and stares. She smiles like a wolf about to bite. "Are you two dating? Finally?"

I say "No" at the same time King says "Yes," and the shack becomes two sizes too small instantly.

"Maybe people should talk more when they don't date." Florence laughs.

Neither King nor I join in. Even nonstop Florence senses the awkward in the air. I hate myself, but I lean over to check the freezers. We're almost sold out. A few scoops of Red, Orange, and Violet left. The last rainbow bowl helped. And when we sell out, we can quit. I can explain to King I didn't exactly mean what I said. Only, maybe I do.

Three dates isn't dating.

Three dates is three dates.

Once an AAA hockey team celebrating their first practice of the season piles back into too few vehicles like circus clowns, we close up the shack.

If Florence understands we're waiting for her to leave, she refuses to play along. She sits on top of one of the picnic tables and says, "Oh my stars, you two. You're both acting off-the-charts oddball. What is going on?"

I glance at King.

But he's watching a white SUV slow on the highway, turn into the lot. King approaches the vehicle to tell them we're closed.

I know the SUV is sporting vanity plates.

FREED.

He's not hiding anymore. This time, the driver rolls down his window. My feet are glued to the land. I can't move, even though what I want is to run. For the safety of the shack. Or toward the trees. Away from here.

Florence lays a hand on my back protectively.

The driver is bearded. Sunglasses conceal his eyes—but I know they're muddy blue. He stares at me, almost through me. My friends don't exist for him. Time slows. The crows in the trees quiet.

King says, "We're sold out for the day. Sorry."

When it was letters, and a ghost SUV stalking the edges of my world, it seemed manageable. But Peter England is flesh and blood.

Bearded. In his forties but graying hard along his sideburns and through his facial hair. His eyes *are* blue.

They're like mine. They could be mine.

His flesh and blood is *mine*.

"I don't really give a damn about desserts," Peter England says before turning to the passenger, that same blond woman. "After we're married, we should build another house out here"—he waves a hand toward the shack, the trees—"by then the new subdivision will be under construction."

My knees lock. Florence's hand butterflies on my back.

I'm combing what I can see of the man in the vehicle, wondering if the sunshine makes him sneeze, if he's an early bird like me, if he has a birthmark on his calf like I do.

Peter England says, "Think on my ask, Louisa. But don't think too long. The weather's turning." Without another word, he reverses hard, right up onto the shoulder of the highway, and leaves us, frozen in place.

CHAPTER 27

August 16

FACT: If ice cream can't fix your problem, we
advise seeking help. Ice cream is a great thing—
don't get us wrong—but friends are better.

It's not what I was expecting. The letters suggested he was mostly keeping his distance. Sitting now, my limbs are weak—as if I've been swimming hard, against a riptide. Florence is tucked close, on top of the picnic table, her feet butted up to my hip. King's facing me. One of his shoes, it's pressed against my flip-flop. Not hard. Just enough pressure to say he's here.

Both of them. They're present.

Eventually, Florence covers her mouth with her hand. It's been maybe two minutes since the white SUV left, but everything is slow. Even Florence, who normally moves double time, she's slowed.

My voice surprises me. It's mine, but it's not. It's distant—rough. "He owns this land. Right here. Under our feet. That man . . . my . . . father . . ."

Florence pushes herself off the table and pulls me into a hug. She hugs hard. Until she stops to invite King. He's watching me.

Sad eyes. I nod over and over until he joins us.

I'm the shortest. And I'm sort of crushed. Though I feel like crying, it's momentary and it's not because of Peter England. It's because I'm going to miss my friends. We're running out of time.

King wipes at his eyes. Even Florence is sniffly.

"We are totally holding it together, aren't we?" Florence asks.

This time, King and I both say, "Right?" and it's sweet.

We live here in the moment, three hearts in sync.

Florence breaks the silence, asks me what I want to do.

I sketch it out. "I want him gone. I want nothing to do with him." I stop, thinking. The strength leaks from my voice. "My family needs to be safe, my uncles—and my mom. He cannot hurt my mom again."

Those truths sit in the air.

"Let's do something all three of us, then." Florence grabs her phone and instructs King to pull out his too.

Together, on the picnic table, we write a statement.

I'm terrified, but I'm not alone. And that's small comfort. Enough that I reclaim control of my body, enough that I find this place where I'm okay again. This land is as much mine as it is Peter England's. And maybe what's more important: The crows up in the trees, watching us, they know me. They know my friends, my family. This land knows me.

The crows, the land, don't know the man in the white SUV for shit.

What we end up with, it's short and to the point and according to Florence's googling, a perfectly fecking legal cease-and-desist letter. She hugs us both again, one at a time, her movements slow, her eyes cloudy, and says, "I really need sleep. I'm beyond drained all of a sudden."

I've watched this happen before. But I said I wouldn't push it. And so, even if she sees the struggle on my face, my lips remain sealed.

But King didn't make those promises. "Florence, I'm going to be real with you. You really need to start taking your meds again, you get me?" It's so matter of fact, without any pressure. It's not something King needs for himself. It's something he wants for her.

She doesn't explode. Doesn't storm off. She just says, "Yeah. I do. Thanks for watching out for me, love."

"Do you want us to drive you home?" I ask.

She smiles—but it doesn't quite breach her eyes. "No, I'm okay."

I have to trust her.

After Florence leaves, King settles next to me on the bench.

"You're a good friend to her," I say.

"You are too." He pauses. "Only she might need something different from you, is all."

"If you can be her take-your-meds person, I'm happy to stop being that person. I can share."

"Good, all right." King drums his knuckles against the picnic table. He's trying to stay cool, but he's not. "Today, I found out we're secret dating? Or we're not dating at all? I'm . . . confused."

"I'm sorry about that."

His eyebrows spike. "Let's be clear, Lou. What exactly are you sorry about? That you said it? That it was confusing? Something else?"

276

The crows chirp at each other. They understand what's going on here.

"You're mad again."

King stretches away from me. If he were wearing a ball cap, he'd be pulling it down hard over his eyes. "Florence is your best friend and you couldn't even tell her."

There's no traffic on the highway, but I'm talking louder. "In case you haven't noticed, I'm kind of a mess."

"Nope. I do not accept that. You owe me a real answer. Damn, the excuses, Lou, are exhausting."

Tell him. If it wouldn't be the worst thing I could possibly do, I would. My voice breaks but I have to say something. "What if I don't know? Because I'm not sure I do."

It's a lie.

I can't have sex with him. With anyone.

King stares across the street, way out there, past the house, into the far distance.

My hands are sticky and I wish I'd washed them before we locked up. I pick at the mess.

"We should print out what Florence typed up and mail it," he says finally. "Get this over with."

"That's what you want to say to me?" It hurts. It does. Because I want him to understand. Even if I can't tell him the truth. I want him to somehow get it anyway.

He shrugs. "For now, yes."

He wants to get this over with. He wants to get away from me. He hasn't said anything about our third date. At all. "Okay. Fine."

But nothing's fine.

"I'll drive." That's the last thing he says and then he's taking big steps away from me toward the Subaru.

He's not talking. I'm not either.

We're almost done. Once the letter is printed, we'll stop. We didn't even get our three dates. He's pulling away from me. Like kisses don't count for enough. Like he knows I won't ever be able to give him what he wants. I'm telling myself it's for the best. The summer's almost over. The end was coming for us.

We swing by King's house to use their printer. I'm happy Dr. Nathan isn't home because he'd suss out the undercurrent running between his son and me instantly.

When we're done, with the letter in hand, stuffed into a plain white envelope, King hands me a pen and I realize we don't have an address. But I know where the England farmstead is. Tyler and I were there after the tornado.

"I'll deliver it. Just take me back to the shack."

"You know where he lives?" King asks. It's not heated; the question is simply there. Like, of course. It's only another thing I haven't told my friends—haven't told him. "That's dangerous, Lou. I'm mildly cheesed at you, but I'm not letting you do this alone. If we're delivering this to that man's doorstep, I'm there alongside."

I cave. Warm a little. Wish that I could give King a proper relationship. We drive almost all the way up to Peter England's house. King's hand lands on the door handle. He's planning on walking the letter up there for me.

Part of me wants to let him. But I can't. Like at the pharmacy—this is mine. Peter England's matching patio furniture is all wicker with heavy white cushions. There's a glass of lemonade sitting on the end table like this is a movie set. My knees lock as I tuck the letter under the glass, even though the glass is sweating and will soak through the envelope soon enough.

King watches from the driver's seat.

Behind me, the screen door creaks open.

I walk down the stairs, slow, as if I'm not running away. I count my steps. One, two, three more left.

Peter England says, "You remind me of your mother. But she was a little younger when I knew her."

I walk all the way back to the passenger door before I turn to face him. He's smiling. I reach for the door handle.

Peter England's voice carries, in the quiet: "I'll be seeing you, Louisa."

I sink into the vehicle, slamming the door hard, and whisper, "Drive, please."

King throws the Subaru into reverse, his three-point turn cresting onto the lawn to escape.

In the rearview and side mirrors, I'm watching the man who fathered me in an act of monstrous violence open the letter, peer at it like it's only another piece of junk mail, and then, deliberately, because he knows I'm watching, he rends it in half.

CHAPTER 28
August 17

FACT: Ice cream can soothe an upset stomach. Unless
you're lactose intolerant, and then, well, ice cream
is going to fuck you up. You could stick to sorbets.
But here at the Michif Creamery, we carry lactase
pills behind the counter. If you want one, ask.

In the morning, I wake because King is outside my tent calling my name. "Rise and shine. I fixed it with your uncles. We're getting out of here for the day."

I rub sleep from my eyes. Peter England had me all twisted up. But I was wrong about King being done with me. We'll have our third date. And I'm thrilled to be wrong. The summer isn't over yet. When I climb out of the tent, I'm wearing the same jean skirt from yesterday, my bralette, a flimsy tank top, and a real smile. It's early morning still. No frost, not yet. But the dew across the grass, and on my tent, shimmers.

I brush my teeth with water from the two-liter bottle, spitting into the field. When I finish with the toothpaste, King is looking at me funny. He's enjoying himself, but he's also holding back.

"About yesterday." He swallows, his Adam's apple jutting up and down. "I was forgetting our deal. I was starting to think I was dating you and you were my girlfriend. That's on me, since you made it clear that's not what you want. So I'm the one who's sorry. And you are so cute, in your tent, brushing your teeth in the semi-wilderness. I can't handle it. The cute. You."

It's the moment, and it's not.

It hits me. I love King Nathan. He's so important to me. He used to be, and now he is again, and things might be different, but he's still the person he was at fifteen, only grown. And like I did at fifteen, I love him. I can't say it aloud, but I can make sure he knows I didn't intend to hurt him.

It comes out in a rush. "I'm sorry too. For being hard and weird, all uptight."

He nods. "So I have an epic date to rival all dates ready to go. If you want. To finish this off."

My heart thuds at "finish this," but I know that's what we have to do. Three has to be enough.

The cows are in the dairy getting milked. Which means Dom is with them. I don't know when King fixed this, or what he said, but right now even though I'm losing another day's salary, I don't care. "I want to."

"The radio is holding this contest," King says as we walk toward the access road where he's parked. He talks with his hands—all excited. "The team to take the most selfies with Alberta's 'Big Things,' you know, all those giant, absurd sculptures every town in this province seems to have—and, worse still, take pride in—that team wins a thousand cash. You game? We have until midnight."

Of course King's been paying attention. Of course he knows I need the money. And I know exactly what he's talking about: no other place I've lived in Canada has ever been so obsessed with giant sculptures of the weird and the historical, all in an empty bid for fame. But all I say is, "Which station?"

"Today's Killer Country," King says sheepishly, then shrugs. "Hey, my dad likes it."

"Your dad," I say, totally unconvinced. The way King's music tastes are all over the board, there's no way he doesn't jam to country sometimes.

King laughs self-consciously. "You know, I was born here. We didn't have Black History Month in Alberta until 2017, but we've always had country music."

Damn, he's pretty cute too. But I'm not telling him that. Yesterday's forgotten. For now. "So . . ."

"So . . . ," he echoes.

"When does the contest start?"

He doubles down on enthusiasm, beaming. "If we leave now, we can be in Vegreville to text our first photo when things open at nine."

In the Subaru, we're listening to the radio station because why not.

We snap both of our faces with the giant brown-and-gold pysanka, a Ukrainian Easter egg tilted on a queer axis, and get a text back saying we're officially in the contest thirty seconds later. The world's largest Easter egg weighs five thousand pounds, but what's cooler: it's a giant jigsaw puzzle, made from interlocking aluminum shapes. The pattern that emerges, it reminds me of my mom's beadwork. It's bittersweet, this realization. I brush it away. Focus on the sun on my face, the careful wind in my hair. Before driving onward, we sidetrack to take a selfie—King smiling and me pointing at the life-size elk sculpture standing guard over the park. We have no idea if it counts, but it's sure big. King's phone buzzes and he does a little dance. It's cute. So cute.

But we don't have time. We head north to Elk Point, and St. Paul, and Vilna—a statue of Peter Fiddler, a British settler from the 1780s who married a Nehiyaw woman and made his life here with her; the largest UFO landing pad (what were Canadians thinking in 1967?); and some funny mushroom sculptures. They're local—Dom would love this, but mushroom ice cream is all wrong.

"Never tell Dom about the local fungi. I'm afraid of what will spark in his strange brain," I say, climbing back into our seats.

"Oof, that's an easy promise." King glances at his phone. "We should head south and hit up what we can before the deadline."

"But we'll miss Bonnyville's Angus Shaw," I say, like it's the best possible thing we could ever see. And maybe it is.

This is fun.

"Your call," he says eventually. "Actually, I'm the driver, you're the navigator. You tell me where we're going. We're good at this. You're in charge, Lou. Always have been."

I really love him. My pulse echoes in my ears, and I wonder if King hears it. If he senses this.

After Bonnyville and to-go coffees from Timmie's, we scoop south, down to Wainwright, and while we catch our breath after running from the parking lot to get close enough for our photo, we admire the big fake bison. It's here because the real bison used to be here, and it's massive and it makes me sad. But there's no time for sadness. To think about what we did to this earth and to the things living here. To think about what it was like when we were at the front of this thing, on our first date and not at the end. In our selfie I'm trying to smile, but I can't, not really—and then we're on our way.

In Castor, we find Paddy the Beaver—but it's not the same five-foot-tall mascot in the photo online; it's been replaced with a recycled metal sculpture that isn't as ridiculous—and in Coronation, a massive white one-dimensional crown, a replica of something the Queen of England wears to state events. I wonder how many people remember whose land this really is? I dwell here as we drive down prairie roads. Hanna has three gray geese and we snap a shot with each of them, and though the wait feels like forever, we get a confirmation that, yes, all three count.

"Hey, we're up to thirteen."

King checks his phone again, too long to simply be checking for the time. He says, "It's noon."

"Where to next?"

"Drumheller?"

I smile big and wide and I don't need to say anything. He programs the next stop into the GPS app. As we drive toward my favorite place in the world, King's singing along to the radio. It's all bad country, catchy and easy to know what's coming next. Trucks, girls, beer.

And heartbreak.

King's voice is deep. It's not pretty; it's something else. It's in my chest, thrumming down in my belly. And I don't want him to stop. Don't want this song to ever end.

But the song ends, as songs do. King clears his throat and drinks his now cold coffee. "Why not four dates, Lou?"

He won't let it go. Can't.

"Why not six? Or thirty?" It could be the singing; it could be something else. King's voice is tight. "Why not?"

The station's gone to commercial. I turn the volume low. "Because I can't do more than three. I . . . I can't be that person. Your girlfriend. And in two weeks you'll be back in Toronto, where you live, with your friends and your sister and your mom. And I don't want to break up with you when you leave. And that's what happens if we push this to four."

He exhales. "You want to be friends. Just friends."

"Yes."

"It's a big ask."

He's keeping his distance. He hasn't touched me once yet today. And I'm noticing it like something important is missing. "Are you changing your mind?"

"Your consent's not a thing I can influence. And I wouldn't try."

I reach my hand out, rest it on his shoulder. "I thought we could walk away easy."

"Can you?"

"I have to."

The radio updates the rankings. We're in second place. My hand falls, shaking, into my lap. Second place.

"Can we forget about what has to happen tomorrow?" I ask, knowing it's too much to ask, but asking it anyhow.

"Sure."

The music returns with another hit. King turns it up.

Even though it takes longer to climb all the way up to the top of Drumheller's T. rex, King insists. And I don't want to say no. She's the world's largest dinosaur. Four and a half times bigger than a real T. rex, because this isn't about accuracy. The museum is for accuracy; this is for the sheer joy of it. When we reach the top of the never-ending stairs, we're breathless. Looking out from the viewing deck on the park below, I pull King close, kiss him for the first time today. In our photo, I'm holding the camera, aiming up, and King's hands are tangled in my hair. We're in the moment— not thinking forward or back.

As we climb down to earth, King asks, "Are you sure?"

"We get to have today. Today is ours."

That's when he smiles. When everything shifts.

In Drumheller, we find the allosaur too.

"You know, if you want, we can quit and tour the museum?" He leans down and kisses me again. My whole body throbs. I'm in my favorite place with one of my best friends.

I want to press pause. To stay.

But I want to win this, too.

If we win, we'll split the cash, and I'll make up for so much of this summer in one day. I don't let him down easy, with a promise of next time. Because there won't be one, and I don't think I can come here with King as friends. "Let's finish what we started. But thanks."

It's not simply the prize money. Money, it always matters. And anyone who says otherwise has too much of it. I pick at my cuticles in the Subaru. It's also that if King takes me to the Royal Tyrrell,

I won't be able to stop dating him. If we go there together, there's too much possibility. I can't picture it. But it's warm and fuzzy. It's something I want.

But can't have. I might like kissing him. But I don't know if I'll ever want anything more. And if King knew, he wouldn't want to date me. It's not that sex is everything, but sex is something, and I haven't met someone yet who feels like I do.

We skip Calgary—both of us avoiding the city we'd planned at fifteen to make ours—and head east toward Medicine Hat, where their giant Saamis Tepee stands high on the prairie. Canada claims to celebrate the Indigenous nations whose territories it occupies, but really, it's these gestures: sculptures on land where bison used to roam. Another beat of sadness fills my heart. We don't know if it counts, but there's a big moose sculpture too. We photograph both.

We're up to seventeen items.

It's seven p.m.

On our way to Lethbridge, we swing through Taber, and by nine thirty we're starving, but we've made it to Bow Island and on to Vauxhall. Car snacks and coffees that go cold before we can finish them aren't fueling us. But stopping for anything else takes too long.

Twilight breaks across the prairie in dramatic oranges and yellows. It's stunning. In that early dark of late summer, we see the Vauxhall potatoes, and we can't stop laughing. One's red and one's brown. They have green hair that could be spinach leaves or collard greens. And the potatoes, they're dancing. This time we send a video, dancing and laughing.

Confirmed: twenty-four entries.

It's ten forty-five, fully dark now, but we capture Vulcan's spaceship with the flash.

Twenty-five.

With an hour and fifteen minutes until midnight, we need two more things to beat the first-place team. I'm scouring the map, comparing it to online lists, searching, searching for our win.

"We can reach Calgary in an hour and eighteen minutes. If we gun it . . ."

King's not convinced. "There's traffic. Speed traps. Police."

"What if we make it?"

"I don't feel good about that, Lou."

He's tense. He's telling me no, in the best way he knows how. He can't go to Calgary with me. There's too much history between us. For him, maybe that's his place where our potential is too much. The radio goes to commercial again. I kick my flip-flops off to sit cross-legged on the grass. I'm scrolling my phone's map with two fingers. The map stops on Drumheller and Rosedale. It hits me. "We missed the Rosedale Miner. Right outside of Drumheller. We were so close."

Then I realize what we missed, what we *really* missed. The town of Drumheller is full of large dinosaurs. On every street corner. In front of every business and in every city park. We could have spent the afternoon collecting them, and laughing, and kissing, and maybe we could have won too. Maybe we could have had it all.

King sinks down to the ground too. Like he's half reading my mind, he presses his lips to my bare shoulder and then my neck.

"Lou, this was supposed to be for us. Did you have fun today?"

"A lot. So much."

"We can't beat the other team."

"Nope."

"Are you starving?"

I nod, admiring his cheeks, his deep-brown eyes.

"Should we go and find a Denny's or something? Sit and eat. We can send our concession speech from there?"

His body is warm. I throw my arms around him and hold on.

Later, we eat.

Our last photo, a double stack of blueberry pancakes, a platter of nachos, a sizzling veggie skillet, and two glasses of Coke. We're next to each other in the booth, close, tight, giddy. It's official. Come midnight, we remain in second place.

King pays our middle-aged Black server, Viola, whose fuchsia hair is the best, who when she first arrived at our table complimented my pink teardrop earrings, asking after where I got them. Even though I'm still angry, I shared my mom's Etsy site, typing it into Viola's phone for her. King tips her well and Viola tells us to be safe on the road.

Outside, I try to offer King some cash. He shakes it off. "Put your wallet away."

"This was a very expensive event."

"I've been saving all summer. You know, there's not much to do in a small town."

I hug him again under a streetlamp. We're in a parking lot far from home and it's nighttime and it's so cold already. My teeth almost chatter. I didn't feel it change.

But it changed. It's not summer anymore. In the morning, the dew covering my tent might freeze.

"So, it's tomorrow," King says as we climb into the Subaru.

We have a five-and-a-half-hour drive home.

"It's tomorrow," I agree.

"This is an epic two-day date. That's how much I like you, Lou."

I should say anything else. But I say, "I know."

He smiles, but it doesn't live in his eyes. We drive, listening to the radio, both of us singing along quietly to the sad songs, the bad songs. We stop for gas once and we're the only people awake in the whole town, it seems.

King fills the tank without speaking.

I stretch, breathing in the cold, reminding my lungs how to expand.

As we drive, it's a rule, the navigator isn't allowed to sleep. We're moving fast again. The stars are out tonight. When the radio loops, playing the same songs we've heard all day, twenty times already, I turn it off.

I break the silence. "Do you remember when we used to make up stories about the stars? When we used to sit on those benches at the park? When we made all those plans for university, about getting out of town together?"

"Yeah. Why?"

"We'd only known each other for . . ." I do the math on my fingers. "January, February, March, April, May, June, July, August . . . eight months when you left."

"Felt like longer. Like you'd lived here forever."

"It did. And not, at the same time."

"You didn't want to move back, did you?"

"Nope, not at all."

"We would never have become friends."

"I wouldn't have lied to you. I wouldn't have lied at all, I don't think. Coming back to the place where it happened, where my mom was violated, where it wasn't safe to be Native in this deep and clear way, to be anything but the default, that's why I did it. I see that now."

"That sounds like more truth."

"King," I ask, even though I shouldn't. "When we were fifteen, back then, did you want to date me?"

He laughs and then sobers. "You were becoming my best friend so fast, and I needed a friend like you. Someone who saw me, who I could trust with all the parts of myself. And honestly, my ma—one of the last things she said before she left with Aliya was that I should be in a relationship with a Black woman. To find a Black woman, I'd have to leave too. And I've always listened to my ma, respected where she was coming from. So no, I didn't want to date you." He laughs quietly. "I wanted to date Sarah Barrable-Tishauer, you know, Liberty from *Degrassi*, even though she was much older."

What he's not saying. I wasn't that person. I lied to him. And later, after he'd left, I brought shame, the police, down on his family. Thinking hard, I stretch my aching feet. When King pulls onto my access road and turns off the engine, I'm wide awake all of a sudden. We both exit the Subaru.

He rubs his temples like he's got a headache. "Lou, I'm not

going to be able to turn off how I feel."

He doesn't ask me if I can do the same. All I say is, "I know that."

He paces a few feet away from me, turns around, still full of energy. "I want for us to hold on . . . longer. I want to kiss you."

I nod and that's enough. King picks me up, right off the ground, his hands on my waist, and I wrap my legs around him because it feels right, because I want to hold on too, and we kiss. Just kiss. His lips and mine.

I feel dizzy. Head-rush runs along my body, like all of me is spinning. It could be the lack of sleep or it could be King.

We break apart to breathe, to rest.

"Okay, okay. You need to put me down now."

He does but keeps me close, a hand tucked against my hip.

The dizziness settles. I wish I could want him back properly. Kissing is good. But kissing isn't enough.

"You need to go on back to your house now."

"I'm not trying to get you naked, Lou. I keep having to say that." He sighs against me roughly. "But doesn't this feel good? Don't you want to stay like this . . . longer before we have to . . . stop?"

He's too close.

Wyatt never asked. Never noticed. But this is too much. If we'd stayed in Drumheller, maybe we could have rewritten our story. But we didn't. We lost.

I don't want to have to say this to King. Our three dates are done. Summer's over. So what I say is only half a lie: "It's not . . . good enough."

He steps away. And away again. "I hear you. I'm listening now."

"Good night," I say.

And all he says is, "It's morning, Lou."

King leaves.

One of my uncles has filled up the jug of water and left heavy wool blankets inside the tent. I fall to the ground, pushing the blankets away. My body throbs still. I'm uncomfortable. My hand runs along bare skin as I strip. Kissing is nice. So nice. I touch myself, tentative. I want to want this—in my head, in my heart. I think I do. At least, I know I should want. I remember my last experiment, when I was trying so hard to be able to desire King the way he does me. Frustrated, I roll onto my side, heaving air. Inhale. Exhale. I want to be able to do this. To kiss him beyond the end of summer. But I don't want what comes next.

I don't work. I've been caught up on why. On thinking this is a side effect, an inheritance, something that's come from the violence of what Peter England did to my mom when she was sixteen. But *why* doesn't matter. All that matters is I don't work.

And worse, my heart is breaking. Because I can't—for a person who, if I could, I'd really like to be able to want in all the ways. Not only as a friend.

On the ground, half crying, I know friendship is all my body— all I—can manage.

CHAPTER 29
August 18

FACT: Ice cream for breakfast isn't okay.
We're telling it straight. But mixing ice cream
with cereal is a pretty decent lunch.

'm scheduled at the shack all day. That was the trade. Open to
close. Me and King. I still haven't showered, haven't done much
more than brush my teeth and rinse my face. Neither of my uncles
is pressing matters beyond making sure I know they're watching.
When it was too cold to sleep, the wool blankets were a comfort.

I can't smell myself yet. But that's got to be coming. Layers of
deodorant cake off each morning as I try pressing more into my
skin.

Worse than that, I'm sick in my heart, fully not at home in my
body, like the morning after Tyler and I burned down O'Reilly's,
when I was afraid of the person I was becoming.

I arrive at the shack first. Instead of waiting, I open the windows
and manage to pin them in place in a totally gymnastics-worthy
move that stretches out my bad shoulder. But finally, after all this
time, it doesn't hurt. I'm not back to pre-injury performance. Part
of that I can blame on my shoulder.

I'm cleaning the counters as if Florence and Elise didn't yesterday, for something to do, when King rolls up ten minutes late, shades on.

We've had four hours of sleep.

He waves hello, goes to hang his hoodie and keys up. As he steps into my space, I leap back.

"I'm not gonna bite," he says.

"I'm tired."

"Yeah," he says.

"Nice hoodie," I offer. It's We the North, with black-and-white lettering.

"It is," he says, navigating around me to plug his iPhone in.

He didn't say it. Bunnyhug. He always corrects me. Since the day we met, in the hallway when I had to stash my hoodie in my locker to meet the dress code. *Around here, it's called a bunnyhug.* He said it like it was the most important thing. Yesterday, we were dating. Today we're suffering through a full shift, with only the two of us on staff, and we've changed.

A line forms, and it doesn't seem like it will ever end. As soon as we get down to the last person, the last family, and there's a break coming for us, more cars turn into the lot.

It's busy. We're slow moving.

Multitasking, we bump into each other too many times. His hip against my side. My arm brushing his. Once we lean in for the same scoop, and his face smashes into my shoulder. And so I start watching for him, making space. That's all.

I'm being careful.

Kind.

A coward too, but it doesn't discount all the other things I'm doing when I get out of King's way and stay out of his way.

At one point, he turns, I step back, and he throws his hands up in the air. His eyes close tight as if he's pained. When he recovers, he switches up the playlist. We're listening to country, maybe for the first time this summer, in here.

It's a weird message. We had so much fun yesterday. These songs. They're tied to good memories. To us.

I asked about his mom and he told me something—as if he trusted me.

"I need a quick break," I say.

He shakes his head like no, then fumbles and starts nodding. "Go. Sorry. I'm . . ."

"What? Tired?"

"Drained."

When I return, I stare out at the line of people waiting to buy my family's ice cream while washing my hands at the sink. It's longer. In the three minutes since I stepped away. Somehow, our stock isn't running out yet. Dom's been working hard, I guess. We return to the madness. We take orders, scoop, and ring them up. It means there's a lot of back-and-forth. A lot of mess. Under my feet, pieces of cones crunch.

But since I started being careful, I haven't touched him once.

It's almost seven at night, and we have Red and Green and Violet left. All I've had to eat today is ice cream—first a scoop of Orange, and later, a Blue sorbet. I'm starving again, craving a big, comforting meal.

As I help a family from out of town with their order—two

Reds and one Violet—the white SUV arrives. This time, Peter England parks. He assists the blond woman, holding her arm formally, like she's his prom date, as they walk toward us. Her shoes are utterly impractical on gravel.

They wait in line.

When they reach the front, I freeze.

"A scoop of strawberry for my lady," Peter England says.

The cold bites my hand. I want to tear into my cuticles, draw blood, breathe air that isn't tainted with his artificial pine aftershave. I want real trees. To curl up in a bear's den and sleep until spring.

Peter England presses a $50 bill into King's hand. "Boy, keep the change."

I taste copper. Realize I'm biting my cheek.

Then, like nothing's happened, Peter England helps the woman back across the gravel, and they drive off.

We run out of Red and then Green follows. Only a few people lounge at the picnic tables. That's when I call it. "Let's close up. Quit for the night."

King starts cleaning, wordlessly.

I close the windows. Alone. I install the "Done for the Day, Try Us Tomorrow" sign while King counts bills into a deposit bag. But when I step back into the almost-dark shack, he says, "Why didn't you . . . ? Why couldn't you . . . ? Lou, you said not a word to him. You could have told him he wasn't welcome, you know? You could have said . . . anything."

I shrug. It's all I can manage.

King says, "I didn't see him well when we were tearing off his property. I kept imagining he'd have a gun. It's . . . silly. But I was afraid."

"Me too."

King deflates. "That man is a monster. Coming here, baiting you."

I haven't said it, claimed him as part of me, out loud before. My voice wavers. "That man is *my father*. He makes up half of me. I'm half of that . . ." I wipe at my eyes.

King steps near me, as if to hug me, and I do the wrong thing: place my hands in front of me like, stop. Please, please, stop. I cover my mouth. My cheek throbs.

King continues, "What is wrong with you? You're acting as if I'm gonna hurt you. I'm your goddamned friend. Exactly like you wanted. So yeah, we've kissed a lot recently. And I get you're not into that. But . . . you keep shying off like I'm . . . You're standing ten fucking feet away."

I stare at the wall behind him. The pictures Florence and I taped up. Shots of last summer, March break when her family took us to West Edmonton Mall and we stayed at the Fantasyland Hotel, sleeping in the creepy western-themed room, and I haven't noticed, but she's added King and Elise too. The newspaper clippings are changing colors, curling at the edges.

"Say something?" he asks. "Anything that's real."

I shake my head, my hand forming a fist, pressing that fist against my mouth until it hurts.

His shoulders fall. His voice grows low and quiet. "Why did you keep kissing me if you didn't want to?"

I don't know what to say, how to tell the truth, how to keep stepping around my body and his, in a space that's almost like lying. A space that doesn't feel nearly as good as when I was younger, when I was in control of my lies.

Now, sometimes, I don't even know if I'm lying to other people or to myself anymore. Not at all.

"Okay, okay. I'll stop," he says.

He steps past me, and he's right—I almost recoil. Is this what I've been doing all day?

"I can't have sex with you," I blurt out. It's inelegant. It's only half truth. But it's what matters.

His face, it's as if I've slapped him. "You haven't been hearing me at all, have you, Lou?" he asks, but he isn't looking for an answer. He rips his bunnyhug over his head hard. When he drives out of the parking lot, though, it's slow and calm. Not angry at all.

In the trees, the crows caw at me, as if in judgment. *Look how you've hurt that good human.* It's not kind, but I'm not feeling kind today: I honk my horn, scaring them off. Eventually, I head home, in the opposite direction, fairly sure all I've done by speaking this truth is make everything worse.

CHAPTER 30
August 23

FACT: Secret ice cream is the best. When you're alone
and you know it's all yours. When you know you don't
have to share. Come on, you agree. You're not a bad
parent/sibling/cousin or whatever if you need your
own ice cream every once in a while. We promise.

After emailing back and forth, Leif Winters agrees to meet but
hates that one of my conditions is we keep it a secret from
my uncle. Leif's in the area, filming in Edmonton, and though he
had planned to fly straight back to Toronto, he's curious enough
about my proposition to delay his flight.

We can't meet at the farm or the shack.

We meet at the Timmie's on the far side of town. It's not as nice
as the one by the mall. It's smaller. If you close your eyes, this place
smells the same as any other Tim Horton's. One day, the franchise
will insist it needs to be renovated, but today isn't that day. This is
where Tyler and I used to hang, when we had enough money for
doughnuts and coffee. When we were using the rig pigs for their
alcohol, once for their drugs. When we didn't care. People who
know me, people who know my uncles, they don't really end up
here. They go to one of the nicer locations.

In my good bag with the leather fringe, I have a stack of incriminating mail I swiped from Dom's bedroom and his recipe book. If anything is Dom's baby, it's not his truck or even the really shiny equipment in the barn, it's Mooreen first, followed directly by this book.

A lined black notebook. Hardback. Old.

I've examined it before, while supervised. It's drawings of plants and herbs Dom finds out on the land, recipes for ice-cream base, and imaginations and thinkings, new flavors and disaster flavors. Sometimes it's a line that makes no sense, something whimsical about cows or ice cream or life.

The early pages are covered with nouhkom's handwriting, in gently fading inks. One day, those words will be gone forever.

Leif's already seated against the window, nearby the door. His facial hair is exactly the same as it was the day I met him—perfect. He's clean and polished, and so very out of place here. Back in June, when King first arrived, he looked the same way, shiny and too perfect. But King has relaxed into this place. He can be at home here, even if at the same time he isn't, not fully.

Leif's shoulders are uptight. He doesn't have that skill, to find a way to be at peace when the world doesn't immediately conform to him.

It's something I realize I'm good at too: not caring what the world thinks, not caring enough that I'm at home here, in this town, where I shouldn't feel *at home*, with Peter England stalking the edges of my life.

"Hi," I say, walking up to Leif's table.

He stands awkwardly, his long, tanned arms hanging at his

sides, stiff. "I don't know if I should shake your hand or hug you."

I smile at his honesty. "The last one of Dom's boyfriends I met, well, I didn't meet him until after they'd broken up, but he was a cop who'd just pulled me over."

"Henry," Leif says, and laughs. It's enough to draw some of the tension out of his body. "Can I get you something?"

"Medium double double. And, if you're expensing things, a doughnut. Vanilla dip, please."

He laughs again. "If this is business, we'll expense it. But then I really should have taken you someplace nicer."

I sit down on the hard-plastic chair, Leif's unintentional little dig, someplace nicer, echoing in my head.

There's a line. One man ahead of Leif. He's wearing a ball cap. He's taller than Leif—Peter England's height. I scan the parking lot. Mostly trucks with extended cabs. A few cars, including Leif's sleek rental. I stand, catch a glimpse of white tucked between two trucks. I can't be sure and sink back into my seat.

Leif returns sooner than I expected, balancing a tray. My coffee, his, my doughnut, and his—maple filled.

"I like this town. The gentleman ahead of me paid for our order."

I search the store.

Along the far wall, sitting alone, is Peter England. He's shed his ball cap. When he catches me staring, as if he knew I'd find him here, he raises his cup in the air.

I fold myself small, shivering as if in reaction to nails on a chalkboard. "Sorry. I thought I saw someone I knew," I lie.

Leif and I drink. He draws me into conversation—even

though Peter England's presence has me all itchy. I can see why my uncle likes Leif. He's friendly and smart and knows food but isn't a food snob. He's been all over the country. And to enough other countries that Florence would be jealous. He's got two nephews, they're five and two, and Leif loves them so hard. It's in the way he talks, the way he pulls out his phone to show me pictures like it's an instinct he can't fight.

Examining the photos, I stealth check the lock screen. It's him and Dom, out in the bush, picking the last of the summer's berries. The sun glitters behind them. And they look . . . so happy.

I'm keeping an eye on Peter England—he's drinking his coffee, reading the paper.

In my bag are three envelopes from Victim Services.

I've memorized the last one:

Dear Ms. Norquay,

This is your final notice.

Upon his release, Peter England will establish residency in Lloyd-minster, Alberta. Your window to lodge a complaint has now closed.

Dom's known since December. Since right before Christmas.

I fall silent. Can't hold up my end of the conversation.

"So, Lou, we can talk like this. It's fine. I won't pressure you. But if you want to discuss your idea, we should." Leif smiles, but not too bright, not too convincingly. He doesn't want to turn out to be the bad guy in this story. "I'm here, in town, and I'm not spending time with your uncle. I'm feeling some guilt."

"The book? Do you want to see it?"

"You have it with you? You said it was Dom's most prized possession."

I reach for my bag with the good fringe, hanging on the back of my chair. "I made a copy."

Leif's eyes squeeze tight, almost closed but not. Lines appear. He's older than he looks. And somehow, that's comforting. He might seem all Hollywood North shiny, but he's a person and he's lived a life and his lock screen is him and my uncle.

"Frankly, I don't know if I should."

"Fair." I release my hold on my bag. "I'll just tell you about it then."

And so I do. It's part recipe book, part book about the land, and about how to care for it, and the things that grow and how they nourish us.

Across the room, Peter England rises from his seat. He approaches as if to leave. Again, every part of me wants to flee—to run—to follow the call of the adrenaline flooding my system. But I don't. I stay exactly where I am, and the world doesn't stop. This town, it's my home too.

Unaware, Leif is nodding along to my speech. Eventually he can't help himself. "Can I see it? Purely as a business thing, not at all as an I'm-your-uncle's-boyfriend thing."

Peter England gets closer, closer. He bypasses the exit.

I pull my bag onto my lap, itching to check my messages for the seven hundredth time since I last actually talked to King. At the shack.

He's not speaking to me. At work, he's *hi* and *bye* and *can you hand me the . . . scoop? that spray bottle?*

He won't even say my name. I want to be sad I ruined our friendship. A second time. But I'm only sad we aren't hanging out.

That he wasn't there snooping through Dom's things with me. Helping me fix this.

My mom is still gone. Even after I stopped texting her, after I moved out of the house.

I miss King with an ache that terrifies me.

Peter England closes in on us, hovering over Leif's shoulder. Leif peers up.

If *he* takes the farm, he takes my family. Without this place, Mom and Maurice and Dom will split again. They'll go back to what they were like before. I have to stop this from happening. Somehow.

"I hope you enjoyed those coffees!" Peter England says.

Leif smiles bright. "We did. Thanks again."

That's it. Peter England leaves, smiling back, contented. All he wanted was to exercise his power. Close up, his teeth aren't as white, as straight, as perfect as they could be.

"I was once a good liar," I say, watching the white SUV pull out of its spot, merge into traffic. "But I'm not anymore. And I can see that you never have been. If you look at this, eventually, you'll have to tell Dom you did, and I recommend sooner, rather than later, if you want to still be Dom's person."

Leif rolls his shoulders back to sit straighter in his chair. "Why isn't he in this meeting?"

"I'm pissed at him right now."

Leif nods and I know he knows.

That stokes a fire. I thought it was gentling. But it's not. Leif Winters, a basic stranger, knows more about my life than I do. And my uncle—Dom, someone I thought was kind of like my friend too—won't tell me the same thing to my face that he's told someone who isn't part of our family.

I want to push my chair away from the table. To scratch against the floor. I want to storm.

But I don't.

This is bigger than whatever's going on. This land is where my ancestors lived once they left the Red River. This is the land where my cows grow. This is the land where I'm sleeping. That rock, it hurts me, but it's part of the land that's been holding me safe at night.

I raise my chin high, swallow my anger, and bite into my doughnut. The sprinkles rile against my teeth. "I'm not happy with him at the moment. But I don't want my family to lose their home, and I don't want my uncle to lose his business."

Leif's eyebrows climb. "The Creamery's a success."

For now.

"That's why we need to do this. The book."

He tidies his hands with a napkin meticulously. "Let me see it. I'll make a few calls and then I'll tell Dom. It'll take a couple days. But I won't allow this to stretch out longer than a week. Fair?"

This time, I savor my sugar. It's the first thing my father has ever bought for me, and it's the last.

CHAPTER 31

August 28

FACT: Ice cream mends broken hearts. It fixes
tummy aches, calms and comforts. It's probably
not something you should eat every day—and listen
up, we're the ice-cream people telling you this. But
ice cream is like medicine. The stuff you get at the
doctor's, what the land offers. Ice cream is powerful.

The moon is sleeping, hidden behind clouds. The stars, they
never had a chance. I'm staring up through the mesh ventila-
tion at what seems like a wide expanse of nothing. Cloud so thick.
Wind pushing the cloud, but never breaking it.

After all this time in the tent, I'm accustomed to the din out
on the road. But when someone turns from the highway onto my
access road, I reach for my Swiss Army knife. It's here, exchanged
when I gave King his sweaty tee back. But the knife isn't tucked
next to my pillow. It's not in the little pocket sewn into the tent.

I fumble in the dark, knowing that if someone is out here, this
late at night, it's either one of my uncles—who I don't want to
see—or Peter England, who, worse, I'm afraid of.

I realize this too late.

I'm afraid of what he'll do to my family. To the people I love.

But I'm afraid of what he'll do to me too. He has power over me. I can't stop thinking about him.

The tent's purple skin is opaque. I can't see anything. The door of a vehicle opens. No squeak. Someone takes care of their ride. Someone is meticulous. Or the SUV is new. So new.

Someone has money. He has white cushions on his porch.

If I were asleep, he'd be sneaking up on me. I'm breathing too loud.

Homer isn't barking. I have no idea if Homer is on this part of the property, or if he's in the house, sleeping on one of the living room couches. I've watched the dogs kill snakes, and once a baby raccoon—and this violence is always horrible, but it's what dogs do. It's instinct.

Even if they were here, the dogs wouldn't be able to stop Peter England.

Footsteps thunder closer and closer. He's not even trying for stealth.

I haven't had reliable access to power lately. My phone battery is dead. I'm kicking myself for being out here alone. And I really am alone. Even with my uncles watching over me, the house is too far off.

I'm alone, except for whoever is out there.

I catch the knife—finally—in my left hand. Grip its red casing. My hands shake too badly to open one of the blades. It's useless.

I can't do violence. Don't want to.

Please. Don't make me.

He clears his throat.

If I scream, will my uncles hear? Maurice will be plugged into his headphones, composing, if he isn't asleep. Dom will be on the phone with Leif, or out in the barn working late, talking to the cows. If I scream, I wonder if my mom will wake—as if from a nightmare, and decide, finally, to come home to me.

I don't know what to do. What I'm going to do.

"Lou, you awake?"

It's King. I melt, release the knife, and swallow. Then I have to hold myself still to stop from gagging. My entire body wants to roll. "You . . . scared me."

"I texted."

"My battery's dead," I say through the tent.

"I needed to see you, to talk with you. And I was sort of hoping you'd want to talk too. And if you didn't—if you don't—I promise I will totally leave . . . I wasn't going to—I shouldn't have come."

He's walking away.

Two options: I can let him go. Or we can talk.

Only one of these things will fix our friendship.

I reach for the zipper. "Get inside before the bugs do."

He bends to unzip the outer cover while I tackle the screen. I'd only closed the outer cover because of the wind. Or I'd have been able to see King from the moment he pulled onto the property. I might never close that flap again. I might never sleep out here again. It's time to return to the farmhouse.

I shift to the far end, using my duffel, filled with mostly dirty clothing, as a backrest. My tent is a two-person. But it's not meant for two people who can't touch each other.

I'm safe. I'm safe, I tell myself while King slips his sneakers off. He climbs inside, zipping the screen behind him. He sits at the head of my bed, far away from me, mirroring my body language. His loose sweatpants are gray. His tee is plain black. His hair is new again, pulled into a puffy bun, the sides trimmed, his edges crisp.

This place is too small. He almost brushes the roof. He's touching both sides. He can't be comfortable.

He's wearing going-to-bed clothes.

So am I.

It's late. After midnight.

"I'm sorry," he says, and drops his head into his hands for a second. "For how I've been acting. You are allowed to feel whatever you feel. And I need to be okay with it. And I'm working on that, being okay. And, well, I want to be your friend, if that's all you want. I've been your friend, and I've not been your friend, and I've been something else, and all I really know for sure, like solidly, is that I don't want to go back to not being your friend. If I have a choice in this matter."

I'm nodding, but I have to say it. "Me too. All of it."

"Good," he says. "That's good."

But he's all serious. He waits for something.

I still want to throw up. My voice is ragged. "You know about . . . my father. You know what happened. The big picture, if not the play-by-play. And I think . . ."

King tosses my pillow at me gently. I hug it. I didn't realize I was shaking.

I can't look at King while I say this. "It's not you. It's not only you. Wyatt was all raging hormones, like all the time. Maybe you don't want to hear this, but—"

"You say what you need to. I'm here to listen. Even if it's about Wyatt and sex."

I nod, but don't look up, worry the corner of my pillowcase. "No matter what we did, what he convinced me or pressured me to do with our bodies, I didn't feel good about it. I . . . I didn't want it."

When I look up, because I have to, King's face is strained. He wants to say something. But still he doesn't.

"No. It wasn't like that. I might not have been enthusiastic, but I sort of consented to what we were doing. Until I didn't and then we broke up." I swing my feet out from under me to hug my knees and the pillow at the same time. Last week, I borrowed Florence's black polish and painted my toenails. Last week, I was trying to distract myself. I chip at the polish, here in the dark, but it won't come off. "The truth is I don't think I want sex. I don't think I *can* want sex. It's my DNA. It wasn't Wyatt. As much as I wish I could blame him, I can't. It's not you, either. It's this part of me that doesn't want to . . . you know . . . keep going."

King says, "Can I ask you something?"

Not trusting my voice, I nod.

"Are you asexual? Like the A in LGBTQIA2S+?"

I've been so stuck on Peter England, and what he could have somehow done to me, like the way you carry trauma from one generation to the next, that I haven't even considered it could be something . . . regular.

Like, maybe I'm perfectly, totally fucking okay enough.

"Maybe?" I get braver. "Yes? I think?"

"So we went about this the wrong way. I assumed things,

which I shouldn't have done." King puts his hands out in front of him, palms facing up. "You know I've kissed guys. Florence's little game made that public news maybe before I wanted it to be. But I should have shared that with you, only with you, before we started . . . dating. I like kissing girls too, obviously. In Toronto, gender isn't a binary—not like they think it is here. And so I'm bi, like Florence. Except not like Florence. She's more fifty-fifty, anyone goes, and I'm like seventy-thirty. I prefer women and people who lean femme. But I find some cis guys attractive. What about you, Lou?"

I open my mouth and close it again fast. I study the tent wall. But really, there's not enough space in here to avoid King's question forever. "Why is this . . . so embarrassing?"

"It's not. It shouldn't be. But if you're feeling it, you're feeling it. Pretend I'm not here?"

"Impossible."

He laughs, big because of how I said it. Because of how I mean it.

"I'm your friend. Can't we talk like we used to do?"

"Okay, okay." I close my eyes. "Don't laugh?"

He sobers. "Promise."

I'm searching for an opening, so I can throw the ball. I'm reaching for the end of the thread, so I can begin untangling the knot. I'm trying to remember what it was like figuring out that of all the things I could study at university, I wanted it to be dinosaur fossils. And that thing, it's Wyatt. It's his country-boy swagger. How he paid so much attention to me. How he didn't ask me out but told me he was picking me up that night to see a movie, in front of everyone in the cafeteria. How when it started, when he focused on me with those blue eyes, I knew he'd do almost anything I asked to spend more time in my company. He wanted me.

"I need to talk about Wyatt again."

King urges me on with a small smile.

"We kissed forty-seven times. Every time, and every single time we did anything else, I was not there. I mean, my body was technically present, but I wasn't into it. At all." I exhale, my heart beating in my temples. But otherwise, I'm okay. I will survive this. "I don't know how many times we kissed, King. Because I wasn't counting."

When I look, he's not smiling. But his shoulders have relaxed. He's not terrified anymore—that he was hurting me.

"Because I liked kissing you. But the rest of me, every time we get too close, the rest of me, the part of me that can think when I'm kissing you, isn't sure about anything else."

I stop talking.

King waits. And then he reaches into his pocket for his phone. "Can I look something up? A friend of mine, back in Toronto, they know the ins and outs of all this stuff. They call themself a kick-ass demi. I think I know what it means, but I want to check."

I nod.

We've been sitting in the dark. But when you're in the dark long enough, your eyes learn how to see. The tent lights up. I'm forced to learn how to look at things all over again.

"There's a lot on here." King scrolls. "And maybe this is something we can't do together, because of, well, the whole three dates thing."

"Don't back out now," I say quickly. "Please."

"Um, okay, nothing with Wyatt ever?"

"Never ever. I was terrified and uncomfortable all the time."

"So being ace—asexual—it's a spectrum. Some people never feel attraction; some do with certain people, like the people they fall in love with—that's Yana, my kick-ass demi friend." King keeps reading. "Some people, they masturbate. Some don't. Some have sex. Some don't. Some . . . have orgasms. Others don't."

My hands clench into fists. It's not until I feel pain that I can articulate it. "But how do I know?"

"I wish I could say." King's hands flutter. "Or that you could just know. But life doesn't work like that."

"How did you figure out you wanted to kiss cis guys?"

He laughs in that nervous way. Smiles, bright. His phone screen dims, fades. "Well, I wanted to."

Now, I'm glad the tent is small.

"I don't know what I want."

The two of us together in the dark. This space is safe.

"You said nothing at all with Wyatt felt good. You didn't want any of it. Own that."

"I didn't want any of it," I say in the way you speak truth with a capital *T.*

"Why?"

The cold breeze from the roof vents flutters in, brushing my cheeks. I've slept without the rain fly all this time, and it hasn't poured once. That's some kind of luck. I still haven't repaired the rip. Haven't even tried. Do I want a downpour? Do I want to suffer?

"I don't think I liked him. At all. He's funny when he's not being an ass. I think I wanted to be the kind of person who could like him."

King swallows.

"I like you," I say fast. "But I don't know if anything comes after kissing for me. And I don't think it's fair to ask you—"

His voice is tight. "But you didn't ask."

He's right. The tent is suddenly too warm. I taste cold on my tongue, but the tent is too, too warm.

"King, you have to tell me if this is outside the line. You're my friend. And I don't want to ruin that, not ever again."

"You didn't," he says.

"I meant when we were young."

"Okay, that you did do. But, Lou, you have to know. I ruined it too. I might have run to my ma's house to escape Kenny Marks, but truth is I stayed to escape you. I didn't have to cut you from my life. You made a mistake, a big one, but you weren't toxic. You can't think that."

I did. I used to. It's hard forgiving yourself, harder than being forgiven. I wonder if King knows this, if he can see it's the same thing with his mom, with what he sees as his betrayal. He needs to forgive himself too. We could get lost here, but if I'm going to take this chance and do it true, I need to keep going. "I like kissing you. A lot."

He smiles, nods, like, *me too*, and his hair, it's so charming like this. Friendly, and aesthetically pleasing.

"So. Because I like kissing you a lot. Would you be okay with trying, real slow—like I'm not asking you to have sex with me, because I don't know if I want to have sex ever, and I want that

315

to be the clearest—but maybe, we could try other things? Like an experiment?"

He stares me down for a long minute. But now it's my turn not to say anything, to let him speak. When he's ready.

Outside, an owl calls.

"You don't ask little things, do you? But yes. Wow. Yeah, let's. You're totally in charge and we . . . Wow—I keep saying that." He stops himself. "Lou, I really like kissing you too."

The tent is small. I push the pillow aside and migrate into his space.

He's letting me touch him. He's not touching me back. I need him to act himself, to be himself. I take his hands and pull them against my shoulders. Then, like my skin is the cure, he's King again. He's gentle and not. He's careful with me and still my blood rushes. We brush the tent with parts of our bodies. We laugh when we do.

This is excellent. This is where me—all of me—is happy.

But always, somehow, I find the line. Eventually, there it is.

I don't exactly think. I push back far enough to pull my shirt over my head and toss it behind me.

"Can I . . . ?"

When I nod, King kisses my neck and down to where my skin meets my bralette. My breathing is already unsteady, but now I'm thinking about it. I'm thinking about if my body's responding, if I want this, if—

"Relax, Lou. I promise I won't do anything you don't want. That means you have to talk to me."

I'm on my knees. He's stopped really touching me. He's pressing his face against my collarbone. Hovering, waiting, on pause.

"Serious question, how do I know if I want it?"

He groans. "Okay, we're not doing this."

He doesn't say it mean. He doesn't push me away or make me feel like I'm teasing him or like I'm wrong because I'm probably very ace.

That's what calms me down. What gets me to try. To find out what kind of ace I am. "King Nathan, honestly, your paying attention makes me feel so much better."

I feel as if I might cry.

Instead, I sink down again and kiss him. I press one of his hands to my chest. He's careful and not at the same time. Soft and not soft. I'm in his lap, almost sitting on him, and I don't let the fact get to my head that eventually I can feel how he wants me.

I pull back a second. Make another decision.

The bralette ends up in the back of the tent too.

"You okay?"

"Yes."

I pull him down onto the sleeping bag. Next to me.

And then I peer down at myself and say, "Well, this isn't fair."

"Life's super unfair, Lou."

We laugh, but King pulls his soft shirt off. We lie on our sides and I spend time exploring him.

"Can I try something?"

"The shorts are staying on," I say.

He kisses my healing shoulder again, traces down my chest,

and I'm not expecting it, not sure I'm not freaked-out, not scared, not everything at the same time, when he starts . . . almost biting me. "Wow."

"Wow, good? Or wow, bad?"

"Honestly? I don't know."

King breathes against my skin. But kisses me a while longer.

When I pull him up until our foreheads are aligned, I smile.

"How do you feel?"

"Weird?" I laugh, all light air, all bubbles. "Good? Happy? You?"

"Good and happy."

Tangled together, somehow, this is how we fall asleep.

CHAPTER 32
August 28

FACT: Ice cream is cold. It's in its nature. And we can't fault things that act exactly as nature intended them to.

"Get up."

I can't place the voice. Not at first. I'm tucked against King. One of his legs is thrown over mine, and his fingers are warm, splayed along my ribs. We're bathed in purple—it's daylight. The voice—"Now! Youse two."—finally registers.

Mom.

My mom is home.

She's outside my tent.

My mom . . . can see us. Like this.

My shirt's lost somewhere by our feet. His too. The sleeping bag is unzipped and thrown across our bottom halves, as if to conceal more nakedness. It looks bad. Very bad.

As soon as he's awake, King pulls away from me. He smashes against the side of the tent with a whoosh and the sleeping bag slides off his legs. His jogging pants are low on his hips, and my mom witnesses all of this too.

She's crouched on the other side of the door, her body turned away slightly, as if to offer us privacy. "Put your clothes on."

King scrambles for my shirt, then his own. We dress in a kind of forced quiet and stumble out of the tent. I slip into my shoes. King stands next to me, his arms hanging by his sides, as if he's waiting for my mom to break us.

She's calmer than I expect, like we're sitting at the kitchen table over Indian tacos and tea. "Where are your condoms? Tell me you two have condoms? And have been using them."

I don't want to look at King. Or at my mom. For entirely different reasons.

I'm still angry at her. No, I haven't stopped being angry with her. Even now, half-asleep, standing in the cold of the morning, my mom trying to shame us, my skin prickles with it. She didn't come home. She left. She left and she didn't return until—

"If you two don't have a box of condoms in that tent, I'm going to—"

"What?" I ask, full of quiet, so she knows I'm serious. "You're going to do what to us?"

King's thumb sweeps the inside of my wrist.

He's right. Pax, for now.

"And you, King Nathan? Nothing to say to me?" my mom asks. She stares him down. It's the piercing auntie stare. The one nobody can ignore.

He shakes his head no, and as he does, his neck falls lower. His thumb quiets on my wrist, until his hand slips away.

She stares him down like she does. It's not enough, his contrition.

When she pays attention to me again, it's to say, "If you get pregnant, at this age, right now, you're going to have a steep uphill struggle, my loves."

My face burns.

If she'd been here this summer, she'd know.

"Go on home, King. Your dad's been calling the house since six, wondering if we've seen you. He's worried. The kind of worry a parent shouldn't ever have to live with."

"I will, ma'am." He doesn't call her Auntie Louisa. King whispers, "Text me? I'm gonna find out how much trouble I'm in."

I can't help myself. I laugh. It's stark, almost ugly, echoing off the Subaru, bleeding into the bank of trees behind me. But it's all mine. "If it's get-sent-to-Toronto kind of trouble, this time, will you at least say goodbye?"

"One hundred percent."

It's my mom. She's standing between King and me. She's trying to cut the threads we've sewn up between each other.

He bends down, gathers his shoes in a hand, and walks to the Subaru on bare feet. He doesn't turn his music up. He executes one of those textbook three-point turns and merges onto the highway, his signal blinking orange.

Once he's gone, my mom sets her eyes on me. "Are you about done with this tantrum, Lou? Do you want to come inside and shower? You've treated your uncles badly."

A truck passes on the road—roaring. I want to rewind to when this was a field covered in darkness, when an owl called and King and I listened.

My mom interrupts. "We should have a talk. Now that I'm home."

I don't know why I don't tell her King and I didn't have sex.

Maybe it's because, in a way, I think we did.

Maybe sex is bigger, too, than what I originally imagined.

All I say is, "Yeah, now that you've bothered."

Her hair is longer. Mine is too. It's been months since we've seen each other on anything but a screen. In front of me, she's more real now. We walk in silence. Inside, she brews tea while I shower. The water running over me burns in that good way. My body is still my own. Nothing's changed at all. I'm not different than I was last night. But little bruises on my skin, from King's teeth, his mouth, are here when they weren't yesterday.

That's something. I don't know what to name it yet.

In the basement, I dress in clothes I haven't worn since the weather turned. A long-sleeve top to hide the marks and a pair of black leggings. It's almost time to store my skirts and dresses for another year. Almost cold enough to hibernate.

When I step into the kitchen, my mom's in her chair, drinking her tea in her mug. Like she never left. My dinosaur mug waits on the table for me. I've missed it. I've missed sitting in this room, surrounded by my family. I've missed the pool, a hard workout, early mornings on Dom's computer checking my blogs for exciting discoveries, seeking that pure wonder my mom unlocked inside me when she brought *The Land before Time* home. All the pieces of my life that have gotten sidetracked this summer.

At first, while I navigate the kitchen, plugging my phone into its charger, pouring myself a glass of iced tea and cutting the last lemon in the fridge into slices, she doesn't say anything. I hold my mug in both hands, like it's hot, like it's warming me, and lean against the counter.

It's not fair I've missed her so much.

"Sit," she says.

It's a command.

"Please," she says.

She softens and so do I.

I slump into Maurice's chair, across from her. I can't bear being too close. And my chair, the one I made mine the day we moved into this house, since we returned here, is right next to hers.

She begins talking in a low, deep-down voice: "There are things I've told you. Things you know. There are things I never wanted to tell you. Things you don't know. In the hospital, the doctor offered me a pill, four doses. It was ninety-three percent effective, he told me, in preventing a pregnancy." My mom sips her tea. "I didn't think about how the newspaper, the rest of the world, would see it. I wanted my body to be mine again. I wanted . . . *him* . . . to burn in Jesus's hell. I wanted sleep."

She knows. Somehow, she knows. I steady my hand, clutch my dinosaur mug harder.

Outside the wind picks up again. The screens rattle and dust carries up into the air.

It appears it might rain.

Finally. The first time since the tornado.

"That's the abortion he used to talk about in the papers. It was no termination. It was four birth control pills, prescribed to prevent pregnancy, an early version of the morning-after pill. I was

323

sixteen, a girl who didn't know . . . anything. And it was not meant to be, because here you are. And I'm thankful every day you are in my life. Even when you're acting the typical teenager—snagging that boyfriend of yours in a camping tent in what amounts to the backyard of your family home."

What she's telling me, it's warm and without jagged edges. But I can't let it go. Can't let it be. "But why didn't you tell me?"

"I couldn't!"

"He owns the land the shack sits on. What else does he own? How much of me is him? Exactly how much?"

We're yelling at each other now. Over our tea. At our kitchen table. This sucks all the fire out of me.

Out of Mom too.

There's been too much anger here lately. This table isn't meant for anger. This land isn't breathing for us to tear into each other with anger.

It's bad.

Bad energy.

"Lou, do you really want to know all of it? You can't unknow it once you know."

I don't think. "Tell me."

She freshens her tea. "His family has money. They own the land. And they have interests in pipelines, like the rich around here do. And they tried to use their money to stop me from getting 'another abortion,' as they called it. How they found out about the birth control pills, I don't know. But they did. And they used it against me."

I'm staring at my dinosaur mug, at the door, at anything but my mom's face while she talks. But her gaze settles on me. She doesn't look away. If she's going to say this, she needs to be looking at me while she does.

"This town," she says. "By the time his family realized he'd probably serve time, that the community was angry he'd hospitalized a sixteen-year-old girl, even a Native one, they started offering me things. To quiet me. To buy me. As if to demonstrate some . . . restitution before sentencing."

"The land."

"It's yours, Lou."

"It's *his*."

"It's supposed to be yours. Your land. Where you can build a house and a life. Maybe trap like we used to do. Buy one of those big aboveground pools and let your kids swim around during our too-short summers. To put in trust, to return it to the hands of its caretakers, or even gift it to the Friendship Center for that language camp they want to build. Whatever you wanted. Forty-seven acres, from the highway and up."

"That's not what the survey says."

"It's in multiple parcels. The land transfer happens after you turn nineteen. Then it's yours, only yours." She sighs. "Lou, baby, what matters to me, to your uncles . . . Are you okay?"

I can't tell what she's asking after. King and last night. This whole summer without her. Peter England and the way, slowly, he's unmade my family by twisting the truth until it tarnished.

"I'm fine," I say, but my voice wavers.

She rises from her chair. Settling behind me, she rests her head on mine. My mom wraps her arms around me. It's awkward, with the chair between us, but this is everything I've been missing. The scent of tanned moosehide from her earrings and her floral shampoo. Her touch. My mom.

"I'll deal with your uncles later. For keeping this from me. It's not something you want to find out by text after your one and only child decides to give you the silent treatment. That your abuser has been released from prison. Lou, why didn't you tell me when you first knew he was back? Has he been . . . Is he hurting you?" She's not angry. She's not unaffected either.

"He is, yes. But I needed to protect you. I wanted to protect us all from him."

Her grip tightens. "Don't you know that goes both ways? We protect each other. That's how it should be."

I let myself cry.

That's when Maurice and Dom tiptoe into the kitchen.

Mom just turns to them and says, "Youse two, sit down."

She's been hanging out with aunties all summer. It's in the way she talks, the way she's looking at all of us—her family—right now.

Her brothers do exactly as she's asked.

"What's been going on, my loves?" my mom asks.

Dom is in my chair. Maurice is in Dom's. Things are topsy-turvy. We're out of balance. We're out of control.

"Who's going to start?"

At first it's none of us, and then it's all of us at once.

Me: "He's threatening to take the farm, the shack, all of it, unless I amend my birth certificate, add his name. Unless I become his daughter."

Dom: "My Food Network boyfriend has gotten me a lightning-fast book deal."

Maurice: "I'm moving to Edmonton."

Mom sits down. Sits right down in her chair and she says, "I caught King and Lou here having relations out in that tent of hers."

My cheeks are hot, so hot, a burning I can't blame on the weather. "Mom!"

She shrugs. "You still live in this house, even if you sleep outside."

Dom laughs but when I glare at him, stops, and has the decency to at least pretend to look guilty. Leif told me he would tell Dom about the book. Underneath it all, my burning cheeks and the little part of me that hoped Leif would tell me first, it's right he did it this way.

Maurice's news, it's old. He's been wanting to do this since Mom and I moved in. But I'm glad too, that Maurice is pursuing what he wants.

"Who's threatening to take the farm?" Dom asks finally. "Do they know how expensive this place is to run?"

Maurice chokes on his laughter.

"Her father," my mom says without humor. "He's out of his prison cell, has been all damn summer. That should not be a thing I learned by text, Dominic."

Maurice and I shift from staring at Mom to her little brother and back again.

"Nimish," Dom says immediately, looking at my mom. He shifts, catching my eyes with his. "And Lou, I don't know why I didn't inform you, both of you, right away."

"Is it considered a lie when you hide the truth? Yes or no?" I ask. "I've been puzzling over this for weeks."

Dom leans back in the chair. He runs his hands through his hair and then sinks forward again. "It was hurting you both so much, being back here, and I wanted you to be happy, and I thought—"

"It worked," my mom says. "I trusted you to handle the official correspondence. I didn't want to have to deal with him. At all. And that was my fault, Dominic. For not facing it."

"You look good," Maurice says to my mom, and she smiles.

Her skin is lightly browned and warm. She's wearing new earrings and she's still in a way I haven't seen her almost ever. Still at heart.

"A book deal, eh?" I say.

"Don't pretend you know nothing about this," Dom chides. "Secret meetings with my boyfriend? Stealing my recipe book?"

I ignore him. "What does Molly think about your moving, Maurice?"

He smiles too, a gesture almost alien to his face. "She's practically a teenager. She's thrilled but trying to hide it."

"And your ex?" Dom asks.

"Lisa's thrilled too."

I raise my eyebrows. Dom's spike as well.

Maurice says nothing else.

And Mom just laughs. Big and bubbling and full, and at the same time, still. She's been gone. She needed to be gone.

She's home and now she's changed.

"One thing I'm still wondering over," she says. "Where are all the mugs? Did a bunch of aunties raid our kitchen?"

Maurice points at me. "This one, she donated them."

"She said we had too many and some people have none," Dom adds.

Mom stares at me, but she's talking to her brothers. "Well, what are we going to do when her boyfriend comes over?"

The three of them laugh. I don't get what's so funny. "I left four extras, for guests."

And my family, they only laugh louder. Mom brews tea for the table, telling stories of her summer and moving around the kitchen like she never left, and this time, I drink mine hot. We're talking, and we're comfortable, and we're family the way we've always been, but now, we're doing it better than we have for the last few months, maybe for years, with the words spoken, the truths in the open.

Outside, the rain starts. My tent, my sleeping bag, will be soaked. It'll be quiet at work, but we don't close because it rains. And here, on the prairies, this should be over soon. We're big thunder and hard rain, but we don't typically brood in it. I check my phone. I have to go. I don't want to, but I have to. I push my chair back and just say, "It's that time."

Dom nods at me, and my mom waves her hand, like, get out of here, you.

And Maurice says, "Have fun."

But Dom stops me. "Wait. Don't leave yet, yaence. I have an idea. Before the summer's over, what do we think about thanking the community? Hosting a party, here?"

"It's a good idea," I say.

Mom agrees and Maurice offers a hearty "why not."

"Okay, okay." Dom stands. "I'll handle the details."

In the mudroom, as I'm pulling on my rain boots, Mom approaches. "And Lou, listen to me now. Listen well. Let me take care of your father."

She says it like she's said this a hundred times, like he didn't spend most of my life in prison, like he's just another person.

And maybe he is.

Florence and Elise sit on the prep counter, painting each other's nails. "Oh, let me do yours next!" Florence squeals when she sees me. She's only brought the sunny colors today.

We sit and laugh, interrupted a couple of times by customers willing to brave the rain. Lightning strikes and thunder rolls and we three guard over the shack like it's precious until it starts to get dark.

This is the first day in weeks we haven't sold out.

"When do you leave?" I ask Florence later, after Elise has gone. It's ten p.m. and my uncles wouldn't say a thing if we closed early, not today, but we don't want to go home yet. We haven't been alone with each other, it seems, all summer.

"My ticket to lovely, rainy Ireland is booked for September sixth. The weather's greeting me early, I see."

"So soon."

"Terribly. But you know I'm coming back. When it's all said and done. This is my home too. You're my home, Lou."

"And you're mine." I press my newly pink nails against the

countertop, to steady myself. I don't want to ruin this moment—push her away before she has to leave me. "But who will take care of you while you're gone?"

Florence's eyes get wet. "Why, you, silly. And King will. And Elise. And my beautiful, wonderful girlfriend must. And my parents, of course, as it's literally their job."

"That's not enough people."

"And," she says, laying her hand over mine. "I will too, promise."

It's not enough. It has to be enough. I wipe my nose on my long sleeves.

"That's an awfully covered-up look," she says, with her regular sharpness.

"It's none of your business."

That's when a green Subaru pulls into the parking lot.

Florence smiles. "Oh, I sincerely hope you've decided you're dating proper now."

"It's a long story. Later?"

"Of course. But don't blow me off."

"I won't."

"I'll even answer the actual phone," she says.

We watch him like we did the first day we saw him, here, together. His jeans are dark, and his button-up top has a handful too many buttons undone. At first it looks perfectly polished. Until I notice the buttons are misaligned.

He climbs into the shack and stands next to me, and like we do this every day, like this is normal, grabs my hand. His palm is dry but he's shaking. I hold on tight.

"What's wrong?" Florence asks.

King sinks to the floor of the shack and I follow him. I don't let go.

Florence crouches down, and then, drops too. "I don't often sit on the ground," she says. "You may notice I prefer perches. But if this is what we're doing, we're doing it together."

"King?"

He steadies. "We need a real lawyer. My dad agrees. Sorry, Florence."

Florence's eyebrows crease. "What did that miserable man do now? And why am I always the last to know? This could get to a woman's ego, you know? This could do permanent harm. Finding out last every time."

"King?" I ask again.

"He was inside my house. On my couch. In my living room. Your father."

Florence gasps.

I grip King's hand. Harder.

"He was drinking one of my dad's Trini beers. In a glass, from our cupboard. He said he'd been waiting. That keeping him waiting was rude. He didn't threaten me. He was polite, even. Used a coaster, and nobody in my house has used a coaster since my ma left. He asked after her—my ma." King swallows.

I reach up, finding my water bottle by touch alone, and pass it to him.

He drinks.

"Are you okay? Is Dr. Nathan okay?" I ask.

"Yes. Your father left. He didn't break anything or hurt me. He said something I can't forget, can't let go of, and he left this for you, Lou." King hands me another letter. "He insisted I deliver it. Directly. That it was imperative I handed this to you myself. He knew I'd do it because I care about you. That's what he said."

Florence puts a hand on King's shoulder. "Oh, that's entirely too much."

I'm holding on to part of the story. The part that hurt King more than the home invasion. "What can't you forget? What is it?"

"Open the letter," King says.

"No, this is more important."

"She's right," Florence says. "Heaven knows you won't let us carry anything alone, King. Now's our turn to hold on to your shite."

King laughs—but it's humorless.

He's not ready to see what Florence has, what I have, that he's always taking care of the people around him, that he needs care too.

"Did you know your father, Lou, he was in the same prison as my ma's old boss?"

"Fill me in," Florence says.

"O'Reilly."

"Oh." She falls silent. She knows enough of the town gossip to know enough, even if she doesn't know it all.

"They shared a cell block. They played ball together in the yard. Fast friends, that's what your father claims. He said O'Reilly often talked about Aliya." King chokes. "My baby sister."

"You can't trust him," I say. "You can't trust a thing he says. He shifts the truth. He bends it. There's only a hint of what's real in his words. Only a small, small part."

"I'm desperate to believe that," King says.

"What about your sister? Exactly?" Florence asks.

"My dad's not her dad. We've always known that. But my ma never could tell us. She still won't. That's partly why Aliya's in foster care—because my sister doesn't have a father, and my ma wasn't suitable, not without my dad helping out." King's face crumples. "He didn't say it. Not exactly. But he implied O'Reilly—"

"He lies."

"But now I can't get the possibility from my head. And what do I do? Do I tell my dad? Do I tell Aliya?"

"He lies," I say again, more forcefully. "It's a lie."

Florence is so quiet.

"What if it isn't?" King asks.

"Talk to your mom," I say. "I—I wish I'd asked mine . . . sooner."

King sighs. Since from what I know, his mom still won't talk to him, even if he wanted to, he can't get that kind of relief. I ache for him.

Sitting next to my two best friends, I rip through the seal on the letter.

THE LAST LETTER

Dear Daughter,

Attached to this document, which I've asked the boy to deliver directly into your hands, is what I'm offering. It's drawn up and ready for you. It's a small thing, my name on your birth certificate, such a small thing to give—but important to the future.

I believe it's a fair exchange. And once we've made it, I can accept this is all you'll offer. I swear it. I regret my previous comments about your family's businesses. I regret how this small thing drives me to express my desires in unsuitable ways.

I anticipate your response. Once we've legally arranged the amendment, the money is yours. But this must conclude soon. It's critical.

Your father

CHAPTER 33
August 29

Note scribbled in the margins of Dom's recipe
book: Sometimes you need to do it yourself.

Neither Florence nor King wants to leave me, but eventually they do. I lie—promising I'll go straight home, and tomorrow we'll speak to a lawyer. And I don't feel even a little bad about it.

I should.

But I can't.

Behind the letter, I find a photocopy of four bank drafts. Each for twenty thousand dollars. Made out to me. It's enough for four years of university. Room and board and books and fees, even inflation. Everything.

It's quarter past twelve. The liquor store in the hotel with the expensive steakhouse is open until two a.m. That's something I learned back when I was running around with Tyler, when I was reckless.

Tonight, the air is bitter and cold. The ground is wet. Overfull.

My heart is heavy.

Eighty thousand dollars. For his name. It doesn't make sense.

It's not a fair exchange. Not something that a man like Peter England would do simply to write his name on a government document. The money's not without strings. And it's the strings that don't add up.

The wind whips debris from the fields across the highway. As I reach town, the speed limit drops, and I slow sharply. Some lessons I've learned proper and well. Some fires are necessary.

When I walk into the liquor store, the bell at the door rings. The lights are too bright, too sterile. Everything is bathed in yellow, except at the back of the store where one of the fluorescents buzzes and flickers. The clerk glances up from his book and nods his chin at me.

He doesn't know me. And I don't know him.

But he recognizes me. It's not the earrings—it's something else. Can he smell my smoke too? Am I suffused with it?

His hair is in two skinny braids. "Searching for something?"

I'm old enough. I have been since my birthday in April. I'm thinking about a white SUV with vanity plates, and how much more I'd like it if it were on fire. "What's the most flammable shit you have?"

He laughs, deep and long. I notice the sharpness of his canines in his wide smile. "One of those nights, eh?"

I like him. I smile back.

He maneuvers through the aisles. When he suddenly stops, he squats down. He hands me a bottle of overproof rum. "This'll burn awhile."

"I'll take it."

"As long as you got the money, cuz," he says, and laughs again.

I don't have a choice. Not anymore.

Peter England walked into Dr. Nathan's house—and he said the worst possible thing, the thing that would destabilize one of the kindest people I know. And he called King "boy," over and over again. Like King doesn't deserve a name, respect, basic fucking human decency.

If I don't stop this, who's next: Florence? Tyler and Cami? Elise? Even if my mom is acting all tough—it's my job to protect her as much as it's hers to protect me. She told me that. But I should have seen it long ago. We hold each other—we ground each other. That's kinship, that's community, that's love.

Brown paper bag in hand, I climb back into my truck and head out to the England farmstead. I shouldn't be this girl, shouldn't sink into the smoke. But this is what I need.

I've spent too long being ashamed of what Tyler and I did. I stopped talking to Ty because I couldn't stand the way bile bubbled into my throat when we hung out after the fire, after the police stopped looking for who did it.

I'm not ashamed anymore.

When I see what's left of the farmhouse the tornado destroyed, I throw my turn signal on. It ticks steadily, another drumbeat to follow. I pull into the England driveway, park a way back from the white SUV, and, staring at it, at the sad declaration FREED, it's like somehow I'm clear. Clearer than I've ever been. I don't need to burn anything. I don't need to ruin his vehicle or take something from him. When I walk up to the door, I leave the rum behind. The fire is content inside me.

I'll empty the bottle later, with Florence and King and Elise — and I'll invite Tyler. Try to mend what I've run from, to build a healthy fire. We'll sit together and while we sit, we'll talk. Maybe we'll talk about this.

On the porch, the smoke surrounds me, warms me like comfort. As I'm about to ring the doorbell, I curl into the smoke for a moment. It would feel so good to let things go to flame. It's a tiny pause, a moment of hesitation.

There aren't any lights on, and maybe my first instinct, setting his car on fire and tearing out of the drive before he wakes, is the best one. Only it's King that stops me from backtracking. He was in King's home, in Dr. Nathan's living room, and no one's safe until I end this. I ring the bell.

Inside, voices, a bit alarmed, pick up. A man and a woman. Shuffling down the hallway.

Peter England opens the big wooden door. He's not dressed for the day, and this way, with a ratty blue robe over his shoulders, he appears older. Worn-out and tired and not the kind of strong I've been faced with all these weeks. He wants to think he has power. To prove to himself he does. When he doesn't have any. It's all posturing, all window dressing: the SUV, the cushions on his porch furniture, this house.

"What is it?" the woman asks, and immediately Peter England says, "Go off now. This isn't your business."

She mutters something, backs away. It's the blond from the shack. Without makeup, her eyebrows aren't as sharply defined. She looks older too, tired. My shoulders relax.

These two, they're only people.

Peter England clears his throat. "Do you want to come inside, Louisa?"

"No."

In the background, the woman stares at me, her eyes narrowing.

He steps out onto the porch but doesn't close the door. "I've been waiting—"

"You're misunderstanding what this is. This is me talking at you, not you talking at me."

He laughs but doesn't try to deliver whatever line he'd been about to drop, all bad-movie-script tough—full of loud, empty threats.

"I don't belong to you." I'm saying each word slow and careful, so he hears me. "You have nothing I want or need. What you're doing, threatening me, my family, my friends, it stops now."

"Louisa—"

"No." I tear the photocopies of all that money into pieces. I drop them on his porch, where they rest between us.

And that's it. I've said it. I turn away from this man, in his worn-out blue housecoat, turn away from those too-white-even-in-the-dark cushions on his matching furniture, and walk off his porch. I drive away. He stands there watching me, but I don't care.

Finally, I don't care.

CHAPTER 34
August 31

FACT: This book is here to help you, because you can
make ice cream alone. But sometimes . . . when it's all
wrong, when things won't come together or your flavor
is off or you know there's not enough salt? Sometimes,
you need a little help. Check out our FAQs, and if those
don't solve your problem, we're online, ready and willing
to lend a hand. After all, ice cream is our family business.

It should be embarrassing welcoming King and Dr. Nathan into
the farmhouse kitchen—after all the kissing and after what
Peter England's done to them. What I've done to them. Though
I haven't told Dr. Nathan about my part in O'Reilly's yet, I know
he'll forgive me.

He's said nothing about the whole his-son-sleeping-in-my-tent
thing, even after my mom had the nerve to recount the whole
story to him on the phone—while I sat in the kitchen, forced to
listen. But he does, quietly, ask me why we didn't come to him
with our problem. He's a good man.

"I wish I had," I say, leading them into the house.

If it was only this easy, inviting one of Dom's buddies—a
lawyer—to the farm, and filling out some forms, maybe I'd have

told my family sooner. But we're not kidding ourselves.

It won't be easy.

Mom and Maurice are drawing other chairs from around the house into the kitchen while Dom brews tea. I'm worried about mugs, if we have enough. I don't regret donating them, but I know we're going to run out today, if everyone shows.

But King is doing his best not to let me worry. He grabs my hand, and Florence, not to be outdone, claims the other. Sitting on the floor, petting the dogs, Elise watches me with careful eyes. I told her she didn't need to come, but she insisted, showing up early with two boxes of doughnuts.

It should be embarrassing, having all these people here. For this reason.

But it isn't.

They're my family. Every one of them.

And together, we're going to stop Peter England from making himself a part of my life. He doesn't get to decide that. Only I do.

Sometimes you need one person—and sometimes you need all your people with you.

Earlier, Dom briefed his lawyer on the phone. The lawyer's the second-to-last person to arrive. He's short and bald, dressed in the nicest suit I've ever seen.

"This is a family meeting," Dom says, standing by the fridge. "Giles is here to offer advice on the legal issues."

"Shall we start?" Giles asks, accepting a mug with thanks. "We're applying for a restraining order as a first step. It should be easy enough to convince a judge that the no-contact order should be reinstated in your—in Lou's—case."

342

I'm still hoping Tyler will show. That she'll want to mend our friendship, that she'll forgive me for running from her. That she'll be here with us all, that later, my friends and I can drink almost-revenge rum on the porch.

"He's not getting anywhere near our Louie ever again," Florence says like she'll claw the eyes out of anyone who might try to hurt me—even from thousands of kilometers away. And she'd do it. Somehow.

"We're applying for another order to do the same for Mr. King Nathan, is that right?" Giles asks.

My mom nods.

"Is that enough to keep them safe?" Dr. Nathan asks. "That man was in our home." His hand is out of the cast now, but the angry lines from where the surgeon cut are raised, thick scars.

My mom shakes her head.

A court appearance will happen later. Since we have to file in Edmonton anyway, it won't interrupt my schooling. None of us think—not even the lawyer—that this will stop Peter England. This is only the beginning.

Through the kitchen window, a plume of dust rises up behind Tyler's old two-door beast. She parks, steps out of her car, and stands there a minute.

Looking out the kitchen window, I smile.

"What does the man want?" Dr. Nathan asks, refusing to call Peter England my father.

"For Lou to amend her birth certificate. To add his name on the file," my mom says.

"And that would invigorate his legal claim to the joint lands if something were to happen to you, Lou," the lawyer says. "His family had a land survey done in the nineties. It's on file. But a lot of those surveys from the nineties weren't precise enough to discover deep oil. It could be this request is to prime another action, that he intends to claim the land solely as his. I shouldn't be saying anything, but there's been some talk—among my colleagues—about England planning a development on the land. Nothing solid. But he's asking questions in the right places, making friendly with operations that conduct seismic mapping."

If something were to happen to you . . .

In the room, the mood drops. We're silent, processing.

The lawyer shrugs out of his navy suit jacket, hanging it off the back of his chair. He knows my mom's history. "You mentioned there's been a threat? Against your business? But no direct threats against Lou and King themselves?"

Dom pushes the letters I still have across the table, letters the whole family has read now. They know everything. What I've been hiding. And they still love me.

Outside, Tyler lights a cigarette.

"I'll be right back." I pull away from King, from Florence. I step out onto the porch with bare feet. "You shouldn't smoke those," I say, climbing down the stairs. When I get close enough, I extend a hand.

Tyler passes me the menthol cigarette. These were banned here ages ago, yet Ty always has a pack. The taste is . . . gross. Somehow, it's what I need in this moment.

To draw us back into orbit.

"I hear once this show is over, you're headed to university?"

"Edmonton's not that far." I pass the cigarette back.

"It's far enough," Tyler says, resigned.

This smoke, it's not the same as the kind I know so well. This is human-made. It will dissolve into the air, won't follow me around. "You could go, you know? To school?"

"Who? Me?" Tyler's laugh is bitter, unconvinced.

She can't see herself like I do. She can't reflect her own light. "Someone once told me that we get to keep growing. That 'badass Native auntie' doesn't always fit everyone and might not fit forever. Maybe 'badass Nehiyaw university student auntie' is next."

"What I have is right for now." She crushes the smoke under her boot. "At least until Cami graduates. This is what she needs."

"But what do you need?"

"I need it too, Lou—promise." Tyler falls quiet, pensive. Eventually, she juts her chin at the house. "Should we join your party?"

"Unless you want to ditch?"

Tyler laughs, a real one this time. "I didn't drive all the way out here not to witness this."

We leave our smoke outside. When we step into the kitchen, Dom smiles brightly at Ty, and my mom pours her tea in a canning jar. Even Florence stands to offer Ty a chair.

The conversation restarts.

"What alternatives do we have?" Dom asks.

"Dominic, you're a friend. I'll tell it to you straight. You have two options—and we can follow them both. Or not. To start, we'll go ahead with filing restraining orders—those will be pieces of paper that say England must not contact your niece or Mr. King Nathan, or come within a certain distance of them, plus the enforcement of the law if England disobeys."

"And the other option?" Dom asks.

The lawyer holds his pen up in the air, like a sword. "You won't like it."

"It's the police, Dominic," my mother says. "We bring a criminal case against him."

The lawyer nods.

No one speaks.

"Henry Reina would listen." I pull my cardigan more tightly around my body. "I think."

"That the police you were dating before the television star?" my mom asks her brother.

Florence laughs. "I adore your family. They're significantly more interesting than mine."

"He helped me out," I add.

The lawyer nods, looking at Dom. "I like the man. And haven't heard anything untoward about him either. But this is your choice."

"No," my mom says. "It's theirs."

Everyone is waiting for King and me to say something. We glance at each other. He smiles. I erupt into motion, dragging King through the crowded kitchen, down the stairs, and across the basement into my bedroom. I don't start talking until the door closes behind us. "Do you want to involve the police?"

"I don't." King shakes his head. "Do you?"

"Honestly, I don't know." I sit on the edge of my bed.

King laughs, sitting next to me. "Well, we've figured out how to get clearer answers, haven't we?"

"You want to make out right now?"

"Always."

I grin.

He's wearing another button-up shirt. But this one's buttoned all the way right. "What if we file a harassment case against him? What happens next?"

"The same thing that happened to my mom. Peter England will dig into our pasts and he'll try to find something that hurts enough to force us to stop."

"What will they find, Lou?"

He's asking me what else I'm holding on to. What else I've been keeping to myself, all the other things I've lied about. "On me?"

King nods. "I know what they're going to dig up on my end. Underage drug stuff, if they talk to the right people, but I'll bet the right people won't talk to them, and a murky, almost-kidnapping that got kept real quiet."

I think. Really do. There's nothing left, nothing King doesn't already know. "Those Molotov cocktails, I told you about."

"You are so tough. So—"

"Don't say cute."

"Cute."

I roll my eyes, but I'm loving it. "You should know, I've recently decided it was a onetime thing, my brief love affair with arson."

King pulls me close and hugs me. "I really, really fucking like you, Lou."

"Same," I say because it's the most I can manage. "So that's what they're going to find. Underage arsonist with a history of major property damage."

347

"Yeah, but arson isn't a summary offense. It's indictable and there's no statute of limitations for those. You and Tyler could go to prison for a really long time."

"Wow, you paid attention in grade-twelve law."

"No, I pay attention to Florence. She's addicted to true-crime stuff."

"And *Drag Race*," I say.

"Florence has most . . . excellent taste."

It's funny. We both laugh.

But we sober up quick.

King asks, "So what do we do?"

"Maybe he won't find our secrets?"

"We have to assume he will."

"What if," I ask, "what if I do what he wants? What if I do this little thing, and then we hope he goes away. The money could do so much for me, for my family. All I have to do is claim him, in the eyes of the government. On a document."

"You heard them upstairs. Once you do that, what stops that man from hurting you? He killed a fellow inmate in prison. Over a minor disagreement. The lawyer confirmed that story when you were outside with Ty."

I lean against his shoulder. I want to stay here, sit here, like this for a long time.

"Money's not worth your life, Lou."

"Not at all. Not ever."

King sighs. It's content. "Our families are waiting."

"We're hiding in my bedroom, eh?"

"I mean, I'm not complaining."

Upstairs, chairs shift, and the kettle's whistling again. There's time. Nothing's going to happen without us. I lean over and, because I can, I draw King—my friend—into a kiss.

When we break apart, he laughs. "Cigarettes, Lou?"

"It was a bonding moment," I offer. "Another one of those one-time things."

"I trust you." King kisses me again.

It's sweet. It's what we deserve. But we have to go upstairs and we have to finish this. Later, I'll draw Dr. Nathan aside, and I'll tell him what I can about the night O'Reilly's burned to the ground. I owe this to him. This truth has been a long time coming.

CHAPTER 35
September 4

FACT: Making ice cream isn't as hard as everyone thinks. Ice cream is about good ingredients, happy cows who live on the land, being free enough to be creative and to take a few risks, and it's about family. That's it. But that's a lot. We're proud to share our family with yours.

The farm is frenetic. It's been raining, but Leif sent along a big red-and-white tent. We've cleaned out one of the barns. Elise is opening the production studio so we can enjoy the last of this season's ice cream before we unplug the freezers for another year.

There isn't much.

But there will be enough.

Maurice tunes his fiddle on the porch.

Leif and Dom are somewhere. Maybe even up in the hayloft.

The invitations say to show up by six p.m., and so far, it's quiet on the road. We don't do balloons because they kill birds, but we've got proper signs down at the major turns to make sure everyone can find us. We've invited the whole town, all of Alberta and Saskatchewan, and cousins Maurice has tracked down from across the prairies.

"Stop worrying," my mom says, coming up behind me. "They'll

show. We've got food and drink and Dom's weird ice cream."

"And music," Maurice offers.

"That too," she adds, leaning close to me. "To tell the Métis from the others tonight, watch the dancing. Our relations won't stop until Maurice breaks all his strings. After, they might carry on, dance without music."

She never used to talk like this, openly. It's nice. It's right.

King and Florence are at the shack. It's the last day of the season. They're supposed to close the doors exactly at six. We'll clean up tomorrow when we shut everything down.

After that, I'm due at university. A dorm room awaits. I have to buy books and find where I'll have my lectures. I'm pushing it close. Blowing off orientation for a few more days at home. Water polo tryouts are the weekend after next. I'm not sure I have what it takes for the competitive team—but I'll show up and give it. I have so many goodbyes to say before I leave. But for now, for now, I have a party to host.

As vehicles start to arrive, the music begins. I'm welcoming community members, Food Network people Leif invited, and I'm waiting. I don't really know what for.

Something good, maybe. Something bad, could be, too. Something balanced in the middle.

King and Florence arrive laughing.

Florence hugs me before breaking off to find her parents. "We need a lake afternoon. Can we have one? You and me, tomorrow? I'll plan all the specifics."

I nod. After we shut down the shack, it's a tradition. "Rain or shine."

King walks up to me slowly, his hair in the same gorgeous man bun. "Are you afraid your father will . . . ?"

"Are you?"

"Naw," he says. "I'm only afraid of your ma. My dad had that horror-story call on speakerphone. I couldn't not listen."

"It was so awkward." I smile up at him. "You should kiss me now."

And he does. On my family farm, and again, like the first time, and every time since, sparks draw up gooseflesh on my arms, and dance along my neck.

"It's selfish," I say, looking over at the party. Grown-ups and kids, they're smiling, talking to each other, laughing.

King stares at me like he can't stop, and I let that push me forward, to say the thing. "It's selfish, but I want to keep dating you."

"Why's that selfish?" he asks.

"Don't try to make me feel better."

"I'm not."

"Good."

"Answer the question."

"Because I might never want to do anything but kiss you. And even if one day I want to, it'll take time. Probably a lot of it. And we don't have enough."

"I'm not afraid of that." King holds a hand out toward me, palm up.

I curl my fingers around his.

"Lou," he says. "I want to put in time with you. Whatever that means."

It's enough, just enough that I know what he's saying without him saying it. But he says it anyway, and that's why he's one of my best friends. "I like waking up next to you—just waking up next to you. But maybe we can work it so your ma isn't our alarm clock, though, please and thanks?"

I break into laughter.

It was horrible.

It was exactly too much.

The whole summer. It's been exactly too much. And exactly enough too. Florence and Elise and King, they've been my people. If Tyler wants it, I'm ready for her to be my person again too.

We stay in the field, welcoming those we know, and those we don't—this old man who swears he knew Nouhkom when she was my age, and I look exactly like her. He promises to email me the photo.

Wyatt's Range Rover rolls up without his characteristic speed.

"Do you need moral support?" King asks after Wyatt's music goes quiet.

"Can you get me something to drink? If Wyatt and I talk alone, it's better, I think."

King trusts me, takes off for the red-and-white tent.

My ex's jeans are low on his hips, his hands buried deep in his pockets. His head is low too. "Lou," he says when he sees me.

"Wyatt."

I'm not going to be mean. But I'm not going to make this easy. He doesn't deserve easy. But he doesn't deserve to be excommunicated either. Not yet.

"I thought I should be here. Since, you know, I'm part of this."

I snort. It's super loud and totally in line with what he deserves.

"I *was* part of this," he corrects himself. When he looks up from his feet, he gives me that classic country-swagger smile, and though I'm immune to his kisses, I'm not immune to his charm. "I've been a jerk."

My eyebrows spike.

"Okay, worse. I've been friends with people who haven't changed since the second grade and whose parents are . . . racist, and so they laugh about that kind of stuff, and then they have a few brews and they become their parents. And then folks get hurt. Folks I like."

"Is that what you came here to say?" I ask, thinking of all the times he didn't listen to me. All the times he pushed me. Of that one time he refused to stop his Range Rover so I could disembark safely.

"Pretty much."

"Okay."

"Okay what?" he asks, almost hopeful.

"Okay, you said it."

"Lou!"

"You didn't ask me to forgive you."

His shoulders sink lower. "I asked Cami. And her sister."

This shocks me.

"What did they say?"

"The first time? I could go suck an egg."

"The second time?"

"Cami was pretty fired up. I don't think I should repeat any of it. She called me a skinny white boy a lot, though."

"The third time?"

He shrugs. "I'll have to keep asking."

"I should know," I say. "It's more than talk. It's doing. It's action. It's being."

The only smoke on the wind is from the barbecues.

"I'll take that to heart. Thanks, Lou," he says, and he turns back toward his wildly expensive vehicle.

"Maybe . . . you should stay, work on being that person who deserves to be forgiven."

"Really?" he asks, though I can tell he regrets asking. Like I might snap, change my mind.

"Yeah."

"Thanks. I mean, what can I say, but thank you?"

He walks past me, but I turn around and he faces me.

"Just so you know. I'm asexual—ace or demi or something."

I don't expect him to know what I'm talking about.

He thinks for a minute. "Like Janeane Garofalo?"

"Is she?"

"Yeah, I think. It's in her comedy. Ah, damn," he says, suddenly, and fiercely. "Our relationship was mostly us watching movies with my dick center stage . . ." He stops himself to peer off into the mid-distance.

I laugh. It's not enough, but it's something. "Enjoy the party. Go."

A few minutes later, King returns. He's carrying my dinosaur mug, filled with iced tea and a lemon slice.

I haven't asked him yet, but I need to. He'll do his legal stuff from Toronto, and I'll do mine from where I'll be. I can't seem to ask him straight on, though. "Are you flying out of Edmonton or Saskatoon?"

He offers me my mug.

I want to smile. Want to hold it and know it's going to be okay, that I'll be okay, and so will King, when this summer ends.

He tilts his head to the side a bit. "I've been meaning to tell you this almost all season. And all these weeks I've held out. I've made excuse after excuse."

"This sounds serious."

"It is."

The party is loud behind us. People are dancing now. Maurice sings and plays the fiddle. My mom's laugh punctuates a note. But I feel cold. Far away from them.

"I deferred a year. From school," King says.

"Why?"

"Don't you get on my dad's side of this—you're my girlfriend," he says.

"I am?"

"We're doing this all wrong again," King says, but he's smiling.

"No. Am I your girlfriend?"

"Wanna be?"

I nod and he comes closer and hugs me. My dinosaur mug is awkward, pressed against King's back. I don't want to spill on his nice shirt. "Okay, okay, but tell me why. For real."

"My dad needs me. And honestly, I like the idea of seeing you on the weekends, of sitting in the bleachers and cheering during water polo games. Of writing the novel I've been too chicken to write, too caught up in my Toronto life to think on clearly."

"You should tell your mom. It's something she ought to know."

We're still hugging, still holding each other close.

"Aliya's saying that ma's softening, that she's asking questions about me, that's she not angry anymore."

"Have you tried to call?"

"Not in a while. She's going to hate that I'm not coming back right away. She's going to think it's some kind of retaliation—me sacrificing something she knows I want in order to get at her. But it's not that. I want to be here, at least for the next year."

"Tell her," I say. "Leave a voice mail if she doesn't pick up."

"That's an idea," he says, peering down at me like I'm a revelation.

My cheeks hurt from smiling.

My mom's voice comes from behind us: "Hey, I was sent to come get you."

We break apart. Like lightning can strike the same place twice.

"Lou," my mom says, and she opens her arms.

I hug her. In the big tent, Dom's at the microphone now.

"You too, King," my mom says, after she lets me go. She's so much shorter than him, but she wraps her arms around his middle tightly. "I love you—you know that, right?"

"I do," he says.

Once she releases him, we walk together.

"Want to know the first thing I did after I found you two that morning?" she asks with a big belly laugh.

Neither King nor I answer her, but she's not waiting for that, not really. She's waiting for us to sweat. I'll tell her soon, I will, but for now, we'll let her say what she needs.

"I planned a party with my brother, and we drove to the Costco to purchase supplies, and while I was there, I stopped by the pharmacy and bought two extremely large boxes of condoms. Use them, my loves," she says, and then we're at the tent, and she's walking away from us—toward one of her nurse friends.

I'm not even blushing.

The crowd sits at the tables we borrowed, drinking wine out of little plastic cups and beer out of longneck bottles. There's iced tea and sodas. Water too.

King grabs my hand again, pulling me closer to him, like he can't get enough of holding me.

Hunched over the microphone, Dom starts speaking. "We wanted to invite you all out here to offer you thanks for how you've supported us the past three years, and how you've helped us grow. The Michif Creamery wouldn't exist without you."

King leans against me and I lean back against him.

This is strange. But it's not bad strange.

"We're happy to announce it here, first, with all of you to celebrate with us. My niece . . ." Dom looks out into the crowd.

I wave from the back of the tent.

I'm not sure if he sees me. The lights.

My mom yells, "She's in back with her boyfriend."

Florence catches my eye, mouthing, "Finally."

Tomorrow, at the lake, I'll tell her everything.

King leans closer, eclipsing everyone else. "Oof, that's super public all of a sudden. You okay with it?"

"I am," I whisper back.

"My niece reminded us of something," Dom says. "And it's the land. It's this land. We've been working the shack for three years now, on other property that we don't own. It's time to bring it home, to bring it here, where we can hold tours and we can let folks pet Mooreen and we can keep our family business where our family lives."

The crowd claps. Someone whoops and cheers a little too loud. When I look, it's Leif.

"Oh, and, I'm not supposed to tell you yet, since we haven't finalized the contract, but we're publishing a book!"

Leif's face breaks into a rather large grimace, then a smile.

"That's a secret," Dom says, smiling back at his boyfriend from the stage. "Big corporations like to do all this in their own way. But we're a family business. We do things our way.

"One last thing, before we get back to the music. Before we continue our celebration. Most of you know about what happened to my sister in this town years ago. We've filed legal papers to stop Peter England from stepping foot on this property and from being anywhere near my niece and her boyfriend. But that's not what I want to say. I want to say . . . I know many of you work for his family. Or have interests that line up with his. But if you're one of those still supporting him, if you're one of the people who have been whispering to him news about my niece, or think he has a right to be anywhere near her, I want you to know you're not welcome here. You should leave. Now."

No one stands. Not that I would expect them to.

If someone like that is here, they'll sneak out quietly, after they finish their drink. Maybe they'll stay all night, eating our good food.

But it feels right to know I'm not in this alone.

I'm not alone.

And I'm not broken.

I'm me.

King leans close again. Night's fallen, somehow, when none of us were paying attention. Hundreds of sparkle lights illuminate the tent. I can't help but check the sky. It's all lit up—full of stars—and later tonight, if we're lucky, we'll see the northern lights. And when King kisses me, when I kiss him back, I don't need to wait—the northern lights are all around me.

This might be enough for me.

This might not be forever.

This family. My friends dancing to the fiddle. King. All of this. I fall into the moment, sink into my body as if slipping into wild water, powerful here, happy here. Right now, this is exactly enough.

A NOTE FROM JEN

I didn't understand I was demisexual in high school, or in university, or even in my late twenties. I wrote Lou's story for teens like me, those of us who could aesthetically appreciate bodies, could see the beautiful and the transcendent, could love a particularly distinct nose or most-excellent eyebrows or find someone's biceps pretty, but didn't really feel attraction.

I was an early reader. When I discovered adult fantasy in the seventh grade, I began to devour books. If I couldn't convince my dad to drive me, I biked from Keele and Sheppard to the Toronto Public Library—Downsview branch, two kilometers away, with a backpack I'd fill to the brim. I biked to the library at least twice a week.

And this is a sad story: The books I was reading—including the ones I was reading for fun—didn't have room for queer teens, or questioning teens, or frankly, characters who didn't engage in very clear, often very problematic, heterosexual relationships. The books I read were very white. Oh so very white. Because whiteness and straightness and allosexuality were the defaults.

From those books, I learned to feel like there was something wrong with me, to sink into colonial relationships with myself and with others.

But I never fell out of love with stories. I started writing my own novels at seventeen, in my basement bedroom, on my HP desktop computer. And what I wrote were basic heterosexual, allosexual relationships for white, skinny, able-bodied, financially well-off people.

You can laugh at me. Really, you can.

Those books, they were really bad books for at least two reasons. But the most important one, as you already know, is that they were so very limited in their understanding of the world.

Lou's complicated relationship with her biracial ancestry also reflects a bit of what I was going through as a teen.

There is safety in conforming to whiteness. Whiteness wants us to feel safe in conforming, too, because it keeps whiteness unchallenged.

In middle school, I didn't feel like I could or should or ought to claim my Michif ancestry and culture. My skin is white—so having been trained by the Canada education system, a system that wants to keep whiteness at the center of stories, to me, that meant I was white. Indigeneity and white skin could not coexist. I lived in Toronto; I went to Beverly Heights Middle School, where as a white-skinned person, I was in the minority, and the Jane Finch Mall was my after-school playground. But despite the fact that my classmates and my friends were BIPOC, and were mixed, I couldn't understand myself as Métis. I lived in a city, my dad was disconnected, my Michif grandmother passed as white, and in the textbooks where I learned "history," Indigenous people didn't exist in the present.

You can see how it took a long while for me to work through this: how colonial Canada was winning if I erased half of my family, half of myself. How I was contributing to the violence done to Native communities by being unable to exist as both white and Métis.

So while my story is different from Lou's, the complicated feelings, the feelings of safety in whiteness, and Lou's eventual coming to her Michif culture, are things I understand in my body.

As someone actively taking back from colonial Canada, rebuilding relationships, reclaiming histories and culture and language, I'm still learning.

The space of learning is a vulnerable one. You have to be willing to make yourself vulnerable to learn.

In that, too, Lou's further along than I was as a teen. And I love that for her.

Let's talk books and representation for a minute.

The first novel I read where I felt *seen* as a Métis/Michif person was Cherie Dimaline's *The Marrow Thieves* in 2017.

The first novel I read where I felt *seen* as demi was Claire Kahn's *Let's Talk about Love* in 2018.

I was in my thirties when I read these books. They were the first I'd ever read with a demi or Métis protagonist.

Oof.

I've yet to read a book with a character who is both demi and Michif.

But I did write one.

I feel like I'm betraying Lou when I tell you that she's not my favorite character—King is. The most common critique of King from early readers was that *he's too good for a teenage boy.* Let me tell you, I have no regrets. King's goodness, his kindness, his heart, those are his superpowers.

Tyler and Cami are other author faves. Their superpowers have been honed by grief. But I love their sharp edges, their anger, their unwillingness to sit down, shut up, and fall apart.

Lou's inherited trauma doesn't make her ace—not at all—that's some problematic bullshit that she has to discard. But her inherited trauma is related to Tyler's and Cami's grief. Violence toward Indigenous women, girls, and two-spirit people is rampant in Canada, and in the United States, and across the world. It's a genocide.

This loss cannot be quantified, but it can be contextualized. I don't do this through numbers, but through relations and through story. Tyler, Cami, and Lou are part of a larger story about how violence is seeded, where it breaks familial bonds, where this violence breaks communities, where it repeats itself again and again under the pervasive, often invisible weight of white supremacy culture.

If this is news to you, to learn more and to participate in action, visit these hashtags: #MMIW, #MMIWG, #MMIWG2S, #NoMoreStolenSisters, #MissingAndMurdered. Find a local organization and share in doing the needed work.

And there is other work to be done. Anti-Blackness is pervasive not only in white spaces, but in Indigenous and POC communities too. Here I also invite you to participate in action, to learn, and to break down anti-Black thoughts, acts, and laws in your hearts and communities.

***

I've come to understand that I could only set this story in Lloyd-minster, Alberta/Saskatchewan. While I only spent two years here (grades ten and eleven), this city was a place of loud contradictions, of good people, and of people who insisted that we do not all deserve basic human rights, that we are not all fully human.

Lou's story is a story of the Canadian prairies, and Lloydminster was for me a place where I ran a bit wild, and friends ran wilder, where the young men who worked in the oil fields spent their off time and their money, where I first experienced the very ugly prairies racism against Indigenous peoples, where I worked for the first time, running a pizza shop with basically no adult oversight, where I fell in love with bison. I see Lloydminster through a very particular lens. It's not sugarcoated, but I do write about this city on the prairies with an honest kind of love.

Love and life, as in the case of most things, tend toward both bitter and sweet.

One truth: we never stop growing, we never stop becoming. If I'd had books that represented queer teens, demi teens, and other ace teens, Michif teens, other Indigenous teens, would I have come to terms with my identity sooner? Maybe. Maybe not. But damn, I would have loved those stories. They would have fed a hunger in my heart.

Another truth: I wrote Lou's story for myself, for awkward, wonderful teen me, but I wrote it for you, too.

To close, a few more truths: My favorite more-than-human

relative is still the bison. My second favorite is the moose. I was once attacked by a cow at a petting zoo just outside of Lloydminster, and my friends, they laughed so hard they cried. I've never scooped ice cream for a summer—I'm a pizza expert. But that's another story.

ACKNOWLEDGMENTS

THE REDS

The team who made this book happen: Rosemary Brosnan, Cynthia Leitich Smith, Courtney Stevenson, Kathryn Silsand, Megan Gendell, and every other person at Heartdrum and HarperCollins Children's Books, every single one of you who had a part in bringing Lou's story to teens, maarsi, because you're the strawberries, the raspberries, all the reds that bring worlds to life.

THE ORANGES

Patricia Nelson, you have been taking care with my work long before you became my agent. Please know how much this brightness has meant to me, and how much it continues to mean. I am honored to be in collaboration with you—now and onward.

To Ellen Oh, Heartdrum's auntie: <3 <3 <3. To We Need Diverse Books, all of you, you're doing the Work, thank you. I'm happy to do the Work alongside.

THE YELLOWS

Like a good dandelion wine, friends are sunshine.

To Jamie Pacton, who told me, *Why don't you write that.* She's to blame for Lou's story being in the world because, in a way, she gave me permission to write about being Métis and white and demi. Thank you, my friend. May your dandelions always bloom, always seed, always return to bloom again.

To Tracy Gold, who has been here and has been cheering me on since 2015, thank you. I know you love your gardens—may your yellows always be bright, and may your words continue to take root.

All those who gave me feedback: Alison Miller, Julie Artz, Jennifer Austin, ReLynn Vaughn, Anna Meriano, Elle Jauffret, Heather Murphy Capps, Michelle Armfield, Sarah Robbins, Sarah White, Amy Parkes, Shanna Walsh, and everyone who my very pandemic-exhausted brain missed, thank you. You've brightened a long process for me with kind, careful critiques.

I can't help but always send love to my PW15 peers: we are writing, we are winning, we are tenacious like dandelions, and we will keep making words happen. Try and stop us. If you ask my dad, who is in a constant fight against the universe to maintain his lawn, he knows dandelions cannot be stopped.

To my Lloydminster friends (you know who you are): You've been living in my head, as this book clearly indicates. We were beautiful messes in high school, like a good patch of dandelions. We still are and will continue to be.

To Euterpe, my room, at La Muse in Labastide-Esparbairenque, and to the humans who were there making art alongside me and sharing in mealtimes on the patio, thanks for the support; especially, Elise, Tara, Nora, and Talia. Also, shout-out to Homer, the dog.

Other friends who have held me up, even under bracing winds: Mike Mammay; Kristin Tartar; Kat Urban; Amanda Reaume; my middle school besties, Priyanka Parshad, Callie Stanley, and

Tanya Lusan; Annisa Maxwell; Ava Homa; Erin Soros; Rickie Legleitner; Cassie Herbert; Ryan Ward; Holly Baker; Valerie Kolbinger; everyone in the 22Debut group; and the good people (only the good people) of Twitter Dot Com, to all of you, thanks.

To my TTJ co-organizers at LMU, thank you. You've taught me a lot and I credit so many of your teachings and kindness for how this book developed in revision. You were a bright light during a hard year, and I'm thankful to be in collaboration with you all.

THE GREENS

To my sensitivity/authenticity readers, Elise Hyrak and Antonio Michael Downing, thank you for your kindness and care in holding me accountable. You've made this a better book. Any mistakes, any places where I've failed, these are on me, and I vow here and now to always, always do better.

To Edward Underhill, and @TypeACreative1, thank you for conaming Mooreen, the udderly delightful Cowntessa de Pasteur.

THE BLUES

Reconnecting to an Indigenous community is hard work, good work, work that needs to be done with care: listening and reflecting and insisting on not claiming space, on letting those who are connected speak. Maarsi to everyone who has reminded me of this, held me to this. Lou's story is only one story of what it means to be a contemporary Métis teen. There are many, many, many more. Seek them out.

To Katherine Crocker, especially, who always asks *How can I support you?*, maarsi. From them I've learned to ask this question, and so, to my Indigenous communities, to our more-than-human relations, to the land, I will always ask, *How can I support you?*, and I will act in accordance.

Reyna Hernandez: Since the first time I saw your art at the University of South Dakota back in the day, I've been in love. You've brought Lou to life, and Indigenous teen girls will see themselves, and their family and friends—their power—on the cover of this book, as they see this in all your paintings and community murals. I am honored, and thankful, for the care you've taken with Lou.

Kim Stewart: it's an honor to have your beadwork on the cover and on the pages of this book.

To everyone keeping Michif alive, and to LearnMichif for helping me with language and spelling in this book: maarsi!

THE INDIGOS

The humans of Coven: The Return, you are my family. I will always be as excited to support you, to hold you when it hurts, to celebrate your wins, to mourn your losses, as I was on the most awesome day when you invited me to the group chat and into your lives.

My family. All of you. Those who have come before and those who are here now. Extra special love to the ones growing: Linky; Owen and Morgane; Caleb; Neko and Nova; Fynn and Davrine; Arbenita; Deven; and the littles yet to come.

THE VIOLETS

They say the last person you should thank in traditional book acknowledgments is the person you are currently having sex with, but hey, demi here, so let's break the mold. The last people I'll thank are instead the people who I do this work for, the ones I'm always advocating for: my students and the BIPOC and queer teens of the world. You are loved, you are cared for, you are, as they say, your ancestors' wildest dreams, and I thank you for everything you're doing to make this world one where everyone can thrive. You are, in a word, or in a few, absolutely, completely fucking incredible. You have all my love and support, always. Thank you.

A NOTE FROM CYNTHIA LEITICH SMITH,
Author-Curator of Heartdrum

Dear Reader,

The Summer of Bitter and Sweet is a lot like ice cream. Like sugar, it provides a rush of emotion, and like cream, it's a challenge to digest. I love how deeply Lou loves, even as she struggles to reconcile relationships gone wrong or to navigate the delicate stages of healing.

Her heart is radiant in moments of joy, friendship, and the romance with King, in familial duty to her mom and uncles, and in personal reinvention, with every step forward and every cool scoop of delicious dessert.

Too many of us are impacted by bigotry, violence—sexual or otherwise—and the intergenerational trauma they bring. As author Jen Ferguson explains, she drew a lot on lived experience in writing this book. She kept you, her audience, in mind with each word, each paragraph and page. I'm hopeful that you found the story illuminating and cathartic.

Reading is a way that we can process harm from a safe distance. If you're hurting, you may also want to reach out to beloved Elders—when I was a teenager, my grandparents were a tremendous source of support—or other trusted healers in your family and community.

Have you read many stories by and about Métis people?

Hopefully, *The Summer of Bitter and Sweet* will inspire you to read more. The novel is published by Heartdrum, a Native-focused imprint of HarperCollins, which offers stories about young Native heroes by Indigenous authors and illustrators.

Take care of yourselves and each other and remember: You're the heroes of your own life stories. We believe in you.

Mvto,

Cynthia Leitich Smith

ABOUT THE AUTHOR

JEN FERGUSON is Michif/Métis and white, an activist, an intersectional feminist, an auntie, and an accomplice armed with a PhD in English and creative writing. Her favorite ice-cream flavor is mint chocolate chip. She currently lives on unceded Gabrielino-Tongva land, where she teaches fiction writing at Loyola Marymount University. Visit her online at www.jenfergusonwrites.com.

ABOUT CYNTHIA LEITICH SMITH

CYNTHIA LEITICH SMITH is the bestselling, acclaimed author of books for all ages, including *Sisters of the Neversea, Rain Is Not My Indian Name, Indian Shoes, Jingle Dancer,* and *Hearts Unbroken,* which won the American Indian Library Association's Youth Literature Award; she is also the anthologist of *Ancestor Approved: Intertribal Stories for Kids.* Most recently, she was named the 2021 NSK Neustadt Laureate. Cynthia is the author-curator of Heartdrum, a Native-focused imprint at HarperCollins Children's Books, and serves as the Katherine Paterson Inaugural Endowed Chair on the faculty of the MFA program in writing for children and young adults at Vermont College of Fine Arts. She is a citizen of the Muscogee (Creek) Nation and lives in Austin, Texas. You can visit Cynthia online at www.cynthialeitichsmith.com.